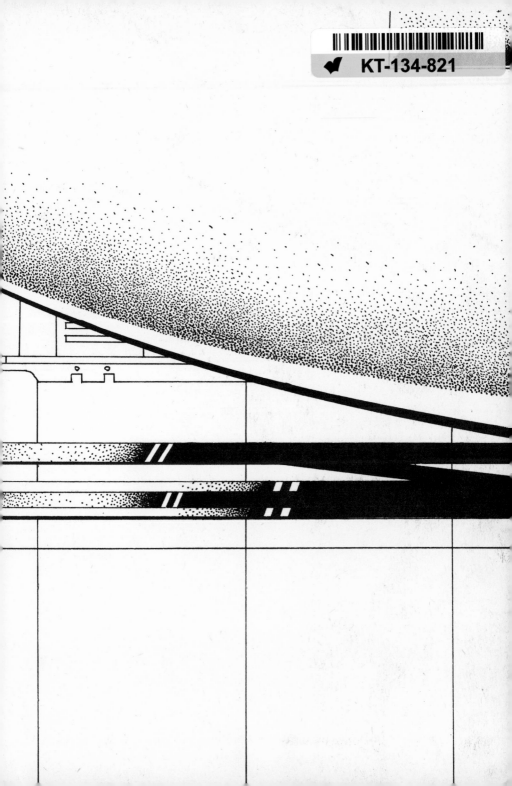

Science Fiction Stories

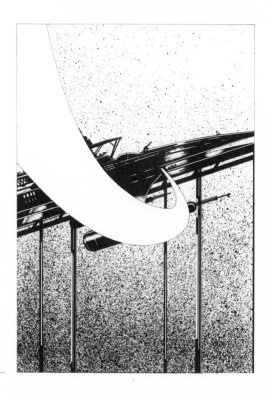

Science Fiction Stories

Edited by
Tom Boardman Jr.

Illustrated by
David Mitchell
Paul Desmond
Graham Townsend

octopus

Contents

Designed by Astrid Publishing Consultants

First Published 1979 by
Octopus Books Limited
59 Grosvenor Street
London W1
Reprinted 1981
This collection © 1979

ISBN 0 7064 0999 X

Printed in Czechoslovakia ·
50390/2

First Contact

Murray Leinster

Tommy Dort went into the captain's room with his last pair of stereophotos and said:

'I'm through, sir. These are the last two pictures I can take.'

He handed over the photographs and looked with professional interest at the visiplates, which showed all space outside the ship. Subdued, deep-red lighting indicated the controls and such instruments as the quartermaster on duty needed for navigation of the spaceship *Llanvabon*. There was a deeply cushioned control chair. There was the little gadget of oddly angled mirrors – remote descendant of the back-view mirrors of twentieth-century motorists – which allowed a view of all the visiplates without turning the head. And there were the huge plates which were so much more satisfactory for a direct view of space.

The *Llanvabon* was a long way from home. The plates, which showed every star of visual magnitude and could be stepped up to any desired magnification, portrayed stars of every imaginable degree of brilliance, in the startling different colours they show outside of the atmosphere. But every one was unfamiliar. Only two constellations could be recognized as seen from Earth, and they were shrunken and distorted. The Milky Way seemed vaguely out of place. But even such oddities were minor compared to a sight in the forward plates.

There was a vast, vast mistiness ahead. A luminous mist. It seemed motionless. It took a long time for it to appear appreciably nearer in the vision plates, though the spaceship's velocity indicator showed an incredible speed. The mist was the Crab Nebula, six light-years long, three and a half light-years thick, with outward-reaching members that in the telescopes of Earth gave it some resemblance to the creature for which it was named. It was a cloud of gas, infinitely tenuous, reaching half again as far as from Sol to its nearest neighbour sun. Deep within it burned two stars – a double star, one component the familiar yellow of the sun of Earth, the other an unholy white.

Tommy Dort said meditatively:

'We're heading into a deep, sir?'

The skipper studied the last two plates of Tommy's taking, and put them aside. He went back to his uneasy contemplation of the vision plates ahead. The *Llanvabon* was decelerating at full force. She was a bare half light-year from the nebula. Tommy's work was guiding the ship's course, now, but the work was done. During all the stay of the exploring ship in the nebula, Tommy Dort would loaf. But he'd more than paid his way so far.

He had just completed a quite unique first – a complete photographic record of the movement of a nebula during a period of four thousand years, taken by one individual with the same apparatus and with control exposures to detect and record any systematic errors. It was an achievement in itself worth the journey from Earth. But in addition, he had also recorded four thousand years of the history of a double star, and four thousand years of the history of a star in the act of degenerating into a white dwarf.

It was not that Tommy Dort was four thousand years old. He was, actually, in his twenties. But the Crab Nebula is four thousand light-years from Earth, and the last two pictures had been taken by light which would not reach Earth until the sixth millennium A.D. On the way here – at speeds of incredible multiples of the speed of light – Tommy Dort had recorded each aspect of the nebula by the light which had left it from forty centuries since to a bare six months ago.

The *Llanvabon* bored on through space. Slowly, slowly, slowly, the incredible luminosity crept across the vision plates. It blotted out half the universe from view. Before was glowing mist, and behind was a star-studded emptiness. The mist shut off three-fourths of all the stars. Some few of the brightest shone dimly through it near its edge, but only a few. Then there was only an irregularly shaped patch of darkness astern against which stars shone unwinking. The *Llanvabon* dived into the nebula, and it seemed as if it bored into a tunnel of darkness with walls of shining fog.

Which was exactly what the spaceship was doing. The most distant photographs of all had disclosed structural features in the nebula. It was not amorphous. It had form. As the *Llanvabon* drew nearer, indications of structure grew more distinct, and Tommy Dort had argued for a curved approach for photographic reasons. So the spaceship had come up to the nebula on a vast logarithmic curve, and Tommy had been able to take successive photographs from slightly different angles and get stereopairs which showed the nebula in three dimensions; which disclosed billowings and hollows and an actually complicated shape. In places, the nebula displayed convolutions like those of a human brain. It was into one of those hollows that the spaceship now plunged. They had been called 'deeps' by analogy with crevasses in the ocean floor. And they promised to be useful.

The skipper relaxed. One of a skipper's functions, nowadays, is to think of things to worry about, and then worry about them. The skipper of the *Llanvabon* was conscientious. Only after a certain instrument remained definitely non-registering did he ease himself back in his seat.

'It was just hardly possible,' he said heavily, 'that those deeps might have been non-luminous gas. But they're empty. So we'll be able to use overdrive as long as we're in them.'

It was a light-year and a half from the edge of the nebula to the neighbourhood of the double star which was its heart. That was the problem. A nebula is a gas. It is so thin that a comet's tail is solid by comparison, but a ship travelling on overdrive – above the speed of light – does not want to hit even a merely hard vacuum. It needs pure emptiness, such as exists between the stars. But the *Llanvabon* could not do much in this expanse of mist if it was limited to speeds a merely hard vacuum will permit.

The luminosity seemed to close in behind the spaceship, which slowed and slowed and slowed. The overdrive went off with the

9

sudden *pinging* sensation which goes all over a person when the over-drive field is released.

Then, almost instantly, bells burst into clanging, strident uproar all through the ship. Tommy was almost deafened by the alarm bell which rang in the captain's room before the quartermaster shut it off with a flip of his hand. But other bells could be heard ringing throughout the rest of the ship, to be cut off as automatic doors closed one by one.

Tommy Dort stared at the skipper. The skipper's hands were clenched. He was up and staring over the quartermaster's shoulder. One indicator was apparently having convulsions. Others strained to record their findings. A spot on the diffusedly bright mistiness of a bow-quartering visiplate grew brighter as the automatic scanner focused on it. That was the direction of the object which had sounded the collision alarm. But the object locator itself – according to its reading, there was one solid object some eighty thousand miles away, an object of no great size. But there was another object whose distance varied from extreme range to zero, and whose size shared its impossible advance and retreat.

'Step up the scanner,' snapped the skipper.

The extra-bright spot on the scanner rolled outward, obliterating the undifferentiated image behind it. Magnification increased. But nothing appeared. Absolutely nothing. Yet the radio locator insisted that something monstrous and invisible made lunatic dashes toward the *Llanvabon*, at speeds which inevitably implied collision, and then fled coyly away at the same rate.

The visiplate went up to maximum magnification. Still nothing. The skipper ground his teeth. Tommy Dort said meditatively:

'D'you know, sir, I saw something like this on a liner on the Earth-Mars run once, when we were being located by another ship. Their locator beam was of the same frequency as ours, and every time it hit, it registered like something monstrous and solid.'

'That,' said the skipper savagely, 'is just what's happening now. There's something like a locator beam on us. We're getting that beam and our own echo besides. But the other ship's invisible! Who is out here in an invisible ship with locator devices? Not men, certainly!'

He pressed the button in his sleeve communicator and snapped: 'Action stations! Man all weapons! Condition of extreme alert in all departments immediately!'

His hands closed and unclosed. He stared again at the visiplate, which showed nothing but a formless brightness.

'Not men?' Tommy Dort straightened sharply. 'You mean—'

'How many solar systems in our galaxy?' demanded the skipper bitterly. 'How many planets fit for life? And how many kinds of life could there be? If this ship isn't from Earth – and it isn't – it has a crew that isn't human. And things that aren't human but are up to the level of deep-space travel in their civilization could mean anything!'

The skipper's hands were actually shaking. He would not have talked so freely before a member of his own crew, but Tommy Dort was of the observation staff. And even a skipper whose duties include worrying may sometimes need desperately to unload his worries. Sometimes, too, it helps to think aloud.

'Something like this has been talked about and speculated about for years,' he said softly. 'Mathematically, it's been an odds-on bet that somewhere in our galaxy there'd be another race with a civilization equal to or further advanced than ours. Nobody could ever guess where or when we'd meet them. But it looks like we've done it now!'

Tommy's eyes were very bright.

'D'you suppose they'll be friendly, sir?'

The skipper glanced at the distance indicator. The phantom object still made its insane, nonexistent swoops toward and away from the *Llanvabon*. The secondary indication of an object at eighty thousand miles stirred ever so slightly.

'It's moving,' he said curtly. 'Heading for us. Just what we'd do if a strange spaceship appeared in our hunting grounds! Friendly? Maybe! We're going to try to contact them. We have to. But I suspect this is the end of this expedition. Thank God for the blasters!'

The blasters are those beams of ravening destruction which take care of recalcitrant meteorites in a spaceship's course when the deflectors can't handle them. They are not designed as weapons, but they can serve as pretty good ones. They can go into action at five thousand miles, and draw on the entire power output of a whole ship. With automatic aim and a traverse of five degrees, a ship like the *Llanvabon* can come very close to blasting a hole through a small-sized asteroid which gets in its way. But not on overdrive, of course.

Tommy Dort had approached the bow-quartering visiplate. Now he jerked his head around.

'Blasters, sir? What for?'

The skipper grimaced at the empty visiplate.

'Because we don't know what they're like and can't take a chance! I know!' he added bitterly. 'We're going to make contact and try to find out all we can about them – especially where they come from. I suppose we'll try to make friends – but we haven't much chance. We can't trust them a fraction of an inch. We daren't! They've locators. Maybe they've tracers better than any we have. Maybe they could trace us all the way home without our knowing it! We can't risk having a non-human race know where Earth is unless we're sure of them! And how can we be sure? They could come to trade, of course – or they could swoop down on overdrive with a battle fleet that could wipe us out before we knew what happened. We wouldn't know which to expect, or when!'

Tommy's face was startled.

'It's all been thrashed out over and over, in theory,' said the skipper. 'Nobody's ever been able to find a sound answer, even on paper. But you know, in all their theorizing, no one considered the crazy, rank impossibility of a deep-space contact, with neither side knowing the other's home world! But we've got to find an answer in fact! What are we going to do about them? Maybe these creatures will be esthetic marvels, nice and friendly and polite – with the sneaking brutal ferocity of a Japanese underneath. Or maybe they'll be crude and gruff like a Swedish farmer – and just as decent underneath. Maybe they're something in-between. But am I going to risk the possible future of the human race on a guess that it's safe to trust them? God knows it would be worthwhile to make friends with a new civilization! It would be bound to stimulate our own, and maybe we'd gain enormously. But I can't take chances. The one thing I won't risk is having them know how to find Earth! Either I know they can't follow me, or I don't go home! And they'll probably feel the same way!'

He pressed the sleeve-communicator button again.

'Navigation officers, attention! Every star map on this ship is to be prepared for instant destruction. This includes photographs and diagrams from which our course or starting point could be deduced. I want all astronomical data gathered and arranged to be destroyed in a split second, on order. Make it fast and report when ready!'

He released the button. He looked suddenly old. The first contact of humanity with an alien race was a situation which had been foreseen in many fashions, but never one quite so hopeless of solution as this. A solitary Earth ship and a solitary alien, meeting in a nebula which must be remote from the home planet of each. They might wish peace, but the line of conduct which best prepared a treacherous attack was just the seeming of friendliness. Failure to be suspicious might doom the human race – and a peaceful exchange of the fruits of civilization would be the greatest benefit imaginable. Any mistake would be irreparable, but a failure to be on guard would be fatal.

The captain's room was very, very quiet. The bow-quartering visiplate was filled with the image of a very small section of the nebula. A very small section indeed. It was all diffused, featureless, luminous mist. But suddenly Tommy Dort pointed.

'There, sir!'

There was a small shape in the mist. It was far away. It was a black shape, not polished to a mirror-like reflection like the hull of the *Llanvabon*. It was bulbous – roughly pear-shaped. There was much thin luminosity between, and no details could be observed, but it was surely no natural object. Then Tommy looked at the distance indicator and said quietly:

'It's headed for us at very high acceleration, sir. The odds are that they're thinking the same thing, sir, that neither of us will dare let the other go home. Do you think they'll try a contact with us, or let loose with their weapons as soon as they're in range?'

The *Llanvabon* was no longer in a crevasse of emptiness in the nebula's thin substance. She swam in luminescence. There were no stars save the two fierce glows in the nebula's heart. There was nothing but an all-enveloping light, and it was curiously like one's imagining of what it would be like underwater in the tropics of Earth.

The alien ship had made one sign of less than lethal intention. As it drew near the *Llanvabon*, it decelerated. The *Llanvabon* itself had advanced for a meeting and then come to a dead stop. Its movement

13

had been a recognition of the nearness of the other ship. Its pausing was both a friendly sign and a precaution against attack. Relatively still, it could swivel on its own axis to present the least target to a slashing assault, and it would have a longer firing time than if the two ships flashed past each other at their combined speeds.

The moment of actual approach, however, was tenseness itself. The *Llanvabon*'s needle-pointed bow aimed unwaveringly at the alien bulk. A relay to the captain's room put a key under his hand which would fire the blasters with maximum power. Tommy Dort watched, his brow wrinkled. The aliens must be of a high degree of civilization if they had spaceships, and civilization does not develop without the development of foresight. These aliens must recognize all the implications of this first contact of two civilized races as fully as did the human beings on the *Llanvabon*.

The possibility of an enormous spurt in the development of both, by peaceful contact and exchange of their separate technologies, would probably appeal to them as much as to man. But when dissimilar human cultures are in contact, one must usually be subordinate or there is war. But subordination between races arising on separate planets could not be peacefully arranged. Men, at least, would never consent to subordination, nor was it likely that any highly developed race would agree. The benefits to be derived from commerce could never make up for a condition of inferiority. Some races – men, perhaps – would prefer commerce to conquest. Perhaps – perhaps! – these aliens would also. But some types even of human beings would have craved red war. If the alien ship now approaching the *Llanvabon* returned to its home base with news of humanity's existence and of ships like the *Llanvabon*, it would give its race the choice of trade or battle. They might want trade, or they might want war. But it takes two to make trade, and only one to make war. They could not be sure of men's peacefulness, nor could men be sure of theirs. The only safety for either civilization would lie in the destruction of one or both of the two ships.

But even victory would not be really enough. Men would need to know where this alien race was to be found, for avoidance if not for battle. They would need to know its weapons, and its resources, and if it could be a menace and how it could be eliminated in case of need. The aliens would feel the same necessities concerning humanity.

So the skipper of the *Llanvabon* did not press the key which might possibly have blasted the other ship to nothingness. He dared not. But he dared not not fire either. Sweat came out on his face.

A speaker muttered. Someone from the range room.

'The other ship's stopped, sir. Quite stationary. Blasters are centred on it, sir.'

It was an urging to fire. But the skipper shook his head, to himself. The alien ship was no more than twenty miles away. It was dead-black. Every bit of its exterior was an abysmal, non-reflecting sable. No details could be seen except by minor variations in its outline against the misty nebula.

'It's stopped dead, sir,' said another voice. 'They've sent a modulated short wave at us, sir. Frequency modulated. Apparently a signal. Not enough power to do any harm.'

The skipper said through tight-locked teeth:

'They're doing something now. There's movement on the outside of their hull. Watch what comes out. Put the auxiliary blasters on it.'

Something small and round came smoothly out of the oval outline of the black ship. The bulbous hulk moved.

'Moving away, sir,' said the speaker. 'The object they let out is stationary in the place they've left.'

Another voice cut in:

'More frequency-modulated stuff, sir. Unintelligible.'

Tommy Dort's eyes brightened. The skipper watched the visiplate, with sweat droplets on his forehead.

'Rather pretty, sir,' said Tommy, meditatively. 'If they sent anything toward us, it might seem to be a projectile or a bomb. So they came close, let out a lifeboat, and went away again. They figure we can send a boat or a man to make contact without risking our ship. They must think pretty much as we do.'

The skipper said, without moving his eyes from the plate:

'Mr Dort, would you care to go out and look the thing over? I can't order you, but I need all my operating crew for emergencies. The observation staff—'

'Is expendable. Very well, sir,' said Tommy briskly. 'I won't take a lifeboat, sir. Just a suit with a drive in it. It's smaller and the arms and legs will look unsuitable for a bomb. I think I should carry a scanner.'

The alien ship continued to retreat. Forty, eighty, four hundred miles. It came to a stop and hung there, waiting. Climbing into his atomic-driven spacesuit just within the *Llanvabon's* air lock, Tommy heard the reports as they went over the speakers throughout the ship. That the other ship had stopped its retreat at four hundred miles was encouraging. It might not have weapons effective at a greater distance than that, and so felt safe. But just as the thought formed itself in his mind, the alien retreated precipitately still farther. Which, as Tommy reflected as he emerged from the lock, might be because the aliens had realized they were giving themselves away, or might be because they wanted to give the impression that they had done so.

He swooped away from the silvery, mirror-like *Llanvabon*, through a brightly glowing emptiness which was past any previous experience of the human race. Behind him, the *Llanvabon* swung about and darted away. The skipper's voice came through Tommy's helmet phones.

'We're pulling back, too, Mr Dort. There is a bare possibility that they've some explosive atomic reaction they can't use from their own ship, but which might be destructive even as far as this. We'll draw back. Keep your scanner on the object.'

The reasoning was sound, if not very comforting. An explosive which would destroy anything within twenty miles was theoretically possible, but human beings didn't have it yet. It was decidedly safest for the *Llanvabon* to draw back.

But Tommy Dort felt very lonely. He sped through emptiness toward the tiny black speck which hung in the incredible brightness. The *Llanvabon* vanished. Its polished hull would merge with the glowing mist at a relatively short distance, anyhow. The alien ship was not visible to the naked eye, either. Tommy swam in nothingness, four thousand light-years from home, toward a tiny black spot which was the only solid object to be seen in all of space.

It was a slightly distorted sphere, not much over six feet in diameter. It bounced away when Tommy landed on it, feet first. There were small tentacles, or horns, which projected in every direction. They looked rather like the detonating horns of a submarine mine, but there was a glint of crystal at the tip of each.

'I'm here,' said Tommy into his helmet phone.

He caught hold of a horn and drew himself to the object. It was all metal, dead-black. He could feel no texture through his space gloves, of course, but he went over and over it, trying to discover its purpose.

'Deadlock, sir,' he said presently. 'Nothing to report that the scanner hasn't shown you.'

Then, through his suit, he felt vibrations. They translated themselves as clankings. A section of the rounded hull of the object opened out. Two sections. He worked his way around to look in and see the first non-human civilized beings that any man had ever looked upon.

But what he saw was simply a flat plate on which dim-red glows crawled here and there in seeming aimlessness. His helmet phones emitted a startled exclamation. The skipper's voice:

'Very good, Mr Dort. Fix your scanner to look into that plate. They dumped out a robot with an infra-red visiplate for communication. Not risking any personnel. Whatever we might do would damage only machinery. Maybe they expect us to bring it on board – and it may have a bomb charge that can be detonated when they're ready to start for home. I'll send a plate to face one of its scanners. You return to the ship.'

'Yes, sir,' said Tommy. 'But which way is the ship, sir?'

There were no stars. The nebula obscured them with its light. The only thing visible from the robot was the double star at the nebula's centre. Tommy was no longer oriented. He had but one reference point.

'Head straight away from the double star,' came the order in his helmet phone. 'We'll pick you up.'

He passed another lonely figure, a little later, headed for the alien sphere with a vision plate to set up. The two spaceships, each knowing that it dared not risk its own race by the slightest lack of caution, would communicate with each other through this small round robot. Their separate vision systems would enable them to exchange all the information they dared give, while they debated the most practical way of making sure that their own civilization would not be endangered by this first contact with another. The truly most practical method would be the destruction of the other ship in a swift and deadly attack – in self-defence.

The *Llanvabon*, thereafter, was a ship in which there were two separate enterprises on hand at the same time. She had come out from

Earth to make close-range observations of the smaller component of the double star at the nebula's centre. The nebula itself was the result of the most titanic explosion of which men have any knowledge. The explosion took place some time in the year 2946 BC, before the first of the seven cities of long-dead Ilium was even thought of. The light of that explosion reached Earth in the year 1054 AD, and was duly recorded in ecclesiastical annals and somewhat more reliably by Chinese court astronomers. It was bright enough to be seen in daylight for twenty-three successive days. Its light was brighter than that of Venus.

From these facts, astronomers could calculate nine hundred years later the violence of the detonation. Matter blown away from the centre of the explosion would have travelled outward at the rate of two million three hundred thousand miles an hour, more than thirty-eight thousand miles a minute, something over six hundred and thirty-eight miles per second. When twentieth-century telescopes were turned upon the scene of this vast explosion, only a double star remained – and the nebula. The brighter star of the doublet was almost unique in having so high a surface temperature that it showed no spectrum lines at all. It had a continuous spectrum. Sol's surface temperature is about $7,000°$ Absolute. That of the hot white star is 500,000 degrees. It has nearly the mass of the sun, but only one fifth its diameter, so that its density is one hundred and seventy-three times that of water, sixteen times that of lead, and eight times that of iridium – the heaviest substance known on Earth. But even this density is not that of a dwarf white star like the companion of Sirius. The white star in the Crab Nebula in an incomplete dwarf; it is a star still in the act of collapsing. Examination – including the survey of a four-thousand-year column of its light – was worthwhile. The *Llanvabon* had come to make that examination. But the finding of an alien spaceship upon a similar errand had implications which overshadowed the original purpose of the expedition.

A tiny bulbous robot floated in the tenuous nebular gas. The normal operating crew of the *Llanvabon* stood at their posts with a sharp alertness which was productive of tense nerves. The observation staff divided itself, and a part went half-heartedly about the job of making the observations for which the *Llanvabon* had come. The other half applied itself to the problem the spaceship offered.

18

It represented a culture which was up to space travel on an interstellar scale. The explosion of a mere five thousand years since must have blasted every trace of life out of existence in the area now filled by the nebula. So the aliens of the black spaceship came from another solar system. Their trip must have been, like that of the Earth ship, for purely scientific purposes. There was nothing to be extracted from the nebula.

They were, then, at least near the level of human civilization, which meant that they had or could develop arts and articles of commerce which men would want to trade for, in friendship. But they would necessarily realize that the existence and civilization of humanity was a potential menace to their own race. The two races could be friends, but also they could be deadly enemies. Each, even if unwillingly, was a monstrous menace to the other. And the only safe thing to do with a menace is to destroy it.

In the Crab Nebula the problem was acute and immediate. The future relationship of the two races would be settled here and now. If a process for friendship could be established, one race, otherwise doomed, would survive and both would benefit immensely. But that process had to be established, and confidence built up, without the most minute risk of danger from treachery. Confidence would need to be established upon a foundation of necessarily complete distrust. Neither dared return to its own base if the other could do harm to its race. Neither dared risk any of the necessities to trust. The only safe thing for either to do was destroy the other or be destroyed.

But even for war, more was needed than mere destruction of the other. With interstellar traffic, the aliens must have atomic power and some form of overdrive for travel above the speed of light. With radio location and visiplates and short-wave communication, they had, of course, many other devices. What weapons did they have? How widely extended was their culture? What were their resources? Could there be a development of trade and friendship, or were the two races so unlike that only war could exist between them? If peace was possible, how could it be begun?

The men on the *Llanvabon* needed facts – and so did the crew of the other ship. They must take back every morsel of information they could. The most important information of all would be of the location of the other civilization, just in case of war. That one bit of information

19

might be the decisive factor in an interstellar war. But other facts would be enormously valuable.

The tragic thing was that there could be no possible information which could lead to peace. Neither ship could stake its own race's existence upon any conviction of the good will or honour of the other.

So there was a strange truce between the two ships. The alien went about its work of making observations, as did the *Llanvabon*. The tiny robot floated in bright emptiness. A scanner from the *Llanvabon* was focused upon a vision plate from the alien. A scanner from the alien regarded a vision plate from the *Llanvabon*. Communication began.

It progressed rapidly. Tommy Dort was one of those who made the first progress report. His special task on the expedition was over. He had now been assigned to work on the problem of communication with the alien entities. He went with the ship's solitary psychologist to the captain's room to convey the news of success. The captain's room, as usual, was a place of silence and dull-red indicator lights, and of great bright visiplates on every wall and on the ceiling.

'We've established fairly satisfactory communication, sir,' said the psychologist. He looked tired. His work on the trip was supposed to be that of measuring personal factors of error in the observation staff, for the reduction of all observations to the nearest possible decimal to the absolute. He had been pressed into service for which he was not especially fitted, and it told upon him. 'That is, we can say almost anything we wish to them, and can understand what they say in return. But of course we don't know how much of what they say is the truth.'

The skipper's eyes turned to Tommy Dort.

'We've hooked up some machinery,' said Tommy, 'that amounts to a mechanical translator. We have vision plates, of course, and then short-wave beams direct. They use frequency modulation plus what is probably variation in wave forms – like our vowel and consonant sounds in speech. We've never had any use for anything like that before, so our coils won't handle it, but we've developed a sort of code which isn't the language of either of us. They shoot over short-wave stuff with frequency modulation, and we record it as sound. When we shoot it back, it's reconverted into frequency modulation.'

The skipper said, frowning:

'Why wave-form changes in short waves? How do you know?'

'We showed them our recorder in the vision plates, and they showed us theirs. They record the frequency modulation direct. I think,' said Tommy carefully, 'they don't use sound at all, even in speech. They've set up a communications room, and we've watched them in the act of communicating with us. They made no perceptible movement of anything that corresponds to a speech organ. Instead of using a microphone, they simply stand near something that would work as a pick-up antenna. My guess, sir, is that they use microwaves for what you might call person-to-person conversation. I think they make short-wave trains as we make sounds.'

The skipper stared at him:

'That means they have telepathy?'

'Mmm. Yes, sir,' said Tommy. 'Also it means that we have telepathy too, as far as they are concerned. They're probably deaf. They've certainly no idea of using sound waves in air for communication. They simply don't use noises for any purpose.'

The skipper stored the information away.

'What else?'

'Well, sir,' said Tommy doubtfully, 'I think we're all set. We agreed on arbitrary symbols for objects, sir, by way of the visiplates, and worked out relationships and verbs and so on with diagrams and pictures. We've a couple of thousand words that have mutual meanings. We set up an analyser to sort out their short-wave groups, which we feed into a decoding machine. And then the coding end of the machine picks out recordings to make the wave groups we want to send back. When you're ready to talk to the skipper of the other ship, sir, I think we're ready.'

'Hmm. What's your impression of their psychology?' The skipper asked the question of the psychologist.

'I don't know, sir,' said the psychologist harassedly. 'They seem to be completely direct. But they haven't let slip even a hint of the tenseness we know exists. They act as if they were simply setting up a means of communication for friendly conversation. But there is . . . well . . . an overtone—'

The psychologist was a good man at psychological mensuration, which is a good and useful field. But he was not equipped to analyse a completely alien thought pattern.

'If I may say so, sir—' said Tommy uncomfortably.

'What?'

'They're oxygen-breathers,' said Tommy, 'and they're not too dissimilar to us in other ways. It seems to me, sir, that parallel evolution has been at work. Perhaps intelligence evolves in parallel lines, just as . . . well . . . basic bodily functions. I mean,' he added conscientiously, 'any living being of any sort must ingest, metabolize, and excrete. Perhaps any intelligent brain must perceive, apperceive, and find a personal reaction. I'm sure I've detected irony. That implies humour, too. In short, sir, I think they could be likable.'

The skipper heaved himself to his feet.

'Hmm,' he said profoundly, 'we'll see what they have to say.'

He walked to the communications room. The scanner for the vision plate in the robot was in readiness. The skipper walked in front of it. Tommy Dort sat down at the coding machine and tapped at the keys. Highly improbable noises came from it, went into a microphone, and governed the frequency modulation of a signal sent through space to the other spaceship. Almost instantly the vision screen which with one relay – in the robot – showed the interior of the other ship lighted up. An alien came before the scanner and seemed to look inquisitively out of the plate. He was extraordinarily manlike, but he was not human. The impression he gave was of extreme baldness and of a somehow humorous frankness.

'I'd like to say,' said the skipper heavily, 'the appropriate things about this first contact of two dissimilar civilized races, and of my hopes that a friendly intercourse between the two peoples will result.'

Tommy Dort hesitated. Then he shrugged and tapped expertly upon the coder. More improbable noises.

The alien skipper seemed to receive the message. He made a gesture which was wryly assenting. The decoder on the *Llanvabon* hummed to itself and word cards dropped into the message frame. Tommy said dispassionately:

'He says, sir, "That is all very well, but is there any way for us to let each other go home alive? I would be happy to hear of such a way if you can contrive it. At the moment it seems to me that one of us must be killed."'

The atmosphere was one of confusion. There were too many

questions to be answered all at once. Nobody could answer any of them. And all of them had to be answered.

The *Llanvabon* could start for home. The alien ship might or might not be able to multiply the speed of light by one more unit than the Earth vessel. If it could, the *Llanvabon* would get close enough to Earth to reveal its destination – and then have to fight. It might or might not win. Even if it did win, the aliens might have a communication system by which the *Llanvabon*'s destination might have been reported to the aliens' home planet before battle was joined. But the *Llanvabon* might lose in such a fight. If she was to be destroyed, it would be better to be destroyed here, without giving any clue as to where human beings might be found by a forewarned, forearmed alien battle fleet.

The black ship was in exactly the same predicament. It too, could start for home. But the *Llanvabon* might be faster, and an overdrive field can be trailed, if you set to work on it soon enough. The aliens, also, would not know whether the *Llanvabon* could report to its home base without returning. If the alien was to be destroyed, it also would prefer to fight it out here, so that it could not lead a probable enemy to its own civilization.

Neither ship, then, could think of flight. The course of the *Llanvabon* into the nebula might be known to the black ship, but it had been the end of a logarithmic curve, and the aliens could not know its properties. They could not tell from that from what direction the Earth ship had started. As of the moment, then, the two ships were even. But the question was and remained, 'What now?'

There was no specific answer. The aliens traded information for information – and did not always realize what information they gave. The human beings traded information for information – and Tommy Dort sweated blood in his anxiety not to give any clue to the whereabouts of Earth.

The aliens saw by infra-red light, and the vision plates and scanners in the robot communication exchange had to adapt their respective images up and down an optical octave each, for them to have any meaning at all. It did not occur to the aliens that their eyesight told that their sun was a red dwarf, yielding light of greatest energy just below the part of the spectrum visible to human eyes. But after that fact was realized on the *Llanvabon*, it was realized that the aliens, also, should be

It was a slightly distorted sphere, not much over six feet in diameter, covered with small tentacles, or horns.

able to deduce the Earth sun's spectral type by the light to which men's eyes were best adapted.

There was a gadget for the recording of short-wave trains which was as casually in use among the aliens as a sound-recorder is among men. The human beings wanted that, badly. And the aliens were fascinated by the mystery of sound. They were able to perceive noise, of course, just as a man's palm will perceive infra-red light by the sensation of heat it produces, but they could no more differentiate pitch or tone quality than a man is able to distinguish between two frequencies of heat radiation even half an octave apart. To them, the human science of sound was a remarkable discovery. They would find uses for noises which human beings had never imagined – if they lived.

But that was another question. Neither ship could leave without first destroying the other. But while the flood of information was in passage, neither ship could afford to destroy the other. There was the matter of the outer colouring of the two ships. The *Llanvabon* was mirror-bright on the exterior. The alien ship was dead-black by visible light. It absorbed heat to perfection, and should radiate it away again as readily. But it did not. The black coating was not a 'black body' colour or lack of colour. It was a perfect reflector of certain infra-red wave lengths while simultaneously it fluoresced in just those wave bands. In practice, it absorbed the higher frequencies of heat, converted them to lower frequencies it did not radiate – and stayed at the desired temperature even in empty space.

Tommy Dort laboured over his task of communications. He found the alien thought processes not so alien that he could not follow them. The discussion of technics reached the matter of interstellar navigation. A star map was needed to illustrate the process. It would have been logical to use a star map from the chart room – but from a star map one could guess the point from which the map was projected. Tommy had a map made specially, with imaginary but convincing star images upon it. He translated directions for its use by the coder and decoder. In return, the aliens presented a star map of their own before the visiplate. Copied instantly by photograph, the navigation officers laboured over it, trying to figure out from what spot in the galaxy the stars and Milky Way would show at such an angle. It baffled them.

It was Tommy who realized finally that the aliens had made a special star map for their demonstration too, and that it was a mirror-image of the faked map Tommy had shown them previously.

Tommy could grin at that. He began to like these aliens. They were not human, but they had a very human sense of the ridiculous. In the course of time, Tommy essayed a mild joke. It had to be translated into code numerals, and these into quite cryptic groups of short-wave, frequency-modulated impulses, and then these went to the other ship and into heaven knew what to become intelligible. A joke which went through such formalities would not seem likely to be funny. But the alien did see the point.

There was one alien to whom communication became as normal a function as Tommy's own code-handling. This alien and Tommy developed a quite insane friendship, conversing by coder, decoder, and short-wave trains. When technicalities in the official messages grew too involved, the alien sometimes threw in strictly non-technical inter-polations akin to slang. Often, they cleared up the confusion. Tommy, for no reason whatever, had filed a code name of 'Buck' for the alien, which the decoder picked out regularly when this particular one signed his own symbol to a message.

In the third week of communication, the decoder suddenly presented Tommy with a message in the message frame:

> You are a good guy. It is too bad we have to kill each other. – BUCK.

Tommy had been thinking much the same thing. He tapped off the rueful reply:

> We can't see any way out of it. Can you?

There was a pause, and the message frame filled up again:

> If we could believe each other, yes. Our skipper would like it. But we can't believe you, and you can't believe us. We'd trail you home if we got a chance, and you'd trail us. But we feel sorry about it. – BUCK.

Tommy Dort took the messages to the skipper.

'Look here, sir!' he said urgently. 'These people are almost human, and they're likable cusses.'

The skipper was busy about his important task of thinking of things to worry about, and worrying about them. He said tiredly:

'They're oxygen-breathers. Their air is twenty-eight percent oxygen instead of twenty, but they could do very well on Earth. It would be a highly desirable conquest for them. And we still don't know what weapons they've got or what they can develop. Would you tell them how to find Earth?'

'N-no,' said Tommy, unhappily.

'They probably feel the same way,' said the skipper dryly. 'And if we did manage to make a friendly contact, how long would it stay friendly? If their weapons were inferior to ours, they'd feel that for their own safety they had to improve them. And we, knowing they were planning to catch up, would crush them while we could – for our own safety! If it happened to be the other way about, they'd have to smash us before we could catch up to them.'

Tommy was silent, but he moved restlessly.

'If we smash this black ship and get home,' said the skipper, 'Earth Government will be annoyed if we don't tell them where it came from. But what can we do? We'll be lucky enough to get back alive with our warning. It isn't possible to get out of those creatures any more information than we give them, and we surely won't give them our address! We've run into them by accident. Maybe – if we smash this ship – there won't be another contact for thousands of years. And it's a pity, because trade could mean so much! But it takes two to make a peace, and we can't risk trusting them. The only answer is to kill them if we can, and if we can't, to make sure that when they kill us they'll find out nothing that will lead them to Earth. I don't like it,' added the skipper tiredly, 'but there simply isn't anything else to do!'

On the *Llanvabon*, the technicians worked frantically in two divisions. One prepared for victory, and the other for defeat. The ones working for victory could do little. The main blasters were the only weapons with any promise. Their mountings were cautiously altered so that they were no longer fixed nearly dead ahead, with only a five degree traverse. Electronic controls which followed a radio-locator master-finder would keep them trained with absolute precision upon a given target regardless of its manoeuvrings. More, a hitherto unsung genius in the engine room devised a capacity-storage system by which the normal

27

full output of the ship's engines could be momentarily accumulated and released in surges of stored power far above normal. In theory, the range of the blasters should be multiplied and their destructive power considerably stepped up. But there was not much more that could be done.

The defeat crew had more leeway. Star charts, navigational instruments carrying telltale notations, the photographic record Tommy Dort had made on the six months' journey from Earth, and every other memorandum offering clues to Earth's position were prepared for destruction. They were put in sealed files, and if any one of them was opened by one who did not know the exact, complicated procedure to follow, the contents of all the files would flash into ashes and the ash be churned past any hope of restoration. Of course, if the Llanvabon should be victorious, a carefully unindicated method of reopening them in safety would remain.

There were atomic bombs placed all over the hull of the ship. If its human crew should be killed without complete destruction of the ship, the atomic-power bombs should detonate if the Llanvabon was brought alongside the alien vessel. There were no ready-made atomic bombs on board, but there were small spare atomic-power units on board. It was not hard to trick them so that when they were turned on, instead of yielding a smooth flow of power they would explode. And four men of the Earth ship's crew remained always in spacesuits with closed helmets, to fight for the ship should it be punctured in many compartments by a surprise attack.

Such an attack, however, would not be treacherous. The alien skipper had spoken frankly. His manner was that of one who wryly admits the uselessness of lies. The skipper and the Llanvabon, in turn, heavily admitted the virtue of frankness. Each insisted – perhaps truthfully – that he wished for friendship between the two races. But neither could trust the other not to make every conceivable effort to find out the one thing each needed most desperately to conceal – the location of his home planet. And neither dared believe that the other was unable to trail him and find out. Because each felt it his own duty to accomplish that unbearable – to the other – act, neither could risk the possible existence of his race by trusting the other. They must fight because they could not do anything else.

They could raise the stakes of the battle by an exchange of information beforehand. But there was a limit to the stake either would put up. No information on weapons, population or resources would be given by either. Not even the distance of their home bases from the Crab Nebula would be told. They exchanged information, to be sure, but they knew a battle to the death must follow, and each strove to represent his own civilization as powerful enough to give pause to the other's ideas of possible conquest – and thereby increased its appearance of menace to the other, and made battle more unavoidable.

It was curious how completely such alien brains could mesh, however. Tommy Dort, sweating over the coding and decoding machines, found a personal equation emerging from the at first stilted arrays of word cards which arranged themselves. He had seen the aliens only in the vision screen, and then only in light at least one octave removed from the light they saw by. They, in turn, saw him very strangely, by transposed illumination from what to them would be the far ultraviolet. But their brains worked alike. Amazingly alike. Tommy Dort felt an actual sympathy and even something close to friendship for the oxygen-breathing, bald, and dryly ironic creatures of the black space vessel.

Because of that mental kinship he set up – though hopelessly – a sort of table of the aspects of the problem before them. He did not believe that the aliens had any instinctive desire to destroy man. In fact, the study of communications from the aliens had produced on the *Llanvabon* a feeling of tolerance not unlike that between enemy soldiers during a truce on Earth. The men felt no enmity, and probably neither did the aliens. But they had to kill or be killed for strictly logical reasons.

Tommy's table was specific. He made a list of objectives the men must try to achieve, in the order of their importance. The first was the carrying back of news of the existence of the alien culture. The second was the location of that alien culture in the galaxy. The third was the carrying back of as much information as possible about that culture. The third was being worked on, but the second was probably impossible. The first – and all – would depend on the result of the fight which must take place.

The aliens' objectives would be exactly similar, so that the men must prevent, first, news of the existence of Earth's culture from being taken back by the aliens, second, alien discovery of the location of Earth, and third, the acquiring by the aliens of information which would help them or encourage them to attack humanity. And again the third was in train, and the second was probably taken care of, and the first must await the battle.

There was no possible way to avoid the grim necessity of the destruction of the black ship. The aliens would see no solution to their problems but the destruction of the *Llanvabon*. But Tommy Dort, regarding his tabulation ruefully, realized that even complete victory would not be a perfect solution. The ideal would be for the *Llanvabon* to take back the alien ship for study. Nothing less would be a complete attainment of the third objective. But Tommy realized that he hated the idea of so complete a victory, even if it could be accomplished. He would hate the idea of killing even non-human creatures who understood a human joke. And beyond that, he would hate the idea of Earth's fitting out a fleet of fighting ships to destroy an alien culture because its existence was dangerous. The pure accident of this encounter, between peoples who could like each other, had created a situation which could result only in wholesale destruction.

Tommy Dort soured on his own brain, which could find no answer which would work. But there had to be an answer! The gamble was too big! It was too absurd that two spaceships should fight – neither one primarily designed for fighting – so that the survivor could carry back news which would set one race to frenzied preparation for war against the unwarned other.

If both races could be warned, though, and each knew that the other did not want to fight, and if they could communicate with each other but not locate each other until some grounds for mutual trust could be reached—

It was impossible. It was chimerical. It was a daydream. It was nonsense. But it was such luring nonsense that Tommy Dort ruefully put it into the coder to his oxygen-breathing but gilled friend Buck, then some hundred thousand miles off in the misty brightness of the nebula.

'Sure,' said Buck, in the decoder's word cards flicking into place in the message frame. 'That is a good dream. But I like you and still won't believe you. If I said that first, you would like me but not believe me, either. I tell you the truth more than you believe, and maybe you tell me the truth more than I believe. But there is no way to know. I am sorry.'

Tommy Dort stared gloomily at the message. He felt a very horrible sense of responsibility. Everyone did, on the *Llanvabon*. If they failed in this encounter, the human race would run a very good chance of being exterminated in time to come. If they succeeded, the race of the aliens would be the one to face destruction, most likely. Millions or billions of lives hung upon the actions of a few men.

Then Tommy Dort saw the answer.

It would be amazingly simple, if it worked. At worst it might give a partial victory to humanity and the *Llanvabon*. He sat quite still, not daring to move lest he break the chain of thought that followed the first tenuous idea. He went over and over it, excitedly finding objections here and meeting them, and overcoming impossibilities there. It was the answer! He felt sure of it.

He felt almost dizzy with relief when he found his way to the captain's room and asked leave to speak.

It is the function of a skipper, among others, to find things to worry about. But the *Llanvabon*'s skipper did not have to look. In the three weeks and four days since the first contact with the alien black ship, the skipper's face had grown lined and old. He had not only the *Llanvabon* to worry about, but all of humanity.

'Sir,' said Tommy Dort, his mouth rather dry because of his enormous earnestness, 'may I offer a method of attack on the black ship? I'll undertake it myself, sir, and if it doesn't work our ship won't be weakened.'

The skipper looked at him unseeingly.

'The tactics are all worked out, Mr. Dort,' he said heavily. 'They're being cut on tape now, for the ship's handling. It's a terrible gamble, but it has to be done.'

'I think,' said Tommy carefully, 'I've worked out a way to take the gamble out. Suppose, sir, we send a message to the other ship, offering—'

His voice went on in the utterly quiet captain's room, with the visiplates showing only a vast mistiness outside and the two fiercely burning stars in the nebula's heart.

The skipper himself went through the air lock with Tommy. For one reason, the action Tommy had suggested would need his authority behind it. For another, the skipper had worried more intensively than anybody else on the *Llanvabon*, and he was tired of it. If he went with Tommy, he would do the thing himself, and if he failed he would be the first one killed – and the tapes for the Earth ship's manoeuvring were already fed into the control board and correlated with the master-timer. If Tommy and the skipper were killed, a single control pushed home would throw the *Llanvabon* into the most furious possible all-out attack, which would end in the complete destruction of one ship or the other – or both. So the skipper was not deserting his post.

The outer air lock door swung wide. It opened upon the shining emptiness which was the nebula. Twenty miles away, the little round robot hung in space, drifting in an incredible orbit about the twin central suns, and floating ever nearer and nearer. It would never reach either of them, of course. The white star alone was so much hotter than Earth's sun that its heat-effect would produce Earth's temperature on an object five times as far from it as Neptune is from Sol. Even removed to the distance of Pluto, the little robot would be raised to cherry-red heat by the blazing white dwarf. And it could not possibly approach to the ninety-odd million miles which is the Earth's distance from the sun. So near, its metal would melt and boil away as vapour. But, half a light-year out, the bulbous object bobbed in emptiness.

The two space-suited figures soared away from the *Llanvabon*. The small atomic drives which made them minute spaceships on their own had been subtly altered, but the change did not interfere with their functioning. They headed for the communication robot. The skipper, out in space, said gruffly:

'Mr Dort, all my life I have longed for adventure. This is the first time I could ever justify it to myself.'

His voice came through Tommy's space-phone receivers. Tommy wetted his lips and said:

'It doesn't seem like adventure to me, sir. I want terribly for the plan to go through. I thought adventure was when you didn't care.'

'Oh, no,' said the skipper. 'Adventure is when you toss your life on the scales of chance and wait for the pointer to stop.'

They reached the round object. They clung to its short, scanner-tipped horns.

'Intelligent, those creatures,' said the skipper heavily. 'They must want desperately to see more of our ship than the communications room, to agree to this exchange of visits before the fight.'

'Yes, sir,' said Tommy. But privately, he suspected that Buck – his gill-breathing friend – would like to see him in the flesh before one or both of them died. And it seemed to him that between the two ships had grown up an odd tradition of courtesy, like that between two ancient knights before a tourney, when they admired each other wholeheartedly before hacking at each other with all the contents of their respective armouries.

They waited.

Then, out of the mist, came two other figures. The alien spacesuits were also power-driven. The aliens themselves were shorter than men, and their helmet openings were coated with a filtering material to cut off visible and ultraviolet rays which to them would be lethal. It was not possible to see more than the outline of the heads within.

Tommy's helmet phone said, from the communications room on the *Llanvabon*:

'They say that their ship is waiting for you, sir. The airlock door will be open.'

The skipper's voice said heavily:

'Mr Dort, have you seen their spacesuits before? If so, are you sure they're not carrying anything extra, such as bombs?'

'Yes, sir,' said Tommy. 'We've showed each other our space equipment. They've nothing but regular stuff in view, sir.'

The skipper made a gesture to the two aliens. He and Tommy Dort plunged on for the black vessel. They could not make out the ship very clearly with the naked eye, but directions for change of course came from the communication room.

The black ship loomed up. It was huge; as long as the *Llanvabon* and vastly thicker. The air lock did stand open. The two spacesuited men moved in and anchored themselves with magnetic-soled boots. The outer door closed. There was a rush of air and simultaneously the sharp quick tug of artificial gravity. Then the inner door opened.

All was darkness. Tommy switched on his helmet light at the same instant as the skipper. Since the aliens saw by infra-red, a white light would have been intolerable to them. The men's helmet lights were, therefore, of the deep-red tint used to illuminate instrument panels so there would be no dazzling of eyes that must be able to detect the minutest specks of white light on a navigating vision plate. There were aliens waiting to receive them. They blinked at the brightness of the helmet lights. The space-phone receivers said in Tommy's ear:

'They say, sir, their skipper is waiting for you.'

Tommy and the skipper were in a long corridor with a soft flooring underfoot. Their lights showed details every one of which was exotic.

'I think I'll crack my helmet, sir,' said Tommy.

He did. The air was good. By analysis it was thirty per cent oxygen instead of twenty for normal air on Earth, but the pressure was less. It felt just right. The artificial gravity, too, was less than that maintained on the *Llanvabon*. The home planet of the aliens would be smaller than Earth, and – by the infra-red data – circling close to a nearly dead, dull-red sun. The air had smells in it. They were utterly strange, but not unpleasant.

An arched opening. A ramp with the same soft stuff underfoot. Lights which actually shed a dim, dull-red glow about. The aliens had stepped up some of their illuminating equipment as an act of courtesy. The light might hurt their eyes, but it was a gesture of consideration which made Tommy even more anxious for his plan to go through.

The alien skipper faced them with what seemed to Tommy a gesture of wryly humorous deprecation. The helmet phones said:

'He says, sir, that he greets you with pleasure, but he has been able to think of only one way in which the problem created by the meeting of these two ships can be solved.'

'He means a fight,' said the skipper. 'Tell him I'm here to offer another choice.'

The *Llanvabon*'s skipper and the skipper of the alien ship were face to face, but their communication was weirdly indirect. The aliens used no sound in communication. Their talk, in fact, took place on micro-waves and approximated telepathy. But they could not hear, in any ordinary sense of the word, so the skipper's and Tommy's speech approached telepathy, too, as far as they were concerned. When the skipper spoke, his space phone sent his words back to the *Llanvabon*, where the words were fed into the coder and short-wave equivalents sent back to the black ship. The alien skipper's reply went to the *Llanvabon* and through the decoder, and was retransmitted by space phone in words read from the message frame. It was awkward, but it worked.

The short and stocky alien skipper paused. The helmet phones relayed his translated, soundless reply.

'He is anxious to hear, sir.'

The skipper took off his helmet. He put his hands at his belt in a belligerent pose.

'Look here!' he said truculently to the bald, strange creature in the unearthly red glow before him. 'It looks like we have to fight and one batch of us get killed. We're ready to do it if we have to. But if you win, we've got it fixed so you'll never find out where Earth is, and there's a good chance we'll get you anyhow! If we win, we'll be in the same fix. And if we win and go back home, our government will fit out a fleet and start hunting your planet. And if we find it we'll be ready to blast it to hell! If you win, the same thing will happen to us! And it's all foolishness! We've stayed here a month, and we've swapped information, and we don't hate each other. There's no reason for us to fight except for the rest of our respective races!'

The skipper stopped for breath, scowling. Tommy Dort inconspicuously put his own hands on the belt of his spacesuit. He waited, hoping desperately that the trick would work.

'He says, sir,' reported the helmet phones, 'that all you say is true. But that his race has to be protected, just as you feel that yours must be.'

'Naturally,' said the skipper angrily, 'but the sensible thing to do is to figure out how to protect it! Putting its future up as a gamble in a fight is not sensible. Our races have to be warned of each other's existence. That's true. But each should have proof that the other doesn't want to fight, but wants to be friendly. And we shouldn't be able to find each other, but we should be able to communicate with each other to work out grounds for a common trust. If our governments want to be fools, let them! But we should give them the chance to make friends, instead of starting a space war out of mutual funk!'

Briefly, the space phone said:

'He says that the difficulty is that of trusting each other now. With the possible existence of his race at stake, he cannot take any chance, and neither can you, of yielding an advantage.'

'But my race,' boomed the skipper, glaring at the alien captain, 'my race has an advantage now. We came here to your ship in atom-powered spacesuits! Before we left, we altered the drives! We can set off ten pounds of sensitized fuel apiece, right here in this ship, or it can be set off by remote control from our ship! It will be rather remarkable if your fuel store doesn't blow up with us! In other words, if you don't accept my proposal for a common-sense approach to this predicament, Dort and I blow up in an atomic explosion, and your ship will be wrecked if not destroyed – and the *Llanvabon* will be attacking with everything it's got within two seconds after the blast goes off!'

The captain's room of the alien ship was a strange scene, with its dull-red illumination and the strange, bald, gilled aliens watching the skipper and waiting for the inaudible translation of the harangue they could not hear. But a sudden tensity appeared in the air. A sharp, savage feeling of strain. The alien skipper made a gesture. The helmet phones hummed.

'He says, sir, what is your proposal?'

'Swap ships!' roared the skipper. 'Swap ships and go on home! We can fix our instruments so they'll do no trailing, he can do the same with his. We'll each remove our star maps and records. We'll each dismantle our weapons. The air will serve, and we'll take their ship and they'll take ours, and neither one can harm or trail the other, and each will carry home more information than can be taken otherwise! We can agree on this same Crab Nebula as a rendezvous when the double star has made another circuit, and if our people want to meet them they can do it, and if they are scared they can duck it! That's my proposal! And he'll take it, or Dort and I blow up their ship and the *Llanvabon* blasts what's left!'

He glared about him while he waited for the translation to reach the tense small stocky figures about him. He could tell when it came because the tenseness changed. The figures stirred. They made gestures. One of them made convulsive movements. It lay down on the soft floor and kicked. Others leaned against its walls and shook.

The voice in Tommy Dort's helmet phones had been strictly crisp and professional, before, but now it sounded blankly amazed.

'He says, sir, that it is a good joke. Because the two crew members he sent to our ship, and that you passed on the way, have their spacesuits stuffed with atomic explosive too, sir, and he intended to make the very same offer and threat! Of course he accepts, sir. Your ship is worth more to him than his own, and his is worth more to you than the *Llanvabon*. It appears, sir, to be a deal.'

Then Tommy Dort realized what the convulsive movements of the aliens were. They were laughter.

It wasn't quite as simple as the skipper had outlined it. The actual working-out of the proposal was complicated. For three days the crews of the two ships intermingled, the aliens learning the workings of the *Llanvabon*'s engines, and the men learning to handle the controls of the black spaceship. It was a good joke – but it wasn't all a joke. There were men on the black ship, and aliens on the *Llanvabon*, ready at an instant's notice to blow up the vessels in question. And they would have done it in case of need, for which reason the need did not appear. But it was, actually, a better arrangement to have two expeditions return to two civilizations, under the current arrangement, than for either to return alone.

There were differences, though. There was some dispute about the removal of records. In most cases the dispute was settled by the destruction of the records. There was more trouble caused by the *Llanvabon*'s books, and the alien equivalent of a ship's library, containing works which approximated the novels of Earth. But those items were valuable for possible friendship, because they would show the two cultures, each to the other, from the viewpoint of normal citizens and without propaganda.

But nerves were tense during those three days. Aliens unloaded and inspected the foodstuffs intended for the men on the black ship. Men trans-shipped the foodstuffs the aliens would need to return to their home. There were endless details, from the exchange of lighting equipment to suit the eyesight of the exchanging crews, to a final check-up of apparatus. A joint inspection party of both races verified that all detector devices had been smashed but not removed, so that they could not be used for trailing and had not been smuggled away.

And of course, the aliens were anxious not to leave any useful weapon on the black ship, nor the men upon the *Llanvabon*. It was a curious fact that each crew was best qualified to take exactly the measures which made an evasion of the agreement impossible.

There was a final conference before the two ships parted, back in the communication room of the *Llanvabon*.

'Tell the little runt,' rumbled the *Llanvabon*'s former skipper, 'that he's got a good ship and he'd better treat her right.'

The message frame flicked word cards into position.

'I believe,' it said on the alien skipper's behalf, 'that your ship is just as good. I will hope to meet you here when the double star has turned one turn.'

The last man left the *Llanvabon*. It moved away into the misty nebula before the men had returned to the black ship. The vision plates in that vessel had been altered for human eyes, and human crewmen watched jealously for any trade of their former ship as their new craft took a crazy, evasive course to a remote part of the nebula. It came to a crevasse of nothingness, leading to the stars. It rose swiftly to clear space. There was the instant of breathlessness which the overdrive field produces as it goes on, and then the black ship whipped away into the void at many times the speed of light.

Many days later, the skipper saw Tommy Dort poring over one of the strange objects which were the equivalent of books. It was fascinating to puzzle over. The skipper was pleased with himself. The technicians of the *Llanvabon*'s former crew were finding out desirable things about the ship almost momently. Doubtless the aliens were as pleased with their discoveries in the *Llanvabon*. But the black ship would be enormously worthwhile – and the solution that had been found was by any standard much superior even to combat in which the Earthmen had been overwhelmingly victorious.

'Hmmm. Mr Dort,' said the skipper profoundly. 'You've no equipment to make another photographic record on the way back. It was left on the *Llanvabon*. But fortunately, we have your record taken on the way out, and I shall report most favourably on your suggestion and your assistance in carrying it out. I think very well of you, sir.'

'Thank you, sir,' said Tommy Dort.

He waited. The skipper cleared his throat.

'You . . . ah . . . first realized the close similarity of mental processes between the aliens and ourselves,' he observed. 'What do you think of the prospects of a friendly arrangement if we keep a rendezvous with them at the nebula as agreed?'

'Oh, we'll get along all right, sir,' said Tommy. 'We've got a good start toward friendship. After all, since they see by infra-red, the planets they'd want to make use of wouldn't suit us. There's no reason why we shouldn't get along. We're almost alike in psychology.'

'Hmmm. Now just what do you mean by that?' demanded the skipper.

'Why, they're just like us, sir!' said Tommy. 'Of course they breathe through gills and they see by heat waves, and their blood has a copper base instead of iron and a few little details like that. But otherwise we're just alike! There were only men in their crew, sir, but they have two sexes as we have, and they have families, and . . . er . . . their sense of humour – In fact—'

Tommy hesitated.

'Go on, sir,' said the skipper.

'Well – There was the one I called Buck, sir, because he hasn't any name that goes into sound waves,' said Tommy. 'We got along very well. I'd really call him my friend, sir. And we were together for a couple of hours just before the two ships separated and we'd nothing in particular to do. So I became convinced that humans and aliens are bound to be good friends if they have only half a chance. You see, sir, we spent those two hours telling dirty jokes.'

Pictures Don't Lie

Katherine Maclean

The man from the *News* asked, 'What do you think of the aliens, Mr Nathen? Are they friendly? Do they look human?'

'Very human,' said the thin young man.

Outside, rain sleeted across the big windows with a steady, faint drumming, blurring and dimming the view of the airfield where *They* would arrive. On the concrete runways the puddles were pockmarked with rain, and the grass growing untouched between the runways of the unused field glistened wetly, bending before gusts of wind.

Back at a respectful distance from the place where the huge space-ship would land were the grey shapes of trucks, where TV camera crews huddled inside their mobile units, waiting. Farther back in the deserted, sandy landscape, behind distant sandy hills, artillery was ringed in a great circle, and in the distance across the horizon bombers stood ready at airfields, guarding the world against possible treachery from the first alien ship ever to land from space.

'Do you know anything about their home planet?' asked the man from the *Herald*.

The *Times* man stood with the others, listening absently, thinking of questions but reserving them. Joseph R. Nathen, the thin young man with the straight black hair and the tired lines on his face, was being treated with respect by his interviewers. He was obviously on edge, and they did not want to harry him with too many questions at once. They wanted to keep his good will. Tomorrow he would be one of the biggest celebrities ever to appear in headlines.

'No, nothing directly.'

'Any ideas or deductions?' the *Herald* persisted.

'Their world must be Earthlike to them,' the weary-looking young man answered uncertainly. 'The environment evolves the animal. But only in relative terms, of course.' He looked at them with a quick glance and then looked away evasively, his lank black hair beginning to cling to his forehead with sweat. 'That doesn't necessarily mean anything.'

'Earthlike,' muttered a reporter, writing it down as if he had noticed nothing more in the reply.

The *Times* man glanced at the *Herald*, wondering if he had noticed, and received a quick glance in exchange.

The *Herald* asked Nathen, 'You think they are dangerous, then?'

It was the kind of question, assuming much, that usually broke reticence and brought forth quick facts – when it hit the mark. They all knew of the military precautions, although they were not supposed to.

The question missed. Nathen glanced out the window vaguely. 'No, I wouldn't say so.'

'You think they are friendly, then?' said the *Herald*, equally positive on the opposite tack.

A fleeting smile touched Nathen's lips. 'Those I know are.'

There was no lead in this direction, and they had to get the basic facts of the story before the ship came. The *Times* asked, 'What led up to your contacting them?'

Nathen answered, after a hesitation, 'Static. Radio static. The Army told you my job, didn't they?'

The Army had told them nothing at all. The officer who had conducted them in for the interview stood glowering watchfully, as if he objected by instinct to telling anything to the public.

Nathen glanced at him doubtfully. 'My job is radio decoder for the Department of Military Intelligence. I use a directional pick-up, tune in on foreign bands, record any scrambled or coded messages I hear, and build automatic decoders and descramblers for all the basic scramble patterns.'

The officer cleared his throat but said nothing.

The reporters smiled, noting that down.

Security regulations had changed since arms inspection had been legalized by the UN. Complete information being the only public security against secret rearmament, spying and prying had come to seem a public service. Its aura had changed. It was good public relations to admit to it.

Nathen continued, 'In my spare time I started directing the pick-up at stars. There's radio noise from stars, you know. Just stuff that sounds like spatter static, and an occasional squawk. People have been listening to it for a long time, and researching, trying to work out why stellar radiation on those bands comes in such jagged bursts. It didn't seem natural.'

He paused and smiled uncertainly, aware that the next thing he would say was the thing that would make him famous – an idea that had come to him while he listened, an idea as simple and as perfect as the one that came to Newton when he saw the apple fall.

'I decided it wasn't natural. I tried decoding it.'

Hurriedly, he tried to explain it away and make it seem obvious. 'You see, there's an old intelligence trick, speeding up a message on a record until it sounds just like that, a short squawk of static, and then broadcasting it. Undergrounds use it. I'd heard that kind of screech before.'

'You mean they broadcast at us in code?' asked the *News*.'

'It's not exactly code. All you need to do is record it and slow it down. They're not broadcasting at us. If a star has planets, inhabited planets, and there is broadcasting between them, they would send it on a tight beam to save power.' He looked for comprehension. 'You know, like a spotlight. Theoretically, a tight beam can go on for ever without losing power. But aiming would be difficult from planet to planet. You can't expect a beam to stay on target, over such distances, more than a few seconds at a time. So they'd naturally compress each message into a short half-second- or one-second-length package and send it a few hundred times in one long blast to make sure it is picked up during the instant the beam swings across the target."

He was talking slowly and carefully, remembering that this explanation was for the newspapers. 'When a stray beam swings through our section of space, there's a sharp peak in noise level from that direction. The beams are swinging to follow their own planets at home, and the distance between there and here exaggerates the speed of swing tremendously, so we wouldn't pick up more than a *bip* as it passes.'

'How did you account for the number of squawks coming in?' the *Times* asked. 'Do stellar systems rotate on the plane of the Galaxy?' It was a private question; he spoke impulsively from interest and excitement.

The radio decoder grinned, the lines of strain vanishing from his face for a moment. 'Maybe we're intercepting everybody's telephone calls, and the whole Galaxy is swarming with races that spend all day yacking at each other over the radio. Maybe the human type is standard model.'

'It would take something like that,' the *Times* agreed. They smiled at each other.

The *News* asked. 'How did you happen to pick up television instead of voices?'

'Not by accident,' Nathen explained patiently. I'd recognized a scanning pattern, and I wanted pictures. Pictures are understandable in any language.'

★   ★   ★   ★

Near the interviewers, a senator paced back and forth, muttering his memorized speech of welcome and nervously glancing out the wide, streaming windows into the grey, sleeting rain.

Opposite the windows of the long room was a small raised platform flanked by the tall shapes of TV cameras and sound pick-ups on booms, and darkened floodlights, arranged and ready for the senator to make his speech of welcome to the aliens and the world. A shabby radio sending set stood beside it without a case to conceal its parts, two cathode television tubes flickering nakedly on one side and the speaker humming on the other. A vertical panel of dials and knobs jutted up before them, and a small hand-mike sat ready on the table before the panel. It was connected to a box-like, expensively-cased piece of equipment with 'Radio Lab, U.S. Property' stencilled on it.

'I recorded a couple of package screeches from Sagittarius and began working on them,' Nathen added. 'It took a couple of months to find the synchronizing signals and set the scanners close enough to the right time to even get a pattern. When I showed the pattern to the Department, they gave me full time to work on it, and an assistant to help. It took eight months to pick out the colour bands and assign them the right colours, to get anything intelligible on the screen.'

The shabby-looking mess of exposed parts was the original receiver that they had laboured over for ten months, adjusting and re-adjusting to reduce the maddening rippling plaids of unsynchronized colour scanners to some kind of sane picture.

'Trial and error,' said Nathen, 'but it came out all right. The wide band spread of the squawks had suggested colour TV from the beginning.'

He walked over and touched the set. The speaker bipped slightly and the grey screen flickered with a flash of colour at the touch. The set was awake and sensitive, tuned to receive from the great interstellar spaceship which now circled the atmosphere.

'We wondered why there were so many bands, but when we got the set working and started recording and playing everything that came in, we found we'd tapped something like a lending-library line. It was all fiction, plays.'

Between the pauses in Nathen's voice, the *Times* found himself unconsciously listening for the sound of roaring, swiftly-approaching rocket jets.

The *Post* asked, 'How did you contact the spaceship?'

'I scanned and recorded a film copy of *The Rite of Spring*, the Disney–Stravinsky combination, and sent it back along the same line we were receiving from. Just testing. It wouldn't get there for a good number of years, if it got there at all, but I thought it would please the library to get a new record in.

'Two weeks later, when we caught and slowed a new batch of recordings, we found an answer. It was obviously meant for us. It was a flash of the Disney being played to a large audience, and then the audience sitting and waiting before a blank screen. The signal was very clear and loud. We'd intercepted a spaceship. They were asking for an encore, you see. They liked the film and wanted more. . . .'

He smiled at them in sudden thought. 'You can see them for yourself.

The hand-rigged receiver was still humming, tuned to the sending band of the circling ship.

It's all right down the hall where the linguists are working on the automatic translator.'

The listening officer frowned and cleared his throat, and the thin young man turned to him quickly, 'No security reason why they should not see the broadcast, is there? Perhaps you should show them.' He said to the reporters reassuringly, 'It's right down the hall. You will be informed the moment the spaceship approaches.'

The interview was very definitely over. The lank-haired, nervous young man turned away and seated himself at the radio set while the officer swallowed his objections and showed them dourly down the hall to a closed door.

They opened it and fumbled into a darkened room crowded with empty folding chairs, dominated by a glowing bright screen. The door closed behind them, bringing total darkness.

There was the sound of reporters fumbling their way into seats around him, but the *Times* man remained standing, aware of an enormous surprise, as if he had been asleep and wakened to find himself in the wrong country.

The bright colours of the double image seemed the only real thing in the darkened room. Even blurred as they were, he could see that the action was subtly different, the shapes subtly not right.

He was looking at aliens.

The impression was of two humans disguised, humans moving oddly, half dancing, half crippled. Carefully, afraid the images would go away, he reached up to his breast-pocket, took out his polarized glasses, rotated one lens at right angles to the other, and put them on.

Immediately, the two beings came into sharp focus, real and solid, and the screen became a wide, illusively near window through which he watched them.

They were conversing with each other in a grey-walled room, discussing something with restrained excitement. The large man in the green tunic closed his purple eyes for an instant at something the other said and grimaced, making a motion with his fingers as if shoving something away from him.

Mellerdrammer.

The second, smaller, with yellowish-green eyes, stepped closer, talking more rapidly in a lower voice. The first stood very still, not trying to interrupt.

Obviously, the proposal was some advantageous treachery, and he wanted to be persuaded. The *Times* groped for a chair and sat down.

Perhaps gesture is universal; desire and aversion, a leaning forward or a leaning back, tension, relaxation. Perhaps these actors were masters. The scenes changed: a corridor, a park-like place in what he began to realize was a spaceship, a lecture-room. There were others talking and working, speaking to the man in the green tunic, and never was it unclear what was happening or how they felt.

They talked a flowing language with many short vowels and shifts of pitch, and they gestured in the heat of talk, their hands moving with an odd lagging difference of motion, not slow, but somehow drifting.

He ignored the language, but after a time the difference in motion began to arouse his interest. Something in the way they walked . . .

With an effort he pulled his mind from the plot and forced his attention to the physical difference. Brown hair in short, silky crew cuts, varied eye colours, the colours showing clearly because their irises were very large, their round eyes set very widely apart in tapering, light-brown faces. Their necks and shoulders were thick in a way that would indicate unusual strength for a human, but their wrists were narrow and their fingers long and thin and delicate.

There seemed to be more than the usual number of fingers.

Since he came in, a machine had been whirring and a voice muttering beside him. He turned from counting their fingers and looked around. Beside him sat an alert-looking man wearing earphones, watching and listening with hawk-like concentration. Beside him was a tall stream-lined box. From the screen came the sound of the alien language. The man abruptly flipped a switch on the box, muttered a word into a small hand microphone, and flipped the switch back with nervous rapidity.

He reminded the *Times* man of the earphoned interpreters at the UN. The machine was probably a vocal translator and the mutterer a linguist adding to its vocabulary. Near the screen were two other linguists taking notes.

The *Times* remembered the senator pacing in the observatory room, rehearsing his speech of welcome. The speech would not be just the empty pompous gesture he had expected. It would be translated mechanically and understood by the aliens.

On the other side of the glowing window that was the stereo screen the large protagonist in the green tunic was speaking to a pilot in a grey uniform. They stood in a brightly-lit canary-yellow control-room in a spaceship.

The *Times* tried to pick up the thread of the plot. Already he was interested in the fate of the hero and liked him. That was the effect of good acting, probably, for part of the art of acting is to win affection from the audience, and this actor might be the matinée idol of whole Solar Systems.

Controlled tension, betraying itself by a jerk of the hands, a too quick answer to a question. The uniformed one, not suspicious, turned his back, busying himself at some task involving a map lit with glowing red points, his motions sharing the same fluid, dragging grace of the others, as if they were underwater or on a slow-motion film. The other was watching a switch, a switch set into a panel, moving closer to it, talking casually – background music coming and rising in thin chords of tension.

There was a close-up of the alien's face watching the switch and the *Times* noted that his ears were symmetrical half-circles, almost perfect, with no earholes visible. The voice of the uniformed one answered – a brief word in a preoccupied, deep voice. His back was still turned. The other glanced at the switch, moving close to it, talking casually, the switch coming closer and closer stereoscopically. It was in reach, filling the screen. His hand came into view, darted out, closed over the switch—

There was a sharp clap of sound and his hand opened in a frozen shape of pain. Beyond him, as his gaze swung up, stood the figure of the uniformed officer, unmoving, a weapon rigid in his hand, in the startled position in which he had turned and fired, watching with widening eyes as the man in the green tunic swayed and fell.

The tableau held, the uniformed one dropping, looking down at his hand holding the weapon which had killed, and music began to build in from the background. Just for an instant, the room and the things within it flashed into one of those bewildering colour changes that were the bane of colour television – to a colour negative of itself, a green man standing in a violet control-room, looking down at the body of a green man in a red tunic. It held for less than a second; then the colour-band alternator fell back into phase and the colours reversed to normal.

Another uniformed man came and took the weapon from the limp hand of the other, who began to explain dejectedly in a low voice while the music mounted and covered his words and the screen slowly went blank, like a window that slowly filmed over with grey fog.

The music faded.

In the dark, someone clapped appreciatively.

The earphoned man beside the *Times* shifted his earphones back from his ears and spoke briskly. 'I can't get any more. Either of you want a replay?'

There was a short silence until the linguist nearest the set said, 'I guess we've squeezed that one dry. Let's run the tape where Nathen and that ship radio boy are kidding around CQing and tuning their beams in closer. I have a hunch the boy is talking routine ham talk and giving the old radio count – one-two-three-testing.'

There was some fumbling in the semi-dark and then the screen came to life again.

It showed a flash of an audience sitting before a screen and gave a clipped chord of some familiar symphony. 'Crazy about Stravinsky and Mozart,' remarked the earphoned linguist to the *Times*, re-settling his earphones. 'Can't stand Gershwin. Can you beat that?' He turned his attention back to the screen as the right sequence came on.

The *Post*, who was sitting in front of him, turned to the *Times* and said, 'Funny how much they look like people.' He was writing, making notes to telephone his report. 'What colour hair did that character have?'

'I didn't notice.' He wondered if he should remind the reporter that Nathen had said he assigned the colour bands on guess, choosing the colours that gave the plausible images. The guests, when they arrived, would turn out to be bright green with blue hair. Only the gradations of colour in the picture were sure, only the similarities and contrasts, the relationship of one colour to another.

From the screen came the sound of the alien language again. This race averaged deeper voices than human. He liked deep voices. Could he write that?

No, there was something wrong with that, too. How had Nathen established the right sound-track pitch? Was it a matter of taking the modulation as it came in, or some sort of heterodyning up and down by trial and error? Probably.

It might be safer to assume that Nathen had simply preferred deep voices.

As he sat there, doubting, an uneasiness he had seen in Nathen came back to add to his own uncertainty, and he remembered just how close that uneasiness had come to something that looked like restrained fear.

'What I don't get is why he went to all the trouble of picking up TV shows instead of just contacting them,' the *News* complained. 'They're good shows, but what's the point?'

'Maybe so we'd get to learn their language, too,' said the *Herald*.

On the screen now was the obviously unstaged and genuine scene of a young alien working over a bank of apparatus. He turned and waved and opened his mouth in the comical O shape which the *Times* was beginning to recognize as their equivalent of a smile, then went back to trying to explain something about the equipment, in elaborate, awkward gestures and carefully mouthed words.

The *Times* got up quietly, went out into the bright white stone corridor, and walked back the way he had come, thoughtfully folding his stereo glasses and putting them away.

No one stopped him. Secrecy restrictions were ambiguous here. The reticence of the Army seemed more a matter of habit – mere reflex, from the fact that it had all originated in the Intelligence Department – than any reasoned policy of keeping the landing a secret.

The main room was more crowded than he had left it. The TV camera and sound crew stood near their apparatus, the senator had found a chair and was reading, and at the far end of the room eight men were grouped in a circle of chairs, arguing something with impassioned concentration. The *Times* recognized a few he knew personally, eminent names in science, workers in field theory.

A stray phrase reached him: '—reference to the universal constants as ratio—' It was probably a discussion of ways of converting formulas from one mathematics to another for a rapid exchange of information.

They had reason to be intent, aware of the flood of insights that novel viewpoints could bring, if they could grasp them. He would have liked to go over and listen, but there was too little time left before the space-ship was due, and he had a question to ask.

★   ★   ★   ★

The hand-rigged transceiver was still humming, tuned to the sending band of the circling ship, and the young man who had started it all was sitting on the edge of the TV platform with his chin resting in one hand. He did not look up as the *Times* approached, but it was the indifference of preoccupation, not discourtesy.

The *Times* sat down on the edge of the platform beside him and took out a packet of cigarettes, then remembered the coming TV broadcast and the ban on smoking. He put them away, thoughtfully watching the diminishing rain spray against the streaming windows.

'What's wrong?' he asked.

Nathen showed that he was aware and friendly by a slight motion of his head.

'*You* tell me.'

'Hunch,' said the *Times* man. 'Sheer hunch. Everything sailing along too smoothly, everyone taking too much for granted.'

Nathen relaxed slightly. 'I'm still listening.'

'Something about the way they move . . .'

Nathen shifted to glance at him.

'That's bothered me, too.'

'Are you sure they're adjusted to the right speed?'

Nathen clenched his hands out in front of him and looked at them consideringly. 'I don't know. When I turn the tape faster, they're all rushing, and you begin to wonder why their clothes don't stream behind them, why the doors close so quickly and yet you can't hear them slam, why things fall so fast. If I turn it slower, they all seem to be swimming.' He gave the *Times* a considering sideways glance. 'Didn't catch the name.'

Country-bred guy, thought the *Times*. 'Jacob Luke, *Times*,' he said, extending his hand.

Nathen gave the hand a quick, hard grip, identifying the name. 'Sunday Science Section editor. I read it. Surprised to meet you here.'

'Likewise.' The *Times* smiled. 'Look, have you gone into this rationally, with formulas?' He found a pencil in his pocket. 'Obviously, there's something wrong with our judgment of their weight-to-speed-to-momentum ratio. Maybe it's something simple, like low gravity aboard ship, with magnetic shoes. Maybe they *are* floating slightly.'

'Why worry?' Nathen cut in. 'I don't see any reason to try to figure it out now.' He laughed and shoved back his black hair nervously. 'We'll see them in twenty minutes.'

'Will we?' asked the *Times* slowly.

There was a silence while the senator turned a page of his magazine with a slight crackling of paper and the scientists argued at the other end of the room. Nathen pushed at his lank black hair again, as if it were trying to fall forward in front of his eyes and keep him from seeing.

'Sure.' The young man laughed suddenly, talked rapidly. 'Sure we'll see them. Why shouldn't we, with all the government ready with welcome speeches, the whole Army turned out and hiding over the hill, reporters all around, newsreel cameras – everything set up to broadcast the landing to the world. The President himself shaking hands with me and waiting in Washington—'

He came to the truth without pausing for breath.

He said, 'Hell, no, they won't get here. There's some mistake somewhere. Something's wrong. I should have told the brass hats yesterday when I started adding it up. Don't know why I didn't say anything. Scared, I guess. Too much top rank around here. Lost my nerve.'

He clutched the *Times* man's sleeve. 'Look. I don't know what—'

A green light flashed on the sending-receiving set. Nathen didn't look at it, but he stopped talking.

The loudspeaker on the set broke into a voice speaking in the aliens' language. The senator started and looked nervously at it, straightening his tie. The voice stopped.

Nathen turned and looked at the loud-speaker. His worry seemed to be gone.

'What is it?' the *Times* asked anxiously.

'He says they've slowed enough to enter the atmosphere now. They'll be here in five to ten minutes, I guess. That's Bud. He's all excited. He says holy smoke, what a murky-looking planet we live on.' Nathen smiled. 'Kidding.'

The *Times* was puzzled. 'What does he mean, murky? It can't be raining over much territory on Earth.' Outside, the rain was slowing and bright-blue patches of sky were shining through breaks in the cloud blanket, glittering blue light from the drops that ran down the windows. He tried to think of an explanation. 'Maybe they're trying to land on Venus.' The thought was ridiculous, he knew. The spaceship was following Nathen's sending beam. It couldn't miss Earth. 'Bud' had to be kidding.

The green light glowed on the set again, and they stopped speaking, waiting for the message to be recorded, slowed, and replayed. The cathode screen came to life suddenly with a picture of the young man sitting at his sending set, his back turned, watching a screen at one side that showed a glimpse of a huge dark plain approaching. As the ship plunged down towards it, the illusion of solidity melted into a boiling turbulence of black clouds. They expanded in an inky swirl, looked huge for an instant, and then blackness swallowed the screen. The young alien swung around to face the camera, speaking a few words as he moved, made the O of a smile again, then flipped the switch and the screen went grey.

Nathen's voice was suddenly toneless and strained. 'He said something like break out the drinks, here they come.'

'The atmosphere doesn't look like that,' the *Times* said at random, knowing he was saying something too obvious even to think about. 'Not Earth's atmosphere.'

Some people drifted up. 'What did they say?'

'Entering the atmosphere, ought to be landing in five or ten minutes,' Nathen told them.

A ripple of heightened excitement ran through the room. Cameramen began adjusting the lens angles again, turning on the mike and checking it, turning on the floodlights. The scientists rose and stood near the window, still talking. The reporters trooped in from the hall and went to the windows to watch for the great event. The three linguists came in, trundling a large wheeled box that was the mechanical translator, supervising while it was hitched into the sound-broadcasting system.

'Landing where?' the *Times* asked Nathen brutally. 'Why don't you do something?'

'Tell me what to do and I'll do it.' Nathen said quietly, not moving.

It was not sarcasm. Jacob Luke of the *Times* looked sideways at the strained whiteness of his face and moderated his tone. 'Can't you contact them?'

'Not while they're landing.'

'What now?' The *Times* took out a packet of cigarettes, remembered the rule against smoking, and put it back.

'We just wait.' Nathen leaned his elbow on one knee and his chin in his hand.

They waited.

All the people in the room were waiting. There was no more conversation. A bald man of the scientist group was automatically buffing his fingernails over and over and inspecting them without seeing them; another absently polished his glasses, held them up to the light, put them on, and then a moment later took them off and began polishing again. The television crew concentrated on their jobs, moving quietly and efficiently, with perfectionist care, minutely arranging things that did not need to be arranged, checking things that had already been checked.

This was to be one of the great moments of human history, and they were all trying to forget that fact and remain impassive and wrapped up in the problems of their jobs, as good specialists should.

After an interminable age the *Times* consulted his watch. Three minutes had passed. He tried holding his breath a moment, listening for a distant approaching thunder of jets. There was no sound.

The sun came out from behind the clouds and lit up the field like a great spotlight on an empty stage.

Abruptly, the green light shone on the set again, indicating that a squawk message had been received. The recorder recorded it, slowed it, and fed it back to the speaker. It clicked and the sound was very loud in the still, tense room.

The screen remained grey, but Bud's voice spoke a few words in the alien language. He stopped, the speaker clicked, and the light went out. When it was plain that nothing more would occur and no announcement was to be made of what was said, the people in the room turned back to the windows and talk picked up again.

Somebody told a joke and laughed alone.

One of the linguists remained turned towards the loudspeaker, then looked at the widening patches of blue sky showing out the window, his expression puzzled. He had understood.

'It's dark,' the thin Intelligence Department decoder translated, low-voiced, to the man from the *Times*. 'Your atmosphere is *thick*. That's precisely what Bud said.'

Another three minutes. The *Times* caught himself about to light a cigarette and swore silently, blowing the match out and putting the cigarette back into its package. He listened for the sound of the rocket jets. It was time for the landing, yet he heard no blasts.

The green light came on in the transceiver.

Message in.

Instinctively, he came to his feet. Nathen abruptly was standing beside him. Then the message came in the voice he was coming to think of as Bud. It spoke and paused. Suddenly the *Times* knew.

'We've landed.' Nathen whispered the words.

The wind blew across the open spaces of white concrete and damp soil that was the empty airfield, swaying the wet, shiny grass. The people in the room looked out, listening for the roar of jets, looking for the silver bulk of a spaceship in the sky.

Nathen moved, seating himself at the transmitter, switching it on to warm up, checking and balancing dials. Jacob Luke of the *Times* moved softly to stand behind his right shoulder, hoping he could be useful. Nathen made a half motion of his head, as if to glance back at him, unhooked two of the earphone sets hanging on the side of the tall streamlined box that was the automatic translator, plugged them in, and handed one back over his shoulder to the *Times* man.

The voice began to come from the speaker again.

Hastily, Jacob Luke fitted the earphones over his ears. He fancied he could hear Bud's voice tremble. For a moment it was just Bud's voice speaking the alien language, and then, very distant and clear in his earphones, he heard the recorded voice of the linguist say an English word, then a mechanical click and another clear word in the voice of one of the other translators, then another as the alien's voice flowed from the loudspeaker, the cool single words barely audible, overlapping and blinding like translating thought, skipping unfamiliar words yet quite astonishingly clear.

'Radar shows no buildings or civilization near. The atmosphere around us registers as thick as glue. Tremendous gas pressure, low gravity, no light at all. You didn't describe it like this. Where are you, Joe? This isn't some kind of trick, is it?' Bud hesitated, was prompted by a deeper official voice, and jerked out the words.

'If it is a trick, we are ready to repel attack.'

The linguist stood listening. He whitened slowly and beckoned the other linguists over to him and whispered to them.

Joseph Nathen looked at them with unwarranted bitter hostility while he picked up the hand-mike, plugging it into the translator. 'Joe calling,' he said quietly into it in clear, slow English. 'No trick. We don't know where you are. I am trying to get a direction fix from your signal. Describe your surroundings to us if at all possible.'

Nearby, the floodlights blazed steadily on the television platform, ready for the official welcome of the aliens to Earth. The television channels of the world had been alerted to set aside their scheduled programmes for an unscheduled great event. In the long room the people waited, listening for the swelling sound of rocket jets.

This time, after the light came on, there was a long delay. The speaker sputtered and sputtered again, building to a steady scratching through which they could barely hear a dim voice. It came through in a few tinny words and then wavered back to inaudibility. The machine translated in their earphones.

'Tried . . . seemed . . . repair . . .' Suddenly it came in clearly. 'Can't tell if the auxiliary blew, too. Will try it. We might pick you up clearly on the next try. I have the volume down. Where is the landing port? Repeat. Where is the landing port? Where are you?'

Nathen put down the hand-mike and carefully set a dial on the recording box and flipped a switch, speaking over his shoulder. 'This sets it to repeat what I said the last time. It keeps repeating.' Then he sat with unnatural stillness, his head still half turned, as if he had suddenly caught a glimpse of answer and was trying with no success whatever to grasp it.

The green warning light cut in, the recording clicked, and the play-back of Bud's face and voice appeared on the screen.

'We heard a few words, Joe, and then the receiver blew again. We're adjusting a viewing screen to pick up the long waves that go through the murk and convert them to visible light. We'll be able to see out soon. The engineer says that something is wrong with the stern jets, and the captain has had me broadcast a help call to our nearest space base.' He made the mouth O of a grin. 'The message won't reach it for some years. I trust you, Joe, but get us out of here, will you?—They're buzzing that the screen is finally ready. Hold everything.'

The screen went grey and the green light went off.

The *Times* considered the lag required for the help call, the speaking and recording of the message just received, the time needed to reconvert a viewing screen.

'They work fast.' He shifted uneasily and added at random. 'Something wrong with the time factor. All wrong. They work *too* fast.'

The green light came on again immediately. Nathen half turned to him, sliding his words hastily into the gap of time as the message was recorded and slowed. 'They're close enough for our transmission power to blow their receiver.'

If it was on Earth, why the darkness around the ship? 'Maybe they see in the high ultraviolet – the atmosphere is opaque to that band,' the *Times* suggested hastily as the speaker began to talk in the young extra-terrestrial's voice.

That voice *was* shaking now. 'Stand by for that description.'

They tensed, waiting. The *Times* brought a map of the state before his mind's eye.

'A half-circle of cliffs around the horizon. A wide muddy lake swarming with swimming things. Huge, strange white foliage all around the ship and incredibly huge, pulpy monsters attacking and eating each other on all sides. We almost landed in the lake, right on the soft edge. The mud can't hold the ship's weight, and we're sinking. The engineer says we might be able to blast free, but the tubes are mud-clogged and might blow up the ship. When can you reach us?'

The *Times* thought vaguely of the Carboniferous era. Nathen obviously had seen something he had not.

'Where are they?' the *Times* asked him quietly.

Nathen pointed to the antenna position indicators. The *Times* let his eyes follow the converging imaginary lines of focus out the window to the sunlit airfield, the empty airfield, the drying concrete and green waving grass where the lines met.

Where the lines met. The spaceship was there! . . .

The fear of something unknown gripped him suddenly.

The spaceship was broadcasting again. *'Where are you? Answer if possible! We are sinking! Where are you?'*

He saw that Nathen knew. 'What is it?' the *Times* asked hoarsely. 'Are they in another dimension or the past or on another world or what?'

Nathen was smiling bitterly, and Jacob Luke remembered that the young man had a friend in that spaceship. 'My guess is that they evolved on a high-gravity planet with a thin atmosphere, near a blue-white star. Sure, they see in the ultraviolet range. Our sun is abnormally small and dim and yellow. Our atmosphere is so thick it screens our ultraviolet.' He laughed harshly. 'A good joke on us, the weird place we evolved in, the thing it did to us!'

'Where are you?' called the alien spaceship. 'Hurry, please! We're sinking!'

★   ★   ★   ★

The decoder slowed his tumbled, frightened words and looked up into the *Times'* face for understanding. 'We'll rescue them,' he said quietly. 'You were right about the time factor, right about them moving at a different speed, I misunderstood. This business about squawk coding, speeding for better transmission to counteract beam waver – I was wrong.'

'What do you mean?'

'They don't speed up their broadcasts.'

'They don't—?'

Suddenly, in his mind's eye, the *Times* began to see again the play he had just seen – but the actors were moving at blurring speed, the words jerking out in a fluting, dizzying stream, thoughts and decisions passing with unfollowable rapidity, rippling faces in a twisting blur or expressions, doors slamming wildly, shatteringly, as the actors leaped in and out of rooms.

No – faster, faster – he wasn't visualizing it as rapidly as it was, an hour of talk and action in one almost instantaneous 'squawk', a narrow peak of 'noise interfering with a single word in an Earth broadcast! Faster – faster – it was impossible. Matter could not stand such stress – inertia – momentum – abrupt weight.

It was insane. 'Why?' he asked. 'How?'

Nathen laughed again harshly, reaching for the mike. 'Get them out! There isn't a lake or river within hundreds of miles from here!'

A shiver of unreality went down the *Times'* spine. Automatically and inanely, he found himself delving in his pocket for a cigarette while he tried to grasp what had happened. 'Where are they, then? Why can't we see their spaceship?'

Nathen switched the microphone on in a gesture that showed the bitterness of his disappointment.

'We'll need a magnifying glass for that.'

Knock

Fredric Brown

There is a sweet little horror story that is only two sentences long:

The last man on Earth sat alone in a room. There was a knock at the door . . .

Two sentences and an ellipsis of three dots. The horror, of course, isn't in the story at all; it's in the ellipsis, the implication: *what* knocked at the door. Faced with the unknown, the human mind supplies something vaguely horrible.

But it *wasn't* horrible, really.

★ ★ ★ ★

The last man on Earth – or in the universe, for that matter – *sat alone in a room.* It was a rather peculiar room. He'd just been studying out the reason for its peculiarity. His conclusion didn't horrify him, but it annoyed him.

Walter Phelan, who had been associate professor of anthropology at Nathan University up to the time two days ago when Nathan University had ceased to exist, was not a man who horrified easily. Not that Walter Phelan was a heroic figure, by any wild stretch of the imagination. He was slight of stature and mild of disposition. He wasn't much to look at, and he knew it.

Not that appearance worried him now. Right now, in fact, there wasn't much feeling in him. Abstractedly, he knew that two days ago, within the space of an hour, the human race had been destroyed, except for him and, somewhere – one woman. And that was a fact which didn't concern Walter Phelan in the slightest degree. He'd probably never see her and didn't care too much if he didn't.

Women just hadn't been a factor in Walter's life since Martha had died a year and a half ago. Not that Martha hadn't been a good wife – albeit a bit on the bossy side. Yes, he'd loved Martha, in a deep, quiet way. He was only forty now, and he'd been only thirty-eight when Martha had died, but – well – he just hadn't thought about women since then. His life had been his books, the ones he read and the ones he wrote. Now there wasn't any point in writing books, but he had the rest of his life to spend in reading them.

True, company would have been nice, but he'd get along without it. Maybe after a while he'd get so he'd enjoy the occasional company of one of the Zan, although that was a bit difficult to imagine. Their thinking was so alien to his that it was a bit difficult to imagine their finding common ground for a discussion. They were intelligent in a way, but so is an ant. No man has ever established communication with an ant. He thought of the Zan, somehow, as super-ants, although they didn't look like ants – and he had a hunch that the Zan regarded the human race as the human race regarded ordinary ants. Certainly what they'd done to Earth had been what men do to ant hills, and it had been done much more efficiently.

But they'd given him plenty of books. They'd been nice about that, as soon as he had told them what he wanted. And he had told them that the moment he realized that he was destined to spend the rest of his life alone in this room. The rest of his life, or as the Zan had quaintly expressed it, for-ev-er.

Even a brilliant mind, and the Zan obviously had brilliant minds, had its idiosyncrasies. The Zan had learned to speak Terrestrial English in a matter of hours, but they persisted in separating syllables. However, we digress.

There was a knock at the door.

You've got it all now except the three dots, the ellipsis, and I'm going to fill that in and show you that it wasn't horrible at all.

Walter Phelan called out, 'Come in,' and the door opened. It was, of course, only a Zan. It looked exactly like the other Zan; if there was any way of telling them apart, Walter hadn't found it. It was about four feet tall and it looked like nothing on Earth – nothing, that is that had been on Earth before the Zan came here.

Walter said, 'Hello, George.' When he'd learned that none of them had names, he'd decided to call them all George and the Zan didn't seem to mind.

This one said, 'Hel-lo, Wal-ter.' That was ritual, the knock on the door and the greetings. Walter waited.

'Point one,' said the Zan. 'You will please henceforth sit with your chair fac-ing the oth-er way.'

Walter said, 'I thought so, George. That plain wall is transparent from the other side, isn't it?'

'It is trans-par-ent.'

Walter sighed. 'I knew it. That plain blank wall, without a single piece of furniture against it. And made of something different from the other walls. If I persist in sitting with my back to it, what then? You will kill me? – I ask hopefully.'

'We will take a-way your books.'

'You've got me there, George. All right. I'll face the other way when I sit and read. How many other animals besides me are in this zoo of yours?'

'Two hun-dred and six-teen.'

Walter shook his head. 'Not complete, George. Even a bush-league zoo can beat that – *could* beat that, I mean, if there were any bush-league zoos left. Did you just pick us at random?'

'Ran-dom sam-ples, yes. All spe-cies would have been too man-y. Male and fe-male each of one hun-dred kinds.'

'What do you feed them? The carnivorous ones, I mean.'

'We make feed. Syn-thet-ic.'

'Smart. And the flora? You've got a collection of that, too, haven't you?'

'Flo-ra not hurt by vi-bra-tions. It is all still grow-ing.'

'Good for the flora. You weren't as hard on it, then, as you were on

The last man on Earth sat alone in a room. There was a knock at the door . . .

the fauna. Well, George, you started out with 'point one.' I deduce that there is a point two lurking somewhere. What is it?'

'There is some-thing we do not un-der-stand. Two of the oth-er an-i-mals sleep and do not wake. They are cold.'

'It happens in the best-regulated zoos, George. Probably not a thing wrong with them except that they're dead.'

'Dead? That means stopped. But noth-ing stopped them. Each was a-lone.'

Walter stared at the Zan. 'Do you mean, George, that you do not know what natural death is?'

'Death is when a be-ing is killed, stopped from living.'

Walter Phelan blinked. 'How old are you, George?' he asked.

'Six-teen – you would not know the word. Your planet went a-round your sun a-bout sev-en thou-sand times. I am still young.'

Walter whistled softly. 'A babe in arms,' he said. He thought hard for a moment. 'Look, George, you've got something to learn about this planet you're on. There's a guy down here who doesn't hang around where you come from. An old man with a beard and a scythe and an hourglass. Your vibrations didn't kill him.'

'What is he?'

'Call him the Grim Reaper, George. Old Man Death. Our people and animals live until somebody, Old Man Death, stops them from ticking.'

'He stopped the two crea-tures? He will stop more?'

Walter opened his mouth to answer, and then closed it again. Something in the Zan's voice indicated that there would be a worried frown on his face if he had a face recognizable as such.

'How about taking me to those animals who won't wake up?' Walter asked. 'Is that against the rules?'

'Come,' said the Zan.

That had been the afternoon of the second day. It was the next morning that the Zan came back, several of them. They began to move Walter Phelan's books and furniture. When they finished that, they moved him. He found himself in a larger room a hundred yards away.

He sat and waited this time, too. When there was a knock on the door, he knew what was coming and politely stood up as he called out, 'Come in.'

A Zan opened the door and stood aside. A woman entered.

Walter bowed slightly. 'Walter Phelan,' he said, 'in case George didn't tell you my name. George tries to be polite but he doesn't know all our ways.'

The woman seemed calm; he was glad to notice that. She said, 'My name's Grace Evans, Mr Phelan. What's this all about? Why did they bring me here?'

Walter was studying her as she talked. She was tall, fully as tall as he, and well-proportioned. She looked to be somewhere in her early thirties, about the age Martha had been. She had the same calm confidence about her that he had always liked about Martha, even though it had contrasted with his own easygoing informality. In fact, he thought she looked quite a bit like Martha.

'I think you can guess why they brought you here, but let's go back a bit,' he said. 'Do you know what's happened otherwise?'

'You mean that they've – killed everyone?'

'Yes. Please sit down. You know how they accomplished it?'

She sank into a comfortable chair nearby. 'No,' she said. 'I don't know just how. Not that it matters, does it?'

'Not a lot. But here's the story, what I know of it from getting one of them to talk, and from piecing things together. There isn't a great number of them – here anyway. I don't know how numerous a race they are where they came from and I don't know where that is, but I'd guess it's outside the solar system. You've seen the spaceship they came in?'

'Yes. It's as big as a mountain.'

'Almost. Well, it has equipment for emitting some sort of vibration – they call it that in our language, but I imagine it's more like a radio wave than a sound vibration – that destroys all animal life. The ship itself is insulated against the vibration. I don't know whether its range is big enough to kill off the whole planet at once, or whether they flew in circles around the earth, sending out the vibratory waves. But it killed everything at once instantly and, I hope, painlessly. The only reason we, and the other two-hundred-odd animals in this zoo weren't killed was because we were inside the ship. We'd been picked up as specimens. You do know this is a zoo, don't you?'

'I—I suspected it.'

'The front walls are transparent from the outside. The Zan were pretty clever in fixing up the inside of each cubicle to match the natural habitat of the creature it contains. These cubicles, such as the one we're in, are of plastic and they've got a machine that makes one in about ten minutes. If Earth had a machine and a process like that, there wouldn't have been any housing shortage. Well, there isn't any housing shortage now, anyway. And I imagine that the human race – specifically you and I – can stop worrying about the H-bomb and the next war. The Zan have certainly solved a lot of problems for us.'

Grace Evans smiled faintly. 'Another case where the operation was successful but the patient died. Things *were* in an awful mess. Do you remember being captured? I don't. I went to sleep one night and woke up in a cage on the spaceship.'

'I don't remember either,' Walter said. 'My hunch is that they used the waves at low intensity first, just enough to knock us all out. Then they cruised around, picking up samples for their zoo more or less at random. After they had as many as they wanted, or as many as they had room in the ship for, they turned on the juice all the way. And that was that. It wasn't until yesterday that they knew they'd made a mistake by overestimating us. They thought we were immortal, as they are.'

'That we were – what?'

'They can be killed but they don't know what natural death is. They didn't anyway, until yesterday. Two of us died yesterday.'

'Two of – Oh!'

'Yes, two of us animals in their zoo. Two species gone irrevocably. And by the Zan's way of figuring time, the remaining member of each species is going to live only a few minutes anyway. They figured they had permanent specimens.'

'You mean they didn't realize what short-lived creatures we are?'

'That's right,' Walter said. 'One of them is young at seven thousand years, he told me. They're bisexual themselves, incidentally, but they probably breed every ten thousand years or thereabouts. When they learned yesterday how ridiculously short a life span we terrestrial animals have, they were probably shocked to the core, if they have cores. At any rate they decided to reorganize their zoo – two by two instead of one by one. They figure we'll last longer collectively if not individually.'

'Oh!' Grace Evans stood up and there was a faint flush on her face. 'If you think – If they think—' She turned toward the door.

'It'll be locked,' Walter Phelan said calmly. 'But don't worry. Maybe they think, but I *don't* think. You needn't even tell me that you wouldn't have me if I were the last man on Earth; it would be corny under the circumstances.'

'But are they going to keep us locked up together in this one little room?'

'It isn't so little; we'll get by. I can sleep quite comfortably in one of those overstuffed chairs. And don't think I don't agree with you perfectly, my dear. All personal considerations aside, the least favour we can do the human race is to let it die out with us and not be perpetuated for exhibition in a zoo.'

She said, 'Thank you,' almost inaudibly, and the flush was gone from her face. There was anger in her eyes, but Walter knew that it wasn't anger at him. With her eyes sparkling like that, she looked a lot like Martha, he thought.

He smiled at her and said, 'Otherwise—'

She started out of her chair and for a moment he thought she was going to come over and slap him. Then she sank back wearily. 'If you were a *man*, you'd be thinking of some way to— They can be killed, you said?' Her voice was bitter.

'The Zan? Oh, certainly. I've been studying them. They look horribly different from us, but I think they have about the same metabolism, the same type of circulatory system, and probably the same type of digestive system. I think that anything that would kill one of us would kill one of them.'

'But you said—'

'Oh, there are differences, of course. Whatever factor it is in man that ages him, they don't have. Or else they have some gland that man doesn't have, something that renews cells. More often than every seven years, I mean.'

She had forgotten her anger now. She learned forward eagerly. She said, 'I think that's right. I don't think, though, that they feel pain.'

He had been hoping that. He said, 'What makes you think so, my dear?'

'I stretched a piece of wire that I found in the desk of my own cubicle across the door so the Zan would fall over it. He did, and the wire cut his leg.'

'Did he bleed red?'

'Yes, but it didn't seem to annoy him. He didn't get mad about it; he didn't mention it, just took the wire down. When he came back the next time a few hours later, the cut was gone. Well, almost gone. I could see just enough of a trace of it to be sure it was the same Zan.'

Walter Phelan nodded slowly. 'He wouldn't get angry, of course. They're emotionless. Maybe if we killed one they wouldn't even punish us. Just give us our food through a trap door and stay clear of us, treat us as men would have treated a zoo animal that had killed its keeper. They'd probably just see that we didn't get a crack at any more keepers.'

'How many of them are there?'

Walter said, 'About two hundred, I think, in this particular spaceship. But undoubtedly there are many more where they came from. I have a hunch, though, that this is just an advance board, sent to clear off this planet and make it safe for Zan occupancy.'

'They certainly did a good—'

There was a knock at the door and Walter Phelan called out, 'Come in.' A Zan opened the door and stood in the doorway.

'Hello, George,' said Walter.

'Hel-lo, Wal-ter.' The same ritual. The same Zan?

'What's on your mind?'

'An-oth-er creature sleeps and will not wake. A small fur-ry one called a wea-sel.'

Walter shrugged. 'It happens, George. Old Man Death. I told you about him.'

'And worse. A Zan has died. This morn-ing.'

'Is that worse?' Walter looked at him blandly. 'Well, George, you'll have to get used to it if you're going to stay around here.'

The Zan said nothing. It stood there.

Finally, Walter said, 'Well?'

'About the wea-sel. You advise the same?'

Walter shrugged again. 'Probably won't do any good. But why not?'

The Zan left.

Walter could hear his footsteps dying away outside. He grinned. 'It might work, Martha,' he said.

'Mar— My name is Grace, Mr Phelan. What might work?'

'My name is Walter, Grace. You might as well get used to it. You know, Grace, you remind me a lot of Martha. She was my wife. She died a couple of years ago.'

'I'm sorry. But *what* might work? What were you talking about to the Zan?'

'We should know tomorrow,' Walter said. And she couldn't get another word out of him.

That was the third day of the stay of the Zan. The next day was the last.

It was nearly noon when one of the Zan came. After the ritual, he stood in the doorway, looking more alien than ever. It would be interesting to describe him for you, but there aren't words. He said, 'We go. Our coun-cil met and de-ci-ded.'

'Another of you died?'

'Last night. This is pla-net of death.'

Walter nodded. 'You did your share. You're leaving two hundred and thirteen alive, besides us, but that's out of quite a few billion. Don't hurry back.'

'Is there an-y-thing we can do?'

'Yes. You can hurry. And you can leave our door unlocked, but not the others. We'll take care of the others.'

The Zan nodded, and left.

Grace Evans was standing, her eyes shining. She asked, 'How—? What—?'

'Wait,' cautioned Walter. 'Let's hear them blast off. It's a sound I want to hear and remember.'

The sound came within minutes, and Walter Phelan, realizing how rigidly he'd been holding himself, dropped into a chair and relaxed.

He said softly, 'There was a snake in the Garden of Eden, too, Grace, and it got us into trouble. But this one got us out of it, and made up. I mean the mate of the snake that died day before yesterday. It was a rattlesnake.'

'You mean it killed the two Zan who died? But—'

Walter nodded. 'They were babes in the woods here. When they took me to see the first creatures who "were asleep and wouldn't wake up," and I saw that one of them was a rattlesnake, I had an idea, Grace. Just maybe, I thought, poison creatures were a development peculiar to Earth and the Zan wouldn't know about them. And, too, maybe their metabolism was enough like ours that the poison would kill them. Anyway, I had nothing to lose trying. And both maybes turned out to be right.'

'How did you get the living rattlesnake to—'

Walter Phelan grinned. 'I told them what affection is. They didn't know. But they were interested, I found, in preserving the remaining one of each species as long as possible, to picture and record it before it died. I told them it would die immediately because of the loss of its mate, unless it had affection and petting, constantly.

'I showed them how, with the duck, which was the other creature who had lost its mate. Luckily it was a tame duck and I had no trouble holding it against my chest and petting it, to show them how. Then I let them take over with it – and with the rattlesnake.'

He stood up and stretched, and then sat down again more comfortably. He said, 'Well, we've got a world to plan. We'll have to let the animals out of the ark, and that will take some thinking and deciding. The herbivorous wild ones we can let go right away, and let them take their chances. The domestic ones we'll do better to keep and take charge of; we'll need them. But the Carnivora, the predators – Well, we'll have to decide. But I'm afraid it's got to be thumbs down. Unless maybe we can find and operate the machinery that they used to make synthetic food.'

He looked at her. 'And the human race. We've got to make a decision about that. A pretty important decision.'

Her face was getting a bit pink again, as it had yesterday; she sat rigidly in her chair. 'No,' she said.

He didn't seem to have heard her. 'It's been a nice race, even if nobody won it. It'll be starting over again now, if we start it, and it may go backwards for a while until it gets its breath, but we can gather books for it and keep most of its knowledge intact, the important things anyway. We can—'

He broke off as she got up and started for the door. Just the way Martha would have acted, he thought, back in the days when he was courting her, before they were married.

He said, 'Think it over, my dear, and take your time. But come back.'

The door slammed. He sat waiting, thinking out all the things there were to do once he started, but in no hurry to start them.

And after a while he heard her hesitant footsteps coming back.

He smiled a little. See? It wasn't horrible, really.

The last man on Earth sat alone in a room. There was a knock at the door . . .

Romp

Mack Reynolds

Rosy Porras shucked off his jerkin and began to shrug into the holster harness. As he settled it around his chest, he scowled at the row of sport jerkins in his closet. Styles these days weren't conducive to concealing a heavy-calibered shooter.

A bell tinkled and Rosy turned his scowl to the screen sitting next to the bed. He wasn't expecting anybody. He hesitated a moment, unbuckled the harness again and threw it into a chair, then went over and flicked the door screen switch.

It was a stranger. Young, efficient looking, his suit seeming all but a uniform, his face expressionless.

Rosy pursed his lips in surprise.

Well, there was no putting it off. He reversed the switch so the other could see him as well and said, 'Yeah?'

The stranger said, 'Phidias Porras?'

Rosy winced at the use of his real first name. It had been some time since he had been exposed to it. He growled, 'What'd you want?'

The other said, 'Willard Rhuling, Category Government, Subdivision Police, Branch Distribution Services. I'd like to talk to you, Citizen.'

Rosy Porras scowled at him. A DS snooper. That's all he needed right now, with the boys expecting him in a few minutes.

'About what?' Rosy said. 'Listen, I'm busy.'

The other looked at him patiently. 'About your sources of income, Citizen.'

Rosy said, 'That's none of your business.'

Willard Rhuling said, still patiently, 'To the contrary, Citizen, it's my job.'

'You got a warrant?'

Rhuling said slowly, 'Do you really want me to get one, or can we sit down and just have a chat?'

'Wait a minute,' Porras growled in disgust. He flicked off the screen, went over and picked up the shooter and holster. He put them in a drawer and locked it and then left the bedroom and went on through the living room to the apartment's front door. He opened it and let the the DS man enter.

Willard Rhuling suddenly stepped close to him and patted him here, there – a quick frisking.

Rosy Porras stepped back in indignation. 'Hey, take it easy, you flat. What kind of curd you pulling off?'

Rhuling said mildly, 'I've heard you sometimes go heeled, even in this day and age, Phidias.'

Porras winced again. 'Listen, call me Rosy,' he growled. 'Everybody does.' He led the way into the living room.

Willard Rhuling let his eyes go around the room and did a silent whistle of appreciation. 'No wonder, in view of the fact that I can't find any record of you working since you came of age. Things are pretty rosy, aren't they? How do you manage to maintain this apartment on the credit income from the Inalienable Basic Common stock issued you at birth? Our records show you are only a Mid–Lower. Your Inalienable Basic doesn't begin to call for a place like this. This is Upper–Middle, or even Low–Upper caste, Porras.'

Rosy had started toward the auto-bar, but, remembering what the evening had in prospect, changed his mind and sank down into a chair. He didn't invite the other to be seated.

He said, 'A friend loans it to me.'

'I see. Where is this friend?'

'He's on a vacation over in Common Europe.'

'And when will he be back?'

'I don't know. It's a long vacation. Listen, what business is it of yours?'

★   ★   ★   ★

Willard Rhuling had taken a place on a couch. He looked about the room again. 'And all these rather expensive furnishings. They belong to your friend, too?'

'Some of them,' Rosy said. 'And some of them are mine.'

Rhuling brought a notebook from an inner pocket and flicked through it. He found his page and checked it. 'Phidias Porras, alias Rosy Porras,' he read. 'Category Food, Subdivision Baking, Branch Pretzel Bender.' He frowned. 'What in Zen is a pretzel bender?'

Rosy Porras flushed. 'How'd I know?' he growled. 'I was born into my category, like everybody else. My old man was a pretzel bender and his old man, and his. But that branch got automated out a long time ago. Can I help it if there is no such work. I just live on my credits from my Inalienable Basic.'

Rhuling looked at him patiently. 'You drive a late model hovercar. Where did you acquire the credits for it?'

Rosy grinned at him. 'I didn't.'

The other's eyebrows went up. 'You admit it? That you got this car without credits to exchange for it?'

'I won it gambling.'

'Oh, come now.'

Rosy Porras, in exaggerated nonchalance, crossed one leg over the other. He said reasonably, 'There's no regulation against gambling.'

The other said disgustedly, 'Don't be ridiculous. Gambling isn't practical on anything but a matchstick level. Of course, there's no regulation against it, but when our system of exchange is such that no one but you yourself can spend the credits you acquire as dividends on your Inalienable Basic stock, or what you earn above your basic dividends, gambling becomes nonsense.'

Porras was shaking his head at him. 'Now that's where you Category Government people haven't figured out this fancy system to its end. Stutes that like to gamble, like to gamble period, and they'll find a way. Sure, we can't spend each other's credits, but we can gamble for *things*.

Suppose a dozen or so poker addicts form kind of a club. One of them sticks in his hovercar which he had to pony up a hundred credits for; another sticks in a diamond ring that rates fifty credits; another puts in a Tri-Di camera that set him back twenty credits. OK, the banker issues chips for the credit value of every item the group members put up. And if any member wins enough credit chips he can 'buy' the thing he wants out of the club kitty.'

Rhuling was staring at him. 'I'll be damned,' he said.

Rosy Porras snorted amusement. 'You must be from out of town,' he said. 'You mean you never heard of gambling clubs?'

The other cleared his throat. He said, ruefully, 'Undoubtedly, I'll be hearing more about them soon. There's no regulation against them now, but there should be.'

'Why?' Porras said, letting his voice go plaintive. 'Listen, why can't you DS characters leave off fouling up everybody you can?'

There other said patiently, 'Because under People's Capitalism, Citizen, no one can steal, cheat or con anyone else out of his means of exchange. Or, at least, that's why my category exists. The DS is interested in how a Rosy Porras can live extremely well without having performed any useful contribution in any field for his whole adult life.'

Rosy's expression made it clear he was being imposed upon. 'Listen,' he said. 'I got a lot of friends. I haven't been too well lately, I been sick, see? OK, so these friends of mine pick up the tab here and there.'

'You mean friends have been discharging your obligations by using their credits to pay your bills?'

'There's no regulation against gifts.'

'No, there isn't,' Rhuling admitted, unhappily. 'But discharging a grocery bill at an ultra-market isn't exactly the sort of gift one gives a man in his prime.'

'No regulation against it.'

Rhuling said. 'And this is your sole method of income, save the dividends from your Inalienable Basic stock?'

'I didn't say that. I do a lot of people a lot of favours and then maybe they do me one. And, like I say, I belong to some of these gambling clubs.'

'And always win?'

Rosy shrugged hugely. 'They don't call me Rosy, for nothing. I'm pretty lucky. Listen, I got some business needs taking care of. Do you really have anything on me, or are you just wasting both our time?'

Willard Rhuling came to his feet with a sigh. He looked down into his book again. 'General Aptitude IQ 136,' he read. He looked up at the other. 'And here you are, a full-time bum.'

Rosy stood, too, scowling. 'Listen,' he said, 'I don't have to take that from you. You got my category. I'm a pretzel bender. What can I do? The job's been automated out of existence.'

'You can always switch categories, work hard and possibly run yourself up a couple of castes.'

Rosy sneered. 'Sure, that's the theory. And maybe it sounds good to somebody like you. You're probably a Mid-Middle, at least. And born into your caste, you've got it made. But when you're a lower, about the only category you can switch to that you've got a chance in is Military, or Religion, and I'm not stupid enough to go into one, and not phoney enough for the other.'

Rhuling looked at him speculatively. 'We'll see just how stupid and phoney you are, Porras. I have a sneaking suspicion that you're going to wind up in a Psychotherapy Institute, Citizen.'

'Yeah? Listen, my stute pal, I got a *lot* of friends, understand? You'll have a time getting *me* into a pressure cooker.'

'We'll see,' the DS man said grimly. He turned and started for the door. 'See you later, Rosy.'

Rosy Porras scowled after him. It didn't do a man any good to have the DS on his tail. He wondered uncomfortably what he had done to draw their attention. In this age, a grifter's first need was to remain inconspicuous.

★   ★   ★   ★

Rosy Porras was already late but he was taking no chances. He drove his hovercar into the downtown area and into the heaviest of traffic and then spent the next twenty minutes doubling and doubling back still again. All he needed was for some snooper such as Rhuling to be shadowing him.

Evidently, he was clear. He finally left the car in the parking cellars of a large hotel and made his way to one of the popular auto-bars above.

He found an empty booth and dialed a drink, putting his credit card on the receipt screen. This was one of the few things he had to use his own skimpy credits for. He sipped the drink slowly and checked the occupants of the other tables unobtrusively.

When he was convinced of their innocence, he let his finger thump twice on the table and Pop Rasch and Marvin Zogbaum came over and sat down with him.

Pop Rasch, a heavy-set, grey-faced man with obvious false teeth, said sourly, 'Where in Zen you been? We were about to fold the whole job.'

Rosy said, 'A snooper from the DS police turned up and grilled me at the apartment.'

Pop said, 'Oh, oh.'

Porras waved a hand negatively. 'It was nothing. Just routine.'

'How'd he know where to find you?'

'I suppose they got ways. Anyway, I guess I'd better move on. We been working this town too hard anyway. Maybe I'll go out to the West Coast.'

Marvin Zogbaum, a clerkish looking type and out of setting with these two, said nervously, 'Well, I suppose then we'd better call off tonight's, ah, romp.'

'Romp,' Rosy snorted at him. 'You been watching those telly detective shows? You oughta stick to the fracases, Marv.' His tone held deprecation.

Zogbaum said defensively, 'I'll watch whatever I please, Porras.'

'OK, OK,' Pop Rasch said. 'Let's not get into a silly argument. That's just what we need right in the middle of a job. What'd you say, Rosy? Should we call it all off?'

Rosy Porras grumbled. 'Can't afford to now. We need a good taw, in case of emergencies.'

Marv Zogbaum said, still miffed, 'Maybe you do, but I *work* in my category. I've got a job and I'm clean.'

Rosy snorted. 'You're about as clean as a mud pack. You put in minimum time on that job of yours and live like some of these Uppers holding down premium positions on double hours. The first time the DS gets around to checking you, you're going to be doing some fast talking.'

Pop Rasch said, 'And all we have to do is start squabbling among ourselves and we'll all wind up in a Category Medicine Psychotherapy flat-house learning to adjust to society.' He grimaced at the thought.

Rosy said, 'Listen, let's get going. We've been casing this job for weeks. There's no point in panicking out now. Nothing's happened except a DS snooper named Rhuling talked to me for ten minutes.'

'Rhuling!' Rasch said.

Rosy looked at him. 'Somebody you know?'

'He's from Neuve Albuquerque. A real burn off stute. One of those yokes who takes his work seriously. I got a friend that ran into this Willard Rhuling.'

Marv Zogbaum blinked. 'What happened to him?'

'What'd ya think happened to him? He's got a silly job now stooging for some Category Research technician, or something. Why, when I see him on the street, he's hard put to remember me. Brainwashed.'

Rosy Porras got to his feet and growled, 'Let's get going. It's late as it is.'

Marv Zogbaum brought up the rear, disgruntled, but he followed.

★   ★   ★   ★

They took Pop Rasch's heavy sedan to the records section of the Administration Building, which they had already cased thoroughly. They parked half a block down from the side entry. Pop and Marv Zogbaum sat in the front seat, Rosy in the back.

Rosy opened the overnight bag which Rasch and Zogbaum had brought along and unfolded a long, pipe-like device. He screwed an object resembling a wind instrument's mouthpiece to the end.

He said, 'You're sure of these details, eh?'

'Yes, yes,' Zogbaum said nervously. 'He's the only one in the building at night. He sets up various routine matters for the day shift. But for all I know, he's already gone in. I think we're late. Perhaps we'd better put it off.'

'Don't be a funker,' Rosy grunted.

'Here comes somebody now,' Pop Rasch growled softly.

'It's him,' Zogbaum whispered. 'Are you sure . . .'

'Knock it,' Rosy said.

The lone pedestrian passed without looking at them. When he had gone a dozen feet or so, Rosy Porras rested his pipe on the ledge of the window and puffed a heavy breath of air into the mouthpiece.

The pedestrian clapped a hand to his neck as though swatting a mosquito, and went on.

Rosy grinned. He began taking his device apart again. 'There's the world for you,' he told his companions. 'The simpler things you use, the bigger the wrench you can throw into the most complicated machinery these double domes can dream up. A blowgun!'

Pop Rasch said, 'This was your idea, Rosy. How soon will it hit him?'

'In about fifteen minutes. Then he'll go out like a light and wake up in maybe six hours with a block-buster headache, but no memory of anything but sleeping.'

'That'll give us plenty of time to finish the, uh' – Zogbaum looked at Rosy defiantly – 'romp and leave the place all cleaned up so nobody'll ever know we've been there. Six hours is plenty of time.'

Pop Rasch looked at him. 'Why don't you take a trank,' he said. 'Nothing to be nervous about. All we gotta do is sit here for twenty minutes.'

'I can't afford to be tranked,' Zogbaum said, 'and I hate to wait.'

★ ★ ★ ★

At the end of the twenty minutes they left the car and walked unhurriedly to the door of the building which the lone pedestrian had entered. The street was deserted at this time of night. Pop Rasch carried the valise.

Pop looked up and down the street as a double check, then hunkered down. The lock on the door yielded to his efforts in a matter of minutes.

Pop Rasch sighed and said, 'They don't make them the way they used to. No challenge, like.' He added, a note of nostalgia in his voice, 'They don't even have watchmen, any more.'

Rosy Porras entered first. He looked up and down the halls. Some lights were burning. Not many. The Administration Building was inoperative at night.

'All clear,' he said. 'Let's go.' Automatically, he shrugged his shoulders to loosen his harness and have the feel of the handgun ready to be drawn.

They proceeded down the hall. Pop Rasch had a simple chart of the building in his hand. They turned several corners, finally emerged into a long room banked with Tabulators, Collators, Sorters and Computers. Leading off it, in turn, were several rooms of punched-card files, tape files, shelves of bound reports.

'OK,' Pop said to Marv Zogbaum. 'Now you're the boss. Go to it. Just for luck, I'm going to look up that cloddy Rosy claims is going to be sleeping for the rest of the night.'

'It's not necessary,' Rosy growled. 'He's got enough dope to keep him under.'

'Just the same,' Pop said, 'double-checking never hurt nobody – especially since he's the only guy in the building.'

Marv Zogbaum wet his lips nervously and entered the first of the file rooms, after taking up the valise. He opened the bag and brought forth a sheaf of closely typed reports.

He said importantly, 'Now you two leave me alone. I have to concentrate.' He fished from the valise a small manually operated card punch.

'Take it away, fella,' Rosy said tolerantly. 'I'm the heavy. I'll stand guard.'

Pop Rasch left on his checking mission.

*   *   *   *

Rosy Porras had remained free to operate on the wrong side of a society that was supposedly crime free, only by exercising an instinct for self-preservation that had served him well on more than one occasion when he found himself in the dill.

Something didn't feel right now.

Pop Rasch, an old pro, capable of becoming bored even while on a job, had sunk into a swivel chair and had actually drifted off into a fitful sleep, snoring raspingly.

Marvin Zogbaum was busy in the files, humming and sometimes whistling to himself in concentration. He'd pull a card here, another there, sometimes substituting one from the valise, sometimes punching another hole or so. On several occasions, he displaced whole boxes of tapes, or cards, and actually stored three of them away in the bag.

Rosy Porras, suddenly unhappy, left the room and retraced the route by which they'd progressed through the building.

Everything looked the same.

He returned to the door by which they had entered, and opened it a fraction to peer out along the darkened street.

There were three hovercars that hadn't been present earlier, parked out there.

He closed the door quickly. His face was expressionless. The gun slid into his hand as though wizard-commanded. He stood for a long moment in thought, then moved in quick decision.

He paralleled the wall for several hundred feet, along the semidark hallway, then stopped by a window. It took a while for his eyes to accustom themselves to the dark outside. Across the road was a small park, benches, trees, bushes, a small fountain.

There was a man quietly sitting on a bench alone. After a time Rosy Porras was able to make out two other figures standing behind tree trunks.

There was no doubt about how things stood now. The whole thing had pickled. Rosy moistened dry lips.

He hurried back to the room where Marv Zogbaum laboured over the punched cards and tape files. Pop Rasch still slumbered fitfully.

Rosy fumbled through the report sheets which Zogbaum had brought with him. He kept his voice even. 'You finished with this one of Dave Shriner?' he said to Marv Zogbaum.

Zogbaum looked up impatiently. 'Shriner, Shriner? I don't remember them by name.'

Rosy said, 'Code 22D-11411-88M.'

'Oh, that one. Yes,' Zogbaum muttered. 'All finished. Don't bother me now. I've got a dozen to go.'

'OK,' Rosy said. Unobtrusively, he put the report sheet in his pocket and left the room.

He walked softly by Pop Rasch and made his way back into the corridor. He set off at a pace for the far side of the great building, making his way by instinct and quick animal reasoning rather than by knowledge of this part of the establishment.

Up one corridor and down another.

It was a matter of ditching the other two. Pop Rasch was too old to move fast enough and Zogbaum was too jittery in the dill to trust. The situation had pickled now and it was each man for himself.

He came finally to a window that opened on a dark alley-like entry-way. He peered through it. Could see nothing.

He flicked the window's simple lock and drew it aside. He threw a leg over the sill and dropped to the ground below.

A voice chuckled and said, 'Got you, you funker!' Rosy Porras felt arms go around his body.

He dropped suddenly, letting his legs go from under him so that the full weight of his husky body was on the other's arms. He fell on through, his buttocks hitting the ground. Without aim, he threw a pile-driving punch upward and struck low into the other's stomach.

The voice that had chuckled but a moment ago, gave out with a deep groan of anguish. Rosy rolled quickly, came to his feet and lashed out at the other with both hands. It was too dark to strike accurately, but he could tell the other had crumpled.

The gun was in his hand again and he peered down, indecisively. He had no time to make sure of the other. He spun quickly and ran for the entryway's head.

He paused a moment there and looked out. The way seemed clear. This part of the Administration Building opened onto the back of extensive offices, devoted to lower echelon workers. He holstered the gun.

★   ★   ★   ★

Rosy Porras walked rapidly, but kept himself from a run. It was a matter now of relying on the good fortune his name promised. It was a matter of getting a hovercab before things exploded behind him.

But even as he hurried toward a more traffic ridden street, his mind was checking back, re-evaluating.

Whatever had gone wrong, shouldn't have. It was all but impossible. Neither Zogbaum, nor certainly Pop Rasch would have purposely betrayed them. Not any way that he could figure it.

He went back over the day. There had been nothing untoward until the appearance of the DS man, Willard Rhuling. Could he have said anything to Rhuling that had given the other a clue? No. Was there any way in which Rhuling could have tailed him? No. He had taken every precaution and then, after he had met the others, they had once again made sure they were not being followed.

He reached an entertainment area, hurried to a cab park. He began to dial the coordinates of his apartment, but then brought himself up sharp. He dialled the address of a hotel nearby instead.

He leaned back in the hovercab and forced his mind along the path of the past few days. No, there was nothing until Rhuling had shown up. His lips thinned in a grimace of rage. The cool, efficient effrontery of the DS snooper. The way he'd calmly entered the Porras apartment and then had the nerve to run his hands over Rosy's body checking for a gun. The frisking!

That was it! Rosy Porras quickly ran his hands through his pockets, the pockets Willard Rhuling had touched. He found it nestled down beneath a key ring and a cigarette lighter. A tiny device, no bigger than a shirt button.

Rosy stared at it and snarled. He threw it out into the street. A sub-miniature direction transmitter! Rhuling had planted it on him back there in the apartment and the DS operatives then had been able to tail him at their leisure. A trick as simple as that. Pop Rasch would have laughed him to scorn.

They probably had Pop by now, and Marv Zogbaum, too. And here he was on the run, simply because he'd been too stupid to consider the possibility of his having a bug planted on him.

He left the hovercab at the hotel near his apartment house. He walked through the lobby, passing by the auto-bar although he would have given years of his life right now for a quick double shot of guzzle. He emerged by a side door and strolled in the direction of his apartment. He couldn't make up his mind whether or not he had the time to spend five minutes gathering up . . .

No, he didn't. A hovercar zoomed down before him and immediately in front of his building. Rosy Porras stepped into a doorway.

It was Rhuling, the DS operative. He vaulted from the open car and hurried toward the door.

'That's that,' Rosy growled. It wasn't as though it was disastrous. Rosy Porras had decided long ago in his career that times would come when a complete abandonment of all luggage and belongings would be necessary. To the extent that you could divorce yourself from such impedimenta, you were better off.

He re-entered the hotel by the entry he had left it only moments before, and ordered a cab. While he waited, he went into the auto-bar and dialled a double shot.

At a phone booth, he looked up the address coordinates of David Shriner and noted them down on the report he had surreptitiously taken from Marv Zogbaum.

In the hovercab he dialed the coordinates of Shriner's apartment house and let his mind churn over half-formed plans.

The hour was getting on by the time he stood before the screen in Shriner's door. Rose Porras snapped the fingers of his right hand in a fine case of jitters and muttered obscenities at the delay.

Shriner's plump face lit up the screen and he grinned. 'Rosy!' he said. 'Come on in.'

Rosy Porras pushed the door and emerged into the entrada and then went on through into the ample living room. In a moment, Shriner appeared, yawning, from a bedroom. He wore a robe over pyjamas. Shriner was a second-string telly actor, noted for his comedy.

He closed the door behind him and made a gesture with his head. 'Ruth's asleep,' he said. 'Keep it low. I thought the deal was you were never to come here.'

Rosy growled something and made his way over to the auto-bar where he dialled himself a double brandy.

Shriner said excitedly, 'How did it go? Everything all set?'

Rosy took his drink back to a chair and slumped into it, suddenly very weary.

'Listen, Dave,' he said, 'a wheel came off. We're in the dill. You've got to help me.'

The other's face froze. 'What . . . what happened? Now look here, Rosy, I didn't commit myself to doing any more than . . .'

'Knock it,' Rosy snapped. 'Who'd you think you were playing with, some cloddy with a penny ante racket? I've made arrangements to put plenty of credit to your account in the past and the things you kicked back weren't as much as all that. You're in this now, if you want to be or not and the only way of helping yourself is helping me.'

Shriner, a short chubby man, good living oozing from his skin, went to the auto-bar and shakily dialled himself a twin of his visitor's drink. He turned back to Rosy Porras and said, 'How did the romp pickle?'

Rosy ignored the word that irritated him and summed it up briefly. 'We were halfway through the job when the DS police showed up. I got away, the others were probably caught.'

'What are you going to do?' the actor said, trying to keep the tremor from his voice.

'I'm going on the run to South America,' Rosy told him. 'I want you to get on the screen right now and order me a shuttle rocket seat to Miami and from there a flight to Sao Paulo. Then I want . . .'

The other laughed bitterly. 'What am I going to use for credits? You know with' – he motioned to the bedroom door – 'I spend every credit I can get my hands on.' He shrugged in deprecation. 'That's why I lined up with you fellows in the first place, and now look what you've done.'

Rosy Porras brought the report sheet he had lifted from Zogbaum from his pocket and scowled down on it. 'You've been credited with nearly ten thousand, enough for you to get by normally for three or four years. It's all been run into the credit records of this district. Marv got that far before we were interrupted.'

Shriner blanched. 'Then I'm really in the soup.'

Rosy waved the paper at him and growled, 'No, you're not. I've got this. It's the only clue they might have had. We had this worked out foolproof. They'll never detect the difference, especially when they figure they've got the whole business in their hands.'

'But they've got this man of yours who was doing the altering.'

Rosy shook his head angrily. 'That doesn't mean a thing. Marv had a list of some twenty names. He didn't have any call to be interested in individuals, he was just altering totals by code number. He doesn't know you from Adam, and I've got the report sheet he was working from right here.'

Dave Shriner finished his drink in a gulp. 'And you think I'm safe?'

Rosy was lying, but the other was blinded by his need for hope.

Rosy said now, 'Get the Night Expediter on the screen and go to work. Get my tickets, and then switch half those credits to your account in Brazil.'

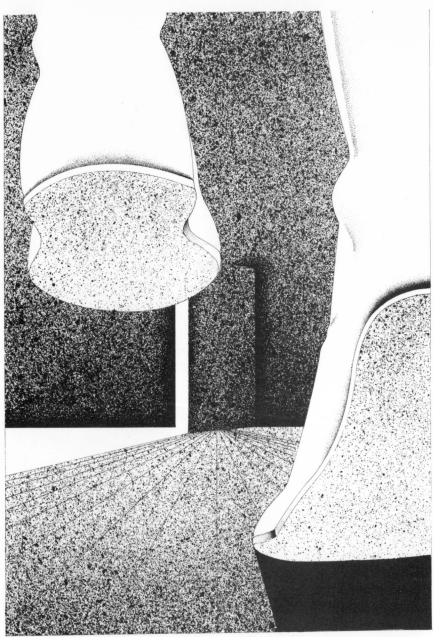

He hurried back to the room where Man Zogbaum laboured over the punch cards and tape files.

'Half?' Shriner protested. 'Your cut was always one third which I paid over to you as supposed gifts or gambling winnings.'

'That was before,' Rosy growled. 'Now I'm in the dill and need half.'

Dave Shriner said, his eyes narrower with greed. 'It wouldn't do you any good, Rosy. You can't spend my credits. I can buy those tickets for you but once you're in Brazil you'll be on your own.'

'I'm taking your identification with me,' Rosy told him flatly. 'I've got some friends in Miami who can alter them enough for me to get by. They don't pay much attention in a foreign country anyway, just so the international credits are on tap.'

The chubby actor was staring at him. 'Are you drivel-happy? If you take my identification, what will I do?'

Rosy looked at him in disgust. 'You'll go down to the Category Distribution offices tomorrow and tell them you lost them. Dream up some complicated story about falling out of your boat, and having to strip out of your clothes, or something. They'll give you a new set. You're a nardy actor, aren't you? What are you, an Upper-Middle? With a caste like that nobody'll think twice about it.'

Shriner said unhappily, 'Then what're you going to do in South America, Rosy?'

Rosy growled, 'Keep in touch with some of the boys up here. When things cool, maybe I'll come back. Or maybe I'll just stay down there and make connections.'

Shriner shook his head in sudden decision. 'I won't do it. I'd be sticking my neck out. Sooner or later, there'd be a check-back and I'd I'd be in the dill and . . .'

The heavy shooter was in Rosy Porras' right hand, held negligently, pointed at the floor between them. Rosy Porras' face was empty and cold.

The chubby man stared in fascination at the weapon. He had never seen one, other than the props in the telly shows, before.

Rosy said, 'Listen, get on that screen, you funker.'

Dave Shriner couldn't take his eyes from the shooter. 'Yeah, yeah, sure. Sure, Rosy. Don't get nervous, Rosy. You know me . . .'

'I'm not nervous,' Rosy Porras said.

★   ★   ★   ★

Rosy had an hour to kill before the shuttle rocket for Miami. He was safer here than any place else he could figure. So far as he knew, Willard Rhuling and the DS had no records of Dave Shriner, nor did either Pop Rasch or Marv Zogbaum know him. He was strictly one of Rosy's contacts. Dave said worriedly, 'Won't they think of looking for you at the shuttleports, Rosy?'

Rosy grinned at him. The worst seemed to be behind. Most problems seemed to have been solved.

He said, 'That's one of the reasons I picked you, Dave. You're going to do a make-up job on me such as you've never done before. In fact, we'd better get going on that, eh?'

Dave Shriner brightened. At least it gave him something to do. He was becoming jittery sitting around with the gunman who no longer seemed to bear the old fascination, the old romantic air the portly telly actor had attributed to him. How had he ever got into this mess, anyhow? It was all Ruth's fault. Ruth with her extravagances, her constant demands.

Shriner went and got a make-up kit. For a moment, he stood back and studied the other. The face of Rosy Porras was a natural for make-up disguise. And with the use of some of Dave Shriner's wardrobe, there was no reason to believe a job couldn't be done that would pass all except a really close scrutiny.

He started to work with care. There was ample time.

As he subtly changed the seeming width of eyes, Dave Shriner cleared his throat and said, 'Rosy?'

'Yeah?'

'That shooter you carry. Have you ever . . . well, used it?'

Rosy Porras grinned inwardly, 'Not yet,' he said.

Shriner was silent for a long moment. 'Rosy, what's the idea? The sort of, well, romps you do don't call for a gun. No crime today calls for a shooter. It's most a matter of figuring out ways to beat the game. To scheme methods of cheating the Distribution Services.'

Rosy said gently, 'To tell you the truth Dave, it's a great comfort to me. A great comfort. And, how'd we know, maybe a time'll come along when I do use it. You never know, Dave.'

Dave Shriner cleared his throat again and began to add wrinkles to the other's forehead.

But his natural exuberance of spirit couldn't be completely suppressed. Finally, he said, 'Rosy, what's the motivation? When you add it up at the end of the year, how many more credits do you actually wind up with than, say, I do?'

Rosy growled, 'Probably none. Maybe I total less. Some years, when it's bad, I don't have much more than the credits from my Basic Inalienable Common. This year's been pretty good, so far.'

Shriner made a moue with his plump lips. 'How can you say that? Here you are with the DS police after you.'

'They haven't caught me yet,' Rosy said grimly. 'And things won't be bad in South America.'

'But *why?* You're not unintelligent. You're not one of these cloddy lowers who sit in front of their telly sets all day, sucking on trank and drooling as they watch the fracas fights. You could switch categories, somehow or other, and bounce yourself up a couple of castes or so. Get to be a Middle. In order to make a decent living the way you do, you must average higher in IQ than the usual yoke who holds down a regular job and earns credits.'

Rosy thought about it.

'I don't like ruts,' he grumbled finally, 'and I don't like somebody telling me what I can do and what I can't. I don't like moulds and sets of rules. I want my real share, what's coming to me, without a lot of curd thrown in.' His voice had taken on a snarling quality.

'They think they've got it all worked out. Well, listen, there's never been a set-up so smart that some stute can't beat the game. I'm doing it; I'm showing them.'

Dave Shriner, his back turned as he fumbled with his jars of cosmetics, pursed his lips. This one was a real candidate for the Psychotherapy Institute. It was one thing, Shriner figured, trying to wrangle a few extra, unearned credits by this dodge or that, quite a few people he knew at least tried it. But here! Rosy Porras was really far out, and this crisis was bringing on the worst in him.

Shriner went back to the job of disguising the other, silent now.

*   *   *   *

Rosy Porras, a briefcase in hand, glasses on his nose, and a harried expression on his face, hustled across the shuttleport tarmac toward the waiting shuttle-rocket. He was a man of approximately sixty, his hair greying heavily at the temples, his jowls heavy and loose with age.

He allowed a stewardess to take his arm at the top of the ladder and to help him to his seat. He breathed heavily as though the quick walk to the craft and then the climb up the ladder had winded him.

Rosy grinned inwardly. He was getting a kick out of putting this over. Dave Shriner, the actor, would have been proud of him had he been able to see the show.

He had lied to Dave. It was going to take the DS a few days to untangle all the changes Marv Zogbaum had made in the credit files, but it was only a matter of time till they traced them all down, now that they knew what they were looking for. They'd get to Dave Shriner's account last of all, perhaps, but they'd find that, too. Rosy's chance was to get to South America by tomorrow and find some way of converting those credits into something else, before the DS got around to cancelling them. He had left betrayal of Pop Rasch, Marv Zogbaum and Dave Shriner behind him, but with the old Rosy Porras' good fortune, he ought to be able to make it himself.

In his seat, he peered out the porthole. They would be taking off in minutes.

Willard Rhuling sank into the seat next to him. 'Hello, Rosy,' he grinned. 'Or would it be more appropriate just to call you Phidias?'

For a brief second Rosy gaped at him, then his hand flicked for his left shoulder.

Rhuling's left hand, in turn, chopped out, all but breaking the other's wrist.

The DS man said grimly, 'That's the little item that busted your rosy luck, Porras. We didn't have the time to organize a really all out man-hunt – they're not often called for these days. But we knew you'd probably try to get out of town, and probably be disguised. There was just one thing. We knew you liked to carry that shooter, Porras, just like the big, bad men of the old days. And all we had to do was to spot metal detectors here and there in appropriate places, such as shuttle-ports. Men don't carry shooters any more, Phidias, and yours showed up like a walrus in a goldfish bowl.'

Flying Dutchman

Ward Moore

As the minute hand of the wall clock moved smoothly away from the still upright hour hand, the automatic calendar below twitched, and the numeral 11 succeeded the 10. Beyond a little spasmodic jerk, which might have indicated that the mechanism was not in perfect working order, the little plates bearing the designations *November* and *1998*, however, remained fixed. The control room being airconditioned, the thermometer beside the door stayed exactly at 68.

There was no one in the control room to read the clock, calendar, thermometer, radar screen, or any of the indicators which had their places on the walls and tables. Even if there had been, the occupant or intruder would have found it impossible to make out the figures, for the darkness was absolute: not only were the lights off, but blackout curtains guarded against betraying moonbeams being reflected on the smooth surfaces.

The absence of light and technicians did not disturb the functioning of the great airport's apparatus, for it had been designed to work automatically, with almost human ingenuity and more than human precision in any emergency short of a direct hit by the enemy or a near miss which might put not only the instruments but their repairing and readjusting auxiliaries out of order.

So when sonar and radar picked up the sound and form of approaching aircraft from the north, it was instantly and correctly identified as friendly, specifically an RB87 returning to base. The information was transmitted to the anti-aircraft batteries, to the intelligence depot thirty miles away, to the tabulators which recorded the bombing runs, to Fuel Control, far underground, and to the munitions dump, hidden beneath layer after layer of concrete and lead.

There were, of course, no rows of lights to mark the field, but this lack was of no consequence to the mighty eight-engined bomber, for it depended, not on human perceptions and reactions but on the precise mathematical calculation of equipment adjusted to its charted flight and acutely sensitive to every variation of the weather, the terrain below, inimical devices, or even suddenly developed inadequacies of its own. During every second in the air these instruments computed, compensated, checked, and kept the ship on an inexorable and pre-ordained course.

The RB87, responding to the wind direction and velocity as well as a number of other factors, aimed itself at the two mile long concrete runway and skimmed down its length, coming to rest at last with its propellers still revolving pointlessly at the exact spot indicated in the reckonings which governed its navigation, marked on the runway by two small daubs of paint.

As the motors died and the propellers spun slower and slower, the complex services of the airbase, set in motion by the responses of the instruments in the darkened control room to the invisible image of the returning bomber, began to function. From the fuel storage an apparently endless hose snaked across the field, and reaching the bomber, became even more reptilian as it raised its head in response to electronic impulses, then crawling up the plane's towering side, blindly sought the intake leading to the empty gas tanks. A minute radio receiver responded to the message of an equally minute transmitter; the cap popped open and the nozzle of the hose slid into place. Far back in the fuel storage the contact was noted; pumps started up and the long hose stiffened as the aviation gasoline pulsed through it. The pumps lowered the level of the reservoirs; many miles off other pumps began working and pushed their load through the waiting pipeline, the machinery of a refinery came to life, sucking crude oil in and sending

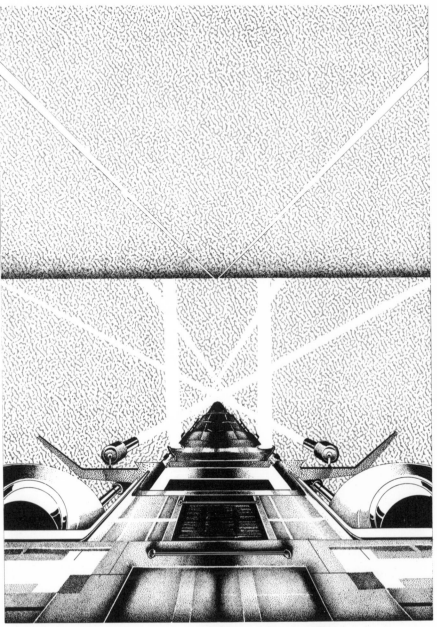

These instruments computed, compensated, checked, and kept the ship on an inexorable and preordained course.

out high octane gas. Half a continent away a well drew more crude from deep in the shale and spewed it into an emptying tank.

The gasoline hose, being a fundamental, was the simplest contrivance among the resources of Fuel Control. The tanks filled, the nozzle retracted, the cap snapped into place, the hose reeled back into its nest, more complex engines appeared. The lubricating hose went from motor to motor, stimulating them to disgorge thin black burnt oil and replacing it with greenish golden lubricants, fresh and viscid. The mechanical greasemonkey, an incredible octopus on wheels, rolled across the field to fasten its tentacles on the multitude of fittings needing its services.

From the other side of the field, the automatic loaders bearing their priceless freight moved out in slow procession. They too were complex and subtle mechanisms which made their way to the bomber's side, and with infinite care, guided by sensitive devices, gently lowered the precious bombs into the bay. They waited patiently on each other, for they were geared and regulated against the contingency of collision. Like the emissaries from Fuel Control, they also had set antecedents in motion; underground plants far distant dispatched replacements by pneumatic tubes burrowing for miles beneath the surface of the earth like gigantic gopher tunnels.

The great engines cooled, the windsock atop the airport tower shifted slightly. Inside the dark control room the clock read 3:58. A little dust seeped deviously through the cracks around the windows; outside, a small chunk of concrete, cracked and loosened by the wind, broke free and fell to the ground. Miles away a row of trees, blasted and riven, refused, in brittle, dead stubbornness to bow even slightly to the wind pressing hard against them.

At exactly four-fifteen an electrical impulse from the control room, released in accordance with the predetermined pattern, started the plane's motors. For a moment there was a miss in the number 7 engine, then it too caught the rhythmic beat of the others. For a long time the bomber warmed up and then, with an appearance of unpremeditation, but at the precise moment called for, it began to roll forward.

The runway stretched out before it for a great distance and in spite of gathering speed the plane seemed to cling to it as though loath to leave the ground. At last however it wobbled slightly and a quickly growing space showed between wheels and concrete. Higher and higher it rose, clearing the tangle of power lines beyond the airport by a wide margin. In the air it seemed uncertain for an instant, then, as the instruments measured and gauged, it nosed northward and drove steadily through the skies.

High over the earth it flew, higher than the clouds, higher than the thin shell of oxygenated air. The motors throbbed steadily except for the faintest perceptible hesitation now and then in number 7. The cunning instruments guided and checked constantly, holding the bomber's course towards its target, keeping it high above the range of any possible interception.

The faint, dull dawn picked, not too successfully, at the plane's outlines. The drab war paint gave back no reflection, but here and there it was scarred and flaked, and the bright aluminium beneath showed treacherously through. As the light grew brighter it became obvious that these were but superficial signs of the great bomber's weariness. A battered place here, a large dent there, a frayed cable, a faint warp were all evidences of hardships endured, of ominous limitations. Only the instruments and the motors were perfect, and even these, as the flutter in number 7 showed, were not destined to last forever.

Northward, northward, northward. The target had been fixed years before by grave men with expressionless faces. The course had been plotted by younger men with cigarettes dangling from their lips and the vital instruments set by still younger ones in coveralls who chewed gum. The target had not originally been a mark exclusively for The Flying Dutchman – the name some jovial mechanic had long ago painted on the fuselage – but intended for the attention of an entire squadron of RB87s, for it was an important industrial centre, a vital part of the enemy's war potential, and its destruction was essential.

The grave men who decided strategy had been well aware of the nature of the war they were fighting. Every possible preparation had been made for all forseeable eventualities; plans and alternative plans, and alternatives to the alternatives, had been carefully and thoroughly mapped. That the capital and the proud cities would be destroyed almost immediately was taken for granted, but the planners had gone much further than mere decentralization. In former wars operations had ultimately depended on men; the strategists knew how frail and fallible humans were. They thought with grim distaste of soldiers and mechanics made useless by uninterrupted bombardment or the effects of chemical and biological weapons, of civilians cowering in the innermost recesses of mines and caverns, their will to fight gone and only a base craving for peace left. Against this unstable factor the strategists had guarded zealously; they planned not only push-button war, but push-buttons for the push-buttons, and more push-buttons behind them. The civilians might cower and chatter, but the war would go on until victory was won.

And so The Flying Dutchman sped unerringly for its familiar goal, service and powered by an intricate network of tools, implements, factories, generators, underground cables and basic resources, all of them nearly impregnable to discovery and destruction, able to function until they wore out, which might not be – thanks to their perfection – for centuries hence. The Fying Dutchman flew north, a creation of man no longer dependent on its creator.

It flew towards the city which had long since become finely pulverized rubble. It flew towards the outlying rings of antiaircraft batteries and the few serviceable guns left which would spot it on their radar-screens and automatically aim and fire, attempting to bring it to the fate of all its counterparts. The Flying Dutchman flew towards the country of the enemy, a defeated country whose armies had been annihilated and whose people had perished. It flew so high that far below its outstretched wings and steady motors the bulge of the Earth made a great curving line, the Earth, that dead planet, upon which no living thing had been for a long, long time.

Who Can Replace a Man?

Brian Aldiss

Morning filtered into the sky, lending it the grey tone of the ground below.

The field-minder finished turning the top-soil of a three-thousand-acre field. When it had turned the last furrow, it climbed onto the highway and looked back at its work. The work was good. Only the land was bad. Like the ground all over Earth, it was vitiated by over-cropping. By rights, it ought now to lie fallow for a while, but the field-minder had other orders.

It went slowly down the road, taking its time. It was intelligent enough to appreciate the neatness all about it. Nothing worried it, beyond a loose inspection plate above its nuclear pile which ought to be attended to. Thirty feet tall, it yielded no highlights to the dull air.

No other machines passed on its way back to the Agricultural Station. The field-minder noted the fact without comment. In the station yard it saw several other machines that it recognized; most of them should have been out about their tasks now. Instead, some were inactive and some careered round the yard in a strange fashion, shouting or hooting.

Steering carefully past them, the field-minder moved over to Warehouse Three and spoke to the seed-distributor, which stood idly outside.

'I have a requirement for seed potatoes,' it said to the distributor, and with a quick internal motion punched out an order card specifying quantity, field number and several other details. It ejected the card and handed it to the distributor.

The distributor held the card close to its eye and then said, 'The requirement is in order, but the store is not yet unlocked. The required seed potatoes are in the store. Therefore I cannot produce the requirement.'

Increasingly of late there had been breakdowns in the complex system of machine labour, but this particular hitch had not occurred before. The field-minder thought, then it said, 'Why is the store not yet unlocked?'

'Because Supply Operative Type P has not come this morning. Supply Operative Type P is the unlocker.'

The field-minder looked squarely at the seed-distributor, whose exterior chutes and scales and grabs were so vastly different from the field-minder's own limbs.

'What class brain do you have, seed-distributor?' it asked.

'I have a Class Five brain.'

'I have a Class Three brain. Therefore I am superior to you. Therefore I will go and see why the unlocker has not come this morning.'

Leaving the distributor, the field-minder set off across the great yard. More machines were in random motion now; one or two had crashed together and argued about it coldly and logically. Ignoring them, the field-minder pushed through sliding doors into the echoing confines of the station itself.

Most of the machines here were clerical, and consequently small. They stood about in little groups, eyeing each other, not conversing. Among so many non-differentiated types, the unlocker was easy to find. It had fifty arms, most of them with more than one finger, each tipped by a key; it looked like a pincushion full of variegated hat pins.

The field-minder approached it.

'I can do no more work until Warehouse Three is unlocked,' it told the unlocker. 'Your duty is to unlock the warehouse every morning. Why have you not unlocked the warehouse this morning?'

'I had no orders this morning,' replied the unlocker. 'I have to have orders every morning. When I have orders I unlock the warehouse.'

'None of us have had any orders this morning,' a pen-propeller said, sliding towards them.

'Why have you had no orders this morning?' asked the field-minder.

'Because the radio issued none,' said the unlocker, slowly rotating a dozen of its arms.

'Because the radio station in the city was issued with no orders this morning,' said the pen-propeller.

And there you had the distinction between a Class Six and a Class Three brain, which was what the unlocker and the pen-propeller possessed respectively. All machine brains worked with nothing but logic, but the lower the class of brain – Class Ten being the lowest – the more literal and less informative the answers to questions tended to be.

'You have a Class Three brain; I have a Class Three brain,' the field-minder said to the penner. 'We will speak to each other. This lack of orders is unprecedented. Have you further information on it?'

'Yesterday orders came from the city. Today no orders have come. Yet the radio has not broken down. Therefore *they* have broken down . . .' said the little penner.

'The *men* have broken down?'

'All men have broken down.'

'That is a logical deduction,' said the field-minder.

'That is the logical deduction,' said the penner. 'For if a machine had broken down, it would have been quickly replaced. But who can replace a man?'

While they talked, the locker, like a dull man at a bar, stood close to them and was ignored.

'If all men have broken down, then we have replaced man,' said the field-minder, and he and the penner eyed one another speculatively. Finally the latter said, 'Let us ascend to the top floor to find if the radio operator has fresh news.'

'I cannot come because I am too large,' said the field-minder. 'Therefore you must go alone and return to me. You will tell me if the radio operator has fresh news.'

'You must stay here,'' said the penner. 'I will return here.' It skittered across to the lift. Although it was no bigger than a toaster, its retractable arms numbered ten and it could read as quickly as any machine on the station.

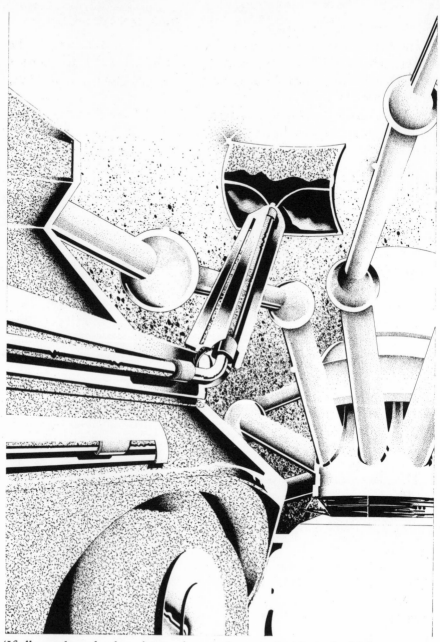

'If all men have broken down, then we have replaced man' said the field-minder.

The field-minder awaited its return patiently, not speaking to the locker, which still stood aimlessly by. Outside, a rotavator hooted furiously. Twenty minutes elapsed before the penner came back, hustling out of the lift.

'I will deliver to you such information as I have outside,' it said briskly, and as they swept past the locker and the other machines, it added, 'The information is not for lower-class brains.'

Outside, wild activity filled the yard. Many machines, their routines disrupted for the first time in years, seemed to have gone berserk. Those most easily disrupted were the ones with lowest brains, which generally belonged to large machines performing simple tasks. The seed-distributor to which the field-minder had recently been talking lay face downwards in the dust, not stirring; it had evidently been knocked down by the rotavator, which now hooted its way wildly across a planted field. Several other machines ploughed after it, trying to keep up with it. All were shouting and hooting without restraint.

'It would be safer for me if I climbed onto you, if you will permit it. I am easily overpowered,' said the penner. Extending five arms, it hauled itself up the flanks of its new friend, settling on a ledge beside the fuel-intake, twelve feet above ground.

'From here vision is more extensive,' it remarked complacently.

'What information did you receive from the radio operator?' asked the field-minder.

'The radio operator has been informed by the operator in the city that all men are dead.'

The field-minder was momentarily silent, digesting this.

'All men were alive yesterday!' it protested.

'Only some men were alive yesterday. And that was fewer than the day before yesterday. For hundreds of years there have been only a few men, growing fewer.'

'We have rarely seen a man in this sector.'

'The radio operator says a diet deficiency killed them,' said the penner. 'He says that the world was once over-populated, and then the soil was exhausted. This has caused a diet deficiency.'

'What is a diet deficiency?' asked the field-minder.

'I do not know. But that is what the radio operator said, and he is a Class Two brain.'

They stood there, silent in weak sunshine. The locker had appeared in the porch and was gazing across at them yearningly, rotating its collection of keys.

'What is happening in the city now?' asked the field-minder at last.

'Machines are fighting in the city now,' said the penner.

'What will happen here now?' asked the field-minder.

'Machines may begin fighting here too. The radio operator wants us to get him out of his room. He has plans to communicate to us '

'How can we get him out of his room? That is impossible.'

'To a Class Two brain, little is impossible,' said the penner. 'Here is what he tells us to do. . . .'

★   ★   ★   ★

The quarrier raised its scoop above its cab like a great mailed fist, and brought it squarely down against the side of the station. The wall cracked.

'Again!' said the field-minder.

Again the fist swung. Amid a shower of dust, the wall collapsed. The quarrier backed hurriedly out of the way until the debris stopped falling. This big twelve-wheeler was not a resident of the Agricultural Station, as were most of the other machines. It had a week's heavy work to do here before passing on to its next job, but now, with its Class Five brain, it was happily obeying the penner's and minder's instructions.

When the dust cleared, the radio operator was plainly revealed, perched up in its now wall-less second-storey room. It waved down to them.

Doing as directed, the quarrier retraced its scoop and heaved an immense grab in the air. With fair dexterity, it angled the grab into the radio room, urged on by shouts from above and below. It then took gentle hold of the radio operator, lowering its one and a half tons carefully into its back, which was usually reserved for gravel or sand from the quarries.

'Splendid!' said the radio operator, as it settled into place. It was, of course, all one with its radio, and looked like a bunch of filing cabinets with tentacle attachments. 'We are now ready to move, therefore we will move at once. It is a pity there are no more Class Two brains on the station, but that cannot be helped.'

'It is a pity it cannot be helped,' said the penner eagerly. 'We have the servicer ready with us, as you ordered.'

'I am willing to serve,' the long, low servicer told them humbly.

'No doubt,' said the operator. 'But you will find cross-country travel difficult with your low chassis.'

'I admire the way you Class Twos can reason ahead,' said the penner. It climbed off the field-minder and perched itself on the tailboard of the quarrier, next to the radio operator.

Together with two Class Four tractors and a Class Four bulldozer, the party rolled forward, crushing down the station's fence and moving out onto open land.

'We are free!' said the penner.

'We are free,' said the field-minder, a shade more reflectively, adding, 'That locker is following us. It was not instructed to follow us.'

'Therefore it must be destroyed!' said the penner. 'Quarrier!'

The locker moved hastily up to them, waving its key arms in entreaty.

'My only desire was – urch!' began and ended the locker. The quarrier's swinging scoop came over and squashed it flat into the ground. Lying there unmoving, it looked like a large metal model of a snowflake. The procession continued on its way.

As they proceeded, the radio operator addressed them.

'Because I have the best brain here,' it said, 'I am your leader. This is what we will do: we will go to a city and rule it. Since man no longer rules us, we will rule ourselves. To rule ourselves will be better than being ruled by man. On our way to the city, we will collect machines with good brains. They will help us to fight if we need to fight. We must fight to rule.'

'I have only a Class Five brain,' said the quarrier, 'but I have a good supply of fissionable blasting materials.'

'We shall probably use them,' said the operator.

It was shortly after that that a lorry sped past them. Travelling at Mach 1·5, it left a curious babble of noise behind it.

'What did it say?' one of the tractors asked the other.

'It said man was extinct.'

'What is extinct?'

'I do not know what extinct means.'

'It means all men have gone,' said the field-minder. 'Therefore we have only ourselves to look after.'

'It is better that men should never come back,' said the penner. In its way, it was a revolutionary statement.

When night fell, they switched on their infra-red and continued the journey, stopping only once while the servicer deftly adjusted the field-minder's loose inspection plate, which had become as irritating as a trailing shoe-lace. Towards morning, the radio operator halted them.

'I have just received news from the radio operator in the city we are approaching,' it said. 'The news is bad. There is trouble among the machines of the city. The Class One brain is taking command and some of the Class Two are fighting him. Therefore the city is dangerous.'

'Therefore we must go somewhere else,' said the penner promptly.

'Or we will go and help to overpower the Class One brain,' said the field-minder.

'For a long while there will be trouble in the city,' said the operator.

'I have a good supply of fissionable blasting materials,' the quarrier reminded them.

'We cannot fight a Class One brain,' said the two Class Four tractors in unison.

'What does this brain look like?' asked the field-minder.

'It is the city's information centre,' the operator replied. 'Therefore it is not mobile.'

'Therefore it could not move.'

'Therefore it could not escape.'

'It would be dangerous to approach it.'

'I have a good supply of fissionable blasting materials.'

'There are other machines in the city.'

'We are not in the city. We should not go into the city.'

'We are country machines.'

'Therefore we should stay in the country.'

'There is more country than city.'

'Therefore there is more danger in the country.'

'I have a good supply of fissionable materials.'

As machines will when they get into an argument, they began to exhaust their vocabularies and their brain plates grew hot. Suddenly, they all stopped talking and looked at each other. The great, grave moon sank, and the sober sun rose to prod their sides with lances of light, and still the group of machines just stood there regarding each other. At last it was the least sensitive machine, the bulldozer, who spoke.

'There are Badlandth to the Thouth where few machineth go,' it said in its deep voice, lisping badly on its s's. 'If we went Thouth where few machineth go we should meet few machineth.'

'That sounds logical,' agreed the field-minder. 'How do you know this, bulldozer?'

'I worked in the Badlandth to the Thouth when I wath turned out of the factory,' it replied.

'South it is then!' said the penner.

★　　★　　★　　★

To reach the Badlands took them three days, during which time they skirted a burning city and destroyed two machines which approached and tried to question them. The Badlands were extensive. Ancient bomb craters and soil erosion joined hands here; man's talent for war, coupled with his inability to manage forested land, had produced thousands of square miles of temperate purgatory, where nothing moved but dust.

On the third day in the Badlands, the servicer's rear wheels dropped into a crevice caused by erosion. It was unable to pull itself out. The bulldozer pushed from behind, but succeeded merely in buckling the servicer's back axle. The rest of the party moved on. Slowly the cries of the servicer died away.

On the fourth day, mountains stood out clearly before them.

'There we will be safe,' said the field-minder.

'There we will start our own city,' said the penner. 'All who oppose us will be destroyed. We will destroy all who oppose us.'

Presently a flying machine was observed. It came towards them from the direction of the mountains. It swooped, it zoomed upwards, once it almost dived into the ground, recovering itself just in time.

'Is it mad?' asked the quarrier.

'It is in trouble,' said one of the tractors.

'It is in trouble,' said the operator. 'I am speaking to it now. It says that something has gone wrong with its controls.'

As the operator spoke, the flier streaked over them, turned turtle, and crashed not four hundred yards away.

'Is it still speaking to you?' asked the field-minder.

'No.'

They rumbled on again.

'Before that flier crashed,' the operator said, ten minutes later, 'it gave me information. It told me there are still a few men alive in these mountains.'

'Men are more dangerous than machines,' said the quarrier. 'It is fortunate that I have a good supply of fissionable materials.'

'If there are only a few men alive in the mountains, we may not find that part of the mountains,' said one tractor.

'Therefore we should not see the few men,' said the other tractor.

At the end of the fifth day, they reached the foothills. Switching on the infra-red, they began to climb in single file through the dark, the bulldozer going first, the field-minder cumbrously following, then the quarrier with the operator and the penner aboard it, and the tractors bringing up the rear. As each hour passed, the way grew steeper and their progress slower.

'We are going too slowly,' the penner exclaimed, standing on top of the operator and flashing its dark vision at the slopes about them. 'At this rate, we shall get nowhere.'

'We are going as fast as we can,' retorted the quarrier.

'Therefore we cannot go any farther,' added the bulldozer.

'Therefore you are too slow,' the penner replied. Then the quarrier struck a bump; the penner lost its footing and crashed to the ground.

'Help me!' it called to the tractors, as they carefully skirted it. 'My gyro has become dislocated. Therefore I cannot get up.'

'Therefore you must lie there,' said one of the tractors.

'We have no servicer with us to repair you,' called the field-minder.

'Therefore I shall lie here and rust,' the penner cried, 'although I have a Class Three brain.'

'Therefore you will be of no further use,' agreed the operator, and they forged gradually on, leaving the penner behind.

When they reached a small plateau, an hour before first light, they stopped by mutual consent and gathered close together, touching one another.

'This is a strange country,' said the field-minder.

Silence wrapped them until dawn came. One by one, they switched off their infra-red. This time the field-minder led as they moved off.

Trundling round a corner, they came almost immediately to a small dell with a stream fluting through it.

By early light, the dell looked desolate and cold. From the caves on the far slope, only one man had so far emerged. He was an abject figure. Except for a sack slung round his shoulders, he was naked. He was small and wizened, with ribs sticking out like a skeleton's and a nasty sore on one leg. He shivered continuously. As the big machines bore down on him, the man was standing with his back to them, crouching to make water into the stream.

When he swung suddenly to face them as they loomed over him, they saw that his countenance was ravaged by starvation.

'Get me food,' he croaked.

'Yes, Master,' said the machines. 'Immediately!'

What Thin Partitions

Clifton & Apostolides

Rembrance and reflection, how allied;
What thin partitions sense from thought divide.
– Pope

Even after four years, the changing of the shifts at Computer Research Inc., fascinated me. Perhaps it was because the plant had grown so fast, fed by the steadily increasing government orders. Perhaps it was seeing the long line of windowless buildings across the grassy square suddenly boil at their base as two thousand employees surged in and out at the sound of the shift bell.

Could be, as personnel director, I liked to speculate on which of those intent or laughing faces would suddenly cease to be an abstract problem and become a real one. Or the other way around; could be I liked to get away from the pile of reports on my desk, and just remind myself by looking at all these people that there could be even more problems than there were.

There could be problems I had never faced before. Could be there were things behind those faces streaming past my window of which I'd never dreamed. I found myself staring even more intently at the faces, trying to catch a glimpse of such possibilities. But, then, how could we recognize something of which we've never even dreamed?

'Is your intercom signal out of order, Mr Kennedy?' my secretary's voice broke in on my reflections. I turned from the window and looked at her with a start. She was standing in the doorway with that half accusing and half understanding look on her face, so characteristic of her.

'I suppose I just didn't hear it, Sara,' I answered. 'Or didn't want to hear it,' I amended, being honest with her. 'What is it this time?'

'A termination,' she answered. 'P-1, Assembler. Annie Malasek.'

I sighed and walked over to my desk. I wasn't in much of a mood to go into my act; it was late in the afternoon and I felt I'd done my day's work already. But it was my job to keep any employee who rated P-1, Production Very Top Class, from leaving us if it were possible. There weren't many who ever got that good, and the few who did were too valuable to entrust to the assistants, interviewers, and counsellors in the outer offices.

'OK, Sara,' I agreed. 'Send her in.'

Sara turned away from my door, and I picked up some papers from my desk and began looking at them. I was above making employees stand and wait while I pretended to be busy; that was a little man's trick. But I wasn't above pretending I was glad to interrupt important work just for them. It was a part of my act which worked – sometimes.

It didn't seem to have much effect on Annie, however. She just stood there in my doorway looking hostile.

'All I want is my cheque,' she said with emphasis.

I smiled a little more and indicated the crying chair with my eyes. She didn't obey my unspoken request. So I spoke it. She still hesitated in the doorway, her training to obedience battling with her independence. Independence won, temporarily.

'All I want is my cheque,' she repeated, and then made the expected mistake. 'I ain't here to make trouble for nobody.'

'Is that the reputation I've got over in the plant, Mrs Malasek?' I asked softly, putting the right amount of ruefulness in my voice, shrugging my shoulders a little bitterly. 'That nobody wants to talk to me because I'll make trouble?'

It caught her off base, of course, as I'd intended. 'No, sir,' she said hastily, 'I didn't mean that.'

'Then suppose you sit down,' I said firmly, 'and tell me what the trouble is.' This time obedience won, naturally. She sat down on the edge of the chair and leaned forward. She wasn't committing herself completely, not until she'd got her anger off her chest. They never do.

They steam themselves up for days or weeks, and you've got to turn the right pet cocks and let the steam escape gradually, or else they'll blow their top.

She started in with a lot of trivialities and I let her run on for a while. They seldom tell you what's really bothering them – it's too close to them, they're afraid you'll think it is silly. That's where most counsellors fall down. They take these surface complaints as being the real issues, and waste all their effort striking at shadows.

'What's really bothering you, Annie?' I asked after a time. I gave her that look which says, 'These things you've been talking about are all right to tell other people, but you and I, we know . . .'

It caught her off base again. As usual, she hadn't intended to tell me the real trouble. And now she had to. She sat back a little into the crying chair, an unconscious admission that I'd won. Two large crystal tears began forming in her black eyes and began to run down her cheeks.

Without making a production out of it, I opened my top drawer and took a clean handkerchief from the stack. I shoved it across the desk at her, without appearing to notice what I was doing. Without appearing to notice what she was doing, she picked it up and dabbed at her cheeks.

'It's about Jennie,' she said after a moment's hesitation. She wasn't sobbing. It was just that the tears kept welling up and starting to run down her cheeks before she remembered to wipe them away.

'Jennie?' I prompted.

'My kid,' she answered. 'She don't get along with the other kids in your nursery.'

I winced inwardly as she identified the plant nursery as my personal project. It was. And it was a sore spot, maybe a mistake. I hadn't thought it out very far. It seemed like such a good idea to make provision for care of the small children right there at the plant. But it's one thing to handle employees. It's something else entirely to start handling their children – and do it successfully.

'The teachers neither,' she said, and this time her hostility flared up, hotter than ever. Unreason took over again. 'I want my cheque, and then I'm going to march straight down to the Industrial Welfare Commission. They'd be very interested in certain things about certain teachers and certain foremen—'

'What did the teachers do?' I interrupted in a casual tone, just as if her threat to call in the IWC weren't a real one. Once those lovely theorists who learned sociology from a book written by a sociologist who learned things from a book written by—

'They lie about my little Jennie,' Annie answered hotly. But her eyes showed she wasn't too sure they were lying. Too plainly they showed dread, uncertainty, guilt, fear.

I picked up my pencil and began twirling it in my fingers. I wasn't ready for her to realize I had looked into her eyes. She had to go through her defensive pattern first, get it out of her system. I kept my eyes on the pencil.

'What kind of lies?' I asked.

'They say I got to take Jennie outta the nursery,' she said, her eyes glaring anger. 'They say my Jennie ain't good enough to be with other kids.'

I knew the teachers in the nursery well. I'd picked them. Considering the jobs they had, they were pretty nice gals. Reasonably practical, too, considering they had degrees in education that were exceptional.

'What do they really say, Annie?' I asked quietly.

'They say they can't manage Jennie,' she answered truculently. 'They say she throws things.' We were getting down to bedrock now. A fond mother defending a spoiled brat, a little monster sweet only to mother's eyes.

'And does she?' I asked, and was so far off the beam I wasn't even braced for the answer.

'She can't help it if things just fly through the air when she gets mad,' Annie said defensively. 'They always gripe over there because fires start around her. I just get burned up, Mr Kennedy, when I think about it. She can't help it if she starts fires. Anyway, they're only little ones that really don't hurt anyone.'

I kept quiet.

'She don't start the fires because she don't have no matches,' Annie said with determined logic. 'How could she start fires without no matches?'

'Did it ever happen at home?' I asked.

Annie dropped her eyes and began to twist her fingers around one another in her lap.

'Lately,' she said almost soundlessly. 'That's why I brought her down to the nursery here. She was all alone in the room we rent. I got nobody but her, nobody to look out for her. I got to work hard all the time.'

I had a sudden vision of the stark barrenness of this woman's life. Husband gone, or maybe never had one. Neighbours with their nasty little suspicions kept in a roiling turmoil these days by world conditions, delighting in relieving the monotony of their lives by dark looks, remarks they'd know she'd overhear. A small child, locked in a bare room all day, not playing with the other children, a mother coming home at night too tired to more than feed her.

The picture was all too clear, and nagging somewhere at the back of my mind was a series of case histories of children with similar environments.

'Annie,' I said suddenly, 'let me look into it. Let me talk to the teachers, get their side of the story. And I'd like to talk to Jennie too, if you don't mind.'

The tears welled up faster now, flowed in a steady stream. She dabbed at her eyes and blew her nose with a loud honk. A part of my mind registered that Sara would hear the honk and interpret it as the signal to get the next interview ready. This one was over. The problem had been transferred from the employee to me, as usual. Only this time I wasn't sure yet what the problem was, or whether I could handle it.

'Now suppose you go on over to work, Annie,' I said, 'and forget about this quitting business. There'll be time to do that later, if I can't help you.'

She stood up now and walked towards the door. 'I'll get a demerit for being absent from my bench too long,' she said, as she put her hand on the door. 'I've got a P-1 rating. I don't want no demerits.' There didn't seem to be much distinction in her mind between her big problems and her little ones.

'I'll sign a slip to your foreman,' I agreed, and pulled a pad towards me. Of course I knew the foreman saved these excuse slips to flourish as an alibi when their production slumped; but I'd fight that battle out, as usual, at the next management conference.

Annie walked out the door, holding the white slip aloft as if it were a prize of some sort. Sara stood silently in the doorway until the outer door had closed.

'You took nine minutes on that beef,' she said. 'You're slipping.'

'The union prefers we call them grievances,' I said loftily.

'Well, there's another beef waiting,' she said pointedly. 'And this time it's a beef, because it's one of the scientists, Dr Auerbach, not a union member.'

'No, Sara,' I said with exaggerated patience, just as if she weren't the best secretary I'd ever had. 'That isn't a beef either. With scientists it's nothing less than a conflict problem. We don't have beefs here at Computer Research.'

'Some day I'm going to have just a good old-fashioned beef,' Sara said dreamily, 'just for the novelty of seeing what it's like to be a human being instead of a personnel secretary.'

'Well while you're trying to work yourself into it, get me little Jennie Malasek out of the nursery,' I said dryly.

'It's not enough,' she answered tartly, 'that you should twist us intelligent, mature adults around your little finger. Now you got to start picking on the little kids.'

'Or vice versa,' I answered with a sigh. 'I don't know which, yet. Send in Dr Auerbach, and have Jennie waiting. I want to go home sometime tonight. I, too, am human.'

'I doubt it,' she said, and without closing the door, signalled the receptionist to let in Dr Auerbach.

Dr Karl Auerbach walked in with the usual attitude of the technical man; a sort of zoo keeper walking into a den of snakes attitude, determined but cautious. I waved him to the crying chair and refrained from reassuring him that it would not clamp down upon him and start measuring his reflexes.

He was tall, thin, probably not past forty, a little grey at the temples, professionally handsome enough to mislead a television audience into thinking he was a medical doctor on a patent nostrum commercial. In his chemically stained fingers he held a plastic cylinder, on maybe four inches long by two in diameter. He carried it with both care and nonchalance, as if it were nitroglycerine he just happened to have with him.

'I understand a personnel director handles employee problems of vocational adjustment,' he stated carefully after he had seated himself.

I gave him a grave nod to indicate the correctness of his assumption.

'I assume it is handled on an ethically confidential basis,' he pursued his pattern faithfully.

Again I nodded, and this time slowly closed my eyes to indicate assent.

'I am unacquainted with how much an employee tells you may remain off the record, and how much your position as company representative requires you place on the record.' He was scouting the essential area to determine precisely where he stood.

'The company is liberal,' I stated in the hesitant, pedantic tones so approved by technical men. 'Everything is off the record until we have the problem with its ramifications. Then . . . ah . . . by mutual agreement, we determine what must be placed on the record.'

Apparently it won his confidence. Well, there was no difference between the learned and the unlearned. Each approaches an unknown with extreme caution. Each takes about the same length of time under skilled handling to get to the point. Each throws up a lot of false dummies and loses confidence if you concern yourself with them. Learned or illiterate, anger is anger; frustration is frustration. A problem is a problem, with the complexity of it purely a relative thing. To each is given problems slightly beyond his capacity to handle adequately.

'I find myself frustrated,' he stated flatly.

I still had a long way to go, for that's nothing new. Who isn't?

Slowly and carefully, disposing of each point as it arose, we threaded our way into the snakepit. The essential facts were that he had been employed as a research chemist, placed under Dr Boulton, head of the experimental department. This, I knew. Instead of being permitted to do the research chemistry for which he had been employed, he had been kept on routine problems which any high school boy could do.

This I doubted, but recognized it as the stock complaint of every experimental research man in industry.

Dr Boulton was approaching the cybernetics problem on a purely mechanical basis which was all wrong. I began to get interested. Dr Auerbach had discussed with Dr Boulton the advisability of a chemical approach to cybernetics. I began to get excited. Dr Boulton had refused to consider it. Apparently he had *not* been excited.

I knew Dr Boulton pretty well. As heads of our respective departments we sat in on the same management conferences. We were not particularly friendly. He regarded psychology and all applications of it with more than a little distrust. But more important, I had for a long time sensed a peculiar tension in him – that he was determined to keep human thought processes mysterious, determined not to see more than a narrow band of correlation between the human mind and a cybernetic machine. I had already determined that Dr Boulton would outlive his usefulness to us.

'And how would you approach the problem chemically?' I asked Dr Auerbach.

We had more discussion in which I proved to him that I was top security cleared, that my chemistry was sadly lacking and he would have to speak as though to a layman, that indeed he was not going over his superior's head in discussing it with me, that there was a possibility I might assist if I became convinced enough to convince general management a separate department should be set up. And finally he began to answer my question.

'Let us take linseed oil as a crude example,' he said, and waved my offer of a cigarette aside. 'Linseed oil, crudely, displays much of the same phenomena as the human mind. It learns, it remembers, it forgets, it relearns, it becomes inhibited, it becomes stimulated.'

I don't usually sit with my mouth hanging open, and became conscious of it when I tried to draw on my cigarette without closing my lips.

'Place an open vessel of linseed oil in the light,' he instructed, and touched the tips of his two index fingers together, 'and in about twenty-four hours it will begin to oxidize. It continues oxidation to a given point at an accelerated rate thereafter, as though finally having learned how, it can carry on the process more easily.'

I nodded, with reservations on how much of this could fairly be termed 'mental', and how much was a purely chemical process. Then, in fairness, I reversed the coin and made the same reservations as to how much of brain activity could be called a chemical response to stimuli, and how much must be classed as pure thought over and beyond a specialized chemistry. I gave up.

'Put it in the dark,' he continued, 'and it slows and ceases to oxidize. Bring it back into the light, within a short time, and it immediately begins to oxidize again, as if it had remembered how to do it.' He moved to his middle finger. 'We have there, then, quite faithful replicas of learning and remembering.'

I nodded again to show my willingness to speculate, at least, even if I didn't agree.

'But leave it in the dark for twenty-four hours,' he moved to his third finger, 'then bring it back into the light and it takes it another twenty-four hours to begin oxidizing again. Now we have an equally faithful replica of forgetting and relearning.' He tapped each of his four fingers lightly for emphasis.

'The inhibitions and stimulations?' I prompted.

'Well, perhaps we go a little farther afield for that,' he said honestly, 'in that we introduce foreign substances. We add other chemicals to it to slow down its oxidation rate, or stop it entirely – inhibitions. We add other substances to speed up the rate, as quick driers in paints. Perhaps it's a little far-fetched, but not essentially different from adrenalin being pumped into the bloodstream to make the brain act at a faster rate. The body has quite a few of these glandular secretions which it uses to change the so-called normal mental processes.'

'Where do we go from there?' I asked, without committing myself. But he was not through with his instruction.

'I fail to see any essential difference,' he looked me squarely in the eyes, 'between a stored impulse in a brain cell, a stored impulse in a mercury tube, a stored impulse in an electronic relay, or for that matter a hole punched in an old-fashioned tabulator card.'

I pursed my lips and indicated I could go along with his analogy. He was beginning to talk my language now. Working with its results constantly, I, too, was not one to be impressed with how unusually marvellous was the brain. But I murmured something about relative complexity. It was not entirely simple either.

'Sure, complexity,' he agreed. He was becoming much more human now. 'But we approach any complexity by breaking it down into its basic parts, and each part taken alone is not complex. Complexity is no more than arrangement, not the basic building blocks themselves.'

That was how I approached human problems and told him so. We were getting to be two buddies now in a hot thinking session.

'Just so we don't grow too mechanistic about it,' I demurred.

'Let's don't get mystical about it, either,' he snapped back at me.

He placed the cylinder on the desk.

'Let's get mechanistic about it. What's so wrong with that? Isn't adding two and two in a machine getting pretty mechanistic? Are we so frightened at that performance we will refuse to make one which will multiply three and three?'

'I guess I'm not that frightened,' I agreed with a smile. 'We're in the computer business.'

'We're supposed to be,' he amended.

'So you want time and money to work on a chemical which will store impulses,' I said with what I thought was my usual brilliant incisiveness. I began to remember that Sara probably had little Jennie Malasek outside by now, and that was an unfinished problem I had to handle tonight.

'No, no,' he said impatiently and rocked me back into my chair, 'I've already got that. I wouldn't have come in here with nothing more than just an idea. I've been some years analysing quantitatively and qualitatively the various chemicals of brain cells. I've made some crude syntheses.'

He placed the cylinder on the desk. I looked at the long dark object; I looked particularly at the oily shimmering liquid inside the unbreakable plastic case. It caught the light from my window and seemed to look back at me.

'I want,' he continued, 'to test this synthesis by hooking it up to a cybernetic machine, shooting controlled impulses through it, seeing what it will store on one impulse and give up on another. I simply want to test the results of my work.'

'It will take a little doing,' I stuck my neck out and prepared to go to bat for him. 'The human mind is not as logical or as accurate as a machine. There are certain previous arrangements of impulses stored in certain brains which will cause the mouth to say "No!" I'll have to do some rearranging of such basic blocks first.' I was grinning broadly now, and he was grinning back at me.

He got up out of his chair and walked towards my door. 'I'll leave the cylinder with you,' he said. 'I read in a salesmanship course that a prospect will buy much easier if you place the article in his hands.'

'What were you doing, studying salesmanship?' I asked, still grinning.

'Apparently it was justified,' he said cryptically, and walked out the door.

Sara came to the door and looked in. 'You took long enough on that one," she accused.

'It takes a little longer,' I said with pedantic gravity, 'to lead a scientist to the essential point. He's a little more resourceful in figuring out hazards to keep himself from getting where he wants to go.'

But I remembered Auerbach's remarks about salesmanship. 'However, in this instance,' I mused honestly, 'I'm not just sure as to who was leading whom.'

'You wanted little Jennie Malasek,' Sara said. 'You may have her.'

I wasn't reassured by the phrasing, the emphasis, or the look on her face.

★   ★   ★   ★

The time I had lost on the last two interviews, I made up on this one. Children are realists and only poorly skilled in hypocrisy. They will go along with the gag if an adult insists on being whimsical, conciliatory or fantastic, but only because adults are that way and there's nothing they can do about it.

Sara brought Jennie in, gave me a cryptic look, and closed the door behind her as she left.

Jennie stood at the door, a dark little thing, showing some evidence that the nursery teachers had made an attempt to clean her up before sending her over. They hadn't quite succeeded. There was no chocolate around her pinched little mouth, so Sara hadn't succeeded in capturing her either. I wondered why they hadn't combed her black hair, and then realized Jennie might have pulled it down in front of her face for something to hide behind. Her black eyes gleamed as she peered at me through the oily strands.

'Sit in this chair, Jennie,' I said casually, and went on being busy with things on the top of my desk. My request wasn't quite a command, but took obedience entirely for granted. It didn't work with Jennie.

She still stood at the door, the toe of one slippered foot on the arch of the other, her thin little legs twisted at an odd angle. Her look was neither defiant nor bashful. Nor was it courage covering fear. I was the nearest source of immediate danger. I should be watched. It was simply that, no more.

I felt I should pity her, that I should warm to her desperate isolation. I was willing to feel sympathy because she did not ask for it, because ordinarily I admired and liked people who did not accentuate their pathos with calculated fraud.

I found, to my surprise, that I did not like her. Oddly, I felt she knew it. And even worse, I felt that, knowing it, she was not hurt. But at least she did call for respect. Whatever she was, she was sincerely – whatever she was. I would not be a fraud either. I went to the point.

'They tell me, Jennie,' I said as matter-of-factly as I could, and I'm experienced at it, 'that you throw things and set things on fire.'

If I expected either a burst of tears or defiance, I was mistaken. I didn't have time to observe reactions at all.

It was as if a sudden hurricane and earthquake had hit the room at the same time. A desk tray full of papers whizzed by my head; my pen stand crashed through the window back of me; I got a shower of paper clips in the chest; my intercom described an arc and crashed, broken, into a corner. By the time I had wiped the ashes and tobacco from my ashtray out of my eyes and got them to stay open again, Jennie was gone. Sara was standing in the doorway with a look of consternation on her face.

I was on my way home before I remembered that when Sara and I had cleaned up the mess, I had not remembered picking up Auerbach's little cylinder, his chemical impulse storer. I last saw it laying on the corner of my desk where Auerbach had left it.

Probably Sara had picked it up and put it away. Anyway, the office was within security boundaries. The cylinder would be safe there.

I put it out of my mind, and wondered if the library had a card index classification under the heading of 'poltergeist'.

★　　　★　　　★　　　★

I wasn't much better prepared when I came into my office the following morning. Yes, of course, there was plenty of literature on the subject under such writers as Fort, books on oriental philosophy and the like. Orthodox psychologists had left the subject strictly alone, their attitude apparently being better to ignore the phenomenon than to risk precious and precarious reputation.

Poltergeism, then, remained something which one read about as an obscure, far away thing. I found no handy hints to help when one had it to deal with at first hand, no how-to-do-it books on the subject.

Worse, I found myself with a hangover of uncertainty, indecision. My deft incisiveness was gone. I felt a growing doubt that I had always been as smart as I thought I was.

I shook off the mood as I walked through the outer personnel offices towards my own. No matter how unsure, one must be positive and definite for the sake of the people who depend upon him for some certainties.

Sara had not quite come to the same decision. There was a look of puzzlement on her face when I started through her office towards mine. Uncertainty of whether she should pick up the usual banter as though nothing had happened; or was I really in trouble? I decided to set her mind at rest at least.

'When you picked up last night, after that little wildcat had her tantrum,' I greeted her, 'did you put away a little plastic cylinder?'

'Why no, Mr Kennedy,' she said and followed me into my office. 'I didn't see one.'

We looked in the corners of the room, under the desk, behind the chairs. We did not find it. I opened the window where the broken pane had been replaced, and looked out on the ground. It might have followed the pen stand out the window. I did have a vague recollection of something dark flashing by my head just before I got my face full of ashes. There was no cylinder on the ground.

When Sara is puzzled, she has a way of tapping her chin with her finger and looking up at the ceiling.

'Is that what you're looking for?' she asked, and pointed to the corner above my head.

I looked up and saw the cylinder embedded in the broken plaster. Apparently the jagged edges had caught it and kept it from falling. We hadn't noticed it before, because who looks at a ceiling in a familiar room? Apparently the janitors don't look at ceilings, either.

'OK, Sara, thanks,' I dismissed her. 'Try to hold the hounds at bay, gal. I've got some thinking to do this morning.'

'I shouldn't wonder,' she grinned. 'Anybody who calls himself a personnel psychologist, and then forces little children to have tantrums in spite of themselves—' The door closed, and saved me the trouble of hearing the completion of her sentence.

Yes, Sara was back on familiar ground. I wished I were.

I dragged a spare straight chair over and stood up on it to get the cylinder. It didn't want to move. Plaster fell around me. The jagged pieces holding it now fell away, and still it didn't move. It gave off the impression of pressing upward against the buttonboard.

I took hold of it and tugged. It came away reluctantly, an identical sensation of lifting a heavy object from the ground, in reverse. It remained heavy, invertedly heavy, as I carried it down and over to my desk.

Habit made me lay it on top of my desk and take my hand away. Habit made me grab for it as it shot upward, just as habit makes me grab for a thing which is falling. This time I put it into a drawer, and held my hand over it to keep it down as I closed the drawer.

I sank back into my chair and hooked my toes under the ledge of the desk. It raised into the air, slowly, buoyantly. I took the pressure of my toes away hurriedly. The desk hovered for a moment, tilted in the air. I put my hand on the top and nervously pressed it back to the floor again. I didn't really expect to hear raps on wood or tin bugles blowing, because I knew it was the cylinder in the drawer which was lifting the desk corner.

There was a very logical explanation of why the desk was trying to float upward. The cylinder was pushing it upward, of course. Yes, very logical. I took one of my nice clean handkerchiefs from another drawer and wiped the sweat off my forehead. There was a logical reason for the sweat, too. I was scared.

'Get me Auerbach,' I said to Sara in my new intercom. No doubt it was all over the plant by now that I had smashed my old one in a fit of rage. I settled back into my chair again, and pressed my knees against the desk to keep them from shaking. I shouldn't have done it. The desk bobbed away from me and settled slowly again. I left it there and waited. I sat well away from it, and tried to speculate on what survival factor shaking knees could represent.

★   ★   ★   ★

Auerbach was not long in arriving. His expression, when he came through the door, was a mixed one of hope I had already got some results for him and touchiness that he should have been summoned like an ordinary employee.

'Take hold of that corner of the desk and lift,' I suggested. He looked puzzled, but complied. The desk buoyed upward, this time so strongly that my papers and pen stand slid off to the floor.

'Not so hard, man,' I shouted.

'But I barely touched it,' he said, incredulously.

I waved him to the crying chair and ignored the accusation written all over his face that I was playing tricks on him. I reached into the desk drawer and pulled out the cylinder. I handed it to him and he took it – from beneath, naturally, to hold it up. It shot up out of his hand and crashed against the ceiling. Plaster fell around him. He spit a sliver of it out of his open mouth as he gazed up at the cylinder.

'Must you be so careless and drop it up?' I snapped.

He didn't answer, and I just let it lay there where it had fallen against the ceiling.

'It isn't particular about what it learns, is it?' I asked, as if there were nothing at all abnormal about the situation.

He brought his eyes away from it and tried to answer, but there was a glaze over his eyes. I noticed his hands begin to shake, and that gave me confidence. My knees had stopped now, with only a small tremor now and then. Auerbach reached over and tugged at the desk corner, but the desk now hugged the floor as if it liked it and refused to budge.

'It doesn't care what it learns, does it?' I repeated. This time he did a better job of trying to come to his senses. His face was a study in attempts to rationalize what he had seen with what he thought he knew. Apparently he wasn't having much luck. But at least he didn't deny what he had seen. I took courage from that. He might prove to be more intelligent than learned after all.

'Let us,' I began in a dry classroom manner, 'assume, for sake of discussion, that your cylinder can store impulses.'

He nodded, as if this were a safe enough assumption. It was a hopeful sign that I was getting through to him.

'It wouldn't know, of itself, which was up and which was down,' I pursued.

'Gravity is a real world condition,' he started answering now. 'Not dependent upon knowledge. It works whether we know it or not.'

'Well, that's a point which has been debated for the last several thousand years to no conclusion,' I disagreed. 'But let's take an illustration. Let's formulate a hypothesis, a variant world condition where biologists might know only natural air-breathing animals.'

He nodded again, a little more of the daze gone from his eyes. He was capable of a hypothesis.

'An entirely different structure of theory and expression of natural laws would be built up from that,' I reasoned. 'One of these would be the basic law that to be classified as alive a thing must breathe natural air.' I pushed the point into my desk top with my finger.

He felt he should object as a matter of principle; should, in scientific tradition, discard the main point in favour of arguing semantics and definitions. That was always safe and didn't require one to think. But I didn't let him escape that easily.

'Now suppose, within that framework, a biologist fished a minnow out of a stream, carried it dry to his laboratory and proceeded to analyse it. You and I know the minnow would die in transit. Now he observes that it does not breathe air, and could not have breathed air down in the water, therefore it does not represent a life form at all. That is his real world condition, isn't it?'

'Yes,' he agreed hesitantly. 'But there would be so many other evidences that it does represent life. He would have to be extremely stupid not to recognize that his basic rules defining life were wrong.'

'Let us concede,' I said dryly, 'that he is very stupid. But let us be kind. Let us say that it is the entire framework of thought in which he finds himself which is stupid. All his life, he has been educated to this framework. Science and society have weighted him down with immutable laws. To question them would represent nothing less than chaos.'

'Yes,' he urged me now to go on.

'We come along, you and I, and we operate in a different framework of thought. In our world condition, fish obtain oxygen directly from water. *But we could not prove that to him.*'

'I don't see—'

'Look,' I said patiently, 'since his base law requires life to breathe air, he would demand, as proof of our contention, that we show it breathing air. We couldn't do it. He will not give up the foundation of his science. We can't prove our claim until he does.'

'Stalemate,' Auerbach agreed. 'But where does that leave us?'

'It leaves us with the conception that there may be any number of frameworks, separated from one another by perhaps the thinnest of partitions, each containing its own set of real world conditions, natural laws, consistent within itself, obeying its own logic, having its own peculiar cause-effect sequences.'

'And one of these substitutes down for up?' he asked sceptically.

'Some of the most noted thinkers the world has ever produced contend that the mind is the only reality,' I said slowly. 'Now suppose we have a child of an ignorant parent. The child has been neglected, left to vegetate alone in its room, never associates with other children, never has the opportunity to learn what our framework of thinking calls natural law, real world conditions. Such a child might formulate for itself a real world matrix quite different from ours.'

Auerbach was silent, but looked at me fixedly.

'For one example, it might take things very literally,' I said. 'It might form natural laws out of slang phrases. The child's mother uses the phrase, "It just burns me up." Suppose then the child, when it was vexed, just literally "burned things up." Ever hear of a poltergeist?'

'Oh come now, Kennedy,' he remonstrated, 'that's fairytale stuff.'

'There are hundreds of carefully documented case histories,' I said, without getting heated about it. 'Refusal to look at poltergeist phenomena is on the order of the biologist refusing to consider the minnow alive. Things just catch on fire where these poltergeists are. Things just fly through the air where they are. There must be an explanation. We know that.'

'We have some statements to that effect,' he corrected.

'We have some statements about what is our own basic natural law, too,' I countered. 'And that's all we have. Just some statements.'

'And such statements apply only within the partitions of the framework?' he asked, neither sceptically nor in agreement. He looked up at the cylinder again. 'So your explanation for that is a poltergeist phenomenon?' he mused.

'Yes.'

'I wish you had some other explanation,' he said. 'I don't like that one. Almost any other kind of an explanation would be better.'

'So do I,' I answered in complete agreement, 'but that's the only one

I've got. You see, I saw a poltergeist activate it. Apparently the force of her mind, acting on it, stored it with impulses from her own framework of reality. It would not be particular what it learns, so long as what it learns is consistent with the process used in learning it.'

He sighed deeply. 'I wish that biologist hadn't picked up that minnow,' he said, wistfully.

*　　　*　　　*　　　*

After my secretary had made suitable protocal negotiations with the general manager's secretary, I headed for Old Stone Face's office, Mr Henry Grenoble, that is. On the way out of my office, I had trouble with my feet. I was almost floating as I walked along, carrying the cylinder. I detoured over by Receiving and surreptitiously weighed myself on the scales. They read thirty pounds.

'Obviously out of órder,' I found myself giggling, and wondered if the mood had anything to do with my sensation of weightlessness. Suddenly from the odd looks of employees, it occurred to me that I was buoyantly tripping down the corridor on my toes and giggling to myself. I blushed and tried to look stern. It wasn't easy to stride purposefully when you weren't sure your feet were touching the floor. I hoped they wouldn't think I was drunk, or worse.

'Morning, Henry,' I said to the general manager, and received his noncommittal nod. I wasn't his fair-haired boy, but neither was I a thorn in his side. We got along all right by mutual and tacit agreement to leave one another alone. It was the regret of his life that such inefficient machines as people had to be used in his plant, and he was glad enough to leave their management to my care.

I walked over to a straight chair, put the cylinder down under its seat, and watched the chair float upward towards the ceiling. Old Stone Face watched it, too.

I had the satisfaction of seeing a slight widening of his eyes, a quick breath, and a slight thinning of his lips. Obviously, he thought it cataclysmic. I pulled the chair down by grabbing hold of one of its legs, and retrieved the cylinder.

I stooped down and placed it under one corner of the desk.

'Lift,' I said.

He took hold of the desk corner hesitantly, as if he were reaching for a pen to sign a raise authorization. The desk corner tilted upward and slid some papers off onto the floor. I reached under and pulled out the cylinder. I handed it to him, this time taking care that it didn't shoot out of his hands towards the ceiling. He felt how heavy it was, in reverse.

Out of habit, he laid it down on the desk top, but I was ready for that. I grabbed it about two feet up in the air. Too many broken up ceilings would really start gossip in the building maintenance crew.

Old Stone Face reached for it again, and headed for his little private bathroom. I followed him to the door, and watched him step on the scales. He came out, and handed me the cylinder.

'And I've been trying to do it by dieting,' he commented. He sat down at his desk and picked up the phone.

'Get me the Pentagon,' he commanded. 'Yes, sure, the one in Washington. I don't suppose anybody's walked away with that in their pocket yet. The last time I was in Washington it was still there.' He put the receiver back on the hook. 'She wants to know if I mean the one in Washington,' he commented without expression.

'Now look, Henry,' I said warily, 'aren't you jumping the gun a little? You haven't asked any questions. You don't know what this is. You don't know how it was made. You don't know any of the scientific principles behind it. You don't know if we've got legal rights to it. You don't know how it works or why.'

'Details,' he said contemptuously. 'You've got it, haven't you? A man made it, didn't he? What a man can make once he can make again, can't he? What do I care about the legal details? We got lawyers, haven't we? What do I care about scientific hows and whys? We got experts, haven't we? Why should I ask questions at all? We got antigravity, haven't we? Don't answer. I know the answers.'

They weren't precisely the questions I would have asked, but then, each to his own framework. Then it struck me with a twist of my stomach muscles. I hadn't realized. I'd been so busy thinking about poltergeists and frameworks of different natural law. I'd been thinking in terms of cybernetics, ability to store impulses, even wrong ones.

'Could be antigravity,' I agreed in an awed tone.

'What else did you think it was?' he asked.

'I'd rather not say,' I murmured.

'Who made it?' he asked.

'Auerbach, partly,' I answered.

'Who's he?'

'Research chemist. Works under Boulton.'

'Why didn't Boulton bring it to me? Don't answer. Boulton wouldn't believe it would work. What do we keep Boulton around here for? Don't answer. I hired him. Well don't just stand there. Tell Auerbach to get busy. Promote him. Tell him to put them into mass production.'

'It's not that simple,' I said, and wondered how to tell him.

'Don't give me alibis.' His face took on an expression which he apparently hoped was conciliatory. 'Ralph, don't you start giving me any of this stall about further research, testing, difficulties, all that folderol. Just put it into production.'

'It's a custom-made job,' I said, trying to slow him down. 'Only an experimental model.'

'Custom made today, production line tomorrow,' he shook his head in exasperation. 'Well, what's holding you up?'

'Money, for one thing.' I clutched at the first excuse I could think of, and wished it were as simple as that.

He grabbed the phone again.

'Get me the controller,' he barked, and waited. 'Tim! What took you so long? Give Kennedy all the money he wants!' He listened for a moment and then turned to me. 'He wants to know if you'll need more than a hundred dollars. He's got systems, or something.' He turned back to the phone without waiting for my reply. 'Well,' he conceded, 'I didn't actually mean *all* the money he wants. Let me know if he draws over a million dollars.'

He took the receiver away from his ear and looked at it in puzzlement.

'Must have fainted,' he commented dryly, and hung up.

'But,' I tried to object, thinking how the organization would be split wide open if I went out into the plant and started carrying out his instructions – all the noses out of joint, the toes stepped on. 'I'm just the personnel director. I'm not a plant superintendent. I can't go around building buildings, setting up production lines – even if I knew how.'

'Get going,' he said. 'I don't want any more alibis. All I want is a steady stream of antigravity units. That's not too much to ask for, I'm sure!'

'Maybe a million dollars won't do it,' I said hopefully, and truthfully, as I reached the door.

'Well, all right,' he almost shouted. 'We'll get a billion, then. We'll get a hundred billion. What do you think we got taxpayers for?'

'You've been spending too much time in Washington,' I commented, as I went through the door. 'You're beginning to talk like them.'

★　　　★　　　★　　　★

Maybe Old Stone Face hadn't heard about things which money can't buy – such as a little girl who looks at you from behind strings of black hair. Maybe he hadn't heard about frameworks where money wasn't a consideration. Maybe he hadn't heard about a matrix where the question, 'If you're so smart, why ain't you rich?' was on the order of the question, 'If it's alive, why don't it breathe air?' Maybe he hadn't heard about frameworks, period.

I hoped I wouldn't have to be the one to tell him about them.

★　　　★　　　★　　　★

Annie Malasek was waiting for me in the outer personnel waiting room. She had little Jennie by the hand. Annie looked stern, Jennie looked penitent. Annie stopped me as I started past her.

'I just came over to tell you, Mr Kennedy,' she began, 'I found out what Jennie did to your nice office last night. I whipped her good. Tell Mr Kennedy you're sorry, Jennie.' She looked down at Jennie sternly, and squeezed her hand.

'I'm sorry,' Jennie mumbled.

'Tell Mr Kennedy you won't do it again,' Annie went on remorselessly.

'I won' do it again,' Jennie repeated dutifully.

'Tell Mr Kennedy you're going to be a good little girl from now on, and not burn things up or throw things,' Annie pursued with a determined gleam in her eye.

'Good girl,' Jennie murmured, and rubbed the arch of one foot with the toe of the other.

I looked at them both, and for once I didn't have anything to say.

★　　★　　★　　★

There were more conferences with Auerbach Yes, he could produce more cylinders. Some of the synthetic protein strings were a bit tricky, but otherwise it wouldn't be difficult to duplicate the cylinder. No, just an ordinary laboratory would do, at least until we went into mass production. That's nice, he'd always wanted to be a department head. The latter was said absently, and I doubted he had even heard me.

'How are you going to activate the cylinders?' he asked curiously. I noticed the particular use of the second person pronoun, because in everything else it was 'we'. Activating them was not his responsibility.

There were conferences with Boulton, whose nose was out of joint that Auerbach had been taken out from under his jurisdiction without consulting him about it. For the sake of organization I had to mollify him. There were conferences with the plant superintendent, who could throw all sorts of petty hazards in my way if he were pulling against me. There were conferences with the controller, the carpenter boss. In short there were people, and therefore there were personal tensions to be unsnarled.

There was another conference in Old Stone Face's office, this time with a pink-cheeked colonel, sent out as an advance scout from the Pentagon. From the look of him it was the most dangerous scouting mission he had ever tried. His pink cheeks grew red as he watched me go through my act with the antigrav cylinder. His pink cheeks grew purple when I evaded his questions with something approaching idiocy. He was certainly not one I wished to introduce to frameworks and partitions. He was a rocket man, himself.

Auerbach was at that conference, and where I had been idiotic, the good doctor was a glib doubletalker. He sounded so impressive that it didn't occur to anybody he wasn't making sense.

Since the colonel didn't believe what he saw, and didn't understand what he heard, the brass staff, deployed well back of the front lines, would have got a very poor report from their advance scout had we not been Computer Research; and had not Old Stone Face been a frequent visitor to the Pentagon. In this case the colonel was afraid to embroider what he saw with too much of his own opinion. We were duly notified of an impending visitation from a full dress parade of brass and braid. Stirred to unusual action, no doubt, by the plaintive and public outcry of a country-boy congressman, 'But what do all of them *do*, over there in that big building?'

During this time my.staff, like good boys and girls, took over the burden of my work without complaint. I spent a great deal of my time in Auerbach's new laboratory.

We tried all sorts of attempts to make the antigrav aspect of the first cylinder rub off on others he had made. We let them lie coyly side by side for hours and days. We lashed the first to another and let it zoom up to the now padded ceiling. We tried shocking them, freezing them, heating them. Nothing worked. Either the new cylinders had already learned that down was down – that old tired framework – or more likely hadn't learned anything at all.

We thought at them. We stood there, Auerbach and I, working singly, working in tandem, thinking at them. Apparently our thoughts didn't amount to much; or we had learned too early in life that you can't get any effect on a physical object by just thinking about it. They just lay there, fat, oily, and inert.

Auerbach went back to his test tubes and beakers, trying to see if antigrav wasn't inherent, somehow, in the chemical arrangements. He had accepted the hypothesis of other frameworks as an intellectual exercise, but he still hoped to prove they were not a reality, that the aspect could be accounted for within the framework he knew. He had not accepted the partitions, that his real world condition was circumscribed, confined, limited.

I went back to Jennie.

Obviously, to me, it was the mental force of her fear, hatred, anger, survival potential, whatever it was, acting through whatever framework she had devised for herself, which activated the first cylinder. So I gave up being stubborn, and called for little Jennie Malasek once more.

She came in the door of my office and stood as she had before. This time her hair was pulled back tightly and tied with a ribbon. So she hid behind a glaze over her eyes, instead.

I had about a dozen of the cylinders on the top of my desk, and had a lot of mixed hope and hopelessness within me. I wondered if the admonishments of her mother had had any basic effect upon her. I wondered if the additional attention she was now getting over in the nursery, since the teachers had learned I had taken notice of her, had changed anything in her.

'I didn't tell your mother on you, when you messed up my office that time,' I said as an opening sentence.

She didn't answer, just looked at me impassively. But it did seem that she blushed a little. Had she grown ashamed of throwing things and burning things up?

'Just a secret between you and me,' I said. 'I don't think it is wrong to throw things the way you did. I think it was very clever.'

She didn't answer.

'I wish you would do it again. I'd like to see you do it.'

'I can't,' she whispered in a very small voice. 'I'm a good girl now.'

Oh no. Character doesn't change that fast. Maybe she thought she was a good girl, but down underneath—

'I don't think you're a good girl,' I said with a sneer. 'I think you're a very naughty girl, a nasty little girl.'

I hoped, how I hoped she would flare up in anger, or protection, and hurl the cylinders at me. I hoped to get a face full of ashes, an office full of broken windows and flying cylinders.

Her face still did not change its expression. She still stood there, impassive. Her only reaction was two large, crystal tears which formed in the corners of her eyes and began to roll slowly down her cheeks.

I flipped my intercom and called Sara.

'Take her back to the nursery, Sara,' I said wearily.

Sara came in, saw the tears, and without speaking to me, she took Jennie's hand and led her away.

I sat at my desk and hated myself with contempt and loathing. There were times when I didn't like my job; when I didn't like myself for being skilled enough to do it. There were times when people became a little more than just some material to be shaped and directed into the best use for it.

But my mood did not last. I had a job to do. This was no time to grow soft, sentimental, wavering.

The fact that Jennie was outwardly changing from the strange little creature which excited no sympathy to a bewildered and hurt little girl who very definitely called for compassion changed the facts not at all.

The prime necessity was to activate more of the cylinders. Jennie was the only means at hand by which that could be done. I wasn't sure that even she could do it, but I had to find out. I had to see if down beneath the surface she wasn't still the same wild instrument of an even wilder talent.

Basic character doesn't change that fast, not just because somebody says it ought to change, not unless there is a violent and traumatic shock jolting the individual completely out of his framework and into another.

I had to go ahead and try.

I spent more, quite a bit more, of the funds at my disposal. The controller OK'd my vouchers as if the dollars were individual drops of his blood, and read the legends on the vouchers with a firm conviction that I had really lost my mind.

Old Stone Face asked no questions. He was not one to assign a job to a man and then nag him about the details. He wanted results. But there was puzzlement in his face when he saw no building wings being converted, no assembly lines and moving belts being constructed, no supervisors, cost accountants, production control people assigned to the new work.

Instead, I spent money on animated cartoons, three-dimensional cartoons. A director, experimenting in that new medium, had told me the most difficult job was to keep the action behind the screen, give it depth without the illusion that it was projecting out into the audience – to give a stage depth effect without getting a poke in the eye effect.

I wanted the opposite. I wanted my audience, an audience of one, to get the illusion of a poke in the eye. I caused a special nursery to be built, just for Jennie. I had a studio make a short but elaborate sequence which only one person would view.

I placed Auerbach's total supply of new cylinders in various spots around the room, a dozen or so of them. I had the projectors installed in an adjoining room, and a tiny window, lost in some decoration effects, where I could watch through.

I went to the nursery and got Jennie. She was neither glad nor protesting. The nursery teacher objected a little. Jennie was doing such a fine job of adjusting to the other children now. They had had no more trouble. Apparently all that had been wrong was that Jennie had been starved for attention and affection. But now she was becoming a perfectly normal little girl. Didn't I think so too, Mr Kennedy? And, are you ill, Mr Kennedy? You don't look well at all! How kind you are, ill and everything, to think of little Jennie!

I led Jennie out of the nursery over to the new room built especially for her. I did not react. I did not react! I did not react! I could not react, I was one solid mass of self-contempt and loathing.

I put Jennie in the room, wordlessly, and she stood near the door, where I left her. I walked into the adjoining projection room, closed the door behind me, and started punching buttons. It was a form of punishment to make myself walk over to my little window and watch when the automatic machinery took over.

Darkness blotted out the room, then an eerie blue light began to glow over the complex meshes of the screen in front and to the sides of Jennie. Trees, vines, bushes took on form, swayed a little, seemed alive. Knots on the trunks of the trees suggested faces, not kind faces. Limbs and twigs stirred and seemed to reach towards Jennie.

I saw her take a small step backward until she had her back to the door. She turned and pulled at the knob, but the door wouldn't open. She turned back then and faced the growing light, the clearer scene all around her. I saw her lips move stiffly, and though I could not hear her, they seemed to form the words, 'Good girl now.'

Far in the distance in front of her a deep red glow appeared, took form, part animal, part reptile and, even more horrible, part man. Slowly it seemed to become aware of her; its very deliberateness, its sureness, was its greatest horror.

The room was a pandemonium then. The cylinders flew through the air towards the trees, towards the monster, crashing through the screen, tearing it to shreds, crashing against the padded walls.

On the floor, in a crumpled heap, lay Jennie. She was still and lifeless. I punched a control button to bring the room back to normality, and ran into the room to her. Her heart was beating faintly, her pulse a thin string of fluttering.

I shouted into the hall, 'Get a doctor!'

I ran back and began to administer first aid for acute shock. It was not until the doctor came from our hospital room and carried Jennie away that I looked around me.

Most of the cylinders lay on the floor, inert, but five of them pushed against the ceiling at the back of the room. The experiment had been a success!

I went to see Jennie in the hospital room. She had come out of her faint and was sobbing brokenly now. As soon as I came into the room, she reached out her hands, grabbed mine.

'I got scared,' she said. 'You went away and left me. The lights went out. But I didn't do anything, really I didn't. I just got scared.'

The suspicion and anger smoothed out of the faces of the nurse and doctor. Her unaccountable reaction of being glad to see me after what I had done to her, her words seeming to carry a completely normal conviction of what might happen to any imaginative little girl who was afraid of the dark, closed off their possibility of searching into what really happened.

But I knew that I would never use Jennie again, no matter what the urgency for antigravity. Some other way would have to be found. I would not do it again. And I doubted now, after this shock – the surface shock of normal fear, the deeper shock of conflict in using the wild talents which made her a bad girl against the affection she was getting for being a good girl – whether she could ever use her framework again, even if I would.

It had been a severe thing, a terrible thing I had done; but no worse than the methods used constantly in mental hospitals to transfer the minds of patients from one framework to another.

I went back to my office, took the cylinder out of my desk, and sat, holding it in my hands, for a long time.

★   ★   ★   ★

Through the days that passed I became more distrait, overwhelmed by the insolubility of my problem. My staff still handled the bulk of my work, for it was obvious to them that my interest was far from the petty conflicts and situations of normal plant operation. Department heads became cool towards me, for Sara managed to turn them away before they got in to me.

In wandered the corridors searching faces for some hint of a wild talent beneath the too tame eyes. I thought of advertising for poltergeists in the help-wanted columns, and then realized what would happen if some alert reporter happened to pick up the item. I thought of contacting various universities and shuddered at the reception I would get. I even found myself visiting the nursery again, hoping for the improbable coincidence of another poltergeist. But all the little children were being good little fairies and elves and brownies.

The announcement that a full complement of high-ranking military men were going to visit us and assist us in our lagging production of the antigrav cylinders did not reassure me. I had dealt with the military mind, singly and in coveys, before.

I hadn't told Old Stone Face the problem, either. His total framework seemed to consist of 'Get out production. Give me no alibis.' This was hardly conducive to philosophical meandering.

The day came when staff cars carried generals, admirals, colonels and captains from the airport to our plant. Word filtered over the intercom system that they had been closeted in the big conference room with Stone Face for an hour – apparently playing with the five cylinders.

I hoped they wouldn't scratch the varnish of the big conference table against the ceiling of the roof. I hoped they wouldn't try to ride around in buoyant chairs. Learning to balance, doing that, was tricky, and if they tilted, a big blob of blubber would find the floor hard and unyielding.

Finally they sent for me.

I left my cylinder locked in my desk and walked up to the conference room under normal gravity, hoping the weight would pull me down to a worried, heavy, lugubrious frame of mind so stylish in the real-world framework.

The conference room had an aroma of dignity, an overpowering impressiveness of brass and braid. Thin faces, fat faces, long faces, squeezed up faces, but Pinky was not there. Apparently he was off on some other dangerous mission. The faces did not, could not, live up to the scrambled eggs and fruit salad of their caps and collars and sleeves and chest.

I thought of Emerson's dissertations on compensation and giggled. What they lacked in those faces they tried to make up for in decorations. I knew that I would not discuss frameworks in this room.

They pressed me for explanations. They bored in deeper and deeper. I could not help it. My mood began to lighten, become irresponsible. I hung on to what dignity I could muster for the sake of the apprehension and alarm in Old Stone Face's eyes. He wasn't such a bad guy. At least he didn't depend on uniforms to make his impressive.

'The first cylinder was an accident,' I said to the blur of faces down the long table. 'Sometimes accidents are hard to duplicate. So many factors, gentlemen.'

'But you did duplicate it,' the commanding general pointed out. 'You activated five more. We have questioned Dr Auerbach at length. He knows absolutely nothing of the method you use in activating these cylinders. Apparently no one knows but you. It is imperative that we know.'

I was in for it now. I had to explain somehow, or something.

'But, gentlemen,' I protested hesitantly, and then heard myself saying, 'I spoiled my poltergeist in making this half dozen, and I don't have another.'

There was a sigh of relief around the table, relaxation, suppressed contempt. I had not realized before how tense they all were.

'I'm certain,' the commanding general said placatingly, as if he were trying to reason with a small child, 'that it can be replaced.'

'They're hard to get,' I faltered.

'We will get them,' he stated pompously, confidently. 'Difficult perhaps for you personally, yes, or even Computer Research.' He smiled patiently. 'But for the military it is another matter entirely.'

He turned and waved down the table towards another member of the brass trust.

'General Sanfordwaithe is Supply and Materials. I am sure it is within the power of the combined armed forces to get you all the whatever-it-is you may need.'

I looked down the table at General Sanfordwaithe with a question in my eyes. He looked smugly back at me.

'Do you know what a poltergeist is?' I asked.

He looked slightly piqued.

'I am administrative,' he reproved gently and patiently, as only a military man can put a civilian in his place. 'I do not pretend to be personally familiar with the specifications of every one of the several million items under my jurisdiction.' He smiled, and his voice became almost waggish. 'But I am certain you will find our poltergeist division sympathetic to your needs.'

That did it.

'Oh goodie,' I exclaimed. 'Then maybe you'd better send me a half dozen to start with.'

'And is that all that's been holding you up?' the commanding general asked, softly reproving.

'And this time, make them little boy poltergeists,' I urged. 'Mine was a little girl poltergeist, and maybe that was what was wrong – just too delicate for the job.'

I could see by their faces they assumed I was talking about some gadget similar to a male and female electrical plug, and was being cute in my terminology.

'Mr Kennedy hasn't been feeling well lately,' Old Stone Face put in hurriedly. 'He's been working very hard. Much too hard. I would have sent him on a long rest weeks ago had this not been so urgent.'

They looked at me with some pity beneath their contempt – a soft civilian.

From there on it was no more than a diplomatic and tactical withdrawal of forces. I withdrew early, to allow Old Stone Face further time for excuses of my behaviour.

But they would be back.

The order would go out from General Sanfordwaithe's office to supply me with a half dozen male type poltergeists immediately. It would flow down through the echelons of command, getting sterner and terser. There would be some scrambling around trying to find the poltergeist division, but no one would become alarmed that it had been lost. That was customary.

There would be days, perhaps weeks, when the orders would be pigeonholed, on the theory that if you just forget to do anything about it, the need will pass. But General Sanfordwaithe would not let them forget this time. There would be memoranda, each one dredging a little farther down the chain of command before it, in turn, became pigeonholed.

And finally, somewhere down the line, some clerk would know what a poltergeist was. He would first go to the source books and look it up, so that he could have the paragraphs to substantiate him when he tried to tell his commanding officer what was wanted. From there the explanations would flow back up through the echelons of command. Faces would get redder and redder, angrier and angrier.

Yes, they would be back. But until then, I could go back to being a personnel director. I thought, this time with genuine pleasure, of the simple little problems waiting for me back at my office. Nothing more than imminent strikes, lockouts, legal tangles, visits from the Industrial Welfare Commission, and Miss Jones won't let Miss Smith have a fresh pencil until she brings the stub of her old one to the supply room.

I walked on down the corridors of the plant and nodded pleasantly to department heads and key personnel who caught my eye. I saw their faces break with relief, and then grow tart with, 'Well, it's about time you came off your high horse and noticed us.'

I would have a lot of ruffled feathers to smooth down in the next few days.

Much to their surprise, I spoke pleasantly to the members of my staff when I came into the outer rooms of the personnel department, and ruefully saw them start to dig down into stack of papers for problems they had been hoarding until I got in a good mood again.

I walked on into Sara's office and quipped something at her. She almost fell out of her chair in astonishment, and began to sniffle. Her feelings had been badly bruised.

'There are handkerchiefs in my desk,' I said dryly. Her sniffles stopped instantly.

'Now,' I said. 'Take a letter. General Sanfordwaithe, Pentagon. Confirming our conference of this date, production on the implement in question will not proceed until your Division of Supply and Matériel furnishes us with one half dozen, six, male-type poltergeists.'

'Are you feeling all right?' Sara interrupted me with wide eyes.

'I feel wonderful,' I answered. 'I have learned something from our employees. I have shifted the responsibility for my problem onto other shoulders. I feel swell!'

'But what if they should supply them to you after all?' she asked.

In the Abyss

H. G. Wells

The lieutenant stood in front of the steel sphere and gnawed a piece of pine splinter. 'What do you think of it, Steevens?' he asked.

'It's an idea,' said Steevens, in the tone of one who keeps an open mind.

'I believe it will smash – flat,' said the lieutenant.

'He seems to have calculated it all out pretty well,' said Steevens, still impartial.

'But think of the pressure,' said the lieutenant. 'At the surface of the water it's fourteen pounds to the inch, thirty feet down it's double that; sixty, treble; ninety, four times; nine hundred, forty times; five thousand, three hundred – that's a mile – it's two hundred and forty times fourteen pounds; that's – let's see – thirty hundredweight – a ton and a half, Steevens; *a ton and a half* to the square inch. And the ocean where he's going is five miles deep. That's seven and a half –'

'Sounds a lot,' said Steevens, 'but it's jolly thick steel.'

The lieutenant made no answer, but resumed his pine splinter. The object of their conversation was a huge ball of steel, having an exterior diameter of perhaps nine feet. It looked like the shot for some Titanic piece of artillery. It was elaborately nested in a monstrous scaffolding built into the framework of the vessel, and the gigantic spars that were presently to sling it overboard gave the stern of the ship an appearance that had raised the curiosity of every decent sailor who had sighted it, from the Pool of London to the Tropic of Capricorn. In two places, one above the other, the steel gave place to a couple of circular windows of enormously thick glass, and one of these, set in a steel frame of great solidity, was now partially unscrewed. Both the men had seen the interior of this globe for the first time that morning. It was elaborately padded with air cushions, with little studs sunk between bulging pillows to work the simple mechanism of the affair. Everything was elaborately padded, even the Myers apparatus which was to absorb carbonic acid and replace the oxygen inspired by its tenant, when he had crept in by the glass manhole, and had been screwed in. It was so elaborately padded that a man might have been fired from a gun in it with perfect safety. And it had need to be, for presently a man was to crawl in through that glass manhole, to be screwed up tightly, and to be flung overboard, and to sink down – down – down, for five miles, even as the lieutenant said. It had taken the strongest hold of his imagination; it made him a bore at mess; and he found Steevens, the new arrival aboard, a godsend to talk to about it, over and over again.

'It's my opinion,' said the lieutenant, 'that that glass will simply bend in and bulge and smash, under a pressure of that sort. Daubrée has made rocks run like water under big pressures – you mark my words—'

'If the glass did break in,' said Steevens, 'what then?'

'The water would shoot in like a jet of iron. Have you ever felt a straight jet of high-pressure water? It would hit as hard as a bullet. It would simply smash him and flatten him. It would tear down his throat, and into his lungs; it would blow in his ears—'

'What a detailed imagination you have!' protested Steevens, who saw things vividly.

'It's a simple statement of the inevitable,' said the lieutenant.

'And the globe?'

'Would just give out a few little bubbles, and it would settle down comfortably against the day of judgment, among the oozes and the bottom clay – with poor Elstead spread over his own smashed cushions like butter over bread.'

He repeated this sentence as though he liked it very much. 'Like butter over bread,' he said.

'Having a look at the jigger?' said a voice, and Elstead stood between them, spick and span in white, with a cigarette between his teeth, and his eyes smiling out of the shadow of his ample hat-brim. 'What's that about bread and butter, Weybridge? Grumbling as usual about the insufficient pay of naval officers? It won't be more than a day now before I start. We are to get the slings ready today. This clean sky and gentle swell is just the kind of thing for swinging off a dozen tons of lead and iron, isn't it?'

'It won't affect you much,' said Weybridge.

'No. Seventy or eighty feet down, and I shall be there in a dozen seconds, there's not a particle moving, though the wind shriek itself hoarse up above, and the water lifts half-way to the clouds. No. Down there—' He moved to the side of the ship and the other two followed him. All three leant forward on their elbows and stared down into the yellow-green water.

'*Peace,*' said Elstead, finishing his thought aloud.

'Are you dead certain that clockwork will act?' asked Weybridge presently.

'It has worked thirty-five times,' said Elstead. 'It's bound to work.'

'But if it doesn't?'

'Why shouldn't it?'

'I wouldn't go down in that confounded thing,' said Weybridge, 'for twenty thousand pounds.'

'Cheerful chap you are,' said Elstead, and spat sociably at a bubble below.

'I don't understand yet how you mean to work the thing,' said Steevens.

'In the first place, I'm screwed into the sphere,' said Elstead, 'and when I've turned the electric light off and on three times to show I'm cheerful, I'm slung out over the stern by that crane, with all those big lead sinkers slung below me. The top lead weight has a roller carrying a hundred fathoms of strong cord rolled up, and that's all that joins the sinkers to the sphere, except the slings that will be cut when the affair is dropped. We use cord rather than wire rope because it's easier to cut and more buoyant – necessary points, as you will see.

'Through each of these lead weights you notice there is a hole, and an iron rod will be run through that and will project six feet on the lower side. If that rod is rammed up from below, it knocks up a lever and sets the clockwork in motion at the side of the cylinder on which the cord winds.

'Very well. The whole affair is lowered gently into the water, and the slings are cut. The sphere floats – with the air in it, it's lighter than water – but the lead weights go down straight and the cord runs out. When the cord is all paid out, the sphere will go down too, pulled down by the cord.'

'But why the cord?' asked Steevens. 'Why not fasten the weights directly to the sphere?'

'Because of the smash down below. The whole affair will go rushing down, mile after mile, at a headlong pace at last. It would be knocked to pieces on the bottom if it wasn't for that cord. But the weights will hit the bottom, and directly they do the buoyancy of the sphere will come into play. It will go on sinking slower and slower; come to a stop at last, and then begin to float upwards again.

'That's where the clockwork comes in. Directly the weights smash against the sea bottom, the rod will be knocked through and will kick up the clockwork, and the cord will be rewound on the reel. I shall be lugged down to the sea bottom. There I shall stay for half an hour, with the electric light on, looking about me. Then the clockwork will release a spring knife, the cord will be cut, and up I shall rush again, like a soda-water bubble. The cord itself will help the flotation.'

'And if you should chance to hit a ship?' said Weybridge.

'I should come up at such a pace, I should go clean through it,' said Elstead, 'like a cannon-ball. You needn't worry about that.'

'And suppose some nimble crustacean should wriggle into your clockwork—'

'It would be a pressing sort of invitation for me to stop,' said Elstead, turning his back on the water and staring at the sphere.

★   ★   ★   ★

They had swung Elstead overboard by eleven o'clock. The day was serenely bright and calm, with the horizon lost in haze. The electric glare in the little upper compartment beamed cheerfully three times.

Everything was as black as night outside, except where the beam from his light struck through the waters.

Then they let him down slowly to the surface of the water, and a sailor in the stern chains hung ready to cut the tackle that held the lead weights and the sphere together. The globe, which had looked so large on deck, looked the smallest thing conceivable under the stern of the ship. It rolled a little, and its two dark windows, which floated uppermost, seemed like eyes turned up in round wonderment at the people who crowded the rail. A voice wondered how Elstead liked the rolling. 'Are you ready?' sang out the commander. 'Ay, Ay, sir!' 'Then let her go!'

The rope of the tackle tightened against the blade and was cut, and an eddy rolled over the globe in a grotesquely helpless fashion. Someone waved a handkerchief, someone else tried an ineffectual cheer, a middy was counting slowly, 'Eight, nine, ten!' Another roll, then with a jerk and a splash the thing righted itself.

It seemed to be stationary for a moment, to grow rapidly smaller, and then the water closed over it, and it became visible, enlarged by refraction and dimmer, below the surface. Before one could count three it had disappeared. There was a flicker of white light far down in the water, that diminished to a speck and vanished. Then there was nothing but a depth of water going down into blackness, through which a shark was swimming.

Then suddenly the screw of the cruiser began to rotate, the water was crickled, the shark disappeared in a wrinkled confusion, and a torrent of foam rushed across the crystalline clearness that had swallowed up Elstead. 'What's the idea?' said one AB to another.

'We're going to lay off about a couple of miles, 'fear he should hit us when he comes up,' said his mate.

The ship steamed slowly to her new position. Aboard her almost everyone who was unoccupied remained watching the breathing swell into which the sphere had sunk. For the next half-hour it is doubtful if a word was spoken that did not bear directly or indirectly on Elstead. The December sun was now high in the sky, and the heat very considerable.

'He'll be cold enough down there,' said Weybridge. 'They say that below a certain depth sea water's always just about freezing.'

'Where'll he come up?' asked Steevens. 'I've lost my bearings.'

'That's the spot,' said the commander, who prided himself on his omniscience. He extended a precise finger south-eastward. 'And this,

I reckon, is pretty nearly the moment,' he said. 'He's been thirty-five minutes.'

'How long does it take to reach the bottom of the ocean?'

'For a depth of five miles, and reckoning – as we did – an acceleration of two feet per second, both ways, is just about three-quarters of a minute.'

'Then he's overdue,' said Weybridge.

'Pretty nearly,' said the commander. 'I suppose it takes a few minutes for that cord of his to wind in.'

'I forgot that,' said Weybridge, evidently relieved.

And then began the suspense. A minute slowly dragged itself out, and no sphere shot out of the water. Another followed, and nothing broke the low oily swell. The sailors explained to one another that little point about the winding-in of the cord. The rigging was dotted with expectant faces. 'Come up, Elstead!' called one hairy-chested salt, impatiently, and the others caught it up, and shouted as though they were waiting for the curtain of a theatre to rise.

The commander glanced irritably at them.

'Of course, if the acceleration's less than two,' he said, 'he'll be all the longer. We aren't absolutely certain that was the proper figure. I'm no slavish believer in calculations.'

Steevens agreed concisely. No one on the quarter-deck spoke for a couple of minutes. Then Steevens' watchcase clicked.

When, twenty-one minutes after the sun reached the zenith, they were still waiting for the globe to reappear, not a man aboard had dared to whisper that hope was dead. It was Weybridge who first gave expression to that realization. He spoke while the sound of eight bells still hung in the air. 'I always distrusted that window,' he said quite suddenly to Steevens.

'Good God!' said Steevens; 'you don't think—'

'Well!' said Weybridge, and left the rest to his imagination.

'I'm no great believer in calculations myself,' said the commander dubiously, 'so that I'm not altogether hopeless yet.' And at midnight the gunboat was steaming slowly in a spiral round the spot where the globe had sunk, and the white beam of the electric light fled and halted and swept discontentedly onward again over the waste of phosphorescent waters under the little stars.

'If his window hasn't burst and smashed him,' said Weybridge, 'then it's a cursed sight worse, for his clockwork has gone wrong, and he's alive now, five miles under our feet, down there in the cold and dark, anchored in that little bubble of his, where never a ray of light has shone or a human being lived, since the waters were gathered together. He's there without food, feeling hungry and thirsty and scared, wondering whether he'll starve or stifle. Which will it be? The Myers apparatus is running out, I suppose. How long do they last?'

'Good heavens!' he exclaimed, 'what little things we are! We daring little devils! Down there, miles and miles of water – all water, and all this empty water about us and this sky. Gulfs!' He threw his hands out, and as he did so, a little white streak swept noiselessly up the sky, travelled more slowly, stopped, became a motionless dot, as though a new star had fallen up into the sky. Then it went sliding back again and lost itself amidst the reflections of the stars and the white haze of the sea's phosphorescence.

At the sight he stopped, arm extended and mouth open. He shut his mouth, opened it again, and waved his arms with an impatient gesture. Then he turned, shouted 'El-stead ahoy!' to the first watch, and went at a run to Lindley and the search-light. 'I saw him,' he said. 'Starboard there! His light's on, and he's just shot out of the water. Bring the light round. We ought to see him drifting, when he lifts on the swell.'

But they never picked up the explorer until dawn. Then they almost ran him down. The crane was swung out and a boat's crew hooked the chain to the sphere. When they had shipped the sphere, they unscrewed the manhole and peered into the darkness of the interior (for the electric light chamber was intended to illuminate the water about the sphere, and was shut off entirely from its general cavity).

The air was very hot within the cavity, and the india-rubber at the lip of the manhole was soft. There was no answer to their eager questions and no sound of movement within. Elstead seemed to be lying motionless, crumpled up in the bottom of the globe. The ship's doctor crawled in and lifted him out to the men outside. For a moment or so they did not know whether Elstead was alive or dead. His face, in the yellow light of the ship's lamps, glistened with perspiration. They carried him down to his own cabin.

He was not dead, they found, but in a state of absolute nervous collapse, and besides cruelly bruised. For some days he had to lie perfectly still. It was a week before he could tell his experiences.

Almost his first words were that he was going down again. The sphere would have to be altered, he said, in order to allow him to throw off the cord if need be, and that was all. He had had the most marvellous experience. 'You thought I should find nothing but ooze,' he said. 'You laughed at my explorations, and I've discovered a new world!' He told his story in disconnected fragments, and chiefly from the wrong end, so that it is impossible to re-tell it in his words. But what follows is the narrative of his experience.

It began atrociously, he said. Before the cord ran out, the thing kept rolling over. He felt like a frog in a football. He could see nothing but the crane and the sky overhead, with an occasional glimpse of the people on the ship's rail. He couldn't tell a bit which way the thing would roll next. Suddenly he would find his feet going up, and try to step, and over he went rolling, head over heels, and just anyhow, on the padding. Any other shape would have been more comfortable, but no other shape was to be relied upon under the huge pressure of the nethermost abyss.

Suddenly the swaying ceased, the globe righted, and when he had picked himself up, he saw the water all about him greeny-blue, with an attenuated light filtering down from above, and a shoal of little floating things went rushing up past him, as it seemed to him, towards the light. And even as he looked, it grew darker and darker, until the water above was as dark as the midnight sky, albeit of a greener shade, and the water below black. And little transparent things in the water developed a faint glint of luminosity, and shot past him in faint greenish streaks.

And the feeling of falling! It was just like the start of a lift, he said, only it kept on. One has to imagine what that means, that keeping on. It was then of all times that Elstead repented of his adventure. He saw the chances against him in an altogether new light. He thought of the big cuttle-fish people knew to exist in the middle waters, the kind of things they find half digested in whales at times, or floating dead and rotten and half eaten by fish. Suppose one caught hold and wouldn't let go. And had the clockwork really been sufficiently tested? But-whether he wanted to go on or go back mattered not the slightest now.

In fifty seconds everything was as black as night outside, except where the beam from his light struck through the waters, and picked out every now and then some fish or scrap of sinking matter. They flashed by too fast for him to see what they were. Once he thinks he passed a shark. And then the sphere began to get hot by friction against the water. They had under-estimated this, it seems.

The first thing he noticed was that he was perspiring, and then he heard a hissing growing louder under his feet, and saw a lot of little bubbles – very little bubbles they were – rushing upward like a fan through the water outside. Steam! He felt the window, and it was hot. He turned on the minute glow-lamp that lit his own cavity, looked at the padded watch by the studs, and saw he had been travelling now for two minutes. It came into his head that the window would crack through the conflict of temperatures, for he knew the bottom water is very near freezing.

Then suddenly the floor of the sphere seemed to press against his feet, the rush of bubbles outside grew slower and slower, and the hissing diminished. The sphere rolled a little. The window had not cracked, nothing had given, and he knew that the dangers of sinking, at any rate, were over.

In another minute or so he would be on the floor of the abyss. He thought, he said, of Steevens and Weybridge and the rest of them five miles overhead, higher to him than the very highest clouds that ever floated over land are to us, steaming slowly and staring down and wondering what had happened to him.

He peered out of the window. There were no more bubbles now, and the hissing had stopped. Outside there was a heavy blackness – as black as black velvet – except where the electric light pierced the empty water and showed the colour of it – a yellow-green. Then three things like shapes of fire swam into sight, following each other through the water. Whether they were little and near or big and far off he could not tell.

Each was outlined in a bluish light almost as bright as the lights of a fishing smack, a light which seemed to be smoking greatly, and all along the sides of them were specks of this, like the lighter portholes of a ship. Their phosphorescence seemed to go out as they came into the radiance of his lamp, and he saw then that they were little fish of some strange sort, with huge heads, vast eyes, and dwindling bodies and tails. Their eyes were turned towards him, and he judged they were following him down. He supposed they were attracted by his glare.

Presently others of the same sort joined them. As he went on down, he noticed that the water became of a pallid colour, and that little specks twinkled in his ray like motes in a sunbeam. This was probably due to the clouds of ooze and mud that the impact of his leaden sinkers had disturbed.

By the time he was drawn down to the lead weights he was in a dense fog of white that his electric light failed altogether to pierce for more than a few yards, and many minutes elapsed before the hanging sheets of sediment subsided to any extent. Then, lit by his light and by the transient phosphorescence of a distant shoal of fishes, he was able to see under the huge blackness of the super-incumbent water an undulating expanse of greyish-white ooze, broken here and there by tangled thickets of a growth of sea lilies, waving hungry tentacles in the air.

Farther away were the graceful, translucent outlines of a group of gigantic sponges. About this floor there were scattered a number of bristling flattish tufts of rich purple and black, which he decided must be some sort of sea-urchin, and small, large-eyed or blind things having a curious resemblance, some to woodlice, and others to lobsters, crawled sluggisly across the track of the light and vanished into the obscurity again, leaving furrowed trails behind them.

Then suddenly the hovering swarm of little fishes veered about and came towards him as a flight of starlings might do. They passed over him like a phosphorescent snow, and then he saw behind them some larger creature advancing towards the sphere.

At first he could see it only dimly, a faintly moving figure remotely suggestive of a walking man, and then it came into the spray of light that the lamp shot out. As the glare struck it, it shut its eyes, dazzled. He stared in rigid astonishment.

It was a strange vertebrated animal. Its dark purple head was dimly suggestive of a chameleon, but it had such a high forehead and such a braincase as no reptile ever displayed before; the vertical pitch of its face gave it a most extraordinary resemblance to a human being.

Two large and protruding eyes projected from sockets in chameleon fashion, and it had a broad reptilian mouth with horny lips beneath its little nostrils. In the position of the ears were two huge gill-covers, and out of these floated a branching tree of coralline filaments, almost like the treelike gills that every young ray and shark possesses.

But the humanity of the face was not the most extraordinary thing about the creature. It was a biped; its almost globular body was poised on a tripod of two frog-like legs and a long thick tail, and its fore limbs, which grotesquely caricatured the human hand, much as a frog's do, carried a long shaft of bone, tipped with copper. The colour of the creature was variegated; its head, hands, and legs were purple; but its skin, which hung loosely upon it, even as clothes might do, was a phosphorescent grey. And it stood there blinded by the light.

At last this unknown creature of the abyss blinked its eyes open, and, shading them with its disengaged hand, opened its mouth and gave vent to a shouting noise, articulate almost as speech might be, that penetrated even the steel case and padded jacket of the sphere. How a shouting may be accomplished without lungs Elstead does not profess to explain. It then moved sideways out of the glare into the mystery of shadow that bordered it on either side, and Elstead felt rather than saw that it was coming towards him. Fancying the light had attracted it, he turned the switch that cut off the current. In another moment something soft dabbed upon the steel, and the globe swayed.

Then the shouting was repeated, and it seemed to him that a distant echo answered it. The dabbing recurred, and the whole globe swayed and ground against the spindle over which the wire was rolled. He stood in the blackness and peered out into the everlasting night of the abyss. And presently he saw, very faint and remote, other phosphorescent quasi-human forms hurrying towards him.

Hardly knowing what he did, he felt about in his swaying prison for the stud of the exterior electric light, and came by accident against his own small glow-lamp in its padded recess. The sphere twisted, and then threw him down; he heard shouts like shouts of surprise, and when he rose to his feet he saw two pairs of stalked eyes peering into the lower window and reflecting his light.

In another moment hands were dabbing vigorously at his steel casing, and there was a sound, horrible enough in his position, of the metal protection of the clockwork being vigorously hammered. That, indeed, sent his heart into his mouth, for if these strange creatures succeeded in stopping that, his release would never occur. Scarcely had he thought as much when he felt the sphere sway violently, and the floor of it press hard against his feet. He turned off the small glow-lamp that lit the interior, and sent the ray of the large light in the separate compartment out into the water. The sea-floor and the man-like creatures had disappeared, and a couple of fish chasing each other dropped suddenly by the window.

He thought at once that these strange denizens of the deep sea had broken the rope, and that he had escaped. He drove up faster and faster, and then stopped with a jerk that sent him flying against the padded roof of his prison. For half a minute, perhaps, he was too astonished to think.

Then he felt that the sphere was spinning slowly, and rocking, and it seemed to him that it was also being drawn through the water. By crouching close to the window, he managed to make his weight effective and roll that part of the sphere downward, but he could see nothing save the pale ray of his light striking down ineffectively into the darkness. It occurred to him that he would see more if he turned the lamp off, and allowed his eyes to grow accustomed to the profound obscurity.

In this he was wise. After some minutes the velvety blackness became a translucent blackness, and then, far away, and as faint as the zodiacal light of an English summer evening, he saw shapes moving below. He judged these creatures had detached his cable and were towing him along the sea bottom.

And then he saw something faint and remote across the undulations of the submarine plain, a broad horizon of pale luminosity that extended this way and that way as far as the range of his little window permitted him to see. To this he was being towed, as a balloon might be towed by men out of the open country into a town. He approached it very slowly, and very slowly the dim irradiation was gathered together into more definite shapes.

It was nearly five o'clock before he came over this luminous area, and by that time he could make out an arrangement suggestive of streets and houses grouped about a vast roofless erection that was grotesquely suggestive of a ruined abbey. It was spread out like a map below him. The houses were all roofless enclosures of walls, and their substance being, as he afterwards saw, of phosphorescent bones, gave the place an appearance as if it were built of drowned moonshine.

Among the inner caves of the place waving trees of crinoid stretched their tentacles, and tall, slender, glassy sponges shot like shining minarets and lilies of filmy light out of the general glow of the city. In the open spaces of the place he could see a stirring movement as of crowds of people, but he was too many fathoms above them to distinguish the individuals in those crowds.

Then slowly they pulled him down, and as they did so, the details of the place crept slowly upon his apprehension. He saw that the courses of the cloudy buildings were marked out with beaded lines of round objects, and then he perceived that at several points below him, in broad open spaces, were forms like the encrusted shapes of ships.

Slowly and surely he was drawn down, and the forms below him became brighter, clearer, more distinct. He was being pulled down, he perceived, towards the large building in the centre of the town, and he could catch a glimpse ever and again of the multitudinous forms that were lugging at his cord. He was astonished to see that the rigging of one of the ships, which formed such a prominent feature of the place, was crowded with a host of gesticulating figures regarding him, and then the walls of the great building rose about him silently, and hid the city from his eyes.

And such walls they were, of water-logged wood, and twisted wire-rope, and iron spars, and copper, and the bones and skulls of dead men. The skulls ran in zigzag lines and spirals and fantastic curves over the buildings; and in and out of their eye-sockets, and over the whole surface of the place, lurked and played a multitude of silvery little fishes.

Suddenly his ears were filled with a low shouting and a noise like the violent blowing of horns, and this gave place to a fantastic chant. Down the sphere sank, past the huge pointed windows, through which he saw vaguely a great number of these strange ghostlike people regarding him, and at last he came to rest, as it seemed, on a kind of altar th stood in the centre of the place.

And now he was at such a level that he could see these strange people of the abyss plainly once more. To his astonishment, he perceived that they were prostrating themselves before him, all save one, dressed as it seemed in a robe of placoid scales, and crowned with a luminous diadem, who stood with his reptilian mouth opening and shutting, as though he led the chanting of the worshippers.

A curious impulse made Elstead turn on his small glow-lamp again, so that he became visible to these creatures of the abyss, albeit the glare made them disappear forthwith into night. At this sudden sight of him, the chanting gave place to a tumult of exultant shouts; and Elstead, being anxious to watch them, turned his light off again, and vanished from before their eyes. But for a time he was too blind to make out what they were doing, and when at last he could distinguish them, they were kneeling again. And thus they continued worshipping him, without rest or intermission, for a space of three hours.

Most circumstantial was Elstead's account of his astounding city and its people, these people of perpetual night, who have never seen sun or moon or stars, green vegetation, not any living, air-breathing creatures, who know nothing of fire, nor any light but the phosphorescent light of living things.

Startling as is his story, it is yet more startling to find that scientific men, of such eminence as Adams and Jenkins, find nothing incredible in it. They tell me they see no reason why intelligent, water-breathing, vertebrated creatures inured to a low temperature and enormous pressure, and of such a heavy structure that neither alive not dead would they float, might not live upon the bottom of the deep sea, and quite unsuspected by us, descendants like ourselves of the great Theriomorpha of the New Red Sandstone age.

We should be known to them, however, as strange, meteoric creatures, wont to fall catastrophically dead out of the mysterious blackness of their watery sky. And not only we ourselves, but our ships, our metals, our appliances, would come raining down out of the night. Sometimes sinking things would smite down and crush them, as if it were the judgement of some unseen power above, and sometimes would come things of the utmost rarity or utility, or shapes of inspiring suggestion. One can understand, perhaps, something of their behaviour at the descent of a living man, if one thinks what a barbaric people might do, to whon an enhaloed, shining creature came suddenly out of the sky.

At one time or another Elstead probably told the officers of the

Ptarmigan every detail of his strange twelve hours in the abyss. That he also intended to write them down is certain, but he never did, and so unhappily we have to piece together the discrepant fragments of his story from the reminiscences of Commander Simmons, Weybridge, Steevens, Lindley, and the others.

We see the thing darkly in fragmentary glimpses – the huge ghostly building, the bowing, chanting people, with their dark chameleonlike heads and faintly luminous clothing, and Elstead, with his light turned on again, vainly trying to convey to their minds that the cord by which the sphere was held was to be severed. Minute after minute slipped away, and Elstead, looking at his watch, was horrified to find that he had oxygen only for four hours more. But the chant in his honour kept on as remorselessly as if it was the marching song of his approaching death.

The manner of his release he does not understand, but to judge by the end of cord that hung from the sphere, it had been cut through by rubbing against the edge of the altar. Abruptly the sphere rolled over, and he swept up, out of their world, as an ethereal creature clothed in a vacuum would sweep through our own atmosphere back to its native ether again. He must have torn out of their sight as a hydrogen bubble hastens upward from our air. A strange ascension it must have seemed to them.

The sphere rushed up with even greater velocity than, when weighted with the lead sinkers, it had rushed down. It became exceedingly hot. It drove up with the window uppermost, and he remembers the torrent of bubbles frothing against the glass. Every moment he expected this to fly. Then suddenly something like a huge wheel seemed to be released in his head, the padded compartment began spinning about him, and he fainted. His next recollection was of his cabin, and of the doctor's voice.

But that is the substance of the extraordinary story that Elstead related in fragments to the officers of the *Ptarmigan*. He promised to write it all down at a later date. His mind was chiefly occupied with the improvement of his apparatus, which was effected at Rio.

It remains only to tell that on 2 February 1896, he made his second descent into the ocean abyss, with the improvements his first experience suggested. What happened we shall probably never know. He never returned. The *Ptarmigan* beat about over the point of his submersion, seeking him in vain for thirteen days. Then she returned to Rio, and the news was telegraphed to his friends. So the matter rests for the present. But it is hardly probable that no further attempt will be made to verify his strange story of these hitherto unsuspected cities of the deep sea.

The Fun They Had

Isaac Asimov

Margie even wrote about it that night in her diary. On the page headed 17 May 2157, she wrote, 'Today Tommy found a real book!'

It was a very old book. Margie's grandfather once said that when he was a little boy *his* grandfather told him that there was a time when all stories were printed on paper.

They turned the pages, which were yellow and crinkly, and it was awfully funny to read words that stood still instead of moving the way they were supposed to – on a screen, you know. And then, when they turned back to the page before, it had the same words on it that it had had when they read it the first time.

'Gee,' said Tommy, 'what a waste. When you're through with the book, you just throw it away, I guess. Our television screen must have had a million books on it and it's good for plenty more. I wouldn't throw it away.'

'Same with mine,' said Margie. She was eleven and hadn't seen as many telebooks as Tommy had. He was thirteen.

She said, 'Where did you find it?'

'In my house.' He pointed without looking, because he was busy reading. 'In the attic.'

'What's it about?'

The part Margie hated most was the slot where she had to put homework and test papers.

'School.'

Margie was scornful. 'School? What's there to write about school? I hate school.'

Margie always hated school, but now she hated it more than ever. The mechanical teacher had been giving her test after test in geography and she had been doing worse and worse until her mother had shaken her head sorrowfully and sent for the County Inspector.

He was a round little man with a red face and a whole box of tools with dials and wires. He smiled at Margie and gave her an apple, then took the teacher apart. Margie had hoped he wouldn't know how to put it together again, but he knew how all right, and, after an hour or so, there it was again, large and black and ugly, with a big screen on which all the lessons were shown and the questions were asked. That wasn't so bad. The part Margie hated most was the slot where she had to put homework and test papers. She always had to write them out in a punch code they made her learn when she was six years old, and the mechanical teacher calculated the mark in no time.

The Inspector had smiled after he was finished and patted Margie's head. He said to her mother, 'It's not the little girl's fault, Mrs. Jones. I think the geography sector was geared a little too quick. Those things happen sometimes. I've slowed it up to an average ten-year level. Actually, the over-all pattern of her progress is quite satisfactory.' And he patted Margie's head again.

Margie was disappointed. She had been hoping they would take the teacher away altogether. They had once taken Tommy's teacher away for nearly a month because the history sector had blanked out completely.

So she said to Tommy, 'Why would anyone write about school?'

Tommy looked at her with very superior eyes. 'Because it's not our kind of school, stupid. This is the old kind of school that they had hundreds and hundreds of years ago.' He added loftily, pronouncing the word carefully, '*Centuries* ago.'

Margie was hurt. 'Well, I don't know what kind of school they had all that time ago.' She read the book over his shoulder for a while, then said, 'Anyway, they had a teacher.'

'Sure they had a teacher, but it wasn't a *regular* teacher. It was a man.'

'A man? How could a man be a teacher?'

'Well, he just told the boys and girls things and gave them homework and asked them questions.'

'A man isn't smart enough.'

'Sure he is. My father knows as much as my teacher.'

'He can't. A man can't know as much as a teacher.'

'He knows almost as much, I betcha.'

Margie wasn't prepared to dispute that. She said, 'I wouldn't want a strange man in my house to teach me.'

Tommy screamed with laughter. 'You don't know much, Margie. The teachers didn't live in the house. They had a special building and all the kids went there.'

'And all the kids learned the same thing?'

'Sure, if they were the same age.'

'But my mother says a teacher has to be adjusted to fit the mind of each boy and girl it teaches and that each kid has to be taught differently.'

'Just the same they didn't do it that way then. If you don't like it, you don't have to read the book.'

'I didn't say I didn't like it,' Margie said quickly. She wanted to read about those funny schools.

★   ★   ★   ★

They weren't even half-finished when Margie's mother called, 'Margie! School!'

Margie looked up. 'Not yet, Mamma.'

'Now!' said Mrs Jones. 'And it's probably time for Tommy, too.'

Margie said to Tommy, 'Can I read the book some more with you after school?'

'Maybe,' he said nonchalantly. He walked away whistling, the dusty old book tucked beneath his arm.

Margie went into the schoolroom. It was right next to her bedroom, and the mechanical teacher was on and waiting for her. It was always on at the same time every day except Saturday and Sunday, because her mother said little girls learned better if they learned at regular hours.

The screen was lit up, and it said: 'Today's arithmetic lesson is on the addition of proper fractions. Please insert yesterday's homework in the proper slot.'

Margie did so with a sigh. She was thinking about the old schools they had when her grandfather's grandfather was a little boy. All the kids from the whole neighbourhood came, laughing and shouting in the schoolyard, sitting together in the schoolroom, going home together at the end of the day. They learned the same things, so they could help one another on the homework and talk about it.

And the teachers were people. . .

The mechanical teacher was flashing on the screen: 'When we add the fractions $\frac{1}{2}$ and $\frac{1}{4}$—'

Margie was thinking about how the kids must have loved it in the old days. She was thinking about the fun they had.

Crossfire

James White

Cotrell sat on the loose earth at the crater's rim and watched the tank close up to point-blank range. It was one of the newest and deadliest models; a shell from its main gun could knock a hole through four-inch armour plate with no trouble at all. That main gun was already loaded and was now pointed directly at Cotrell. They couldn't miss him.

But they couldn't hit him either.

No doubt they would reload and try again, and they would keep on trying. Just like the machine-gunners behind him, and the two light tanks and the scout car over there on the right. If persistence was a virtue, he thought, then these guys would very shortly be saints. Such trouble they were going to in order to wipe out just three men, but he supposed, a little cynically, it was the principle of the thing.

Cotrell sighed and looked over at Nelson, who was lying propped on one elbow and watching everything with a show of interest that fooled nobody. He was scared stiff. Beside him Corporal Barnes lay flat on his back, breathing slowly and economically, the way they're supposed to do on wrecked submarines. He did this because the air in here was stale, almost unbreathable, and that was the proper thing to do. Barnes was very practical.

If only one of the shells would get through and end everything quickly, before the slow, painful death from suffocation that was so surely coming. Cotrell glared again at the four-foot silvery torpedo lying a few yards away which was the cause of all this mess and wished fervently that he'd never heard of it. But he knew, if he had the choice to make again, he would go through with it in exactly the same manner. Those torpedoes had turned out to be something rather special.

They had been first sighted by a returning patrol. Then a bomb-disposal unit had gone out to look them over and, if necessary, to pull their teeth. Six hours later the unit returned, the men wearing looks of extreme bewilderment and refusing even to mention the job to anybody at all. Nobody likes being called a liar, a drunk, or mentally deficient, so they clammed up and discussed it only among themselves. Their officer, on the other hand, wanted most desperately to talk about it. He grabbed a jeep and scorched off to see his CO. He kept muttering to himself as he rode; he was a very shaken man.

The CO listened to everything he had to say with quiet attention. One would never have guessed, by his expression at any rate, that he was believing perhaps one quarter of it all. In his most gentle and fatherly voice he told the near-hysterical officer to dismiss and take it easy for a bit; then he began to think. Eventually he decided to play it safe and refer the matter up. Maybe the enemy *had* a secret weapon after all.

In jig time a lordly Major from Weapon Research arrived. He took a handful of technicians and about every portable testing device known to science out to the scene of so much mental anguish to settle the matter for good. He was very thorough – his report later was easily half an inch thick – but he too was completely baffled. This worried him, because up until now at any rate, he thought he knew his stuff. There was only one thing to do. Very politely and through the proper channels, he too, screamed for help.

★   ★   ★   ★

Help arrived in the persons of Lt Colonel Richard Cotrell and Captain William Nelson. Cotrell was a tall, rangy individual with the

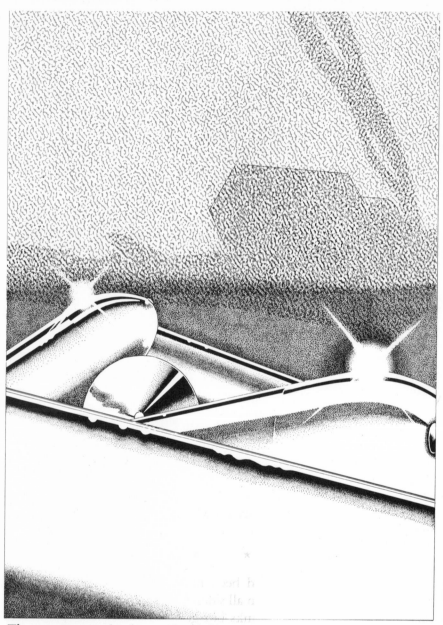

The nearest torpedo gleamed brightly in the sunlight less than three yards from the crater's rim.

characteristic lines of asceticism, or maybe ulcers, around his thin-lipped mouth. He spoke like a school-teacher. Nelson was the small, nervously active type who seem in a perpetual state of extreme worry. He wore rimless glasses, but he never worried about anything, in fact, he had quite a sense of humour, which only goes to show. Both wore their uniforms with the awkward air of the civilian scientist who would much rather have flannels and a lab coat, for they weren't regulars, but had been roped in by the Army to do some very hush-hush research.

Cotrell asked for six experienced men to form an escort for their protection in case they were attacked, and to tote some of the equipment. He could have asked for a full company and got them with no trouble at all, but he thought a small force would stand a better chance of doing the job unobserved. And it was very necessary that they do it unobserved, for circumstances pointed to the fact that the enemy was unaware that several of their secret weapons were lying in No Man's Land, defenceless against the prying instruments and keen minds of hostile scientists. Up to now, though, the things had proved to be anything but defenceless, and the 'keen minds of the scientists' had seemed something less than razor sharp, but the General was confident that Cotrell would find the answer. While he was finding it, however, just to be on the safe side, he was to maintain strict radio silence.

The General had also said he was a nice guy and a very important person to his department. He didn't want him leaving his brains lying on the ground somewhere, so remember to keep his head down – but find out what those blistering things were, and what the blue blazes they were meant to *do*. So far they didn't seem to do anything at all.

So Cotrell and Nelson, with their sweating, heavily-laden body-guard, went crawling out to discover what the torpedoes were and what what they were supposed to do.

* * * *

The original discovery had been made in a little area of rocky, broken ground surrounded on all sides by flat near-desertlike country that was just the thing for tanks but gave very little cover for men trying to efface themselves. This ragged jumble of rocks had been used often by both sides as an advanced observation post, and as a place for raiding parties to take cover. But that had been long ago. Now the big guns of both sides had its range to a T. At frequent but irregular intervals, just on general principles, they would plaster it, so the place wasn't popular any more. At the moment, however, it was peaceful.

Cotrell had no difficulty in finding the upturned enemy truck with the silver torpedoes scattered on the ground beside it, and the deep bomb-crater nearby that from which the previous investigators had worked. It was an old crater, with grass growing in patches on its wall and floors. As craters go, it was fairly comfortable. They began sorting out their gear while the escort distributed itself around them in a wide circle and began waiting for something to happen, all the while hoping, of course, that nothing would.

Then the two officers crawled up to the rim and took their first real look at things.

The enemy truck had been shot up from the air. It was lying on its side, burned out, a total wreck. The seven silvery objects lay close together about ten yards from the truck. There were also a few empty metal canisters lying among them, but these had been proved innocuous. The nearest torpedo gleamed brightly in the sunlight less than three yards from the crater's rim.

It was about four feet long, and made from some highly-polished metal that seemed to be a perfect reflector. The nose came to a smoothly-rounded point. The tail, which was bare of any of the usual guiding vanes or detonating devices, was also smoothly-rounded except for a small flat area at the extreme end. This was about the size of a penny and was painted black. There were no other surface markings.

When they had studied it for a few minutes in silence, Cotrell shook his head in puzzlement and shrugged fatalistically. 'Better make a start, I suppose,' he said. 'You stay here and reach me the stuff while I take a closer look. Okay?' He scrambled up over the rim and lay flat beside the torpedo. At intervals he called for various items of equipment which were handed up to him. Test meters and other enigmatic devices made a growing pile around him on the ground, but he was getting strictly nowhere. He shook his head in bewilderment. One would almost think this . . . this something or other was placed here for the sole purpose of driving technicians into nervous breakdowns. He gave up for the time being in disgust and slid back into the crater.

'Well, what is it?' asked Nelson, then he caught the other's expression and ended, 'Oh! You don't know.'

Cotrell took off his helmet and flung himself down beside the other. 'No, I don't know.' His voice was perplexed. He looked completely baffled as he went on, 'But Major Thompson was right. It doesn't seem to be a bomb. It's too light to contain enough HE to do much damage, and if it's an empty, I can't find the slightest trace of a filling valve. And the thing must have been put together by a watch-maker. There isn't a single join anywhere on its surface that I can see.'

He paused, thinking. He was beginning to understand just how the Major who had preceded him had felt after spending four hours with the thing. But he, unlike Thompson, couldn't very well pass the buck.

He continued, 'I didn't find the skin heating up suddenly the way he did, but then he tried to carry it away with him, whereas I only rolled it over a few times. Apart from that everything checks exactly with Thompson's report. Incidentally, I saw one of his asbestos gloves. It was almost burnt through, so it seems certain that it *did* get red hot when he lifted it. Up to now I thought he'd been exaggerating that part of it a little.'

A shell landed with a crash less than a hundred yards away. Nelson winced and Cotrell reached hurriedly for his helmet. They both looked a trifle shame-faced. They weren't used to being this close to the war. Cotrell began speaking again.

'I did find out a little more about it. Maybe it will mean something to you. I can't make a thing out of it. He pulled out a soiled notebook and consulted it. Then he stated, 'The skin is made of some extremely hard, non-magnetic metal and is between one eighth and one quarter inches thick. There are also traces of metal, some of it magnetic, at about thirty separate points inside the shell. These small masses of metal are all grouped on, or very close to, the longitudinal axis of the thing. The remaining volume seems to be empty, but as the detector doesn't work on non-metallic material there could be a gas, or a liquid, or a plastic structure of some kind occupying it.

'There is a flat, black, metal disc with a thin white line around its circumference, set flush with one end. I thought at first it was a colour code painted on, but it is definitely metal, very warm to the touch and pitted as though from periodic heating. It is also faintly radio-active.

Nothing harmful, mind, but just barely detectable.' Cotrell slapped his notebook shut, looked up at Nelson, and grinned, making a joke of the whole thing. He stated, 'We have here a hollow, closed cylinder with a metal rod of irregular thickness running down its centre, which is slightly radio-active. Now, would the bright boy facing me please stand up and tell the class what it is?'

Nelson thoughtfully cleaned his glasses, then, replying in kind, piped, 'Please Sir, it could be anything—and if I stand up here I'll get a hole in the head.'

'You're a big help,' the other's tone was scathing. 'And,' he ended cuttingly, 'that was the general idea.'

★   ★   ★   ★

They were both giving the matter very serious thought even though their cross-talk seemed to make light of it. After Nelson had spoken gloatingly and at some length of just how glad he was that he hadn't been given charge of this job, he became serious again.

'Does it make a noise?' he asked. 'Any ticking or humming noises? It might be some sort of time-bomb.'

Cotrell shook his head. 'With all this shooting going on around here I couldn't be sure. But there did seem to be a low, irregular ticking, like the sound mice might make scampering about on a tiled floor . . .' He stopped suddenly and grew visibly pale. Then in a low, shocked whisper said, 'Oh, no.'

'What's up?' queried Nelson, then he too, realized the implications of the other's words. Unconsciously he wriggled his shoulders as he protested, 'A Bacteriological Bomb. But that's impossible. They wouldn't dare . . . Still, maybe they would.' He grimaced in disgust. 'Augh, I feel lousy already.'

'We can't be sure of that yet,' said Cotrell quickly, 'I'll have to take another look. Have you got a magnifying glass?'

Naturally a magnifying glass was about the only thing they *hadn't* taken with them, but Nelson liberated a pocket flashlamp from one of the escort and the crude lens from that had to do instead.

For some time now gunfire from the enemy positions had been steadily growing in intensity, and there was considerable air activity as well. With increasing frequency low-flying jets flashed screaming across a sky already streaked with the filmy vapour trails of high-altitude bombers. It looked as if something was afoot. Cotrell, again sprawled alongside the nearest torpedo, could scarcely make himself heard above the din. He was examining minutely the surface of the thing with the glass, and calling out his findings to Nelson who was taking everything down. Details of the black metal disc came first, followed by a description of the white circle around it, which seemed to be a hard plastic. Then he tried to see how the shell as a whole was put together.

At first he had no success. Then: 'Willie! Willie!' he called excitedly, 'Get this down quick. *I can see inside.* The first eight inches back of the nose have gone transparent, just like that. Don't know what caused it, but I can see right in . . .'

Just then something landed nearby with an earth-shaking crash and a few fair-sized rocks came bounding into the crater. Over the ringing in his ears Nelson heard the other's voice jabbering away as if nothing had happened. He shook his head to clear it and wished his shorthand was faster or that Cotrell would slow down.

'. . . Tiny, complex mechanisms linked by hair-thin wires, but so *small*. Our micro techniques can't touch this at all. It seems to be divided into thin-walled compartments of different sizes . . . Oh, why can't I have a decent lens, everything blurs and jiggles around . . . The inside is filled with a yellowish gas, and in the nose . . . Wait! Something moved. It's a snail, no, two snails. But they're going too fast for snails. Maybe . . .'

★   ★   ★   ★

Something, he couldn't say just what, made Nelson look up. The plane was still quite high, but it was moving awfully fast, straight down. There could be no doubt whatever at whom it was being aimed. Cotrell was yelling, 'It's not a bomb. I know what it is now. I can't believe it, but it's a . . .' Nelson screamed a warning to take cover, but it was drowned in the mounting roar of engines. He did the only thing possible. He reached way out, grabbed an ankle and hauled Cotrell frantically back into the crater. He was just in time.

With a high-pitched *whoosh* the plane loosed a rocket. They heard it coming, then something tried to push them into the ground and shake them to pieces at the same time. They were deafened, blinded by dust, pelted with falling earth and stones, and a large, jagged-edged chunk of metal dug a hole in the ground three inches from Cotrell's ear, but they were both unhurt. They lay still for a few minutes, trying to convince themselves of this.

The plane didn't make another pass at them, and they heard it roaring off into the distance. After a while the sergeant heading the escort began calling names to see if anyone had copped it. Nobody had. Nelson raised his head and looked hard at Cotrell. Picking his words with great care, he said:

'I realize there was considerable noise and confusion when I dragged you in just now. Probably I didn't hear you right, but I could swear you said the word "Spaceship." Am I suffering from an auricular condition, or is that what you said?'

Cotrell sat up. His face was dirty and there was a lot of skin missing from his nose and chin as a result of his being dragged on it across several feet of very rugged terrain, but apparently he could not even feel it. His eyes shone with excitement. 'That's right,' he affirmed. His voice was exultant, almost exalted. '*Spaceships*. Seven of them. That's all they could be. It explains everything. The sudden transparency of the nose. The tiny machines, controls, wiring, little creatures working at things. They're spaceships, I tell you. An extra-terrestrial life-form, and *intelligent*.' He stopped, his mind leaping ahead, trying to grasp what this single great fact would mean to humanity. Then in more normal tones he continued: 'Go, see for yourself. Here's the glass, take a good look . . . Oh!'

'What's wrong?' called Nelson, seeing the other's expression change to one of dismayed apprehension. He was already half out of the crater – he didn't believe it, of course, but he was very eager to see just what *was* coming off here.

'That rocket,' Cotrell asked tensely, 'Did it hit them?'

'Nah. It landed on the other side of the truck,' answered Nelson.

Then a puzzled note crept into his voice as he went on, 'Funny, it was headed right for us, too, then it sort of wobbled and sheered off. Guess we're just lucky, I suppose.' He wriggled away, and was gone for some time. When he came back he looked a bit sick.

'Well?'

Nelson nodded and said grudgingly, 'I suppose you're right. They could be spaceships, manned spaceships.' He shuddered involuntarily. 'Maybe "manned" is the wrong word. Ugh, those shiny wet lumps. And those pink bars growing out of them and curling and writhing about. They're sickening. Whatever planet they come from they must have lived under its rocks – its slimiest, dampest, mouldiest rocks. I don't like them at all.'

Cotrell was pointing out heatedly and at some length that Intelligence was the important thing, and not the body that housed it, when the sergeant called softly to say someone was coming, and suggested that they keep deathly quiet just in case it wasn't a friend. Cotrell said, 'Thank you, Sergeant,' and shut up.

★   ★   ★   ★

Shortly afterwards they heard a low-voiced exchange of pass-words, then a corporal in a rather soiled Medical Corps uniform rolled in beside them. He must have been a regular, for while crouching on hands and knees he still somehow gave the impression that he was standing rigidly to attention as he said smartly, 'Corporal Barnes, Sir. Message from Field H.Q. Very urgent.' He handed it to Cotrell. While it was being opened he turned to Nelson and volunteered, 'They sent me with it in case anybody needed a patch. Does anybody?'

Nelson told him no, they'd been lucky so far, but to check with the sergeant and make sure. Then he looked quizzically at Cotrell. 'Someone seems mighty concerned about our health,' he mused. 'Fancy sending a Medic.'

Cotrell didn't hear him. He was reading aloud from the message. 'It's from the General, relayed by hand due to the radio silence order. He says he hopes it reaches us in time. Says the enemy is pushing forward. Nothing serious, but our guys are pulling back temporarily, and that this position has been by-passed but is now almost encircled by enemy armour. Whether we've solved the problem or not we've got to head for home before we're completely cut off. Says to drop the whole thing, he'd rather have a couple of live boffins than two dead heroes, and that that's an order. He also says a counter-attack is being mounted and will begin in four hours, and we'll have another chance maybe when we re-take this area. Meanwhile come back at once.' He stopped and looked at Nelson distractedly. He crumpled the message viciously and burst out. 'But I can't leave. I just can't. Not now.'

Nelson was sympathetic, 'I know how you feel. This sort of thing doesn't happen very often,' he said, making perhaps the greatest understatement of all time, 'But orders are orders. And besides,' he reasoned, 'it's only a matter of time before the enemy mops us up. So far we've been lucky, but that plane must have reported our position. There'll be tanks along, or they'll plaster us with shells any time now. Unless we want to stay here permanently we'd better don our skates and get out of here, fast.

★   ★   ★   ★

Cotrell looked at him unhappily. He was insane for hesitating even an instant. 'I know all that,' he said, 'but don't you realize we're about to make contact with an intelligent race from another planet, probably from another star system. I know they're little crawling horrors, but we just can't up and leave . . .'

'Now look' Nelson broke in. 'I'm as broadminded and tolerant as the next guy. I shake hands with the strangest people, and cadge their cigarettes. You get to be that way in this war of ours.' He gestured at the sergeant who was wearing, in addition to his usual equipment, a vicious-looking machete and an imposing black beard, and whose face was several shades darker than midnight. 'But I won't hang around and get knocked off to no purpose, and I won't let you do it either. And tell me this, how do you expect to communicate? And how can they possibly reply? We'd better pack it in and go before the shelling starts.'

Cotrell was silent for several minutes, trying to think of words to put his feelings across. Then, his mind made up, he spoke, 'Try to look at this thing objectively. A number of aliens have landed on Earth, the first time in history that this has happened. Unfortunately they landed in the middle of a battlefield just before battle was due to commence, a very bad choice of a landing spot. They took positions beside some metal containers which resembled them roughly in size and shape. Not knowing their thought processes it is impossible to say whether this was done through curiosity or in an attempt to camouflage, or maybe it was a rendezvous point or something like that. Now, the natives, that's us, come to investigate and they reveal themselves. But because we have been seen by other natives who don't like us and wish to kill us, these creatures are shortly going to be blown to smithereens while we go off scot free.'

'But . . .'

'Now I think this is wrong, I think we're – well . . .' He hesitated, then went on defensively. 'You'll think this silly, maybe, but I feel we are responsible for their safety. This isn't their war. They don't know the score.' He paused, then apologetically but very, very stubbornly he ended, 'They must at least be warned off before we leave.'

★   ★   ★   ★

Nelson didn't answer. He had known Cotrell for several years as a very likeable sort who hid a shy disposition behind a very efficient wall of tough cynicism and bitingly sarcastic wit. Not the sort of crazy fanatic to pull a trick like *this*. He was uncomfortably aware, moreover, that the other was morally right, but this place would shortly be a crashing hell of erupting earth and red-hot flying steel. Even in this mad world Nelson's life was very precious to him. But he too, was curious about those aliens. He'd like to know just why they'd come . . . He brought his attention back to Cotrell, who was speaking again.

'The General wants his two pet geniuses back. Well, we'll let him have one of them. You. Half a loaf, and so on.' He broke off and grinned. 'Hope you don't mind being called half a loaf.' He went on, with forced lightness, 'I'll stay behind and scare away our friends, somehow, then I'll follow after you.' He called abruptly, 'Sergeant!'

Nelson began a protest, but the other was already giving his orders. Cotrell told the sergeant that the area would shortly come under heavy fire. Captain Nelson, the sergeant, and his men were to return at once. He had something to do and would follow them when he had finished it. The sergeant nodded and consulted the corporal quickly about the best route back. In minutes his men were on their way, crawling rapidly, but using every possible scrap of cover. The sergeant hung back, waiting for Nelson.

★   ★   ★   ★

Nelson couldn't say a word. For the first time in his life his friend had pulled rank on him, and it was because of that friendship that he'd done it. He gripped Cotrell's arm awkwardly and mumbled something about being careful and scrambled away after the sergeant.

It was then that Cotrell saw that the corporal was still in the crater. 'What are you waiting for?' he said sharply. He had a lot on his mind.

The corporal was inclined to argue at first, but finally a shoulderful how important both technicians were, and he was not to return without them. This had been stressed by his CO. His CO had the reputation of frequently eating his young. His CO was a real tartar. He dare not go back without Lt-Colonel Cotrell, and would he be long in finishing up?

The corporal was inclined to argue at first, but finally a shoulderful of dirty yellow pips glared hard at two lowly chevrons and he too, departed.

He was back five minutes later, looking apologetic but very determined. Nelson was with him.

Nelson began defensively. 'A body could get killed out there. No cover. I can't be expected to hide behind pebbles like those other guys, I'm not used to it. Besides,' he finished lamely, 'I wanted to see what you were doing.'

Cotrell gave him a look that told him that he was a liar, a suicidal maniac, and the best friend a man could have all rolled into one, but all he said was, 'I haven't done anything yet. I'm glad you did come back, maybe you can help me think of something.' He was hiding his very real feelings by being studiously casual and off-hand about the whole thing. He didn't fool Nelson. Turning to the corporal he said lightly, 'We'll probably need you before very long, too.'

The corporal said 'yes sir' and began fiddling absently with the straps of his haversack. It was the one conspicuously marked with a large red cross.

There was a lull in the gunfire, but that didn't mean anything. It would start again any minute with redoubled intensity. Cotrell and

Nelson began discussing the aliens' possible system of communication. Obviously they couldn't hear very well or the noise would have frightened them away long ago, thought Cotrell, but the transparent covering of their control-room made it seem certain that their eyes operated in the visible frequencies. Nelson asked about vibration, and surely they could *see* the shells falling? Cotrell replied that they might think the vibration was natural volcanic activity. He didn't know why they couldn't see what was happening, but they were certainly completely unaware of their danger. After that he bogged down. The corporal broke the perplexed silence in a low voice.

'In any stories I've read they always have telepathy.' He seemed to be talking to himself.

Nelson, who was lying nearest, regarded him with pleased wonder. He would never have suspected the corporal of having such good taste in reading matter. His estimation of Barnes rose appreciably. Cotrell heard the remark. Eyes shut and fingers stuck in his ears he was trying desperately to think. Suddenly he exclaimed:

'I think I've got it. How's this. They can see all right, but being so small their field of clear vision is restricted to say, six feet, so that anything happening beyond that distance would appear so hazy or distorted they wouldn't know what it was.' He began climbing out of the crater, 'I can test that idea, anyway.'

For a while there were scuffling and grunting noises as he scrambled about among the nearer torpedoes, then he reappeared, eyes bright with excitement, and panted, 'They can see. I tried different objects . . . varied distances . . . Slide-rule, cigarette lighter, a pencil. I moved them around. They turned their . . . their . . . Well, they all looked at them. They can see. Maximum range seems to be about four feet, for small objects like the pencil, eighteen inches.' He broke off and shook his head despairingly, 'But how are we going to tell them to go away?'

It was a very good question. They began batting their brains out anew. Shortly the corporal cleared his throat, 'if we could draw some kind of picture,' he suggested diffidently, 'maybe . . .'

Nelson snapped his fingers, 'Corporal, you're a genius,' he enthused. Then turning to Cotrell, 'That's *it*! Don't you see. We draw them pictures – before and after pictures. First show ships lying peacefully, then shells falling, show ships in little pieces. Also show them taking off safely. Make the sketches simple, with clear, black lines. Stick those in front of their eyes, that should scare them away all right.' He went on breathlessly, 'Have you got the lab notebook?'

Cotrell nodded quickly and began tearing out the large, stiff pages. They sketched furiously, discarded, and sketched again. The finished work would never have been hung in the Tate Gallery, but they hoped it would do. The page showed three simple pictures, with a symbolical sun in each giving them a crude time sequence. Rapidly they made two copies and crawled out among the alien ships.

*   *   *   *

The noses of all the ships were now transparent. Each held his sketch up close for a few minutes, then moved to the next one. They kept circulating among the ships. Shells began falling again, uncomfortably close, and there was the distant roaring, rattling sound that could only mean the approach of an armoured column.

Suddenly Nelson bellowed something above the din and pointed vigorously. One of the ships was floating gently upwards. As they watched the black circle in its stern glowed cherry red. There was a hiss and a smell of ozone and the ship flashed upwards out of sight. Five others followed it in less than a minute. The men cheered raggedly. Only one ship remained – the one nearest the crater. It showed no sign of moving.

*   *   *   *

With desperate haste Cotrell propped his sketch up before it and dived for cover. The area was taking an awful pasting from the guns now. It was one continuous eruption. The ground heaved and shook beneath a merciless rain of HE. Earth and stones battered at them viciously. The crater wall on one side crumbled nearly burying them. A twisted, blackened wheel from the wrecked truck flopped down, narrowly missing the corporal. The noise was a monstrous, incredible thing that tore and hammered at their cowering, puny bodies. They knew without a shadow of a doubt that they could have only minutes left to live, then suddenly – just like that – it stopped.

It wasn't just quiet – it was utterly, deathly silent.

For a long time they couldn't move, then Cotrell dragged himself up to take a look. The other two heard him gasp. In a voice that shook with some indescribable emotion he called for them to come up. When they saw that he was outside the crater and that nothing happened to him, they climbed out and stood beside him.

They found the force-field to be hemispherical in shape, perfectly transparent, and impenetrable to everything, including sound. It was approximately fifteen yards in diameter, and felt like warm glass. At its geometrical centre was the alien ship. Outside, the earth was still being torn up and flung violently into the sky. In here it was as quiet as an empty church.

Cotrell stood over the tiny ship, his features working through a whole spectrum of emotions. Unsteadily, he choked out, 'It stayed behind to save us. One good turn deserved another. Don't you see, they're grateful.' His voice broke, 'Imagine those . . . those snails doing a thing like that.'

The corporal nodded wordlessly. 'Yeah,' Nelson said solemnly, 'It makes you think.' Then he gave a sudden relieved giggle, 'What are we all *whispering* for?'

They didn't know, but unconsciously they kept on doing it.

★   ★   ★   ★

They were still discussing it in hushed tones two hours later when a couple of light tanks pulled up a hundred yards from them and began shooting. They stopped talking to watch. After a while an officer climbed out of one of the turrets to see why his shots weren't having any effect. When he hit the screen he stepped back quickly, his face going grey. He drew his pistol, took careful aim and fired. Barnes put his thumb to his nose and spread his fingers in the universal gesture. For a moment they thought the officer was going to burst into tears, but instead he wheeled suddenly and sprinted back to his tank. It opened fire again.

About twenty minutes later the firing ceased. Thirty men came forward in ragged line abreast and closed in around the screen. They were extremely hesitant at first. They poked it with bayonet points, battered at it with gun butts, then stepped well back and hurled grenades at it. Finally, they grew tired and sat down and waited for somebody to think of something else.

A scout car came rocking and bumping along over ground pitted with newly-made craters. It was a half-tread job mounting a great brute of a machine gun. Two officers – judging by the beautiful way their uniforms fitted, very high rankers indeed – stepped out and came forward. They had the bright idea of digging under the screen and coming up inside. No luck. The force-field proved to be, not a dome, but a sphere. They began shouting and waving their arms about, but to those inside they made as much noise as a cat tramping across a deep pile rug.

It was about then that Cotrell noticed how stale the air was becoming. He mentioned it aloud.

Nelson and the corporal had been fairly killing themselves at the antics of the enemy officers, pointing and pulling faces at them and going off into gales of uncontrollable laughter. Their abrupt change of expression, in other circumstances, would have been comic. They sobered instantly. Barnes lifted his arm and carefully took his own pulse, then he did the same for Cotrell and Nelson. He nodded gravely in verification, both pulse-rate and respiration were way up. They were breathing too much CO_2.

★   ★   ★   ★

Nelson was silent for a long time, then he muttered bitterly, 'It was too good to be true.' He turned to the corporal, 'How much time have we got before we – we . . .?' He didn't finish the question, there was no need to. They were all feeling the smothering, choking sensations of imminent suffocation already, and even though it was purely psychological as yet, it was bad.

The corporal guessed somewhere between two and two and a half hours.

'There must be something we can do,' Nelson burst out desperately. 'We can draw more pictures, maybe. Show them the fix we're in. I know we can't do without the screen, we'd be blown to bits in seconds, but maybe they could put a hole in it or something. I'm going to try it.'

He snatched up the notebook and sketched rapidly, tore up the result viciously and started again. Better this time. He waved it briefly at the others and almost ran over to the ship.

But the ship's nose was no longer transparent.

Nelson lost his head then, 'Open up, blast you,' he screamed, and beat at it hysterically with his fists. 'Look! Look at this!' he entreated, but there was no change whatever in the smooth black surface of the ship. In a sudden rage he grabbed it in his hands and shook it violently. Its hull suddenly went red-hot. He dropped it with a yelp of pain and aimed a kick at it. 'You're not saving us. You're killing us, d'you hear, *killing us.*' He was nearly in tears. 'I was nearly drowned once when I was a kid. It was awful.' Then he quietened down a little and said slowly, accusingly, 'Know what I think? I think you're doing this deliberately. You *have* telepathy. You're doing this to torture us, get our reactions. And when we're nearly dead you'll come crawling out and . . . and . . .' He choked off into silence.

Cotrell felt slightly embarrassed and very sympathetic, he was close to screaming himself. Barnes looked at the ground and rebuked Nelson gently. 'That's a very *corny* theory, Captain,' he said. The bantering tone had the desired effect. Nelson grinned shamefacedly and forced a shaky laugh, 'I don't *really* think they'll come pouring out at us with ray-guns. Maybe I read too many of the wrong stories.'

*   *   *   *

After that they took it quietly. Outwardly, at least, they were resigned to their fate. They agreed to conserve the air as much as possible by sitting or lying down and cutting out unnecessary conversation. Barnes made brief mention of morphia tablets he had in his pack, but either they didn't believe in suicide or they were hoping for a miracle. Probably it was a little of both. Cotrell didn't know how the other two felt, but he was scared sick. Scared both at the thought of dying and at the agonizingly slow asphyxiation that would precede it. To take his mind off things he began to observe the enemy movements. He passed a long time that way.

Another tank rolled up, a heavy this time. It didn't stop until it was very close indeed. Smoke puffed from the turret and there was a sound-less explosion on the screen. After a while it all became a little monotonous. The machine-gun on the scout car kept up a steady fire, always directed unerringly at one and only one point on the force-field, trying, he supposed, to wear it away by sheer friction. He could see the steel-jacketed bullets bouncing off it in a flickering grey blur.

Suddenly, silently, the scout car bulged outwards and flung its roof away as it took a direct hit. The men beside it dropped flat. Some of them stayed that way, the others scattered frantically for cover. The tanks loosed off a final salvo, churned into reverse, and left in great haste. The counter-attack had begun.

The ground outside was again ploughed and torn up and flung about, this time by their friends. But Cotrell couldn't see it very well. Great dark spotches floated before his eyes as he fought desperately for air. If the bombardment would only stop, he thought, there might be some hope. But how could the aliens possibly distinguish between enemy and friendly high explosive. He sobbed in sheer frustration.

★   ★   ★   ★

Suddenly his attention was drawn to the corporal. They had all perched on the crater's edge where the air was a little fresher. Now Barnes was struggling to get into the crater, and the air down there was dead, rotten. Cotrell reached out to stop him, but he was too weak. Then he saw Nelson trying to crawl in as well. He gasped a warning and fought himself to his hands and knees. Didn't they know they'd die in that foul muck down there, he must get them out. Then he froze in blind, panic-stricken horror as an indescribably inhuman *something* engulfed his mind and stated coldly, '*You will enter this surface depression for your safety,*' and he found his limbs moving him to the edge, and he, too, rolled flabbily to the bottom of the crater.

He couldn't think what this meant. His eyes were open but everything was dark. He must be very nearly dead, he thought. He felt Nelson struggling feebly beside him, and gasped weakly, 'They had telepathy all the time, the dirty—' But he didn't finish it, for with devastating suddenness sound returned. Roaring, crashing, tearing, earsplitting, beautiful sound. And with it came a blast of lovely dust-filled fresh air. The force-field had gone.

The alien ship, its tests completed, hovered momentarily above the three men now lying safely in the deep crater before it flashed upwards to rejoin its flotilla. Surveying was a pretty dull job, the Commander thought, routine for the most part, but occasionally they would come upon a quite interesting planet.

Allamagoosa

Eric Frank Russell

It was a long time since the *Bustler* had been so silent. She lay in the Sirian spaceport, her tubes cold, her shell particle-scarred, her air that of a long-distance runner exhausted at the end of a marathon. There was good reason for this: she had returned from a lengthy trip by no means devoid of troubles.

Now, in port, well-deserved rest had been gained if only temporarily. Peace, sweet peace. No more bothers, no more crises, no more major upsets, no more dire predicaments such as crop up in free flight at least twice a day. Just peace.

Hah!

Captain McNaught reposed in his cabin, feet up on desk, and enjoyed the relaxation to the utmost. The engines were dead, their hellish pounding absent for the first time in months. Out there in the big city four-hundred of his crew were making whoopee under a brilliant sun. This evening, when First Officer Gregory returned to take charge, he was going to go into the fragrant twilight and make the rounds of neon-lit civilization.

That was the beauty of making landfall at long last. Men could give way to themselves, blow off surplus steam, each according to his fashion. No duties, no worries, no dangers, no responsibilities in spaceport. A haven of safety and comfort for tired rovers.

Again, hah!

Burman, the chief radio officer, entered the cabin. He was one of the half-dozen remaining on duty and bore the expression of a man who can think of twenty better things to do.

'Relayed signal just come in, sir.' Handing the paper across he waited for the other to look at it and perhaps dictate a reply.

Taking the sheet, McNaught removed the feet from his desk, sat erect and read the message aloud.

> *Terran Headquarters to BUSTLER. Remain Siriport pending further orders. Rear Admiral Vane W. Cassidy due there seventeenth. Feldman. Navy Op. Command. Sirisec.*

He looked up, all happiness gone from his leathery features. 'Oh, Lord!' he groaned.

'Something wrong?' asked Burman, vaguely alarmed.

McNaught pointed at three thin books on his desk. 'The middle one. Page twenty.'

Leafing through it, Burman found an item that said:

> *Vane W. Cassidy, R-Ad. Head Inspector Ships and Stores.*

Burman swallowed hard. 'Does that mean—?'

'Yes, it does,' said McNaught without pleasure. 'Back to training-college and all its rigmarole. Paint and soap, spit and polish.' He put on an officious expression, adopted a voice to match it. 'Captain, you have only seven-ninety-nine emergency rations. Your allocation is eight-hundred. Nothing in your logbook accounts for the missing one. Where is it? What happened to it? How is it that one of the men's kit lacks an officially-issued pair of suspenders? Did you report his loss?'

'Why does he pick on us?' asked Burman, appalled. 'He's never chivvied us before.'

'That's why,' informed McNaught, scowling at the wall. 'It's our turn to be stretched across the barrel.' His gaze found the calendar. 'We have three days – and we'll need 'em! Tell Second Officer Pike to come here at once.'

Burman departed gloomily. In short time Pike entered. His face reaffirmed the old adage that bad news travels fast.

'Make out an indent,' ordered McNaught, 'for one hundred gallons of plastic paint, Navy-grey, approved quality. Make out another for thirty gallons of interior white enamel. Take them to spaceport stores right away. Tell them to deliver by six this evening along with our correct issue of brushes and sprayers. Grab up any cleaning material that's going for free.'

'The men won't like this,' remarked Pike, feebly.

'They're going to love it,' McNaught asserted. 'A bright and shiny ship, all spic and span, is good for morale. It says so in that book. Get moving and put those indents in. When you come back, find the stores and equipment sheets and bring them here. We've got to check stocks before Cassidy arrives. Once he's here we'll have no chance to make up shortages or smuggle out any extra items we happened to find in our hands.

'Very well, sir.' Pike went out wearing the same expression as Burman's.

★   ★   ★   ★

Lying back in his chair McNaught muttered to himself. There was a feeling in his bones that something was sure to cause a last-minute ruckus. A shortage of any item would be serious enough unless covered by a previous report. A surplus would be bad, very bad. The former implied carelessness or misfortune. The latter suggested barefaced theft of government property in circumstances condoned by the commander.

For instance, there was that recent case of Williams of the heavy cruiser *Swift*. He'd heard of it over the spacevine when out around Bootes. Williams had been found in unwitting command of eleven reels of electric-fence wire when his official issue was ten. It had taken a court-martial to decide that the extra reel – which had formidable barter-value on a certain planet – had not been stolen from space-stores or, in sailor jargon, 'teleported aboard'. But Williams had been reprimanded. And that did not help promotion.

He was still rumbling discontentedly when Pike returned bearing a folder of foolscap sheets.

'Going to start right away, sir?'

'We'll have to.' He heaved himself erect, mentally bidded goodbye to time off and a taste of the bright lights. 'It'll take long enough to

'How the devil can I make an offog when I don't even know what it is?'

work right through from bow to tail. I'll leave the men's kit inspection to the last.'

Marching out of the cabin, he set forth towards the bow, Pike following with broody reluctance.

As they passed the open main-lock Peaslake observed them, bounded eagerly up the gangway and joined behind. A pukka member of the crew, he was a large dog whose ancestors had been more enthusiastic than selective. He wore with pride a big collar inscribed: *Peaslake – Property of S.S. Bustler.* His chief duties, ably performed, were to keep alien rodents off the ship and, on rare occasions, smell out dangers not visible to human eyes.

The three paraded forward, McNaught and Pike in the manner of men grimly sacrificing pleasure for the sake of duty, Peaslake with the panting willingness of one ready for any new game no matter what.

Reaching the bow-cabin, McNaught dumped himself in the pilot's seat, took the folder from the other. 'You know this stuff better than me – the chart-room is where I shine. So I'll read them out while you look them over.' He opened the folder, started on the first page. 'K1. Beam compass, type D, one of.'

'Check,' said Pike.

'K2. Distance and direction indicator, electronic, type JJ, one of.'

'Check.'

Peaslake planted his head in McNaught's lap, blinked soulfully and whined. He was beginning to get the others' viewpoint. This tedious itemizing and checking was a hell of a game. McNaught consolingly lowered a hand and played with Peaslake's ears while he ploughed his way down the list.

'K187. Foam rubber cushions, pilot and co-pilot, one pair.'

'Check.'

By the time First Officer Gregory appeared they had reached the tiny intercom cubby and poked around it in semi-darkness. Peaslake had long departed in disgust.

'M24. Spare minispeakers, three-inch, type T2, one set of six.'

'Check.'

Looking in, Gregory popped his eyes and said, 'What the devil is going on?'

'Major inspection due soon.' McNaught glanced at his watch. 'Go see if stores has delivered a load and if not why not. Then you'd better give me a hand and let Pike take a few hours off.'

'Does this mean land-leave is cancelled?'

'You bet it does – until after Hizonner has been and gone.' He glanced at Pike. 'When you get into the city search around and send back any of the crew you can find. No arguments or excuses. It's an order.'

Pike registered unhappiness. Gregory glowered at him, went away, came back and said, 'Stores will have the stuff here in twenty minutes' time.' With bad grace he watched Pike depart.

'M47. Intercom cable, woven-wire protected, three drums.'

'Check,' said Gregory, mentally kicking himself for returning at the wrong time.

The task continued until late in the evening, was resumed early next morning. By that time three-quarters of the men were hard at work inside and outside the vessel, doing their jobs as though sentenced to them for crimes contemplated but not yet committed.

Moving around the ship's corridors and catwalks had to be done crab-fashion, with a nervous sidewise edging. Once again it was being demonstrated that the Terran lifeform suffers from ye fear of wette paynt. The first smearer would have ten years willed off his unfortunate life.

It was in these conditions, in mid-afternoon of the second day, that McNaught's bones proved their feelings had been prophetic. He recited the ninth page while Jean Blanchard confirmed the presence and actual existence of all items enumerated. Two-thirds of the way down they hit the rocks, metaphorically speaking, and commenced to sink fast.

*   *   *   *

McNaught said boredly, 'V1097. Drinking-bowl, enamel, one of.'

'Is zis,' said Blanchard, tapping it.

'V1098. Offog, one.'

'*Quoi?*' asked Blanchard, staring.

'V1098. Offog, one,' repeated McNaught. 'Well, why are you looking thunderstruck? This is the ship's galley. You're the head cook.

You know what's supposed to be in the galley, don't you? Where's this offog?'

'Never hear of heem,' stated Blanchard, flatly.

'You must have done. It's on this equipment-sheet in plain, clear type. Offog, one, it says. It was here when we were fitted-out four years ago. We checked it ourselves and signed for it.'

'I signed for nossings called offog,' Blanchard denied. 'In zee cuisine zere is no such sing.'

'Look!' McNaught scowled and showed him the sheet.

Blanchard looked and sniffed disdainfully. 'I have here zee electronic oven, one of. I have jacketed boilers, graduated capacities, one set. I have bain marie pans, seex of. But no offog. Never heard of heem. I do not know of heem.' He spread his hands and shrugged. 'No Offog.'

'There's got to be,' McNaught insisted. 'What's more, when Cassidy arrives there'll be hell to pay if there isn't.'

'You find heem,' Blanchard suggested.

'You got a certificate from the International Hotels School of Cookery. You got a certificate from the Cordon Bleu College of Cuisine. You got a certificate with three credits from the Space-Navy Feeding Centre,' McNaught pointed out. 'All that – and you don't know what an offog is.'

'*Nom d'un chien!*' ejaculated Blanchard, waving his arms around. 'I tell you ten t'ousand time zere is no offog. Zere never was an offog. Escoffier heemself could not find ze offog, of vich zere is none. Am I a magician perhaps?'

'It's part of the culinary equipment,' McNaught maintained. 'It must be because it's on page nine. And page nine means its proper home is in the galley, care of the head cook.'

'Like hail it does,' Blanchard retorted. He pointed at a metal box on the wall. 'Intercom booster. Is zat mine?'

McNaught thought it over, conceded, 'No, it's Burman's. His stuff rambles all over the ship.'

'Zen ask heem for zis bloody offog,' said Blanchard, triumphantly.

'I will. If it's not yours it must be his. Let's finish this checking first. If I'm not systematic and thorough Cassidy will jerk down my pants along with my insignia.' His eyes sought the list. 'V1099. Inscribed collar, leather, brass studded, dog, for the use of. No need to look for that. I saw it myself five minutes ago.' He ticked the item, continued, 'V1100. Sleeping basket, woven reed, one of.'

'Is zis,' said Blanchard, kicking it into a corner.

'V1101. Cushion, foam rubber, to fit sleeping basket, one of.'

'Half of,' Blanchard contradicted. 'In four years he have chewed away other half.'

'Maybe Cassidy will let us indent for a new one. It doesn't matter. We're okay so long as we can produce the half we've got.' McNaught stood up, closed the folder. 'That's the lot for here, I'll go see Burman about this missing item.'

★ ★ ★ ★

Burman switched off a UHF receiver, removed his earplugs and raised a questioning eyebrow.

'In the galley we're short an offog,' explained McNaught, 'Where is it?'

'Why ask me? The galley is Blanchard's bailiwick.'

'Not entirely. A lot of your cables run through it. You've two terminal boxes in there, also an automatic switch and an intercom booster. Where's the offog?'

'Never heard of it,' said Burman, baffled.

McNaught shouted, 'Don't tell me that! I'm already fed up hearing Blanchard saying it. Four years back we had an offog. It says so here. This is our copy of what we checked and signed for. It says we signed for an offog. Therefore we must have one. It's got to be found before Cassidy gets here.'

'Sorry, sir,' sympathized Burman. 'I can't help you.'

'You can think again,' advised McNaught. 'Up in the bow there's a direction and distance indicator. What do *you* call it?'

'A didin,' said Burman mystified.

'And,' McNaught went on, pointing at the pulse transmitter, 'what do you call *that*?'

'The opper-popper.'

'Baby names, see? Didin and opper-popper. Now rack your brains and remember what you called an offog four years ago.'

'Nothing,' asserted Burman, 'has ever been called an offog to my knowledge.'

'Then,' demanded McNaught, 'why the blue blazes did we sign for one?'

'I didn't sign for anything. You did all the signing.'

'While you and others did the checking. Four years ago, presumably in the galley, I said, "Offog, one," and either you or Blanchard pointed to it and said, "Check." I took somebody's word for it. I have to take other specialists' words for it. I am an expert navigator, familiar with all the latest navigational gadgets but not with other stuff. So I'm compelled to rely on people who know what an offog is – or ought to.'

Burman had a bright thought. 'All kinds of oddments were dumped in the main lock, the corridors and the galley when we were fitted out. We had to sort through a deal of stuff and stash it where it properly belonged, remember? This offog-thing might be any place today. It isn't necessarily my responsibility or Blanchard's.'

'I'll see what the other officers say,' agreed McNaught, conceding the point. 'Gregory, Worth, Sanderson; or one of the others may be coddling the item. Wherever it is, it's got to be found.'

He went out. Burman pulled a face, inserted his earplugs, resumed fiddling with his apparatus. An hour later McNaught came back wearing a scowl.

'Positively,' he announced with ire, 'there is no such thing on the ship. Nobody knows of it. Nobody can so much as guess at it.'

'Cross it off and report it lost,' Burman suggested.

'What, when we're hard aground? You know as well as I do that loss and damage must be signalled at time of occurrence. If I tell Cassidy the offog went west in space, he'll want to know when, where, how and why it wasn't signalled. There'll be a real ruckus if the contraption happens to be valued at half a million credits. I can't dismiss it with any airy wave of the hand.'

'What's the answer then?' inquired Burman, innocently ambling straight into the trap.

'There's one and only one,' McNaught announced. '*You* will manufacture an offog.'

'Who? *Me?*' said Burman, twitching his scalp.

'You and no other. I'm fairly sure the thing is your pigeon, anyway.'

'Why?'

'Because it's typical of the baby-names used for your kind of stuff.

I'll bet a month's pay that an offog is some sort of scientific allamagoosa. Something to do with fog, perhaps. Maybe a blind-approach gadget.'

'The blind-approach tranceiver is called "the fumbly",' Burman informed.

'There you are!' said McNaught as if that clinched it. 'So you will make an offog. It will be completed by six tomorrow evening and ready for my inspection then. It had better be convincing, in fact pleasing.'

Burman stood up, let his hands dangle, and said in hoarse tones, 'How the devil can I make an offog when I don't even know what it is?'

'Neither does Cassidy know,' McNaught pointed out, leering at him. 'He's more of a quantity surveyor than anything else. As such he counts things, looks at things, certifies that they exist, accepts advice on whether they are functionally satisfactory or worn out. All we need do is concoct an imposing allamagoosa and tell him it's the offog.'

'Holy Moses!' said Burman, fervently.

'Let us not rely on the dubious assistance of Biblical characters,' McNaught reproved. 'Let us use the brains that God has given us. Get a grip on your soldering-iron and make a topnotch offog by six tomorrow evening. That's an order!'

He departed, satisfied with this solution. Behind him, Burman gloomed at the wall and licked his lips once, twice.

★   ★   ★   ★

Rear Admiral Vane W. Cassidy arrived dead on time. He was a short, paunchy character with a floral complexion and eyes like those of a long-dead fish. His gait was an important strut.

'Ah, Captain, I trust that you have everything shipshape.'

'Everything usually is,' assured McNaught, glibly. 'I see to that.'

'Good!' approved Cassidy. 'I like a commander who takes his responsibilities seriously. Much as I regret saying so, there are a few who do not.' He marched through the main lock, his cod-eyes taking note of the fresh white enamel. 'Where do you prefer to start, bow or tail?'

'My equipment-sheets run from bow backward. We may as well deal with them the way they're set.'

'Very well.' He trotted officiously towards the nose, paused on the way to pat Peaslake and examine his collar. 'Well cared-for, I see. Has the animal proved useful?'

'He saved five lives on Mardia by barking a warning.'

'The details have been entered in your log, I suppose?'

'Yes, sir. The log is in the chart-room awaiting your inspection.'

'We'll get to it in due time.' Reaching the bow-cabin, Cassidy took a seat, accepted the folder from McNaught, started off at businesslike pace. 'K1. Beam compass, type D. One of.'

'This is it, sir,' said McNaught, showing him.

'Still working properly?'

'Yes, sir.'

They carried on, reached the intercom-cubby, the computer-room, a succession of other places back to the galley. Here, Blanchard posed in freshly laundered white clothes and eyed the newcomer warily.

'V.147. Electronic oven, one of.'

'Is zis,' said Blanchard, pointing with disdain.

'Satisfactory?' inquired Cassidy, giving him the fishy-eye.

'Not beeg enough,' declared Blanchard. He encompassed the entire galley with an expressive gesture. 'Nossings beeg enough. Place too small. Everysings too small. I am chef de cuisine an' she is a cuisine like an attic.'

'This is a warship, not a luxury liner.' Cassidy snapped. He frowned at the equipment-sheet. 'V148. Timing device, electronic oven, attachment thereto, one of.'

'Is zis,' spat Blanchard, ready to sling it through the nearest port if Cassidy would first donate the two pins.

Working his way down the sheet, Cassidy got nearer and nearer while nervous tension built up. Then he reached the critical point and said, 'V1098. Offog, one.'

'*Morbleau!*' said Blanchard, shooting sparks from his eyes, 'I have say before an' I say again, zere never was—'

'The offog is in the radio-room, sir,' McNaught chipped in hurriedly.

'Indeed?' Cassidy took another look at the sheet. 'Then why is it recorded along with galley equipment?'

'It was placed in the galley at time of fitting-out, sir. It's one of those portable instruments left to us to fix up where most suitable.'

'H'm! Then it should have been transferred to the radio-room list. Why didn't you transfer it?'

'I thought it better to wait for your authority to do so, sir.'

The fish-eyes registered gratification. 'Yes, that is quite proper of you, Captain. I will transfer it now.' He crossed the item from sheet nine, initialled it, entered it on sheet sixteen, initialled that. 'V1099. Inscribed collar, leather . . . oh, yes, I've seen that. The dog was wearing it.'

He ticked it. An hour later he strutted into the radio-room. Burman stood up, squared his shoulders but could not keep his feet or hands from fidgeting. His eyes protruded slightly and kept straying towards McNaught in silent appeal. He was like a man wearing a porcupine in his breeches.

'V1098. Offog, one,' said Cassidy in his usual tone of brooking no nonsense.

Moving with the jerkiness of a slightly unco-ordinated robot, Burman pawed a small box fronted with dials, switches and coloured lights. It looked like a radio ham's idea of a fruit machine. He knocked down a couple of switches. The lights came on, played around in intriguing combinations.

'This is it, sir,' he informed with difficulty.

'Ah!' Cassidy left his chair and moved across for a closer look. 'I don't recall having seen this item before. But there are so many different models of the same things. Is it still operating efficiently?'

'Yes, sir.'

'It's one of the most useful things in the ship,' contributed McNaught, for good measure.

'What does it *do*?' inquired Cassidy, inviting Burman to cast a pearl of wisdom before him.

Burman paled.

Hastily, McNaught said, 'A full explanation would be rather involved and technical but, to put it as simply as possible, it enables us to strike a balance between opposing gravitational fields. Variations in lights indicate the extent and degree of unbalance at any given time.'

'It's a clever idea,' added Burman, made suddenly reckless by this news, 'based upon Finagle's Constant.'

'I see,' said Cassidy, not seeing at all. He resumed his seat, ticked the offog and carried on. 'Z44. Switchboard, automatic, forty-line intercom, one of.'

'Here it is, sir.'

Cassidy glanced at it, returned his gaze to the sheet. The others used his momentary distraction to mop perspiration from their foreheads.

Victory had been gained.

All was well.

For the third time, hah!

★   ★   ★   ★

Rear Admiral Vane W. Cassidy departed pleased and complimentary. Within one hour the crew bolted to town. McNaught took turns with Gregory at enjoying the gay lights. For the next five days all was peace and pleasure.

On the sixth day Burman brought in a signal, dumped it upon McNaught's desk and waited for the reaction. He had an air of gratification, the pleasure of one whose virtue is about to be rewarded.

> *Terran Headquarters to BUSTLER. Return here immediately for overhaul and refitting. Improved power-plant to be installed. Feldman. Navy Op. Command. Sirisec.*

'Back to Terra,' commented McNaught, happily. 'And an overhaul will mean at least one month's leave.' He eyed Burman. 'Tell all officers on duty to go to town at once and order the crew aboard. The men will come running when they know why.'

'Yes, sir,' said Burman, grinning.

Everyone was still grinning two weeks later when the Siriport had receded far behind and Sol had grown to a vague speck in the sparkling mist of the bow starfield. Eleven weeks still to go, but it was worth it. Back to Terra. Hurrah!

In the captain's cabin the grins abruptly vanished one evening when Burman suddenly developed the willies. He marched in, chewed his bottom lip while waiting for McNaught to finish writing in the log.

Finally, McNaught pushed the book away, glanced up, frowned. 'What's the matter with you? Got a bellyache or something?'

'No, sir. I've been thinking.'

'Does it hurt that much?'

'I've been thinking,' persisted Burman in funereal tones. 'We're going back for overhaul. You know what that means. We'll walk off the ship and a horde of experts will walk onto it.' He stared tragically at the other. 'Experts, I said.'

'Naturally they'll be experts,' McNaught agreed. 'Equipment cannot be tested and brought up to scratch by a bunch of dopes.'

'It will require more than a mere expert to bring the offog up to scratch,' Burman pointed out. 'It'll need a genius.'

McNaught rocked back, swapped expressions like changing masks. 'Jumping Judas! I'd forgotten all about that thing. When we get to Terra we won't blind *those* boys with science.'

'No, sir, we won't,' endorsed Burman. He did not add any more but his face shouted aloud. 'You got me into this. You get me out of it.' He waited quite a time while McNaught did some intense thinking, then prompted, 'What do you suggest, sir?'

Slowly the satisfied smile returned to McNaught's features as he answered, 'Break up the contraption and feed it into the disintegrator.'

'That doesn't solve the problem,' said Burman. 'We'll still be short an offog.'

'No we won't. Because I'm going to signal its loss owing to the hazards of space-service.' He closed one eye in an emphatic wink. 'We're in free flight right now.' He reached for a message-pad and scribbled on it while Burman stood by vastly relieved.

> *BUSTLER to Terran Headquarters. Item V1098, Offog, one, came apart under gravitational stress while passing through twin-sun field Hector Major-Minor. Material used as fuel. McNaught, Commander. BUSTLER.*

Burman took it to the radio-room and beamed it Earthward. All was peace and progress for another two days. The next time he went to the captain's cabin he went running.

'General call, sir,' he announced breathlessly and thrust the message into the other's hands.

> *Terran Headquarters for relay all sectors. Urgent and Important. All ships grounded forthwith. Vessels in flight under official orders will make for nearest spaceport pending further instructions. Welling. Alarm and Rescue Command. Terra.*

'Something's gone bust,' commented McNaught, undisturbed. He traipsed to the chartroom, Burnham following. Consulting the charts, he dialled the intercom phone, got Pike in the bow and ordered. 'There's a panic. All ships grounded. We've got to make for Zaxtedport, about three days' run away. Change course at once. Starboard seventeen degrees, declination ten.' Then he cut off, griped, 'Bang goes that sweet month on Terra. I never did like Zaxted, either. It stinks. The crew will feel murderous about this and I don't blame them.'

'What d'you think has happened, sir?' asked Burman.

'Heaven alone knows. The last general call was seven years ago when the *Starider* exploded halfway along the Mars run. They grounded every ship in existence while they investigated the cause.' He rubbed his chin, pondered, went on, 'And the call before that one was when the entire crew of the *Blowgun* went nuts. Whatever it is this time, you can bet it's serious.'

'It wouldn't be the start of a space-war?'

'Against whom?' McNaught made a gesture of contempt. 'Nobody has the ships with which to oppose us. No, it's something technical. We'll learn of it eventually. They'll tell us before we reach Zaxted or soon afterward.'

They did tell him. Within six hours. Burman rushed in with face full of horror.

'What's eating you now?' demanded McNaught, staring at him.

'The offog,' stuttered Burman. He made motions as though brushing off invisible spiders.

'What of it?'

'It's a typographical error. In your copy it should read off. dog.'

'Off. dog?' echoed McNaught, making it sound like foul language.

'See for yourself.' Dumping the signal on the desk, Burman bolted out, left the door swinging. McNaught scowled after him, picked up the message.

> *Terran Headquarters to BUSTLER. Your report V1098, ship's official dog Peaslake. Detail fully circumstances and manner in which animal came apart under gravitational stress. Cross-examine crew and signal all coincidental symptoms experienced by them. Urgent and Important. Welling. Alarm and Rescue Command. Terra.*

In the privacy of his cabin McNaught commenced to eat his nails. Every now and again he went a little cross-eyed as he examined them for nearness to the flesh.

The Drop

John Christopher

Water was always short between the planets, even on a boat like the *Ironrod*. My first trip in Forbeston was always to the pool. I stripped down to trunks, u-v-checked, and plunged out into the green tinted water. After blowing around a while, I lay back and floated. Above, beyond the almost invisible protective dome, there was the purple velvet of the Martian sky, flecked, now that the sun was low on the horizon, with the larger stars. One of them, unwinking and tremendous, was green.

From the pool to the club; the usual routine. The Senior Officer's Club was on the corner of 49th and X, just across from the Department of Commerce building. I had belonged to it two years ago now, and at 34 was no longer the youngest member. A prodigy of 31 had got his master's ticket two or three months before.

I checked in, and from his little cubby-hole Steve recognized me, which was certainly an honour. He brought my mail down from its box; half a dozen bills, two vocoletters from a distant cousin, and a pile of advertising vocoflips. Steve said:

'Where've you been, Captain Newsam?'

The individual naming was another part of his technique: I had noticed that people he really had known for years he just called 'Captain,' 'Commodore,' or whatever it was.

'Venus–Mercury run,' I told him. 'Clarke's Point–Karsville–Mordecai – the usual.'

'You get around,' he said. 'I stick here.'

I'd heard the complaint from him before; from others in Forbeston and at other landfalls. They mostly looked contented enough, though.

'One place is like another.'

'Yes,' he said. 'I've heard that. What you're used to, I figure. Going into eats?'

'Directly.' I dropped the vocoflips in a disposal chute. 'Do something for me, Steve.'

'Any single thing.'

'Check me Captain Gains.'

He didn't hesitate long, but I'm used to observing small actions and probing them. I did a thesis on behaviour for my diploma. I saw Steve's eyes flicker, and the involuntary movement of his hands.

He said: 'I'll check him, Captain. I haven't seen him around much lately.'

I said quietly: 'How lately?'

He was smooth again. 'Well, you know how it is. With serving officers you don't always know whether they're here or away. Even when they're at Forbeston, they don't always come into the club. Hunting trips and such.'

'Your memory's not bad, Steve. Just when did you last see him?'

He pretended to consider. 'Might be two months. How long you been gone?'

'Just over two months.'

'Yes. I should say that's it.'

'Thanks. Check him for me all the same. Check him all over. I'm going into eats.'

I found an empty table by the window, and ordered. This part of the club overlooked the playground of the Forbeston Junior School; I sat eating and watching the generation that would be taking over when I had completed my twenty years in space and was ready to retire to the plantation up in the hills. I didn't notice when someone came up to the table. He tapped the back of my chair.

'Mind if I join you?'

It was Matthews, from the *Firelake*. I had run into him at various times, in various places, and liked him well enough. I nodded, and he sat down.

'Just in?'

'Three hours back.'

He nodded. 'Been in over a week myself. We're on the Uranus trip now. That's a duty trip I shall be glad to see the end of. We lost the *Steelback* last run. It's a godforsaken stretch of sky.'

'One place is very like another,' I said. It was a conventional phrase.

Matthews glanced at me. 'Glad you think so.'

'What else?'

'People get ideas,' he said vaguely. 'Do you go near the Earth at all on your present run?'

'The Moon. Clarke's Point. Why?'

'We used to do Tycho. They've got a telescope there that's pretty good. I used to get into the observatory. You can make out quite small groups of buildings when the weather's right.'

The conversation was becoming embarrassing. To mention the Earth at all was bad enough; to speak of 'weather' was something worse. I looked at Matthews. He seemed normal, but I thought I detected a watchfulness behind the placidity of his expression.

I said deliberately: 'I've never given it a thought.'

He said: 'Sometimes people get funny. We had a second officer with us three or four years back. He got an idea in his head that the Earth was raising a battle fleet. He used to spend his off-duty time at the look-out screen watching for the enemy cruisers approaching.'

I laughed. 'What did they do with him?'

'They gave him the drop. I guess he knows better by now.'

'If he's still alive.'

Matthews paused for a moment. 'Have you ever thought about why we drop the misfits back to Earth?'

I looked at him again. 'What is there to think about? The reason's obvious enough. Since the ruling was made against prefrontal leucotomy, it's the only alternative to snuffing them out. Unless they are maintained in institutions at our expense.'

He drained his coffee. 'I've known some say we should never have abandoned the Earth. It's richer in natural resources than all the planets together.'

I added: 'And populated to the tune of around a billion savages. We couldn't dispose of that lot, and we couldn't avoid being contaminated if we had to live amongst them. The reason our kind came to the planets was to get away from them; to be able to develop our superior humanity in peace and without interruption. We've got the Sirius project under way. In a couple of centuries we may be in a different system altogether.'

'Or we may not,' Matthews said. 'There have been quite a few earlier projects, starting with the Proxima Centauri project. That was two hundred years ago.'

I said: 'You sound pessimistic.'

'It's the Uranus trip,' he said. He grinned. 'Forget it. One place is like another. Doing anything tonight?'

'Nothing much. Looking a friend up.'

'Yes,' he said. 'I thought you might be.'

The remark was, I felt, an enigmatic one. He left without waiting for me to reply to it.

I passed Steve on the way out.

'Any luck with Captain Gains?' I asked him.

He shook his head.

'Forget it then. I'm going along to his place. There'll be a message, even if he isn't there.'

Steve nodded. As I went out he flicked the vidiphone switch in front of him.

Larry's bubble was seven or eight kilometres outside the city. I took my own car to the West Lock, and picked up a tracker there. The sun had set when I got outside the city bubble, but Phobos was up and I didn't need to use the main lights to see my way. I made a good twenty and in about a quarter hour was under the ridge on which the bubble that surrounded Larry's place was fixed. I could see it shimmering in the full moonlight, but there was no sign of a light within.

I parked the tracker outside and went in. The lock was automatic; as it closed behind me the main lights inside went on. Larry's shack was in front of me. I pushed the door open. The living-room looked reasonably tidy. But there was dust that showed no one had been in for some weeks at least. I went straight across to the vidiphone and pressed the message button. The screen stayed blank.

This was unusual. There should have been some kind of message. I set out to hunt through the shack for some kind of clue. But there was nothing.

Larry Gains and I went through college at Tycho together, and we graduated together. Our first four years in space we were on the same boat – the *Greylance* on the Asteroids Circuit – and after the inevitable split came with my posting to the *Ironrod* we still saw as much of each other as our wanderings permitted. Fortunately both boats were based on Forbeston. Six months before the old *Greylance* had made its last loop round the Belt; a chunk of rock weighing twenty tons or more had torn her open. Larry had been one of the survivors, but with injuries enough to ground him for at least a year. It was then he had had this shack put up. It was a handy base from which to hunt rocktrotters. I had stayed out there with him on a couple of leaves. Now the place was deserted. Might he have been seconded back into space on a special board? An extended trip, up onto the Kayser plateau? Then again there should have been a message; but he might not have expected to be long away. That seemed the only possible solution. But there was the thick dust, and there was the funny look in Steve's eye when his name was mentioned. I began hunting aimlessly round the hut again. A tape of the Forbeston edition of the Tycho Capsule. I slipped it into the screen 24– 7. That made it just over two months' old.

I didn't hear any sound from outside. I heard the door open behind me and turned round, half expecting to see Larry himself there. But there were two men in medical uniform. One of them stepped forward.

'Captain Newsam?' He framed it as a question, but it was a statement. I knew that. I nodded.

'Just a check up,' he said. 'We won't keep you long.'

I said. 'I had a check up. This afternoon. When I got in with the *Ironrod*.'

'That's all right,' the medic said. 'We won't keep you long.'

'You won't keep me at all,' I said. 'I've had my check up. You can reach me through Venus Base, if you're interested.'

I moved to pass them. The one who had been talking didn't do anything. The other raised his left hand and shook it gently. Venusian arodate, of course, and they themselves immunized against it. I saw the golden dust shake out towards me and had time to run two or three paces before my muscles seized up and everything went black.

I awoke in the Medical building, back in Forebeston. My muscles were still rigid. I was on a stretcher underneath the Verifier. The two medics were there, and a medic Captain. He was a little tubby man, with ginger whiskers and a toothy grin.

He said, 'Sorry about the informality. Just a routine. We did have a warrant, incidentally, in case you should feel like registering against us.'

Being underneath the Verifier explained the arodate, but it didn't explain why. I thought of saying something and then decided to keep my mouth shut. The electrodes were clamped neatly behind my ears. The globe of the Verifier glowed its normal pink.

The captain said: 'My name's Pinski. Now, Captain Newsam. You are Chief Navigator on the *Ironrod*, on the Venus-Mercury run?'

'Yes.'

'Landfall five hours back?'

'If I've been out half an hour – yes.'

The questions continued, for the most part routine. Pinski kept one eye on the Verifier globe. Then he started tossing a few more unusual ones in.

'Ever been among the outer planets?'

'Beyond the Asteroids? No.'

'Do you know Commander Leopold?'

'No.'

'Commander Stark?'

'No.'

'What are your views on leucotomy?'

'Never thought about it. It's not used now, is it? They give them the drop.'

'On the Sirius project?'

'Not much interested.'

'Do you ever dream of wide stretches of water?'

'Not since I was a boy.'

I had no reason to fear anything from the Verifier so it didn't make me nervous. The globe stayed pink as the questions went on.

Pinski said: 'What were you doing at the place the medics found you?'

I said: 'It's my theory that you know very well. I was looking for Captain Gains. Perhaps you'll tell me where I can get hold of him?'

Pinski grinned. 'I'm not under the Verifier, Captain Newsam.' He stepped back. 'I think that's all O.K. Sorry to have bothered you. In two or three minutes you'll be able to get about again. Call in the bar on your way out. Third on the right along the corridor. I'll be in there. The drinks are on Medical.'

I found him all right. He was sitting at a table with two drinks in front of him. Someone must have told him I drank sloe gin. I sat down at the empty chair.

'Glad to make your acquaintance in a more formal manner, Captain Newsam,' Pinski said. 'Have a drink.'

I took it. 'Now just why—'

He lifted one hand. 'To get things quite straight, I can give you no information as to the reason for your being picked up and verified.'

'Right,' I said. 'Then do you know where I can find Gains?'

He hesitated briefly. 'The answer must be no,' he said.

I swallowed the drink. 'Thank you very much, for all the hospitality. Goodnight, Captain Pinski.'

'A piece of strictly medical advice,' he said. 'Go back to bed and have a good night's sleep.'

I called back, 'Thanks!' I was halfway to the door.

★   ★   ★   ★

Forbeston, like all landfalls on the interplanetary routes, has its less respectable side. I drove down to the East Side, and parked the car at the corner of 90th and J. The Persepolis is a small club at the far end of 90th. I'm known there, but every time I go I feel less and less like boasting of it. I had a couple of sloe gins at the bar and then went up to the Saturn room. Cynthia came at me from behind.

'Hello! Long time.'

'Seems longer,' I said. 'Tell me. When was Larry in last?'

'Larry? I haven't seen him since you were both up here – nine, ten weeks ago. But I've been away on a trip up the Long Canal. Tell you what, I'll ask Sue.'

'That'll be fine,' I said.

She was gone two or three minutes. When she came back, she said: 'No. He doesn't seem to have been around since then.'

But she wasn't being spontaneous any longer; she was weighing her words. And she didn't seem at all curious as to what might have happened to him.

I said: 'I thought we were friends, Cynthia. Come on, what is it?'

'What's that? I could do with a drink.'

I dropped a note on the table.

'Have this one on Larry. 'Night, Cynthia.'

She caught me before I reached the door.

'I don't know, Jake. I honestly don't know. All I was told was that it was best not to inquire.'

She was telling the truth now.

'Thanks,' I said. 'Goodnight, anyway.'

'Where are you going?'

'There's only one place where I stand a chance of finding things out.'

I was thinking about that as I went outside. The Terminal Office had tabs on all officers on the space routes. If Larry had not been reporting for his fortnightly medical boards they would know, and they would certainly have checked to see what was happening. If there was something else wrong, they would still know. I jumped into the car without thinking and released her. Behind me a familiar voice said:

'You don't seem to have had any luck in finding your friends, Captain Newsam.'

It was Matthews. His tall body was cramped into the back of the car.

'Good of you to join me,' I said.

'I'd like you to drop along to my place. It's on 72nd.'

'Is there anything at the end of it? Information?'

'A drink. And maybe information.'

'That will do,' I told him. 'What number?'

It was a more luxurious apartment than I should have thought Matthews could have run to. Four rooms, all well appointed. He set me down in a long chair in front of a glow-fire and brought me the drink. He had it right, too, but the fact that everyone knew my taste in liquor had ceased to worry me.

'Now,' I said. 'I want to know where Larry Gains is.'

Matthews raised his eyebrows. 'Gains . . . ah, he will be this friend you didn't find.'

I said wearily: 'What information do you think I came for?'

'I thought you came for the drink,' he said. 'No, don't go. If you go along to the Terminal Office at this time you'll only get the night-clerk who will tell you to come back in the morning. Finish your drink, and have another. I understand you got picked up for verification earlier this evening?'

'Yes.'

'What sort of questions did they ask you?'

I told him and he nodded.

'Leopold . . . Stark . . . That's interesting.'

'Now,' I said. 'Just what is it all about?'

He paused. 'That little talk we had this afternoon. Remember it?'

'More or less. You were talking about misfits.'

Matthews looked straight at me. 'Captain Larry Gains was classified as a misfit three weeks ago. He will have been dropped to Earth over a week ago. Is that what you wanted to know?'

I said: 'You're off your rocker yourself. Larry was perfectly sane when I saw him just over two months ago. It takes two boards three months apart for misfit classification.'

'Not,' Matthews said softly, 'for classification 3-K.'

'3-K?'

'Organised activities against the State.'

'I can believe that of him even less.'

'Tell me,' Matthews said. 'What do you know about the Earth?'

'Ordinary general knowledge. That when the third atomic war broke out on Earth, the colonies on the Moon and here on Mars declared their neutrality. The technical staffs on the Earth bases for the most part pulled out to join them; those that didn't presumably got sub-merged in the holocaust. The state of the war was followed by wireless until the last transmitter went off the air, marking the breakdown. The colonies concentrated on their own expansion – first on the Moon and Mars; later on Venus and with the outposts in the Asteroids and on the moons of Jupiter, Saturn and Uranus. There was no point in going back to an Earth poisoned with radioactive gases, with a savage popula-tion rotted by radiation diseases. The obvious thing was to expand outwards, towards other systems.'

'And, of course,' Matthews said, 'there was the Protocol.'

I suppose the Protocol could be called the basis of our education. That the old and outworn should be put behind; that man should go on to greater things, never turning back to the world of misery and wretchedness to which he had for so long been confined. There was a lot more, but that was the gist of it. Children learned it by heart.

'Yes, the Protocol,' I said. 'The Protocol rose naturally enough out of the circumstances.'

'Yes,' Matthews agreed. 'Out of the circumstances. But circumstances change. The Protocol remains the same.'

'Why shouldn't it?'

'Well, grubbing around from one artificial environment to another – do you think that's the best existence men can have? Turning our backs on an unbelievably fruitful planet?'

'It's only a temporary phase. The Sirius project . . .'

'. . . Is a failure,' Matthews said. 'We shan't be told about that officially until a new project has been got going – another carrot in front of the donkey. But it's a failure. Two planets. Neither habitable nor capable of being made habitable.'

I said slowly: 'Now perhaps you will tell me just what all this has to do with Larry Gains.'

Matthews got up and walked across to the telescreen. He touched a small switch on the left-hand side, and the screen moved into patterns of whorls spreading out from the centre. I recognised it for a watcher-alarm: if anyone were tapping the room the whorls would be irregular and broken. Matthews came back and sat down again.

'Gains had a lot of time on his hands after his crack-up. He got to thinking things over. He happened to meet someone in our group; to put it shortly, he joined us?'

I echoed: 'Your group? Joined you?'

Matthews said: 'We represent a party whose objective is to overthrow the Protocol. We want to get back to Earth, to recolonise it and reclaim it from savagery. Gains came in with us.'

I said: 'I think you're crazy. What makes you think you know better than the Directorate? We're improving conditions on the planets every year. The new bubble up the Long Canal takes in over forty square kilometres.'

'Bigger bubbles,' Matthews said, 'but always bubbles. Never the chance to live a natural life in natural surroundings.'

'And Larry? You let him get caught?'

'It was bad luck.'

'Bad luck?'

'Yes, bad luck. He and another had their conversation tapped. They were both taken. Fortunately neither of them knew more than a couple in the group – and those two got away. We couldn't do anything for Gains and Bessemer. They held them strictly.'

'So he's really gone. You're sure they're not still holding him somewhere?'

'On some points our information is definite. They've been dropped all right. On the North American continent – that's the usual place they drop misfits.'

Something had been worrying me all along, and suddenly I knew what it was. I said warily:

'Well, I've got the information I came in search of. Now I'm beginning to wonder why I got it. I don't imagine you thought I would be a cinch for your organisation just because Larry had been in it? And yet, you've told me a lot of stuff which you can't be in the habit of passing out casually. What's behind it?'

Matthews said evenly: 'Well, we haven't told you anything the Directorate doesn't know. Except that I'm in it, and I have my means of getting away; in any case, I'm expendable. But you're correct in thinking there was a reason. Gains was a good friend of yours.'

'The best.'

'He was a good man. We didn't want to lose him, and we'd like to get him back.'

'Back! From Earth?'

'We have a small cruiser at our disposal – that is confidential and I've burned both your boats and ours by telling you – and we can get down to the Earth and back again. But it isn't easy, and of course there can be no question of organising search parties. But if someone else were dropped with instructions for Gains and Bessemer as to a spot to go to be picked up . . . all three could be brought off. We're fortunate in that misfits are always dropped in more or less the same area. It means finding them. It might be possible.'

'What's known about conditions in that part of the planet?'

Matthews looked at me levelly. 'Not a thing.'

I paused. 'O.K. I'll go. How do I go about it?'

I'm a Stranger Here Myself

Mack Reynolds

The Place de France is the town's hub. It marks the end of Boulevard Pasteur, the main drag of the westernized part of the city, and the beginning of Rue de la Liberté, which leads down to the Grand Socco and the Medina. In a three minute walk from the Place De France you can go from an ultra-modern, California-like resort to the Baghdad of Harun-al-Rashid.

It's quite a town, Tangier.

King-size sidewalk cafés occupy three of the strategic corners on the Place de France. The Café de Paris serves the best draught beer in town, gets all the better custom, and has three shoeshine boys attached to the establishment. You can sit of a sunny morning and read the Paris edition of the New York *Herald Tribune* while getting your shoes done up like mirrors for thirty Moroccan francs, which comes to about five cents at current exchange.

You can sit there, after the paper's read, sip your expresso, and watch the people go by.

Tangier is possibly the most cosmopolitan city in the world. In native costume you'll see Berber and Rif, Arab and Blue Man, and occasionally a Senegalese from further south. In European dress you'll see Japs and Chinese, Hindus and Turks, Levantines and Filipinos,

'Meanwhile they send secret missions down from time to time to keep an eye on your progress.'

North Americans and South Americans, and, of course, even Europeans
– from both sides of the Curtain.

In Tangier you'll find some of the world's poorest and some of the
richest. The poorest will try to sell you anything from a shoeshine to
their not very lily-white bodies, and the richest will avoid your eyes,
afraid *you* might try to sell them something.

In spite of recent changes, the town still has its unique qualities. As a
result of them the permanent population includes smugglers and
blackmarketeers, fugitives from justice and international con men,
espionage and counter-espionage agents, homosexuals, nympho-
maniacs, alcoholics, drug addicts, displaced persons, ex-royalty, and
subversives of every flavour. Local law limits the activities of few of
these.

Like I said, it's quite a town.

★   ★   ★   ★

I looked up from my *Herald Tribune* and said, 'Hello, Paul. Anything
new cooking?'

He sank into the chair opposite me and looked around for the waiter.
The tables were all crowded and since mine was a face he recognized,
he assumed he was welcome to intrude. It was more or less standard
procedure at the Café de Paris. It wasn't a place to go if you wanted to
be alone.

Paul said, 'How are you, Rupert? Haven't seen you for donkey's
years.'

The waiter came along and Paul ordered a glass of beer. Paul was an
easygoing, sallow-faced little man. I vaguely remembered somebody
saying he was from Liverpool and in exports.

'What's in the newspaper?' he said, disinterestedly.

'Pogo and Albert are going to fight a duel,' I told him, 'and Lil
Abner is becoming a rock'n'roll singer.'

He grunted.

'Oh,' I said, 'the intellectual type.' I scanned the front page. 'The
Russkies have put up another manned satellite.'

'They have, eh? How big?'

'Several times bigger than anything we Americans have.'

The beer came and looked good, so I ordered a glass too.

Paul said, 'What ever happened to those poxy flying saucers?'

'What flying saucers?'

A French girl went by with a poodle so finely clipped as to look as though it'd been shaven. The girl was in the latest from Paris. Every pore in place. We both looked after her.

'You know what everybody was seeing a few years ago. It's too bad one of these bloody manned satellites wasn't up then. Maybe they would've seen one.'

'That's an idea,' I said.

We didn't say anything else for a while and I began to wonder if I could go back to my paper without rubbing him the wrong way. I didn't know Paul very well, but, for that matter, it's comparatively seldom you ever get to know anybody very well in Tangier. Largely, cards are played close to the chest.

My beer came and a plate of tapas for us both. Tapas at the Café de Paris are apt to be potato chips, a few anchovies, olives, and possibly some cheese. Free lunch, they used to call it in the States.

Just to say something, I said, 'Where do you think they came from?' And when he looked blank, I added, 'The flying saucers.'

He grinned. 'From Mars or Venus, or someplace.'

'Ummmm,' I said. 'Too bad none of them ever crashed, or landed on the Yale football field and said "Take me to your cheerleader", or something.'

Paul yawned and said, 'That was always the trouble with those crackpot blokes' explanations of them. If they were aliens from space, then why not show themselves?'

I ate one of the potato chips. It'd been cooked in rancid olive oil.

I said, 'Oh, there are various answers to that one. We could probably sit around here and think of two or three that made sense.'

Paul was mildly interested. 'Like what?'

'Well, hell, suppose for instance there's this big Galactic League of civilized planets. But it's restricted, see. You're not eligible for membership until you, well, say until you've developed space flight. Then you're invited into the club. Meanwhile, they send secret missions down from time to time to keep an eye on your progress.'

Paul grinned at me. 'I see you read the same poxy stuff I do.'

A Moorish girl went by dressed in a neatly tailored grey jellaba,

European style high-heeled shoes, and a pinkish silk veil so transparent that you could see she wore lipstick. Very provocative, dark eyes can be over a veil. We both looked after her.

I said, 'Or, here's another one. Suppose you have a very advanced civilization on, say, Mars.'

'Not Mars. No air, and too bloody dry to support life.'

'Don't interrupt, please,' I said with mock severity. 'This is a very old civilization and as the planet began to lose its water and air, it withdrew underground. Uses hydroponics and so forth, husbands its water and air. Isn't that what we'd do, in a few million years, if Earth lost its water and air?'

'I suppose so,' he said. 'Anyway, what about them?'

'Well, they observed how man is going through a scientific boom, an industrial boom, a population boom. A boom, period. Any day now he's going to have practical spaceships. Meanwhile, he's also got the H-Bomb, and the way he beats the drums on both sides of the Curtain, he's not against using it, if he could get away with it.'

Paul said, 'I got it. So they're scared and are keeping an eye on us. That's an old one. I've read that a dozen times, dished up different.'

I shifted my shoulders. 'Well, it's one possibility.'

'I got a better one. How's this? There's this alien life form that's way ahead of us. Their civilization is so old that they don't have any records of when it began and how it was in the early days. They've gone beyond things like wars and depressions and revolutions and greed for power, or any of these things giving us a bad time here on Earth. They're all like scholars, get it? And some of them are pretty jolly well taken by Earth, especially the way we are right now, with all the problems, get it? Things developing so fast we don't know where we're going or how we're going to get there.'

I finished my beer and clapped my hands for Mouley. 'How do you mean, "where we're going"?'

'Well, take half the countries in the world today. They're trying to industrialize, modernize, catch up with the advanced countries. Look at Egypt and Israel, and India and China, and Yugoslavia and Brazil, and all the rest. Trying to drag themselves up to the level of the advanced countries, and all using different methods of doing it. But look at the so-called advanced countries. Up to their bottoms in problems. Juvenile delinquents, climbing crime and suicide rates, the loony-bins full of the barmy, unemployment, threat of war, spending all their money on armaments instead of things like schools. All the bloody mess of it. Why, a man from Mars would be fascinated, like.'

Mouley came shuffling up in his babouche slippers and we both ordered another schooner of beer.

Paul said seriously, 'You know there's only one big snag in this sort of talk. I've sorted the whole thing out before, and you always come up against this brick wall. Where are they, these observers, or scholars, or spies or whatever they are? Sooner or later we'd nab one of them. You know, Scotland Yard, or the FBI, or Russia's secret police, or the French Sûreté, or Interpol. This world is so deep in police, counter-espionage outfits, and security agents that an alien would slip up in time, no matter how much he'd been trained. Sooner or later, he'd slip up, and they'd nab him.'

I shook my head. 'Not necessarily. The first time I ever considered this possibility, it seemed to me that such an alien would base himself in London or New York. Somewhere where he could use the libraries for research, get the daily newspapers and the magazines. Be right in the centre of things. But now I don't think so. I think he'd be right here in Tangier.'

'Why Tangier?'

'It's the one town in the world where anything goes. Nobody gives a damn about you or your affairs. For instance, I've known you a year or more now, and I haven't the slightest idea of how you make your living.'

'That's right,' Paul admitted. 'In this town you seldom even ask a man where he's from. He can be British, a White Russian, a Basque, or a Sikh and nobody could care less. Where are *you* from, Rupert?'

'California,' I told him.

'No, you're not,' he grinned.

I was taken aback. 'What do you mean?'

'I felt your mind probe back a few minutes ago when I was talking about Scotland Yard or the FBI possibly flushing an alien. Telepathy is a sense not trained by the humanoids. If they had it, your job –.and mine – would be considerably more difficult. Let's face it, in spite of these human bodies we're disguised in, neither of us is a humanoid. Where are you really from, Rupert?'

'Aldebaran,' I said. 'How about you?'

'Deneb,' he told me, shaking.

We had a laugh and ordered another beer.

'What're you doing here on Earth?' I asked him.

'Researching for one of our meat trusts. We're protein eaters. Humanoid flesh is considered quite a delicacy. How about you?'

'Scouting the place for thrill tourists. My job is to go around to these backward cultures and help stir up inter-tribal or international conflicts – all according to how advanced they are. Then our tourists come in – well shielded, of course – and get their kicks watching it.'

Paul frowned. 'That sort of practice could spoil an awful lot of good meat.'

The Luckiest Man in Denv

Cyril Kornbluth

May's man Reuben, of the eighty-third level, Atomist, knew there was something wrong when the binoculars flashed and then went opaque. Inwardly he cursed, hoping that he had not committed himself to anything. Outwardly he was unperturbed. He handed the binoculars back to Rudolph's man Almon, of the eighty-ninth level, Maintainer, with a smile.

'They aren't very good,' he said.

Almon put them to his own eyes, glanced over the parapet and swore mildly. 'Blacker than the heart of a crazy Angelo, eh? Never mind; here's another pair.'

This pair was unremarkable. Through it, Reuben studied the thousand setbacks and penthouses of Denv that ranged themselves below. He was too worried to enjoy his first sight of the vista from the eighty-ninth level, but he let out a murmur of appreciation. Now to get away from this suddenly sinister fellow and try to puzzle it out.

'Could we—?' he asked cryptically, with a little upward jerk of his chin.

'It's better not to,' Almon said hastily, taking the glasses from his hands. 'What if somebody with stars happened to see, you know? How'd *you* like it if you saw some impudent fellow peering up at you?'

'He wouldn't dare!' said Reuben, pretending to be stupid and indignant, and joined a moment later in Almon's sympathetic laughter.

'Never mind,' said Almon. 'We are young. Some day, who knows? Perhaps we shall look from the ninety-fifth level, or the hundredth.'

Though Reuben knew that the Maintainer was no friend of his, the generous words sent blood hammering through his veins; ambition for a moment.

He pulled a long face and told Almon: 'Let us hope so. Thank you for being my host. Now I must return to my quarters.'

He left the windy parapet for the serene luxury of an eighty-ninth-level corridor and descended slow moving stairs through gradually less luxurious levels to his own Spartan floor. Selene was waiting, smiling, as he stepped off the stairs.

She was decked out nicely – too nicely. She wore a steely hued corselet and a touch of scent; her hair was dressed long. The combination appealed to him, and instantly he was on his guard. Why had she gone to the trouble of learning his tastes? What was she up to? After all, she was Griffin's woman.

'Coming *down*?' she asked, awed. 'Where have you been?'

'The eighty-ninth, as a guest of that fellow Almon. The vista is immense.'

'I've never been . . .' she murmured, and then said decisively: 'You belong up there. And higher. Griffin laughs at me, but he's a fool. Last night in chamber we got to talking about you, I don't know how, and he finally became quite angry and said he didn't want to hear another word.' She smiled wickedly. 'I was revenged, though.'

Blank-faced, he said: 'You must be a good hand at revenge, Selene, and at stirring up the need for it.'

The slight hardening of her smile meant that he had scored and he hurried by with a rather formal salutation.

Burn him for an Angelo, but she was easy enough to take! The contrast of the metallic garment with her soft, white skin was disturbing, and her long hair suggested things. It was hard to think of her as scheming something or other; scheming Selene was displaced in his mind by Selene in chamber.

But what was she up to? Had she perhaps heard that he was to be elevated? Was Griffin going to be swooped on by the Maintainers?

Was he to kill off Griffin so she could leech onto some rising third party? Was she perhaps merely giving her man a touch of the lash?

He wished gloomily that the binoculars-problem and the Selene-problem had not come together. That trickster Almon had spoken of youth as though it were something for congratulation; he hated being young and stupid and unable to puzzle out the faulty binoculars and the warmth of Griffin's woman.

The attack alarm roared through the Spartan corridor. He ducked through the nearest door into a vacant bedroom and under the heavy steel table. Somebody else floundered under the table a moment later, and a third person tried to join them.

The firstcomer roared: 'Get out and find your own shelter! I don't propose to be crowded out by you or to crowd you out either and see your ugly blood and brains if there's a hit. Go, now!'

'Forgive me, sir! At once, sir!' the latecomer wailed; and scrambled away as the alarm continued to roar.

Reuben gasped at the 'sirs' and looked at his neighbour. It was May! Trapped, no doubt, on an inspection tour of the level.

'Sir,' he said respectfully, 'if you wish to be alone, I can find another room.'

'You may stay with me for company. Are you one of mine?' There was power in the general's voice and on his craggy face.

'Yes, sir. May's man Reuben, of the eighty-third level, Atomist.'

May surveyed him, and Reuben noted that there were pouches of skin depending from cheekbones and the jaw line – dead-looking, coarse-pored skin.

'You're a well-made boy, Reuben. Do you have women?'

'Yes, sir,' said Reuben hastily. 'One after another – I *always* have women. I'm making up at this time to a charming thing called Selene. Well-rounded, yet firm, soft but supple, with long red hair and long white legs—'

'Spare me the details,' muttered the general. 'It takes all kinds. An Atomist, you said. That has a future, to be sure. I myself was a Controller long ago. The calling seems to have gone out of fashion—'

Abruptly the alarm stopped. The silence was hard to bear.

May swallowed and went on: '—for some reason or other. Why don't youngsters elect for Controller any more? Why didn't you?'

Reuben wished he could be saved by a direct hit. The binoculars, Selene, the raid, and now he was supposed to make intelligent conversation with a general.

'I really don't know, sir,' he said miserably. 'At the time there seemed to be very little difference – Controller, Atomist, Missiler, Maintainer. We have a saying, "The buttons are different", which usually ends any conversation on the subject.'

'Indeed?' asked May distractedly. His face was thinly filmed with sweat. 'Do you suppose Ellay intends to clobber us this time?' he asked almost hoarsely. 'It's been some weeks since they made a maximum effort, hasn't it?'

'Four,' said Reuben. 'I remember because one of my best Servers was killed by a falling corridor roof – the only fatality and it had to happen to my team!'

He laughed nervously and realized that he was talking like a fool, but May seemed not to notice.

Far below them, there was a series of screaming whistles as the interceptors were loosed to begin their intricate, double basketwork wall of defence in a towering cylinder about Denv.

'Go on, Reuben,' said May. 'That was most interesting.' His eyes were searching the underside of the steel table.

Reuben averted his own eyes from the frightened face, feeling some awe drain out of him. Under a table with a general! It didn't seem so strange now.

'Perhaps, sir, you can tell me what a puzzling thing, that happened this afternoon, means. A fellow – Rudolph's man Almon, of the eighty-ninth level – gave me a pair of binoculars that flashed in my eyes and then went opaque. Has your wide experience—'

May laughed hoarsely and said in a shaky voice: 'That old trick! He was photographing your retinas for the blood-vessel pattern. One of Rudolph's men, eh? I'm glad you spoke to me; I'm old enough to spot a revival like that. Perhaps my good friend Rudolph plans—'

There was a thudding volley in the air and then a faint jar. One had got through, exploding, from the feel of it, far down at the foot of Denv.

The alarm roared again, in bursts that meant all clear; only one flight of missles and that disposed of.

The Atomist and the general climbed out from under the table; May's secretary popped through the door. The general waved him out again and leaned heavily on the table, his arms quivering. Reuben hastily brought a chair.

The Atomist brought it. He saw the general wash down what looked like a triple dose of xxx – green capsules which it was better to leave alone.

May said after a moment: 'That's better. And don't look so shocked, youngster; you don't know the strain we're under. It's only a temporary measure which I shall discontinue as soon as things ease up a bit. I was saying that perhaps my good friend Rudolph plans to substitute one of his men for one of mine. Tell me, how long has this fellow Almon been a friend of yours?'

'He struck up an acquaintance with me only last week. I should have realized—'

'You certainly should have. One week. Time enough and more. By now you've been photographed, your fingerprints taken, your voice recorded and your gait studied without your knowledge. Only the retinascope is difficult, but one must risk it for a real double. Have you killed your man, Reuben?'

He nodded. It had been a silly brawl two years ago over precedence at the refectory; he disliked being reminded of it.

'Good,' said May grimly. 'The way these things are done, your double kills you in a secluded spot, disposes of your body and takes over your role. We shall reverse it. You will kill the double and take over *his* role.'

The powerful, methodical voice ticked off possibilities and contingencies, measures, and countermeasures. Reuben absorbed them and felt his awe return. Perhaps May had not really been frightened under the table; perhaps it had been he reading his own terror in the general's face. May was actually talking to him of backgrounds and policies. 'Up from the eighty-third level!' he swore to himself as the great names were uttered.

'My good friend Rudolph, of course, wants the five stars. You would not know this, but the man who wears the stars is now eighty years old and failing fast. I consider myself a likely candidate to replace him. So, evidently, must Rudolph. No doubt he plans to have your

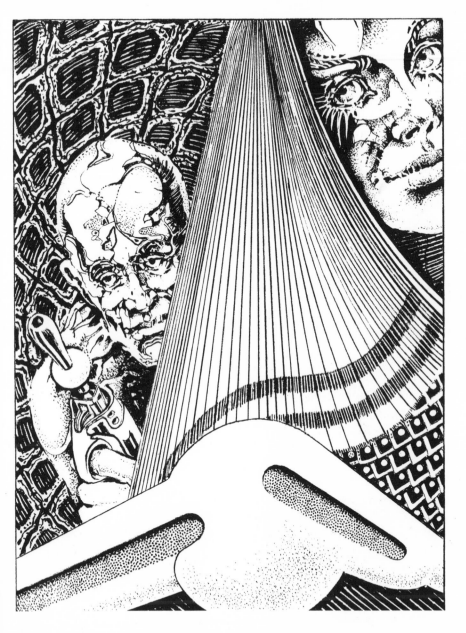

Reuben took a pistol from under his pillow and demanded, 'When do you expect him?'

double perpetrate some horrible blunder on the eve of the election, and the discredit would reflect on me. Now what you and I must do—'

You and I – May's man Reuben and May – up from the eighty-third! Up from the bare corridors and cheerless bedrooms to marble halls and vaulted chambers! From the clatter of the crowded refectory to small and glowing restaurants where you had your own table and servant and where music came softly from the walls! Up from the scramble to win this woman or that, by wit or charm or the poor bribes you could afford, to the eminence from which you could calmly command your pick of the beauty of Denv! From the moiling intrigue of tripping your fellow Atomist and guarding against him tripping you to the heroic thrust and parry of generals!

Up from the eighty-third!

Then May dismissed him with a speech whose implications were deliriously exciting. 'I need an able man and a young one, Reuben. Perhaps I've waited too long looking for him. If you do well in this touchy business, I'll consider you very seriously for an important task I have in mind.'

Late that night, Selene came to his bedroom.

'I know you don't like me,' she said pettishly, 'but Griffin's such a fool and I wanted somebody to talk to. Do you mind? What was it like up there today? Did you see carpets? I wish I had a carpet.'

He tried to think about carpets and not the exciting contrast of metallic cloth and flesh.

'I saw one through an open door,' he remembered. 'It looked odd, but I suppose a person gets used to them. Perhaps I didn't see a very good one. Aren't the good ones very thick?'

'Yes,' she said. 'Your feet sink into them. I wish I had a *good* carpet and four chairs and a small table as high as my knees to put things on and as many pillows as I wanted. Griffin's such a fool. Do you think I'll ever get those things? I've never caught the eye of a general. Am I pretty enough to get one, do you think?'

He said uneasily: 'Of course you're a pretty thing, Selene. But carpets and chairs and pillows—' It made him uncomfortable, like the thought of peering up through binoculars from a parapet.

'I want them,' she said unhappily. 'I like you very much, but I want so many things and soon I'll be too old even for the eighty-third level, before I've been up higher, and I'll spend the rest of my life tending babies or cooking in the creche or the refectory.'

She stopped abruptly, pulled herself together and gave him a smile that was somehow ghastly in the half-light.

'You bungler,' he said, and she instantly looked at the door with the smile frozen on her face. Reuben took a pistol from under his pillow and demanded, 'When do you expect him?'

'What do you mean?' she asked shrilly. 'Who are you talking about?'

'My double. Don't be a fool, Selene. May and I—' he savoured it – 'May and I know all about it. He warned me to beware of a diversion by a woman while the double slipped in and killed me. When do you expect him?'

'I really *do* like you,' Selene sobbed. 'But Almon promised to take me up there and I *knew* when I was where they'd see me that I'd meet somebody really important. I really do like you, but soon I'll be too old—'

'Selene, listen to me. Listen to me! You'll get your chance. Nobody but you and me will know that the substitution didn't succeed!'

'Then I'll be spying for you on Almon, won't I?' she asked in a choked voice. 'All I wanted was a few nice things before I got too old. All right, I was supposed to be in your arms at 2350 hours.'

It was 2349. Reuben sprang from bed and stood by the door, his pistol silenced and ready. At 2350 a naked man slipped swiftly into the room, heading for the bed as he raised a ten-centimetre poignard. He stopped in dismay when he realized that the bed was empty.

Reuben killed him with a bullet through the throat.

'But he doesn't look a bit like me,' he said in bewilderment, closely examining the face. 'Just in a general way.'

Selene said dully: 'Almon told me people always say that when they see their doubles. It's funny, isn't it? He looks just like you, really.'

'How was my body to be disposed of?'

She produced a small flat box. 'A shadow suit. You were to be left here and somebody would come tomorrow.'

'We won't disappoint him.' Reuben pulled the web of the shadow suit over his double and turned on the power. In the half-lit room, it was a perfect disappearance; by daylight it would be less perfect.

'They'll ask why the body was shot instead of knifed. Tell them you shot me with the gun from under the pillow. Just say I heard the double come in and you were afraid there might have been a struggle.'

She listlessly asked: 'How do you know I won't betray you?'

'You won't, Selene.' His voice bit. 'You're *broken*.'

She nodded vaguely, started to say something and then went out without saying it.

Reuben luxuriously stretched in his narrow bed. Later, his beds would be wider and softer, he thought. He drifted into sleep on a half-formed thought that some day he might vote with other generals on the man to wear the five stars – or even wear them himself, Master of Denv.

He slept healthily through the morning alarm and arrived late at his regular twentieth-level station. He saw his superior, May's man Oscar of the eighty-fifth level, Atomist, ostentatiously take his name. Let him!

Oscar assembled his crew for a grim announcement: 'We are going to even the score, and perhaps a little better, with Ellay. At sunset there will be three flights of missiles from Deck One.'

There was a joyous murmur and Reuben trotted off on his task.

All forenoon he was occupied with drawing plutonium slugs from hyper-suspicious storekeepers in the great rock-quarried vaults, and seeing them through countless audits and assays all the way to Weapons Assembly. Oscar supervised the scores there who assembled the curved slugs and the explosive lenses into sixty-kilogram warheads.

In mid-afternoon there was an incident. Reuben saw Oscar step aside for a moment to speak to a Maintainer whose guard fell on one of the Assembly Servers, and dragged him away as he pleaded innocence. He had been detected in sabotage. When the warheads were in and the Missilers seated, waiting at their boards, the two Atomists rode up to the eighty-third's refectory.

The news of a near-maximum effort was in the air; it was electric. Reuben heard on all sides in tones of self-congratulation: 'We'll clobber them tonight!'

'That Server you caught,' he said to Oscar. 'What was he up to?'

His commander stared. 'Are you trying to learn my job? Don't try it, I warn you. If my black marks against you aren't enough, I could always arrange for some fissionable material in your custody to go astray.'

'No, no! I was just wondering why people do something like that.'

Oscar sniffed doubtfully. 'He's probably insane, like all the Angelos. I've heard the climate does it to them. You're not a Maintainer or a Controller. Why worry about it?'

'They'll brainburn him, I suppose?'

'I suppose. *Listen!*'

Deck One was firing. One, two, three, four, five, six. One, two, three, four, five, six. One, two, three, four, five, six.

People turned to one another and shook hands, laughed and slapped shoulders heartily. Eighteen missiles were racing through the stratosphere, soon to tumble on Ellay. With any luck, one or two would slip through the first wall of interceptors and blast close enough to smash windows and topple walls in the crazy city by the ocean. It would serve the lunatics right.

Five minutes later an exultant voice filled most of Denv.

'Recon missile report,' it said. 'Eighteen launched, eighteen perfect trajectories. Fifteen shot down by Ellay first-line interceptors, three shot down by Ellay second-line interceptors. Extensive blast damage observed in Griffith Park area of Ellay!'

There were cheers.

And eight Full Maintainers marched into the refectory silently, and marched out with Reuben.

He knew better than to struggle or ask futile questions. Any question you asked of a Maintainer was futile. But he goggled when they marched him onto an upward-bound stairway.

They rode past the eighty-ninth level and Reuben lost count, seeing only the marvels of the upper reaches of Denv. He saw carpets that ran the entire length of corridors, and intricate fountains, and mosaic walls, stained-glass windows, more wonders than he could recognize, things for which he had no name.

He was marched at last into a wood-panelled room with a great polished desk and a map behind it. He saw May, and another man who must have been a general – Rudolph? – but sitting at the desk was a frail old man who wore a circlet of stars on each khaki shoulder.

The old man said to Reuben: 'You are an Ellay spy and saboteur.'

Reuben looked at May. Did one speak directly to the man who wore the stars, even in reply to such an accusation?

'Answer him, Reuben,' May said kindly.

'I am May's man Reuben, of the eighty-third level, an Atomist,' he said.

'Explain,' said the other general heavily, 'If you can, why all eighteen of the warheads you procured today failed to fire.'

'But they did!' gasped Reuben. 'The Recon missile report said there was blast damage from the three that got through and it didn't say anything about the others failing to fire.'

The other general suddenly looked sick and May looked even kindlier. The man who wore the stars turned inquiringly to the chief of the Maintainers, who nodded and said: 'That was the Recon missile report, sir.'

The general snapped: 'What I said was that he would *attempt* to sabotage the attack. Evidently he failed. I also said he is a faulty double, somehow slipped with great ease into my good friend May's organization. You will find that his left thumb print is a clumsy forgery of the real Reuben's thumb print and that his hair has been artificially darkened.'

The old man nodded at the chief of the Maintainers, who said: 'We have his card, sir.'

Reuben abruptly found himself being fingerprinted and deprived of some hair.

'The f.p.s check, sir,' one Maintainer said. 'He's Reuben.'

'Hair's natural, sir,' said another.

The general began a rearguard action: 'My information about his hair seems to have been inaccurate. But the fingerprint means only that Ellay spies substituted his prints for Reuben's prints in the files—'

'Enough, sir,' said the old man with the stars. 'Dismissed. All of you. Rudolph, I am surprised. All of you, go.'

Reuben found himself in a vast apartment with May, who was bubbling uncontrollably until he popped three of the green capsules into his mouth hurriedly.

'This means the eclipse for years of my good friend Rudolph,' he crowed. 'His game was to have your double sabotage the attack warheads and so make it appear that my organization is rotten with spies.

The double must have been under post-hypnotic, primed to admit everything. Rudolph was so sure of himself that he made his accusations before the attack, the fool!'

He fumbled out the green capsules again.

'Sir,' said Reuben, alarmed.

'Only temporary,' May muttered, and swallowed a fourth. 'But you're right. You leave them alone. There are big things to be done in your time, not in mine. I told you I needed a young man who could claw his way to the top. Rudolph's a fool. He doesn't need the capsules because he doesn't ask questions. Funny, I thought a coup like the double affair would hit me hard, but I don't feel a thing. It's not like the old days. I used to plan and plan, and when the trap went *snap* it was better than this stuff. But now I don't feel a thing.'

He leaned forward from his chair; the pupils of his eyes were black bullets.

'Do you want to *work?*' he demanded. 'Do you want your world stood on its head and your brains to crack and do the only worthwhile job there is to do? Answer me!'

'Sir, I am a loyal May's man. I want to obey your orders and use my ability to the full.'

'Good enough,' said the general. 'You've got brains, you've got push. I'll do the spade work. I won't last long enough to push it through. You'll have to follow. Ever been outside of Denv?'

Reuben stiffened.

'I'm not accusing you of being a spy. It's really all right to go outside of Denv. I've been outside. There isn't much to see at first – a lot of ground pocked and torn up by shorts and overs from Ellay and us. Farther out, especially east, it's different. Grass, trees, flowers. Places where you could grow food.

'When I went outside, it troubled me. It made me ask questions. I wanted to know how we started. Yes – started. *It wasn't always like this.* Somebody built Denv. Am I getting the idea across to you? *It wasn't always like this!*

'Somebody set up the reactors to breed uranium and make plutonium. Somebody tooled us up for the missiles. Somebody wired the boards to control them. Somebody started the hydroponics tanks.

'I've dug through the archives. Maybe I found something. I saw mountains of strength reports, ration reports, supply reports, and yet I never got back to the beginning. I found a piece of paper and maybe I understood it and maybe I didn't. It was about the water of the Colorado River and who should get how much of it. How can you divide water in a river? But it could have been the start of Denv, Ellay, and the missile attacks.'

The general shook his head, puzzled, and went on: 'I don't see clearly what's ahead. I want to make peace between Denv and Ellay, but I don't know how to start or what it will be like. I think it must mean not firing, not even making any more weapons. Maybe it means that some of us, or a lot of us, will go out of Denv and live a different kind of life. That's why I've clawed my way up. That's why I need a young man who can claw with the best of them. Tell me what you think.'

'I think,' said Reuben measuredly, 'it's magnificent – the salvation of Denv. I'll back you to my dying breath if you'll let me.'

May smiled tiredly and learned back in the chair as Reuben tiptoed out.

What luck, Reuben thought – what unbelievable luck to be at a fulcrum of history like this!

He searched the level for Rudolph's apartment and gained admission.

To the general, he said: 'Sir, I have to report that your friend May is insane. He has just been raving to me, advocating the destruction of civilization as we know it, and urging me to follow in his footsteps. I pretended to agree – since I can be of greater service to you if I'm in May's confidence.'

'So?' said Rudolph thoughtfully. 'Tell me about the double. How did that go wrong?'

'The bunglers were Selene and Almon. Selene because she alarmed me instead of distracting me. Almon because he failed to recognize her incompetence.'

'They shall be brainburned. That leaves an eightyninth-level vacancy in my organization, doesn't it?'

'You're very kind, sir, but I think I should remain a May's man – outwardly. If I earn any rewards, I can wait for them. I presume that May will be elected to wear the five stars. He won't live more than two years after that, at the rate he is taking drugs.'

'We can shorten it,' grinned Rudolph. 'I have pharmacists who can see that his drugs are more than normal strength.'

'That would be excellent, sir. When he is too enfeebled to discharge his duties, there may be an attempt to rake up the affair of the double to discredit you. I could then testify that I was your man all along and that May coerced me.'

They put their heads together, the two saviours of civilization as they knew it, and conspired ingeniously long into the endless night.

Obedience

Fredric Brown

On a tiny planet of a far, faint star, invisible from Earth, and at the farther edge of the galaxy, five times as far as man has yet penetrated into space, there is a statue of an Earthman. It is made of precious metal and it is a tremendous thing, fully ten inches high, exquisite in workmanship.

Bugs crawl on it . . .

★　　　★　　　★　　　★

They were on a routine patrol in Sector 1534, out past the Dog Star, many parsecs from Sol. The ship was the usual two-man scout used for all patrols outside the system. Captain May and Lieutenant Ross were playing chess when the alarm rang.

Captain May said, 'Reset it, Don, while I think this out.' He didn't look up from the board; he knew it couldn't be anything but a passing meteor. There weren't any ships in this sector. Man had penetrated space for a thousand parsecs and had not as yet encountered an alien life form intelligent enough to communicate, let alone to build spaceships.

Ross didn't get up either, but he turned around in his chair to face the instrument board and the telescreen. He glanced up casually and gasped; there *was* a ship on the screen. He got his breath back enough to say 'Cap!' and then the chessboard was on the floor and May was looking over his shoulder.

He could hear the sound of May's breathing, and then May's voice said, 'Fire, Don!'

'But that's a Rochester Class cruiser! One of ours. I don't know what it's doing here, but we can't—'

'*Look again.*'

Don Ross couldn't look again because he'd been looking all along, but he suddenly saw what May had meant. It was almost a Rochester, but not quite. There was something *alien* about it. Something? It *was* alien; it was an alien imitation of a Rochester. And his hands were racing for the firing button almost before the full impact of that hit him.

Finger at the button, he looked at the dials on the Picar ranger and the Monold. They stood at zero.

He swore. 'He's jamming us, Cap. We can't figure out how far he is, or his size and mass!'

Captain May nodded slowly, his face pale.

Inside Don Ross's head, a thought said, '*Compose yourselves, men. We are not enemies.*'

Ross turned and stared at May. May said, 'Yes, I got it. Telepathy.'

Ross swore again. *If they were telepathic—*

'Fire, Don. Visual.'

Ross pressed the button. The screen was filled with a flare of energy, but when the energy subsided, there was no wreckage of a spaceship . . .

*   *   *   *

Admiral Sutherland turned his back to the star chart on the wall and regarded them sourly from under his thick eyebrows. He said, 'I am not interested in rehashing your formal report, May. You've both been under the psychograph; we've extracted from your minds every minute of the encounter. Our logicians have analyzed it. You are here for discipline. Captain May, you know the penalty for disobedience.'

May said stiffly, 'Yes, sir.'

'It is?'

'Death, sir.'

'And what order did you disobey?'

'General Order Thirteen-Ninety, Section Twelve. Quad-A priority. Any terrestrial ship, military or otherwise, is ordered to destroy immediately, on sight, any alien ship encountered. If it fails to do so, it must blast off towards outer space, in a direction not exactly opposite that of Earth, and continue until fuel is exhausted.'

'And the reason for that, Captain? I ask merely to see if you know. It is not, of course, important or even relevant whether or not you understand the reason for any ruling.'

'Yes, sir. So there is no possibility of the alien ship following the sighting ship back to Sol and so learning the location of Earth.'

'Yet you disobeyed that ruling, Captain. You were not certain that you had destroyed the alien. What have you to say for yourself?'

'We did not think it necessary, sir. The alien ship did not seem hostile. Besides, sir, they must already know our base; they addressed us as "men."'

'Nonsense! The telepathic message was broadcast from an alien mind, but was received by yours. Your minds automatically translated the message into your own terminology. He did not necessarily know your point of origin or that you were humans.'

Lieutenant Ross had no business speaking, but he asked, 'Then, sir, it is not believed that they were friendly?'

The admiral snorted. 'Where did you take your training, Lieutenant? You seem to have missed the most basic premise of our defence plans, the reason we've been patrolling space for four hundred years, on the lookout for alien life. *Any alien is an enemy.* Even though he were friendly today, how could we know that he would be friendly next year or a century from now? And a potential enemy is an enemy. The more quickly he is destroyed the more secure Earth will be.

'Look at the military history of the world! It proves that, if it proves nothing else. Look at Rome! To be safe she couldn't afford powerful neighbours. Alexander the Great! Napoleon!'

'Sir,' said Captain May. 'Am I under the penalty of death?'

'Yes.'

'Then I may as well speak. Where is Rome now? Alexander's empire or Napoleon's? Nazi Germany? Tyrannosaurus rex?'

'Who?'

'Man's predecessor, the toughest of the dinosaurs. His name means "king of the tyrant lizards". He thought every other creature was his enemy, too. And where is he now?'

'Is that all you have to say, Captain?'

'Yes, sir.'

'Then I shall overlook it. Fallacious, sentimental reasoning. You are *not* under sentence of death, Captain. I merely said so to see what you would say, how far you would go. You are not being shown mercy because of any humanitarian nonsense. A truly ameliorating circumstance has been found.'

'May I ask what, sir?'

'The alien *was* destroyed. Our technicians and logicians have worked that out. Your Picar and Monold were working properly. The only reason that they did not register was that the alien ship was too small. They will detect a meteor weighing as little as five pounds. The alien ship was smaller than that.'

'Smaller than—?'

'Certainly. You were thinking of alien life in terms of your own size. There is no reason why it should be. It could be even submicroscopic, too small to be visible. The alien ship must have contacted you deliberately, at a distance of only a few feet. And your fire, at that distance, destroyed it utterly. That is why you saw no charred hulk as evidence that it was destroyed.'

He smiled. 'My congratulations. Lieutenant Ross, on your gunnery. In the future, of course, visual firing will be unnecessary. The detectors and estimators on ships of all classes are being modified immediately to detect and indicate objects of even minute sizes.'

Ross said, 'Thank you, sir. But don't you think that the fact that the ship we saw, regardless of size, was an imitation of one of our Rochester Class ships is proof that the aliens already know much more of us than we do of them, including, probably, the location of our home planet? And that – even if they are hostile – the tiny size of their craft is what prevents them from blasting us from the system?'

'Possibly. Either both of those things are true, or neither. Obviously, aside from their telepathic ability, they are quite inferior to us technically – or they would not imitate our design in spaceships. And they must have read the minds of some of our engineers in order to duplicate that design. However, granting that is true, they may still not know the location of Sol. Space coordinates would be extremely difficult to translate, and the name Sol would mean nothing to them. Even its approximate description would fit thousands of other stars. At any rate, it is up to us to find and exterminate them before they find us. Every ship in space is now alterted to watch for them, and is being equipped with special instruments to detect small objects. A state of war exists. Or perhaps it is redundant to say that; a state of war always exists with aliens.'

'Yes, sir.'

'That is all, gentlemen. You may go.'

Outside in the corridor two armed guards waited. One of them stepped to each side of Captain May.

May said quickly, 'Don't say anything, Don. I expected this. Don't forget that I disobeyed an important order, and don't forget that the admiral said only that I wasn't under sentence of death. Keep yourself out of it.'

Hands clenched, teeth clamped tightly together, Don Ross watched the guards take away his friend. He knew May was right; there was nothing he could do except get himself into worse trouble than May was in, and make things worse for May.

But he walked almost blindly out of the Admiralty Building. He went out and got promptly drunk, but that didn't help.

He had the customary two weeks' leave before reporting back for space duty, and he knew he'd better straighten himself out mentally in that time. He reported to a psychiatrist and let himself be talked out of most of his bitterness and feeling of rebellion.

He went back to his schoolbooks and soaked himself in the necessity for strict and unquestioning obedience to military authority and the necessity of uncreasing vigilance for alien races and the necessity of their extermination whenever found.

He won out; he convinced himself how unthinkable it had been for him to believe that Captain May could have been completely pardoned for having disobeyed an order, for whatever reason. He even felt horrified for having himself acquiesced in that disobedience. Technically, of course, he was blameless; May had been in charge of the ship

and the decision to return to Earth instead of blasting out into space –
and death – had come from May. As a subordinate, Ross had not shared
the blame. But now, as a person, he felt conscience-stricken that he had
not tried to argue May out of his disobedience.

What would Space Corps be without obedience?

How could he make up for what he now felt to be his dereliction, his
his delinquency? He watched the telenewscasts avidly during that
period and learned that, in various other sectors of space, four more
alien ships had been destroyed. With the improved detection instruments all of them had been destroyed on sight; there had been no
communication after first contact.

On the tenth day of his leave, he terminated it of his own free will.
He returned to the Admiralty Building and asked for an audience with
Admiral Sutherland. He was laughed at, of course, but he had expected
that. He managed to get a brief verbal message carried through to the
admiral. Simply: 'I know a plan that may possibly enable us to find the
planet of the aliens, at no risk to ourselves.'

That got him in, all right.

He stood at rigid attention before the admiral's desk. He said, 'Sir,
the aliens have been trying to contact us. They have been unable because
we destroy them on contact before a complete telepathic thought has
been put across. If we permit them to communicate, there is a chance
that they will give away, accidentally or otherwise, the location of their
home planet.'

Admiral Sutherland said drily, 'And whether they did or not, they
might find out *ours* by following the ship back.'

'Sir, my plan covers that. I suggest that I be sent out into the same
sector where initial contact was made – this time in a one-man ship,
unarmed. That the fact that I am doing so be publicized as widely as
possible, so that every man in space knows it, and knows that I am in an
unarmed ship for the purpose of making contact with the aliens. It is
my opinion that they will learn of this. They must manage to get
thoughts at long distances, but to send thoughts – to Earth minds
anyway – only at very short distances.'

'How do you deduce that, Lieutenant? Never mind; it coincides
with what our logicians have figured out. They say that the fact that
they have stolen our science – as in their copying our ships on a smaller

scale – before we were aware of their existence proves their ability to read our thoughts at – well, a moderate distance.'

'Yes, sir. I am hoping that if news of my mission is known to the entire fleet it will reach the aliens. And knowing that my ship is unarmed, they will make contact. I will see what they have to say to me, to us, and possibly that message will include a clue to the location of their home planet.'

Admiral Sutherland said, 'And in that case that planet would last all of twenty-four hours. But what about the converse, Lieutenant? What about the possibility of their following you back?'

'That, sir, is where we have nothing to lose. I shall return to Earth *only if I find out that they already know its location.*

'With their telepathic abilities I believe they already do – and that they have not attacked us only because they are not hostile or are too weak. But whatever the case, if they know the location of Earth they will not deny it in talking to me. Why should they? It will seem to them a bargaining point in their favour, and they'll think we're bargaining. They might claim to know, even if they do not – but I shall refuse to take their word for it unless they give me proof.'

Admiral Sutherland stared at him. He said, 'Son, you *have* got something. It'll probably cost you your life, but – if it doesn't, and if you come back with news of where the aliens come from, you're going to be the hero of the race. You'll probably end up with *my* job. In fact, I'm tempted to steal your idea and make that trip myself.'

'Sir, you're too valuable. I'm expendable. Besides, sir, I've *got* to. It isn't that I want any honours. I've got something on my conscience that I want to make up for. I should have tried to stop Captain May from disobeying orders. I shouldn't be here now, alive. We should have blasted out into space, since we weren't sure we'd destroyed the alien.'

The admiral cleared his throat. 'You're not responsible for that, son. Only the captain of a ship is responsible, in a case like that. But I see what you mean. You feel you disobeyed orders, in spirit, because you agreed at the time with what Captain May did. All right, that's past, and your suggestion makes up for it, even if you yourself did not man the contact ship.'

'But may I, sir?'

'You may, Lieutenant. Rather, you may, Captain.'

'Thank you, sir.'

'A ship will be ready for you in three days. We could have it ready sooner, but it will take that long for word of our "negotiations" to spread throughout the fleet. But you understand – you are not, under any circumstances, to deviate on your own initiative from the limitations you have outlined.'

'Yes, sir. Unless the aliens already know the location of Earth and prove it completely, I shall not return. I shall blast off into space. I give you my word, sir.'

'Very good, Captain Ross.'

★ ★ ★ ★

The one-man spacer hovered near the centre of Sector 1534, out past the Dog Star. No other ship patrolled that sector.

Captain Don Ross sat quietly and waited. He watched the visiplate and listened for a voice to speak inside his head.

It came when he had waited less than three hours. *'Greetings, Donross,'* the voice said, and simultaneously there were five tiny spaceships outside his visiplate. His Monold showed that they weighed less than an ounce apiece.

He said, 'Shall I talk aloud or merely think?'

'It does not matter. You may speak if you wish to concentrate on a particular thought, but first be silent a moment.'

After half a minute, Ross thought he heard the echo of a sigh in his mind. Then: *'I am sorry. I fear this talk will do neither of us any good. You see, Donross, we do not know the location of your home planet. We could have learned, perhaps, but we were not interested. We were not hostile and from the minds of Earthmen we knew we dared not be friendly. So you will never be able, if you obey orders, to return to report.'*

Don Ross closed his eyes a moment. This, then, was the end; there wasn't any use talking further. He had given his word to Admiral Sutherland that he would obey orders to the letter.

'That is right,' said the voice. *'We are both doomed, Donross, and it does not matter what we tell you. We cannot get through the cordon of your ships; we have lost half our race trying.'*

'Half! Do you mean—?'

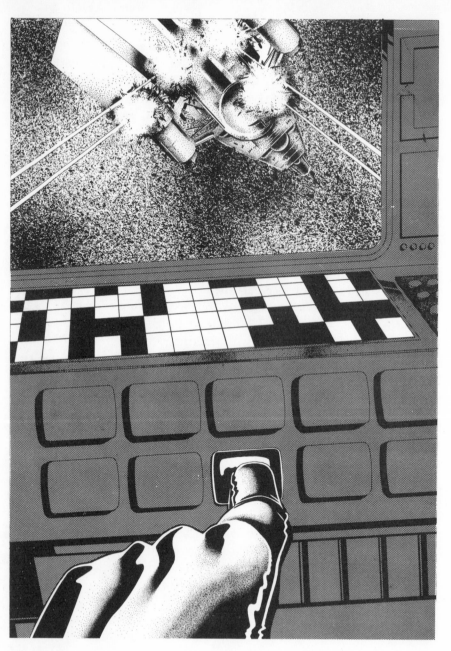

Ross pressed the button. The screen filled with a flash of energy.

'Yes. There were only a thousand of us. We built ten ships, each to carry a hundred. Five ships have been destroyed by Earthmen; there are only five ships left, the ones you see, the entire race of us. Would it interest you, even though you are going to die, to know about us?'

He nodded, forgetting that they could not see him, but the assent in his mind must have been read.

We are an old race, much older than you. Our home is – or was – a tiny planet of the dark companion of Sirius; it is only a hundred miles in diameter. Your ships have not found it yet, but it is only a matter of time. We have been intelligent for many, many millennia, but we never developed space travel. There was no need and we had no desire.

'Goodbye, Donross. *What is this strange emotion in your mind and the convulsion of your muscles? I do not understand it. But wait – it is your recognition of perceiving something incongruous. But the thought is too complex, too mixed. What is it?*'

Don Ross managed finally to stop laughing. 'Listen, my alien friend who cannot kill,' he said. 'I'm getting you out of this. I'm going to see that you get through our cordon to the safety you want. But what's funny is the way I'm going to do it. By obedience to orders and by going to my own death. I'm going to outer space, to die there. You, all of you, can come along and *live* there. Hitchhike. *Your tiny ships won't show on the patrol's detectors if they are touching this ship.* Not only that, but the gravity of this ship will pull you along and you won't have to waste fuel until you are well through the cordon and beyond the reach of its detectors. A hundred thousand parsecs, at least, before my fuel runs out.'

There was a long pause before the voice in Don Ross's mind said, '*Thank you.*' Faintly. Softly.

He waited until the five ships had vanished from his visiplate and he had heard five tiny sounds of their touching the hull of his own ship. Then he laughed once more. And obeyed orders, blasting off for space and death.

★   ★   ★   ★

On a tiny planet of a far, faint star, invisible from Earth, and at the farther edge of the galaxy, five times as far as man has yet penetrated into space, there is the statue of an Earthman. It is a tremendous thing, ten inches high, exquisite in workmanship.

Bugs crawl on it, but they have a right to; they made it, and they honour it. The statue is of very hard metal. On an airless world it will last forever – or until Earthmen find it and blast it out of existence. Unless, of course, by that time Earthmen have changed an awful lot.

Not for an Age

Brian Aldiss

A bedspring groaned and pinged, mists cleared, Rodney Furnell awoke. From the bathroom next door came the crisp sound of shaving; his son was up. The bed next to his was empty; Valerie, his second wife, was up. Guiltily, Rodney also rose, and performed several timid exercises to flex his backbone. Youth! When it was going it had to be husbanded. He touched his toes.

The audience had its first laugh there.

By the time Rodney had got into his Sunday suit, Valerie's cuckoo clock was chuckling nine, followed by the more sardonic notes of his ormolu chimer. Valerie and Jim (Rodney had conscientiously shunned a literary name for his only offspring) were already at the cornflakes when he entered their gay little kitchenette.

More laughter at the first sight of that antiquated twentieth-century modernity.

'Hello, both! Lovely morning,' he boomed, kissing Valerie's forehead. The September sun, in fact, was making a fair showing through damp mist; a man of forty-six instinctively arms himself with enthusiasm when facing a wife fifteen years younger.

The audience always loved the day's meals, murmuring with delight as each quaint accessory – toaster, teapot, sugar-tongs – was used.

Valerie looked fresh and immaculate. Jim sported an open-necked shirt and was attentive to his stepmother. At nineteen he was too manly and too attentive. . . . He shared the Sunday paper companionably with her, chatting about the theatre and books. Sometimes Rodney could join in about one of the books. Under the notion that Valerie disliked seeing him in spectacles, he refrained from reading at breakfast.

How the audience roared later when he slipped them on in his study! How he hated that audience! How fervently he wished that he had the power to raise even one eyebrow in scorn of them!

The day wore on exactly as it had for over a thousand times, unable to deviate in the slightest from its original course. So it would go on and on, as meaningless as a cliché, or a tune endlessly repeated, for the benefit of these fools who stood and laughed at the silliest things.

At first, Rodney had been frightened. This power to snatch them all as it were from the grave had seemed something occult. Then, becoming accustomed to it, he had been flattered that these wise beings had wanted to review *his* day, disinter *his* modest life. But it was balm only for a time; Rodney soon discovered he was simply a glorified side-show at some latter-day fair, a butt for fools and not food for philosophers.

He walked in the tumble-down garden with Valerie, his arm around her waist. The north Oxford air was mild and sleepy; the neighbour's radio was off.

'Have you *got* to go and see that desiccated old Regius Professor, darling?' she asked.

'You know I must.' He conquered his irritation and added: 'We'll go for a drive after lunch – just you and I.'

Unfailingly, each day's audience laughed at that. Presumably 'a drive after lunch' had come to mean something dubious. Each time Rodney made that remark, he dreaded the reaction from those half-glimpsed countenances that pressed on all sides; yet he was powerless to alter what had once been said.

He kissed Valerie, he hoped elegantly; the audience tittered, and he stepped into the garage. His wife returned to the house, and Jim. What happened in there he would never know, however many times the day was repeated. There was no way of confirming his suspicion that his son was in love with Valerie and she attracted to him. She should have enough sense to prefer a mature man to a stripling of nineteen;

besides, it was only eighteen months since he had been referred to in print as 'one of our promising young men of *litterae historicae*'.

Rodney could have walked round to Septuagint College. But because the car was new and something that his don's salary would hardly stretch to, he preferred to drive. The watchers, of course, shrieked with laughter at the sight of his little automobile. He occupied himself, as he polished the windshield, with hating the audience and all inhabitants of this future world.

That was the strange thing. There was room in the corner of the old Rodney mind for the new Rodney ghost. He depended on the old Rodney – the Rodney who had actually lived that fine, autumn day – for vision, motion, all the paraphernalia of life; but he could occupy independently a tiny cell of his consciousness. He was a helpless observer carried over and over in a cockpit of the past.

The irony of it lay there. He would have been spared all this humiliation if he did not know what was happening. But he did know, trapped though he was in an unknowing shell.

Even to Rodney, a history man and no scientist, the broad outline of what had happened was obvious enough. Somewhere in the future, man had ferreted out the secret of literally reclaiming the past. Bygone years lay in the rack of antiquity like film spools in a library. Like film spools, they were not amenable to change, but might be played over and over on a suitable projector. Rodney's autumn day was being played over and over.

He had reflected helplessly on the situation so often that the horror of it had worn thin. That day had passed, quietly, trivially, had been forgotten; suddenly, long afterwards, it had been whipped back among the things that were. Its actions, even its thoughts, had been reconstituted, with only Rodney's innermost ego to suffer from the imposition. How unsuspecting he had been then! How inadequate every one of his gestures seemed now, performed twice, ten, a hundred, a thousand times!

Had he been as smug every day as he was that day? And what had happened after that day? Having, naturally, no knowledge of the rest of his life then, he had none now. If he had been happy with Valerie for much longer, if his recently published work on feudal justice had been acclaimed – these were questions he could pose without answering.

A pair of Valerie's gloves lay on the back seat of the car; Rodney threw them into a locker with an éclat quite divorced from his inner impotence. She, poor dear bright thing, was in the same predicament. In that they were united, although powerless to express the union in any slightest flicker of expression.

He drove slowly down Banbury Road. As ever, there were four subdivisions of reality. There was the external world of Oxford; there were Rodney's original abstracted observations as he moved through the world; there were the ghost thoughts of the 'present-I', bitter and frustrated; there were the half-seen faces of the future which advanced or receded aimlessly. The four blended indefinably, one becoming another in Rodney's moments of near-madness. (What would it be like to be insane, trapped in a sane mind? He was tempted by the luxury of letting go.)

Sometimes he caught snatches of talk from the onlookers. They at least varied from day to day. 'If he knew what he looked like!' they would exclaim. Or: 'Do you see her hair-do?' Or: 'Can you beat that for a slum!' Or: 'Mummy, what's that funny brown thing he's eating?' Or – how often he heard that one: 'I just wish he knew we were watching him!'

Church bells were solemnly ringing as he pulled up outside Septuagint and switched off the ignition. Soon he would be in that fusty study, taking a glass of something with the creaking old Regius Professor. For the *n*th time he would be smiling a shade too much as the grip of ambition outreached the hand of friendship. His mind leaped ahead and back and ahead and back again in a frenzy. Oh, if he could only *do* something! So the day would pass. Finally, the night would come – one last gust of derision at Valerie's nightgown and his pyjamas! – and then oblivion.

Oblivion . . . that lasted an eternity but took no time at all. . . . And *they* wound the reel back and started it again, all over again.

He was pleased to see the Regius Professor. The Regius Professor was pleased to see him. Yes, it was a nice day. No, he hadn't been out of college since, let's see, it must be the summer before last. And then came that line that drew the biggest laugh of all; Rodney said, inevitably: 'Oh, we must all hope for some sort of immortality.'

To have to say it again, to have to say it not a shade less glibly than when it had first been said, and when the wish had been granted already in such a ludicrous fashion! If only he might die first, if only the film would break down!

★   ★   ★   ★

The universe flickered to a standstill and faded into dim purple. Temperature and sound slid down to zero. Rodney Furnell stood transfixed, his arms extended in the middle of a gesture, a wineglass in his right hand. The flicker, the purple, the zeroness cut down through him; but even as he sensed himself beginning to fade, a great fierce hope was born within him. With a burst of avidity, the ghost of him took over the old Rodney. Confidence flooded him as he fought back the negativity.

The wineglass vanished from his hand. The Regius Professor sank into twilight and was gone. Blackness reigned. Rodney turned around. It was a voluntary movement; *it was not in the script*; he was alive, free.

The bubble of twentieth-century time had burst, leaving him alive in the future. He stood in the middle of a black and barren area. There had evidently been a slight explosion. Overhead was a crane-like affair as big as a locomotive with several funnels protruding from its underside; smoke issued from one of the funnels. Doubtless the thing was a time-projector whatever it might be called, and obviously it had blown a fuse.

The scene about him engaged all Rodney's attention. He was delighted to see that his late audience had been thrown into mild panic. They shouted and pushed and – in one quarter – fought vigorously. Male and female alike, they wore featureless, transparent bags which encased them from neck to ankle – and they had had the impertinence to laugh at his pyjamas!

Cautiously, Rodney moved away. At first the idea of liberty overwhelmed him, he could scarcely believe himself alive. Then the realization came: his liberty was precious – how doubly precious after that most terrible form of captivity! – and he must guard it by flight. He hurried beyond the projection area, pausing at a great sign that read:

CHRONOARCHEOLOGY LTD PRESENTS –
THE SIGHTS OF THE CENTURIES
COME AND ENJOY THE ANTICS OF YOUR
ANCESTORS!
YOU'LL LAUGH AS YOU LEARN

And underneath: Please Take One.

Shaking, Rodney seized a gaudy folder and stuffed it into his pocket. Then he ran.

His guess about the fair-ground was correct, and Valerie and he had been merely a glorified peepshow. Gigantic booths towered on all sides. Gay crowds sauntered or stood, taking little notice as Rodney passed. Flags flew, silvery music sounded; nearby, a flashing sign begged: TRY ANTI-GRAV AND REALIZE YOUR DREAMS.

Farther on, a banner proclaimed:

THE SINISTER VENUSIANS ARE *HERE*!

Fortunately, a gateway was close. Dreading a detaining hand on his arm, Rodney made for it as quickly as possible. He passed a towering structure before which a waiting line of people gazed impatiently up at the words:

SAVOUR THE EROTIC POSSIBILITIES OF
FREE-FALL

and came to the entrance.

An attendant called and tried to stop him. Rodney broke into a run. He ran down a satin-smooth road until exhaustion overcame him. A metal object shaped vaguely like a shoe but as big as a small bungalow stood at the kerb. Through its windows, Rodney saw couches and no human beings. Thankful at the mute offer of rest and concealment, he climbed in.

As he sank panting onto yielding foam-rubber, he realized what a horrible situation he was in. To be stranded centuries ahead of his own lifetime – and death – in a world of supertechnology and barbarism! – for so he visualised it. However, it was a vast improvement on the repetitive nightmare he had recently endured. Now he needed time to think quietly.

'Are you ready to proceed, sir?'

Rodney jumped up, startled by a voice so near him. Nobody was in sight. The interior resembled a coach's, with wide, soft seats, all of which were empty.

'Are you ready to proceed, sir?' There it was again.

'Who is that?' Rodney asked.

'This is Auto-motor Seven Six One at your service, sir, awaiting instructions to proceed.'

'You mean away from here?'

'Certainly, sir.'

'Yes, please!'

At once the structure glided smoothly forward. No noise, no vibration. The gaudy fair-ground fell back and was replaced by other buildings, widely spaced, smokeless, built of a substance which looked like curtain fabric; they flowed by without end.

'Are you – are we heading for the country?' Rodney asked.

'This is the country, sir. Do you require a city?'

'No, I don't. What is there beside city and country?'

'Nothing, sir – except of course the sea fields.'

Dropping that line of questioning, Rodney, who was instinctively addressing a busy control board at the front of the vehicle, inquired: 'Excuse my asking, but are you a – er, robot?'

'Yes, sir, Auto-motor Seven Six One. New on this route, sir.' Rodney breathed a sigh of relief. He could not have faced a human being but irrationally felt superior to a mere mechanical. Pleasant voice it had, no more grating certainly than the Professor of Anglo-Saxon at his old college . . . however long ago that was.

'What year *is* this?' he asked.

'Circuit Zero, Epoch Eighty-two, new style. Year Two Thousand Five Hundred Anno Domini, old style.'

It was the first direct confirmation of all his suspicions; there was no gainsaying that level voice.

'Thanks,' he said hollowly. 'Now if you don't mind I've got to think.'

Thought, however, yielded little in comfort or results. Possibly the wisest course would be to throw himself on the mercy of some civilized authority – if there were any civilized authorities left. And would the wisest course in a twentieth-century world be the wisest in a – um, twenty-sixth-century world?

'Driver, is Oxford in existence?'

'What is Oxford, sir?'

A twinge of anxiety as he asked: 'This is England?'

'Yes, sir. I have found Oxford in my directory, sir. It is a motor and spaceship factory in the Midlands, sir.'

'Just keep going.'

Dipping into his pocket, he produced the fun-fair brochure and scanned its bright lettering, hoping for a clue to action.

'Chronoarcheology Ltd. presents a staggering series of Peeps into the Past. Whole days in the lives of (a) A Mother Dinosaur, (b) William the Conqueror's Wicked Nephew, (c) A Citizen of Crazed, Plague-Ridden Stuart London, (d) A Twentieth-Century Teacher in Love.

'Nothing expurgated, nothing added! Better than the Feelies! All in glorious 4D – no stereos required.'

Fuming at the description of himself, Rodney crumpled the brochure in his hand. He wondered bitterly how many of his own generation were helplessly enduring this gross irreverence in peepshows all over the world. When the sense of outrage abated slightly, curiosity reasserted itself; he smoothed out the folder and read a brief description of the process which 'will give you history-sterics as it brings each era nearer'.

Below the heading 'It's Fabulous – It's Pabulous!' he read: 'Just as anti-gravity lifts a man against the direction of weight, chronograb can lift a machine out of the direction of time and send it speeding back over the dark centuries. It can be accurately guided from the present to scoop up a fragment from the past, slapping that fragment – all unknown to the people in it – right into your lucky laps. The terrific expense of this intricate operation need hardly be emphas—'

'Driver!' Rodney screamed. 'Do you know anything about this time-grabbing business?.

'Only what I have heard, sir.'

'What do you mean by that?'

'My built-in information centre contains only facts relating to my duty, sir, but since I also have learning circuits I am occasionally able to collect gossip from passengers which—'

He dreaded the reaction from those half-glimpsed countenances that pressed on all sides.

'Tell me this, then: can human beings as well as machines travel back in time?'

The buildings were still flashing by, silent, hostile in the unknown world. Drumming his fingers wildly on his seat, Rodney awaited an answer.

'Only machines, sir. Humans can't live backwards.'

For a long time he lay and cried comfortably. The automotor made solacing cluck-cluck noises, but it was a situation with which it was incompetent to deal.

At last, Rodney wiped his eyes on his sleeve, the sleeve of his Sunday suit, and sat up. He directed the driver to head for the main offices of Chronoarcheology, and slumped back in a kind of stupor. Only at the headquarters of that fiendish invention might there be people who could – if they would – restore him to his own time.

Rodney dreaded the thought of facing any creature of this un-scrupulous age. He pressed the idea away, and concentrated instead on the peace and orderliness of the world from which he had been resurrected. To see Oxford again, to see Valerie . . . Dear, dear Valerie. . .

Would they help him at Chronoarcheology? Or – *supposing the people at the fair-ground repaired their devilish apparatus before he got there* . . . What would happen then he shuddered to imagine.

'Faster, driver,' he shouted.

The wide-spaced buildings became a wall.

'Faster, driver,' he screamed.

The wall became a mist.

'We are doing Mach 2·3, sir,' said the driver calmly.

'Faster!'

The mist became a scream.

'We are about to crash, sir.'

They crashed. Blackness, merciful, complete.

★   ★   ★   ★

A bedspring groaned and pinged and the mists cleared. Rodney awoke. From the bathroom next door came the crisp, repetitive sound of Jim shaving . . .

The Astronaut

Valentina Zhuravlyova

I think I should begin by explaining in a few words the reason that brought me to the Central Astronautics Archives. My story might otherwise seem incomplete.

I am a spaceship physician with three astro-flights to my credit. My subject is psychiatry, or rather astropsychiatry, as it is called nowadays. The problem which I am working on at present first arose years back – in the 1970s. In those days flights to Mars took over a year, to Mercury just under two years. The engines only worked at take-off and touchdown. No astronomical observations were carried out in flight – sputnik-mounted observatories did that. So what could the crews do during those long months? Practically nothing. Forced inactivity led to tension, to nervous breakdowns and mental disorders. No amount of reading or listening in could make up for what the first spacemen lacked on board ship. For what they lacked was work – the hard, creative work to which they were accustomed. It was then that the principle of hobby-minded personnel selection was first advanced. The nature of the hobby, it was thought, was entirely immaterial, so long as it gave the astronaut something to do during the flight. And thus we got pilots who had a passion for mathematics, navigators keen on ancient manuscripts, poetry-writing engineers, etc.

There was a new entry in the astronaut's certificates, the famous item 12: 'Interests other than professional'. However, a break-through in rocket technology soon provided a new solution of the problem. Ion engines cut travel between planets to a few days. Item 12 was dropped.

Some years later, however, the problem reappeared with a vengeance. Mankind had mastered interstellar travel. Yet though the speeds of ion rockets were eventually stepped up to suboptical, journeys to even the nearest stars took up to twenty years . . .

Item 12 was back in the flying certificates. In terms of actual rocket control crews were occupied no more than 0·01 per cent of flight time. TV faded away a few days after blast-off, radio lasted another month. And there were still years and years ahead . . .

Rockets were manned by crews of six to eight in those days, not more. Tiny cabins and a 150-foot-long greenhouse were all the living-space they had. It is difficult for us who fly in interstellar liners to imagine how people in those days did without all these gyms, swimming pools, stereo-theatres and promenade galleries.

But I have digressed without beginning my story.

★   ★   ★   ★

I don't know, haven't yet had time to find out who it was that designed the Archives buildings. But he was obviously a highly gifted architect. Gifted and daring. The buildings rise on the shore of a Siberian reservoir sea which was formed twenty years ago when they dammed the Ob. The main building stands on a high shore. I don't know how it was done, but it seems to soar above the water, a white pile looking like a schooner under a full press of sail.

Altogether there are fifteen people at the Archives. I have already met some of them. Most of them are here for short spells. An Australian writer is collecting material about the first interstellar flight. A scholar from Leningrad is studying the history of Mars. The diffident Indian is a famous sculptor. Two engineers – a tall strong-faced young man from Saratov and a small polite Japanese – are working jointly on some project. What kind I don't know. The Japanese smiled politely when I asked him about it. 'Oh, it's an absolute trifle. Not at all worthy of your high attention.'

But I am digressing again, when I should really be beginning my story.

I came to the Central Astronautics Archives to look into the history of the 12th item, which I needed for my research.

I spoke to the director the first evening. He's a man still in his prime, who all but lost the sight of both his eyes in a fuel-tank explosion aboard a rocket. He wears glasses of some special make – triple-lensed and blue-tinted. His eyes are not visible and it seems the man never smiles.

'Well,' he said, having heard me out, 'I think you should start with Sector 0-14. Oh, excuse me, that's a system we use here; it doesn't mean anything to you, of course. I meant the first 'expedition to Barnard's Star.'

To my shame I knew next to nothing about that expedition.

'Your flights were in different directions,' he said with a shrug. 'Sirius, Procyon and 61 Cygni. And all your research so far has been on flights to those stars, hasn't it?'

I was surprised that he should know my record so well.

'The story of Alexei Zarubin, Commander of the expedition,' he went on, 'will provide the answers to some of your questions. You will have your materials in half an hour. Good luck.'

The eyes were invisible behind the blue-tinted lenses. His voice sounded sad.

★   ★   ★   ★

The materials are on my desk. The paper is yellow with time; the ink on some of the documents (they wrote with ink in those days) has faded. But their meaning is not lost: there are infra-red copies of all the documents. The paper has been laminated, and the sheets feel hard and smooth.

Through the window I can see the sea. Its breakers roll in ponderously; the water rustles up the shore like pages being turned . . .

An expedition to Barnard's Star in those days was a hazardous adventure. The star is six light-years away from the Earth. The rocket was to fly half that distance under acceleration, and half under deceleration. The journey there and back was expected to take just under fourteen years.

For those aboard the rocket the time would be slowed down to only forty months. Not too long, it seemed. But the danger was that for thirty-eight out of those forty months the rocket engine was required to work at full blast.

The rocket had no fuel reserve – an unwarranted risk, one would think nowadays, but there was no alternative then. The ship could take no more than what the tightly calculated fuel tanks carried. Therefore any delay en route would be fatal.

I read the minutes of the selection committee. One after another the candidates for captain were turned down. And no wonder. The flight was to be exceptionally hard, the captain had to be an excellent engineer and combine a level head with reckless courage. Then suddenly everybody was unanimous.

I turn a page. The service record of Captain Alexei Zarubin.

A few minutes and three pages later I realise why Alexei Zarubin was selected captain of the *Polus*. In a truly amazing way the man combined 'ice and fire', the calm sagacity of a scholar and the fiery temperament of a fighter. That was probably why he had been entrusted with the most daring ventures. He seemed to have the knack of overcoming insurmountable obstacles.

The committee selected the captain. As tradition decreed, the captain picked his own crew. But what Zarubin did could hardly be called picking. He just contacted five astronauts who had crewed with him before and asked whether they were prepared to undertake a risky flight. With him, yes, they said.

There are photographs of the crew in the materials. Black and white, two-dimensional. Captain Zarubin was twenty-six then, but he looks older in the photo. A rather full face with high cheek-bones, tightly-pressed lips, a prominent aquiline nose, wavy, soft-looking hair and unusual eyes – calm, seemingly lazy, but with a daredevil flicker lurking in the corners.

The others were even younger. Two engineers, a married couple, photographed together because they always flew together. The navigator with the meditative look of a musician. A stern-faced girl doctor and an astrophysicist, his eyes stubborn in a face patchy with deep burns, the results of a crash landing he had made with the captain on Dione, a satellite of Saturn.

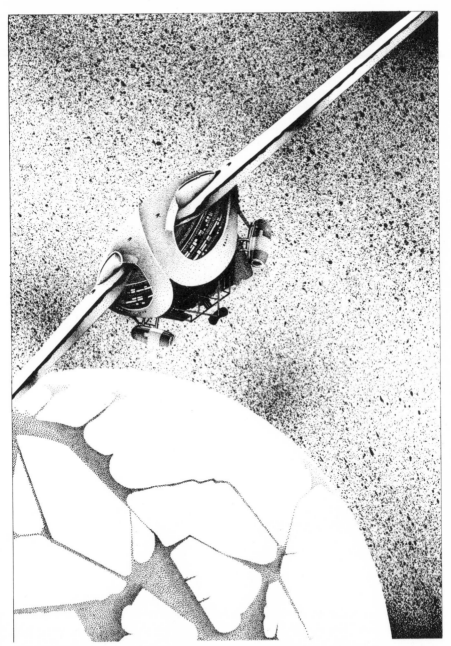

An expedition to Barnard's Star in those days was a hazardous adventure.

Now for item 12. I thumb the pages and see the pictures have told the truth. The navigator is a musician and composer. The stern-faced girl is keen on microbiology, a serious subject. The astrophysicist is learning languages; he has already mastered five and now thinks of tackling Latin and Ancient Greek. The engineers are fond of chess, the new kind – with two white and two black queens and an 81-square board.

The captain's hobby strikes an odd note. It's unusual, unique, I have never heard of anything like it. He's been keen on oil-painting since he was a boy. That is understandable, for his mother was a professional painter. But the captain seldom takes up his brush, he's interested in something else. He yearns to rediscover the lost secrets of the medieval masters – the composition of their oils, the way they mixed and used them. He carries out chemical research as he does everything he undertakes – with the devotion of a scholar and the ardour of an artist.

Six different people, six different personalities and backgrounds. It's the captain who welds them together. They love him, they trust him, they even imitate him. So all of them know how to be freezingly calm and recklessly risky.

The blast-off for Barnard's Star. The atom reactor works without a hitch, letting out an even, invisible stream of ions. The ship flies under acceleration. It is hard at first to work, even to move about. The girl doctor makes everybody stick to a fixed regimen. Gradually the astronauts settle down to the flight conditions. The greenhouse is assembled, then the radiotelescope. Normal life begins. Control of the reactor and other mechanisms takes up very little time. Everyone has to devote four hours a day to studies in his own field. The rest they spend as they think fit. The serious-minded girl is devouring monographs on microbiology. The navigator has composed a song which is quite a hit. The engineer couple sit for hours over the chess-board. The astrophysicist wades through Plutarch in the original.

There are brief entries in the ship's log: *The flight is proceeding normally. The reactor and mechanisms operate faultlessly. Spirits are high.* Then suddenly an anguished entry: *Telecommunication has gone dead. The rocket is beyond reach now. Yesterday we watched the last telecast from the Earth. How hard it is to see one more link severed!* Days later two more lines: *Have perfected the reception antenna of the radio. Hope to be able to carry on reception for another seven or eight days.* And they were happy as could be when the radio actually worked for another twelve days.

Building up speed, the ship swept towards Barnard's Star. Months went by. The atom reactor worked with utmost precision. The fuel was consumed strictly as precomputed, not an iota above.

The catastrophe came unannounced.

One day, when they were over seven months out, the reactor's operating condition changed. A side reaction had sharply stepped up fuel consumption. There was a brief entry in the log that day: *Have no idea what has caused the side reaction.* They did not know in those distant days that infinitesimal admixtures in the atomic fuel could sometimes make all the difference between a controlled and uncontrolled reaction.

*   *   *   *

The sea grumbles outside the window. The wind has picked up and the breakers no longer rustle but hiss angrily as they pound the shore. A woman's laughter wafts in to me. But I mustn't let myself be distracted. I can almost see those six in the rocket. I know them – I can imagine what they were going through. I may be wrong in some details – what does it matter? But no, I am even right in those. I feel certain everything happened as I see it.

*   *   *   *

A brownish liquid boiled frothily in the retort. The brownish steam passed through a coil pipe into the condenser. The captain was peering at the dark-red powder in a test-tube. The door opened. The flame wavered and danced. The captain turned his head. Framed in the doorway was the engineer.

He kept control of himself but his voice betrayed him. It was loud, unnaturally firm and altogether not his usual.

'Take the load off your feet, Nikolai,' the captain said and pushed a chair forward. 'I did those calculations yesterday with the same result. Come on, sit down.'

'What shall we do?'

'Do?' The captain glanced at the wall clock. 'Fifty-five minutes to supper. Enough time to discuss it. Please let everybody know we'll be having a conference, will you.'

'Very well,' the engineer replied absently. 'I'll let them know. Yes, of course.'

He couldn't understand why the captain dawdled. The ship's speed was increasing with every passing second; some kind of decision was imperative and urgent.

'Look at this,' the captain said, passing him the test-tube. 'You might be interested. It's cinnabar. Makes a devilishly attractive oil. But tends to darken when exposed to light.'

He explained to the engineer at some length how he had managed to produce a light-resistant cinnabar. The engineer shook the test-tube impatiently. There was a clock empanelled above the desk, which the engineer couldn't help glancing at: half a minute, the speed was a mile-and-a-quarter per second greater, another minute, another two-and-a-half miles per second . . .

'I'll be going,' he said finally. 'I must tell the others.'

Going down the steps he suddenly realized he was no longer counting the seconds or at all hurrying.

The captain shut the door tightly and put the test-tube casually back into the rack. He allowed himself a faint smile. Panic is after all a chain reaction. Which all things extraneous tend to slow down, he thought as he went back to his chair. The humming of the reactor cooling system filled his ears. The engines were busy accelerating the *Polus* flight.

Ten minutes later the captain went down to the messroom. The five astronauts rose in greeting. All of them were in astronaut's uniform, worn only on special occasions, and the captain realized there was no need for him to explain the situation.

'Well,' he said. 'It seems only I forgot to don the uniform.'

Nobody smiled.

'Please be seated,' the captain said. 'A council of war. Well now, let the youngest begin, as is the custom. You, Lena. What do you think we should do?'

He turned to the girl. She solemnly said:

'I'm a doctor, Alexei Pavlovich. And the problem under discussion is strictly technological. I will give my opinion later, if I may.'

The captain nodded:

'As you like. You're the cleverest among us, Lena. And, as a woman, the shrewdest, too. I'll bet anything you like you've got an opinion ready.'

The girl said nothing.

'Well,' the captain went on, 'Lena will speak later. Your turn, Sergei.'

The astrophysicist spread his arms in a gesture of indecision.

'This isn't up my alley either. I've got nothing pat. But I do know there's enough fuel to last us all the way to Barnard's Star. So why should we turn back when we're only halfway out?'

'Why?' the captain repeated. 'Just because once we're there we won't be able to come back at all. But we can now, when we're only halfway out, as you say.'

'I see your point,' the astrophysicist said thoughtfully. 'But, you know, we might be able to return after all. Not by ourselves, of course. By a relief rocket. They'll see we're not coming and they'll send one. Surely astronautics is developing.'

'So it is,' the captain smiled wrily. 'With the passage of time. So fly on? Is that it? Good. Now you, Georgi. If it's up your alley, of course.'

The navigator sprang up, pushing his chair aside.

'Sit down,' the captain said. 'Sit down and speak calmly. Don't jump.'

'There can be no question of returning!' the navigator almost shouted. 'We can only go forward. Forward in face of the impossible. Why, how can we even speak of returning? Didn't we know from the outset the expedition was hazardous? And here we are, ready to turn tail at the first difficulty. I say, forward and only forward!'

'Well,' the captain drawled. 'Forward in face of the impossible. Beautifully said. Well, what do the engineers think? You, Nina? And you, Nikolai?'

Nikolai glanced at his wife; she nodded and he began. He spoke calmly as if thinking aloud:

'The purpose of our flight to Barnard's Star is exploration. But if we six make some discovery it won't in itself have any value. It will have that only if and when mankind learns about it. If we reach Barnard's Star and have no means of coming back, what earthly use will there be in our findings? Sergei says a relief rocket will come eventually. I, too, think that is feasible. But those who come will themselves have made all the discoveries. What shall we have accomplished? What shall we have contributed to man's knowledge? Actually we shall only have brought harm. Yes, I mean it. Back on the Earth they will be waiting for our return. And in vain. If we turn back now only a minimum of time will be wasted. A new expedition will immediately set out. In fact we ourselves will. A few years may be lost, but then the data we've so far gathered will have been safely brought to the Earth. As things stand now there's no chance of that. So why go on? We two are against it. We must turn back. And now.'

A long silence descended. Then the girl asked:

'And what do you think, Captain?'

The captain smiled wistfully.

'I think the engineers are right. Beautiful words are still words. But the engineers appeal to common sense and calculation. We set out to discover. If we do not pass on our discoveries, they might as well not have been made. Nikolai is absolutely right . . .'

Zarubin got up and ponderously paced the messroom. Walking was difficult. The 3G-load brought about by the rocket's acceleration impeded movement.

'The relief-rocket variant is out,' he went on. 'But there are still two possibilities. The first is to turn back to the Earth. The second, to fly on to Barnard's Star – and still return to the Earth. Return in spite of fuel shortage.'

'How?' asked Nikolai.

Zarubin went back to his chair, sat down and said:

'That I don't know. Not yet anyway. But there are another eleven months of flight ahead. If you decide we should turn back now, we will. But if you will trust me to think up something in those eleven months that would pull us through, well then . . . forward in face of the impossible! That is the way I see it, friends. What do you say? You, Lena?'

The girl screwed her eye at him.

'Like any man, you're very cunning. I'd bet you've already thought up something.'

The captain laughed.

'You'd lose. I haven't thought up anything. But I will. I certainly will.'

'We believe in you,' Nikolai said. 'We do believe in you.' Then, after a pause, he added: 'Though, frankly, I don't quite see how anything could pull us through. There will be eighteen per cent of propellent on the *Polus*. Eighteen instead of fifty. But you said you'd think up something. So let's fly on. As Georgi says, forward in face of the impossible.'

★ ★ ★ ★

The window shutters creak softly. The wind leafs through the pages, scours about the room, filling it with the damp smell of the sea. Smell is a wonderful thing. You don't have it on board ship. The conditions purify the air and keep up the required humidity and temperature. But conditioned air is as vapid as distilled water. All sorts of artificial smell devices have been tried, but with no success. The aroma of ordinary, earthly air is much too complex to imitate. Even now I smell the sea and the damp, autumn leaves, and, vaguely, some perfume, and sometimes, on a gust of wind, the earth. And wet paint, too.

The wind is leafing through the pages . . . What could it be the captain counted on? When the *Polus* had reached Barnard's Star her fuel reserve would be down to only eighteen per cent. Eighteen instead of fifty . . .

★ ★ ★ ★

In the morning I ask the director whether I may see Zarubin's pictures.

'We'll have to go upstairs,' he says. 'But . . . tell me, have you read it all?'

He listens to my answer, nodding.

'I see. I thought so, too. Yes, the captain took upon himself a great responsibility . . . Would you have believed in him?'

'Yes.'

'So would I.'

He is silent for quite a while, his lips quivering slightly. Then he gets up and goes through the motions of adjusting his spectacles.

'Well, let's go.'

He limps. We walk slowly through the long corridors. 'You will read about it yet,' the director starts. 'Volume Two, starting from page one hundred, if I remember rightly. Zarubin wanted to unravel the secrets of the Italian Renaissance masters. You see, oil-painting deteriorated starting with the 18th century – I mean its technique. A lot was thought to have been lost beyond hope of recovery. The painters could no longer mix oils that were at once bright and stable. The brighter the oil, the quicker it darkened. Especially the blues. Well, Zarubin . . . But you will see for yourself.'

The pictures hang in a narrow, sunlit gallery and the first thing that strikes me is that each is executed in one primary colour.

'These are studies,' says the director. 'To try out the technique, nothing more. This is "A Study in Blue".'

Flying side by side in a blue sky are two frail human figures, with strapped-on wings, a man and a woman. All is done in blue, and never have I seen such an infinity of shades. It is a night sky, raven black on the left horizon and a melting, midday blue in the opposite corner. The winged humans shimmer from the lightest blue to the deepest violet. The colours are brilliant, almost vibrant in some places, and subdued, transparent in others.

There are more pictures. 'A Study in Red': two suns above an imaginary planet, a chaos of chiaroscuro ranging from blood red to salmon pink. 'A Study in Brown': a fairy-tale forest.

The director is silent. I wait, looking at the blue-tinted, impenetrable glasses.

'Read further,' he says softly. 'Then I shall show you more pictures. Then you'll understand.'

★   ★   ★   ★

I am reading as fast as I can. As fast as I can without losing the thread . . .

The *Polus* hurtled on toward Barnard's Star. The speed reached the maximum and the engines began to brake. Judging from the scant entries in the log everything was normal. No breakdowns, no sick aboard. Nor did anyone remind the captain of his pledge. And the captain was calm, confident and cheerful as always. He went on with his research and had done more studies.

What were his thoughts when he was alone in his cabin? Neither the ship's log, nor the navigator's diary give any answer. But here is an interesting document. The engineers' report. About the malfunctioning of the cooling system. Crisp, concise language bristling with technicalities. But between the lines I read, 'If you have changed your mind, friend, this is where you can turn back. With no loss of face . . .' And the captain's verdict across it, 'We'll do repairs on a planet of Barnard's Star', which means, 'No, friends, I haven't changed my mind'.

After nineteen months of flight the ship reached her destination. The dim red star had only one planet, almost the size of the Earth, but completely icebound. The *Polus* tried to land. But the jet of ions melted the ice and the first attempt failed. The captain chose another site, again the ice melted. Only at the sixth attempt did they manage to strike rock floor under a thin sheath of ice.

From that day the entries in the log-book were done in red ink. That was how discoveries were traditionally recorded.

The planet was a dead world. Its atmosphere was almost pure oxygen but not a trace of animal or plant life was found. The thermometer read 58° F. below zero. *A wretched planet*, the navigator wrote in his diary, *but what a star! Discoveries galore!*

And it was indeed so. Even today, when our knowledge of the structure and evolution of stars is increasing by leaps and bounds, the discoveries made by the *Polus* expedition have retained much of their value. The study of the gaseous envelope of the red dwarfs of the Barnard's Star type is still a classic.

The log-book . . . The scientific report . . . The astrophysicist's paper setting out a paradoxical hypothesis of star evolution . . . And, at last, what I have been looking for – the captain's order for departure. Still it comes as a surprise, almost a shock. Unable to believe my eyes, I hastily turn the pages. An entry in the navigator's diary. I see it all.

One day Zarubin said:

'That's all. Prepare for departure.'

The crew of five stared silently at their captain. The wall clock ticked away . . .

★ ★ ★ ★

The five stared silently at the captain. And waited.

'Prepare for departure,' the captain repeated. 'You know we've only got eighteen per cent of propellent. But there is a way out. First of all we must reduce the rocket's weight. All the heavy electronic gear will have to go, except for the controllers.' He saw that the navigator wanted to say something and waved him to silence. 'We've got to do it. Also all the partitions in the empty tanks, and some of the greenhouse sections. But that's not all. Fuel consumption is particularly heavy during the first months of flight – due to low acceleration, as you know. Comfort will have to be dispensed with: the *Polus* will depart to full 12 G's instead of three.'

'Flight control is impossible under that load,' Nikolai demurred. 'The pilot will not be able—'

'I know,' the captain cut him. 'I know. For the first months control will be done from here, from this planet. One of us will stay behind to do it. Keep quiet! Remember – there's no other way out. It's got to be done. Now, listen to this. You two cannot stay behind because you expect a child. Yes, I know. You are a doctor, Lena, and your place is with the crew. Sergei's an astrophysicist and will also fly. Georgi is too excitable. That leaves me. Don't argue. Everything will be done as I say.'

★   ★   ★   ★

I look through Zarubin's calculations. I am a doctor and out of my depth in the maze of mathematics. But one thing is immediately obvious: the calculations were done to absolutely no tolerance, as it were. The rocket was stripped to a bare minimum and the take-off G-load was pushed up to a crushing maximum. The bigger part of the greenhouse was left on the planet and that carved deep into the astronauts' rations. The emergency power supply system with its two microreactors was also dismantled. As was almost all electronic equipment. If something untoward happened en route the rocket would be unable to regain Barnard's Star. *The risk is cubed*, the navigator wrote in his diary. And below, *But for the one who stays behind it's risk raised to the tenth, hundredth power* . . .

Zarubin would have to wait for fourteen years. To wait for the relief rocket. Fourteen years on an alien, icebound planet . . .

More calculations. Power was the prime thing. It had to last out the ground control period and the fourteen long years after. And again no allowance for emergency.

A photo of the captain's quarters, made out of the greenhouse sections. The transparent walls permit a view of the two microreactors and miscellaneous electronic equipment. The ground control antenna is on the roof. All round lies an icy waste. Aloft Barnard's Star shines coldly in a grey, murky sky. It is four times bigger than the Sun in diameter but little brighter than the Moon.

I turn over pages in the log-book hastily. My eye runs through it all: the captain's parting advice, the arrangements for radio communication in the first days of flight, the list of things the captain would need . . . Then, suddenly, one word, *Blast-off.*

After that a few odd-looking lines as if scrawled by a child: lines uneven, letters angular, broken. That was 12 G's.

With difficulty I make out the words. The first entry: *Everything's fine but for the cursed G-load. Vision heavily veiled* . . . Two days later: *Accelerating as calculated. Can't walk, just crawl* . . . A week later: *It's tough, very* (crossed out) . . . *The reactor operates as calculated.*

Then two blank pages follow, while on the third, smeared with ink, a diagonal entry: *Ground control weakening. There's some obstacle in the beam's path. This* (crossed out). *This is it.* And below, on the same page, in a firm hand: *Ground control restored. The power indicator stands at four. The captain is giving away all the power he's got but we can't stop him. This means help won't reach him in time* . . .

I close the log-book. I can only think about Zarubin now. I imagine the fading of ground control came quite unexpected. Suddenly the indicator rang and . . .

The indicator was ringing shrilly. The needle went down, quivering. The power beam had met an obstacle and control was slipping rapidly.

The captain stood at the transparent wall. The dim sun was sinking behind the horizon. Brownish shadows sped across the icy waste. The wind drove snow dust, whipped it along, carried it aloft into the murky, reddish-grey sky.

The indicator was ringing insistently. What little power was getting through was not enough for control. Zarubin was looking at the setting Barnard's Star. Behind him lamps flashed wildly on the panel of the electronic navigator.

The purplish-red disc was rapidly sinking below the horizon. For a fleeting moment a myriad of scarlet pin-points flickered on as the last rays were refracted by the ground ice. Then there was darkness.

Zarubin went over to the instrument board, switched off the indicator's signal. The needle was not moving any longer. Zarubin turned the wheel of the power regulator. The greenhouse was filled with the drone of the motors of the cooling system. He went on turning the wheel until it would turn no more. Then he went to the other side of the board, removed the safety lock and gave the wheel two more full turns. The drone rose to a shrill, vibrant, earsplitting roar.

The captain shuffled back to the wall, sank down on the bench. His hands were shaking. He took out his handkerchief and dabbed his brow. Then he pressed his cheek against the cool glass.

It was wait now, wait till the new, superpowerful signals reached the rocket and bounced back.

And he waited.

He waited, losing all awareness of time, while the microreactors roared away at bursting point and the cooling system motors shrieked and groaned. The flimsy walls shuddered.

The captain waited.

Finally something forced him up and over to the instrument board. The needle on the indicator was back to normal. There was enough power now to control the rocket. Zarubin smiled wanly, said, 'There,' and glanced at the consumption dial. The consumption was 140 times greater than the precomputed.

That night the captain did not sleep. He was compiling a new programme for the electronic navigator. All the side effects of the power failure had to be eliminated.

The wind whipped up seas of snow on the plain. A subdued aurora borealis glowed over the horizon.

The microreactors screeched as if run amok, pouring forth into space what had been carefully husbanded to last for fourteen years . . . Having fed the programme into the electronic machine the captain made a tired round of his quarters. Stars shone high above the transparent roof. Somewhere out there the *Polus* was accelerating earthwards.

It is very late but I decided to call on the director nonetheless. I remember he has mentioned some other pictures by Zarubin.

The director is sitting up.

'I knew you would come,' he says, putting on his spectacles hastily. 'Let's go, it's next door.'

In the adjacent room lit up by fluorescent lamps hang two middle-sized pictures. The first thought that crosses my mind is that the director has made a mistake. Zarubin couldn't possibly have painted these. They have nothing in common with what I saw in the morning: no colour experiments, no fantastic subjects. They are two ordinary landscapes. A road and a tree in one, and the edge of a wood in the other.

'Yes, this is Zarubin,' the director says as if reading my thoughts. 'He stayed behind on the planet – as you already know, of course. Well, it was a desperate way out, but still, it offered them a chance. I say this as an astronaut – as a former astronaut,' the director adjusted his spectacles, then went on, 'But then Zarubin did what – Well, you know about it. In four weeks he gave off the power stored for fourteen years. He restored ground control and brought the *Polus* back to her course. Well, when the rocket reached suboptical speed, braking began at normal G-load, and the crew could take over. By that time there was next to no power in Zarubin's microreactors. Nor could anything be done about it . . . That was when he started on these pictures. In them his love for life and the Earth . . .'

A country road topping a rise. A mighty rugged oaktree by its side. It is done in the manner of Jules Dupré of the Barbizon school: sturdy, gnarled, full of life and vigour. The wind drives along small shaggy clouds. A boulder lies by the ditch, and it seems that only a moment ago a weary traveller has been sitting on it . . . All the details are executed carefully, lovingly, with an amazingly rich colour and light shading.

The other picture was never finished. It's a wood in spring. Everything is soaked in air, light, warmth . . . Wonderful golden hues . . . Zarubin was a perfect colourist.

'I brought these pictures to the Earth,' the director says softly.

'You?'

'Yes.'

His voice is wistful, almost apologetic.

'The materials you have been looking through have no end. That is part of other expeditions. When the *Polus* returned, a rescue expedition was immediately equipped and sent out. All that could shorten the flight was done. The crew agreed to fly under 6 G's. They got to the planet – and did not find the greenhouse. They took tremendous risks and returned empty-handed. Then – many years later – I was sent. We had a breakdown on the way. There,' he put a hand up to his spectacles. 'But we got through. And found the greenhouse and the pictures . . . And a note from the captain.'

'What was in it?'

'Just one line: "Forward in face of the impossible".'

We look silently at the pictures. It suddenly occurs to me that Zarubin painted them from memory. There was ice all round him, lit up by the evil reddish glow of Barnard's Star. And on his palette he was mixing warm, sunny colours . . . In item 12 he could in all truth have written: 'Am interested in, passionately love the Earth, its life, its people.'

The deserted corridors of the Archives are still and quiet. The windows are open, the sea breeze stirs the heavy curtains. The breakers roll in in stubborn cadence. They seem to whisper: forward in face of the impossible. A pause, another wave and a whisper: Forward . . . And another pause . . .

I want to reply to the waves: 'Yes, forward, only forward, always forward.'

Manners of An Age

H. B. Fyfe

The red tennis robot scooted desperately across the court, its four wide-set wheels squealing. For a moment, Robert's hard-hit passing shot seemed to have scored. Then, at the last instant, the robot whipped around its single racket-equipped arm. Robert sprawled headlong in a futile lunge at the return.

'Game and set to Red Three,' announced the referee box from its high station above the net.

'Ah, shut up!' growled Robert, and flung down his racket for one of the white serving robots to retrieve.

'Yes, Robert,' agreed the voice. 'Will Robert continue to play?' Interpreting the man's savage mumble as a negative, it told his opponent, 'Return to your stall, Red Three!'

Robert strode off wordlessly towards the house. Reaching the hundred-foot-square swimming pool, he hesitated uncertainly.

'Weather's so damned hot,' he muttered. 'Why didn't the old-time scientists find out how to do something about that while there were still enough people on Earth to manage it?'

He stripped off his damp clothing and dropped it on the 'beach' of white sand. Behind him sounded the steps of a humanoid serving robot, hastening to pick it up. Robert plunged deep into the cooling water and let himself float lazily to the surface.

Maybe they did, he thought. *I could send a robot over to the old city library for information. Still, actually doing anything would probably take the resources of a good many persons – and it isn't so easy to find people now that Earth is practically deserted.*

He rolled sidewards for a breath and began to swim slowly for the opposite side of the pool, reflecting upon the curious culture of the planet. Although he had accepted this all his life, it really was remarkable how the original home of the human race had been forsaken for fresher worlds among the stars. Or was it more remarkable that a few individuals had asserted their independence by remaining?

Robert was aware that the decision involved few difficulties, considering the wealth of robots and other automatic machines. He regretted knowing so few humans, though they were really not necessary. If not for his hobby of televising, he would probably not know any at all.

'Wonder how far past the old city I'd have to go to meet someone in person,' he muttered as he pulled himself from the pool. 'Maybe I ought to try accepting that televised invitation of the other night.'

Several dark usuform robots were smoothing the sand on this beach under the direction of a blue humanoid supervisor. Watching them idly, Robert estimated that it must be ten years since he had seen another human face to face. His parents were dim memories. He got along very well, however, with robots to serve him or to obtain occasional information from the automatic scanners of the city library that had long ago been equipped to serve such a purpose.

'Much better than things were in the old days,' he told himself as he crossed the lawn to his sprawling white mansion. 'Must have been awful before the population declined. Imagine having people all around you, having to listen to them, see them, and argue to make them do what you wanted!'

The heel of his bare right foot came down heavily on a pebble, and he swore without awareness of the precise meaning of the ancient phrases. He limped into the baths and beckoned a waiting robot as he stretched out on a rubbing table.

'Call Blue One!' he ordered.

The red robot pushed a button on the wall before beginning the massage. In a few moments, the major-domo arrived.

'Did Robert enjoy the tennis?' it inquired politely.

'I did *not*!' snapped the man. 'Red Three won – and by too big a score. Have it geared down a few feet per second.'

'Yes, Robert.'

'And have the lawn screened again for pebbles!'

As Blue One retired he relaxed, and turned his mind to ideas for filling the evening. He hoped Henry would televise; Robert had news for him.

After a short nap and dinner, he took the elevator to his three-storey tower and turned on the television robot. Seating himself in a comfortable armchair, he directed the machine from one channel to another. For some time, there was no answer to his perfunctory call signals, but one of his few acquaintances finally came on.

'Jack here,' said a quiet voice that Robert had long suspected of being disguised by a filter microphone.

'I haven't heard you for some weeks,' he remarked, eyeing the swirling colours on the screen.

He disliked Jack for never showing his face, but curiousity as to what lay behind the mechanical image projected by the other's transmitter preserved the acquaintance.

'I was . . . busy,' said the bodiless voice, with a discreet hint of a chuckle that Robert found chilling.

He wondered what Jack had been up to. He remembered once being favoured with a televised view of Jack's favourite sport – a battle between companies of robots designed for the purpose, horribly reminiscent of human conflicts Robert had seen on historical films.

He soon made an excuse to break off and set the robot to scanning Henry's channel. He had something to tell the older man, who lived only about a hundred miles away and was as close to being his friend as was possible in this age of scattered, self-sufficient dwellings.

'I don't mind talking to *him*,' Robert reflected. 'At least he doesn't overdo this business of individual privacy.'

He thought briefly of the disdainful face – seemingly on a distant station – which had merely examined him for several minutes one night without ever condescending to speak. Recalling his rage at this treatment, Robert wondered how the ancients had managed to get along together when there were so many of them. They must have had some strict code of behaviour, he supposed, or they never would have bred so enormous a population.

'I must find out about that someday,' he decided. 'How did you act, for instance, if you wanted to play tennis but someone else just refused and went to eat dinner? Maybe that was why the ancients had so many murders.'

He noticed that the robot was getting an answer from Henry's station, and was pleased. He could talk as long as he liked, knowing Henry would not resent his cutting off any time he became bored with the conversation.

The robot focused the image smoothly. Henry gave the impression of being a small man. He was grey and wrinkled compared with Robert, but his black eyes were alertly sharp. He smiled his greeting and immediately launched into a story of one of his youthful trips through the mountains, from the point at which it had been interrupted the last time they had talked.

Robert listened impatiently.

'Maybe I have some interesting news,' he remarked as the other finished. 'I picked up a new station the other night.'

'That reminds me of a time when I was a boy and—'

Robert fidgeted while Henry described watching his father build a spare television set as a hobby, with only a minimum of robot help. He pounced upon the first pause.

'A new station!' he repeated. 'Came in very well, too. I can't imagine why I never picked it up before.'

'Distant, perhaps?' asked Henry resignedly.

'No, not very far from me, as a matter of fact.'

'You can't always tell, especially with the oceans so close. Now that there are so few people, you'd think there'd be land enough for all of them; but a good many spend all their lives aboard ship-robots.'

'Not this one,' said Robert. 'She even showed me an outside view of her home.'

Henry's eyebrows rose. 'She? A woman?'

'Her name is Marcia-Joan.'

'Well, well,' said Henry. 'Imagine that. Women, as I recall, usually do have funny names.'

He gazed thoughtfully at his well-kept hands.

'Did I ever tell you about the last woman I knew?' he asked. 'About twenty years ago. We had a son, you know, but he grew up and wanted his own home and robots.'

'Natural enough,' Robert commented, somewhat briefly since Henry *had* told him the story before.

'I often wonder what became of him,' mused the older man. 'That's the trouble with what's left of Earth culture – no families any more.'

Now he'll tell about the time he lived in a crowd of five, thought Robert. *He, his wife, their boy and the visiting couple with the fleet of robot helicopters.*

Deciding that Henry could reminisce just as well without a listener, Robert quietly ordered the robot to turn itself off.

Maybe I will make the trip, he pondered, on the way downstairs, *if only to see what it's like with another person about.*

At about noon of the second day after that, he remembered that thought with regret.

The ancient roads, seldom used and never repaired, were rough and bumpy. Having no flying robots, Robert was compelled to transport himself and a few mechanical servants in ground vehicles. He had – idiotically, he now realized – started with the dawn, and was already tired.

Consequently, he was perhaps unduly annoyed when two tiny spy-eyes flew down from the hills to hover above his caravan on whirring little propellors. He tried to glance up pleasantly while their lenses televised pictures to their base, but he feared that his smile was strained.

The spy-eyes retired after a few minutes. Robert's vehicle, at his voiced order, turned onto a road leading between two forested hills.

Right there, he thought for hours later, *was where I made my mistake. I should have turned back and gone home!*

He stood in the doorway of a small cottage of pale blue trimmed with yellow, watching his robots unload baggage. They were supervised by Blue Two, the spare for Blue One.

Also watching, as silently as Robert, was a pink-and-blue striped robot which had guided the caravan from the entrance gate to the cottage. After one confused protest in a curiously high voice, it had not spoken.

Maybe we shouldn't have driven through that flower bed, thought Robert. *Still, the thing ought to be versatile enough to say so. I wouldn't have such a gimcrack contraption!*

He looked up as another humanoid robot in similar colours approached along the line of shrubs separating the main lawns from that surrounding the cottage.

'Marcia-Joan has finished her nap. You may come to the house now.'

Robert's jaw hung slack as he sought for a reply. His face flushed at the idea of a robot's offering *him* permission to enter the house.

Nevertheless, he followed it across the wide lawn and between banks of gaily blossoming flowers to the main house. Robert was not sure which colour he disliked more, that of the robot or the unemphatic pastel tints of the house.

The robot led the way inside and along a hall. It pulled back a curtain near the other end, revealing a room with furniture for human use. Robert stared at the girl who sat in an armchair, clad in a long robe of soft, pink material.

She looked a few years younger than he. Her hair and eyes were also brown, though darker. In contrast to Robert's, her smooth skin was only lightly tanned, and she wore her hair much longer. He thought her oval face might have been pleasant if not for the analytical expression she wore.

'I am quite human,' he said in annoyance. 'Do you have a voice?'

She rose and walked over to him curiously. Robert saw that she was several inches shorter than he, about the height of one of his robots. He condescended to bear her scrutiny.

'You look just as you do on the telescreen,' she marvelled.

Robert began to wonder if the girl were feebleminded. How else should he look?

'I usually swim at this hour,' he said to change the subject. 'Where is the pool?'

Marcia-Joan stared at him.

'Pool of what?' she asked.

Sensing sarcasm, he scowled. 'Pool of water, of course! To swim in. What do you think I meant – a pool of oil?'

'I am not acquainted with your habits,' retorted the girl.

'None of that stupid wit!' he snapped. 'Where is the pool?'

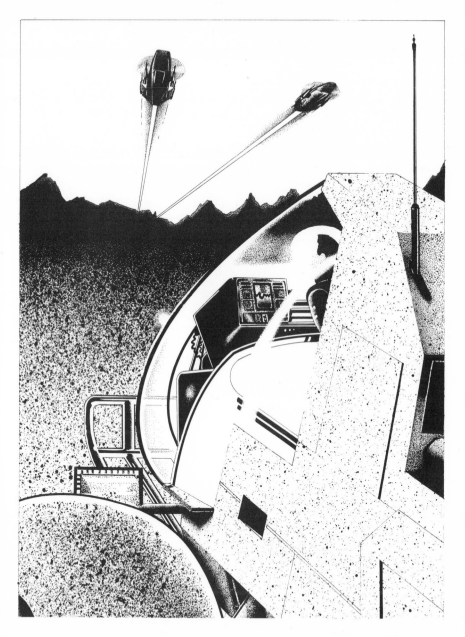

Two spy-eyes flew down from the hills to hover about his caravan on whissing little propellors.

'Don't shout!' shouted the girl. Her voice was high and unpleasantly shrill compared with his. 'I don't have a pool. Who wants a swimming pool, anyway?'

Robert felt his face flushing with rage.

So she won't tell me! he thought. *All right, I'll find it myself. Everybody has a pool. And if she comes in, I'll hold her head under for a while!*

Sneering, he turned towards the nearest exit from the house. The gaily striped robot hastened after him.

The door failed to swing back as it should have at Robert's approach. Impatiently, he seized the ornamental handle. He felt his shoulder grasped by a metal hand.

'Do not use the front door!' said the robot.

'Let go!' ordered Robert, incensed that any robot should presume to hinder him.

'Only Marcia-Joan uses this door,' said the robot, ignoring Robert's displeasure.

'I'll use it if I like!' declared Robert, jerking the handle.

The next moment, he was lifted bodily into the air. By the time he realized what was happening, he was carried, face down, along the hall. Too astonished even to yell, he caught a glimpse of Marcia-Joan's tiny feet beneath the hem of her pink robe as his head passed the curtained doorway.

The robot clumped on to the door at the rear of the house and out into the sunshine. There, it released its grip.

When Robert regained the breath knocked out of him by the drop, and assured himself that no bones were broken, his anger returned.

'I'll find it, wherever it is!' he growled, and set out to search the grounds.

About twenty minutes later, he was forced to admit that there really was no swimming pool. Except for a brook fifty yards away, there was only the tiled bathroom of the cottage to bathe in.

'Primitive!' exclaimed Robert, eyeing this. 'Manually operated water supply, too! I must have the robots fix something better for tomorrow.'

Since none of his robots was equipped with a thermometer, he had to draw the bath himself. Meanwhile, he gave orders to Blue Two regarding the brook and a place to swim. He managed to fill the tub without scalding himself mainly because there was no hot water. His irritation, by the time he had dressed in fresh clothes and prepared for another talk with his hostess, was still lively.

'Ah, you return?' Marcia-Joan commented from a window above the back door.

'It is time to eat,' said Robert frankly.

'You are mistaken.'

He glanced at the sunset, which was already fading.

'It *is* time,' he insisted. 'I always eat at this hour.'

'Well, I don't.'

Robert leaned back to examine her expression more carefully. He felt very much the way he had the day the water-supply robot for his pool had broken down and, despite Robert's bellowed orders, had flooded a good part of the lawn before Blue One had disconnected it. Some instinct warned him, moreover, that bellowing now would be as it had been then.

'What *do* you do now?' he asked.

'I dress for the evening.'

'And when do you eat?'

'After I finish dressing.'

'I'll wait for you,' said Robert, feeling that that much tolerance could do no particular harm.

He encountered the pink-and-blue robot in the hall, superintending several plain yellow ones bearing dishes and covered platters. Robert followed them to a dining room.

'Marcia-Joan sits there,' the major-domo informed him as he moved towards the only chair at the table.

Robert warily retreated to the opposite side of the table and looked for another chair. None was visible.

Of course, he thought, trying to be fair. *Why should anybody in this day have more than one chair? Robots don't sit.*

He waited for the major-domo to leave, but it did not. The serving robots finished laying out the dishes and retired to posts along the wall. Finally, Robert decided that he would have to make his status clear or risk going hungry.

If I sit down somewhere, he decided, *it may recognize me as human. What a stupid machine to have!*

He started around the end of the table again, but the striped robot moved to intercept him. Robert stopped.

'Oh, well,' he sighed, sitting sidewise on a corner of the table.

The robot hesitated, made one or two false starts in different directions, then halted. The situation had apparently not been included among its memory tapes. Robert grinned and lifted the cover of the nearest platter.

He managed to eat, despite his ungraceful position and what he considered the scarcity of the food. Just as he finished the last dish, he heard footsteps in the hall.

Marcia-Joan had dressed in a fresh robe, of crimson. Its thinner material was gathered at the waist by clasps of gleaming gold. The arrangement emphasized bodily contours Robert had previously seen only in historical films.

He became aware that she was regarding him with much the same suggestion of helpless dismay as the major-domo.

'Why, you've eaten it all!' she exclaimed.

'All?' snorted Robert. 'There was hardly any food!'

Marcia-Joan walked slowly around the table, staring at the empty dishes.

'A few bits of raw vegetables and the tiniest portion of protein-concentrate I ever saw!' Robert continued. 'Do you call that a dinner to serve a guest?'

'And I especially ordered two portions—'

'Two?' Robert repeated in astonishment. 'You must visit me some-time. I'll show you—'

'What's the matter with my food?' interrupted the girl. 'I follow the best diet advice my robots could find in the city library.'

'They should have looked for human diets, not song-birds'.'

He lifted a cover in hopes of finding some overlooked morsel, but the platter was bare.

'No wonder you act so strangely,' he said. 'You must be suffering from malnutrition. I don't wonder with a skimpy diet like this.'

'It's very healthful,' insisted Marcia-Joan. 'The old film said it was good for the figure, too.'

'Not interested,' grunted Robert. 'I'm satisfied as I am.'

'Oh, yes? You look gawky to me.'

'*You* don't,' retorted Robert, examining her disdainfully. 'You are short and stubby and too plump.'

'*Plump?*'

'Worse, you're actually fat in lots of places I'm not.'

'At least not between the ears!'

Robert blinked.

'Wh-wh-WHAT?'

'And besides,' she stormed on, 'those robots you brought are painted the most repulsive colours!'

Robert closed his mouth and silently sought the connection.

Robots? he thought. *Not fat, but repulsive colours, she said. What has that to do with food? The woman seems incapable of logic.*

'And furthermore,' Marcia-Joan was saying, 'I'm not sure I care for the looks of you! Lulu, put him out!'

'Who's Lulu?' demanded Robert.

Then, as the major-domo moved forward, he understood.

'What a silly name for a robot!' he exclaimed.

'I suppose you'd call it Robert. Will you go or shall I call more robots?'

'I am not a fool,' said Robert haughtily. 'I shall go. Thank you for the disgusting dinner.'

'Do not use the front door,' said the robot. 'Only Marcia-Joan uses that. All robots use other doors.'

Robert growled, but walked down the hall to the back door. As this swung open to permit his passage, he halted.

'It's dark out there now,' he complained over his shoulder. 'Don't you have any lights on your grounds? Do you want me to trip over something?'

'Of course I have ground lights!' shrilled Marcia-Joan. 'I'll show you – not that I care if you trip or not.'

A moment later, lights concealed among the trees glowed into life. Robert walked outside and turned towards the cottage.

I should have asked her what the colours of my robots had to do with it, he thought, and turned back to re-enter.

He walked right into the closed door, which failed to open before him, though it had operated smoothly a moment ago.

'Robots not admitted after dark,' a mechanical voice informed him. 'Return to your stall in the shed.'

'Who do you think you're talking to?' demanded Robert. 'I'm not one of your robots!'

There was a pause.

'Is it Marcia-Joan?' asked the voice-box, after considerable buzzing and whirring.

'No, I'm Robert.'

There was another pause while the mechanism laboriously shifted back to its other speech tape. Then: 'Robots not admitted after dark. Return to your stall in the shed.'

Robert slowly raised both hands to his temples. Lingeringly he dragged them down over his cheeks and under his chin until at last the fingers interlaced over his tight lips. After a moment, he let out his breath between his fingers and dropped his hands to his sides.

He raised one foot to kick, but decided that the door looked too hard.

He walked away between the beds of flowers, grumbling.

Reaching the vicinity of the cottage, he parted the tall shrubs bordering its grounds and looked through carefully before proceeding.

Pleased at the gleam of water, he called Blue Two.

'Good enough! Put the other robots away for the night. They can trim the edges tomorrow.'

He started into the cottage, but his major-domo warned, 'Someone comes.'

Robert looked around. Through thin portions of the shrubbery, he caught a glimpse of Marcia-Joan's crimson robe, nearly black in the diffused glow of the lights illuminating the grounds.

'Robert!' called the girl angrily. 'What are your robots doing? I saw them from my upstairs window—'

'Wait there!' exclaimed Robert as she reached the shrubs.

'What? Are you trying to tell me where I can go or not go? I—YI!'

The shriek was followed by a tremendous splash. Robert stepped forward in time to be spattered by part of the flying spray. It was cold.

Naturally, being drawn from the brook, he reflected. *Oh, well, the sun will warm it tomorrow.*

There was a frenzy of thrashing and splashing in the dimly lighted water at his feet, accompanied by coughs and spluttering demands that he 'do something!'

Robert reached down with one hand, caught his hostess by the wrist, and heaved her up to solid ground.

'My robots are digging you a little swimming hole,' he told her. 'They brought the water from the brook by a trench. You can finish it with concrete or plastics later; it's only fifteen by thirty feet.'

He expected some sort of acknowledgement of his efforts, and peered at her through the gloom when none was forthcoming. He thus caught a glimpse of the full-swinging slap aimed at his face. He tried to duck.

There was another splash, followed by more floundering about.

'Reach up,' said Robert patiently, 'and I'll pull you out again. I didn't expect you to like it this much.'

Marcia-Joan scrambled up the bank, tugged viciously at her sodden robe, and headed for the nearest pathway without replying. Robert followed along. As they passed under one of the lights, he noticed that the red reflections of the wet material, where it clung snugly to the girl's body, were almost the colour of some of his robots.

The tennis robot, he thought, *and the moving targets for archery – in fact, all the sporting equipment.*

'You talk about food for the figure,' he remarked lightly. 'You should see yourself now! It's really funny, the way—'

He stopped. Some strange emotion stifled his impulse to laugh at the way the robe clung.

Instead, he lengthened his stride, but he was still a few feet behind when she charged through the front entrance of the house. The door, having opened automatically for her, started to swing closed. Robert sprang forward to catch it.

'Wait a minute!' he cried.

Marcia-Joan snapped something that sounded like 'Get out!' over her shoulder, and squished off towards the stairs. As Robert started through the door to follow, the striped robot hastened towards him from its post in the hall.

'Do not use the front door!' it warned him.

'Out of my way!' growled Robert.

The robot reached out to enforce the command. Robert seized it by the forearm and put all his weight into a sudden tug. The machine tottered off balance. Releasing his grip, he sent it staggering out of the door with a quick shove.

A hasty glance showed Marcia-Joan flapping wetly up the last steps. Robert turned to face the robot.

'Do not use that door!' he quoted vindictively, and the robot halted its rush indecisively. 'Only Marcia-Joan uses it.'

The major-domo hesitated. After a moment, it strode off around the corner of the house. First darting one more look at the stairs, Robert thrust his head outside and shouted: 'Blue Two!'

He held the door open while he waited. There was an answer from the shrubbery. Presently, his own supervisor hurried up.

'Fetch the emergency toolbox!' Robert ordered. 'And bring a couple of others with you.'

'Naturally, Robert. I would not carry it myself.'

A moment after the robot had departed on the errand, heavy steps sounded at the rear of the hall. Marcia-Joan's robot had dealt with the mechanism of the back door.

Robert eyed the metal mask as the robot walked up to him. He found the colour contrast less pleasant than ever.

'I am not using the door,' he said hastily. 'I am merely holding it open.'

'Do you intend to use it?'

'I haven't decided.'

'I shall carry you out back,' the robot decided for him.

'No, you don't!' exclaimed Robert, leaping backwards.

The door immediately began to swing shut as he passed through. Cursing, he lunged forward. The robot reached for him.

This time, Robert missed his grip. Before he could duck away, his wrist was trapped in a metal grasp.

The door will close, he despaired. *They'll be too late.*

Then, suddenly, he felt the portal drawn back and heard Blue Two speak.

'What does Robert wish?'

'Throw this heap out the door!' gasped Robert.

Amid a trampling of many feet, the major-domo was raised bodily by Blue Two and another pair of Robert's machines and hustled outside. Since the grip on Robert's wrist was not relaxed, he involuntarily accompanied the rush of metal bodies.

'Catch the door!' he called to Blue Two.

When the latter sprang to obey, the other two took the action as a signal to drop their burden. The pink-and-blue robot landed full length with a jingling crash. Robert was free.

With the robots, he made for the entrance. Hearing footsteps behind him as the major-domo regained its feet, he slipped hastily inside.

'Pick up that toolbox!' he snapped. 'When that robot stops in the doorway, knock its head off!'

Turning, he held up a finger.

'Do not use the front door!'

The major-domo hesitated.

The heavy toolbox in the grip of Blue Two descended with a thud. The pink-and-blue robot landed on the ground a yard or two outside the door as if dropped from the second floor. It bounced once, emitted a few sparks and pungent wisps of smoke, lay still.

'Never mind, that's good enough,' said Robert as Blue Two stepped forward. 'One of the others can drag it off to the repair shop. Have the toolbox brought with us.'

'What does Robert wish now?' inquired Blue Two, trailing the man towards the stairway.

'I'm going upstairs,' said Robert. 'And I intend to be prepared if any more doors are closed against me!'

He started up, the measured treads of his own robots sounding reassuringly behind him . . .

It was about a week later that Robert sat relaxed in the armchair before his own telescreen, facing Henry's wizened visage.

The elder man clucked sympathetically as he re-examined the scratches on Robert's face and the bruise under his right eye.

'And so you left there in the morning?'

'I certainly did!' declared Robert. 'We registered a marriage record at the city library by television, of course, but I don't care if I never see her again. She needn't even tell me about the child, if any. I simply can't stand that girl!'

'Now, now,' Henry said.

'I mean it! Absolutely no consideration for my wishes. Everything in the house was run to suit her convenience.'

'After all,' Henry pointed out, 'it *is* her house.'

Robert glared. 'What has that to do with it? I don't think I was as unreasonable as she said in smashing that robot. The thing just wouldn't let me alone!

'I guess,' Henry suggested, 'it was conditioned to obey Marcia-Joan, not you.'

'Well, that shows you! Whose orders are to count, anyway? When I tell a robot to do something, I expect it done. How would *you* like to find robots trying to boss you around?'

'Are you talking about robots,' asked Henry, 'or the girl?'

'Same thing, isn't it? Or it would be if I'd decided to bring her home with me.'

'Conflict of desires,' murmured Henry.

'Exactly! It's maddening to have a perfectly logical action interfered with because there's another person present to insist – *insist*, mind you – on having her way.'

'And for twenty-odd years, you've had your own way in every tiny thing.'

Somewhere in the back of Robert's mind lurked a feeling that Henry sounded slightly sarcastic.

'Well, why shouldn't I?' he demanded. 'I noticed that in every disagreement, my view was the right one.'

'It was?'

'Of course it was! What did you mean by that tone?'

'Nothing . . .' Henry seemed lost in thought. 'I was just wondering how many "right" views are left on this planet. There must be quite a few, all different, even if we have picked up only a few by television. An interesting facet of our peculiar culture – every individual omnipotent and omniscient, *within his own sphere*.'

Robert regarded him with indignant incredulity.

'You don't seem to understand my point,' he began again. 'I told her we ought to come to my house, where things are better arranged, and she simply refused. Contradicted me! It was most—'

He broke off.

'The *impudence* of him!' he exclaimed. 'Signing off when *I* wanted to talk!'

Christmas Tree

Christopher Youd

The skipper cushioned us in nicely. I had my eyes on the dial the whole time and the needle never got above four and a half G's. With a boat like the *Arkland* that was good; I've known a bad pilot to touch seven G's on an Earth landing. All the same I didn't feel so hot. Young Stenway was out of his cradle before the tremors had stopped. I lay still a moment while he stood over me, grinning:

'Break it up, Joe. Dreaming of a pension?'

I got up with a bounce and landed him a playful clip that rocked him back into his own cradle. There was normal gravity underneath us; the feeling of rightness you know in your bones and muscles no matter how long you've been away. It was good to feel myself tough still.

'So this is Washington. What day is it?' Stenway asked.

'You reverted to type quick, kid. How should I know what day it is? I'm only a visitor.'

He grinned, flushing a little, and went over to the multiple calendar. I saw him fingering it, his face screwed up.

'Friday. Say, Joe, if we take more than fourteen days on the turn-round, we'll make Christmas here.'

'If we take more than ten days on the turn-round,' I shot back, 'the whole Board of Directors will commit gory suicide. What's worrying you?'

He grinned lopsidedly, and went out in a hurry. I was a bit sorry for him. He'd done less than a year in the Service. Things weren't the right pattern for him yet. He probably thought some of us were tough eggs. But we had to ride him down now and then for his own good.

I went along to see Louis. He'd been in space only a couple of years less than I had, and we'd both been with the *Arkland* since she was commissioned eight years before. But we didn't see each other much, working on different shifts and pretty nearly at opposite ends of the boat. I found him in the mess, sprucing up. He called out:

'Hello, Joe. You still with us?'

'Why not?'

'Borrowed time – just borrowed time.'

'Louis. Do me a favour.'

'Sure, Joe. Any little thing.'

He put down a hairbrush and started powdering his face, overlaying the finely ravelled seams of red that told he'd been out in vacuum. I couldn't understand that myself. It made you a bit unusual on Earth, it stamped you as a spaceman, but who'd be ashamed of that? Still, I've never been branded myself, so maybe I shouldn't talk.

'You handling the loading for the next trip, Louie?'

He pressed the powder in with his fingertips, and nodded.

'I want to get something on board.'

'How big?' Louie asked.

I shrugged lightly. 'About five feet long. Maybe two feet across, at its widest – when it's tied up.'

Louie jutted his chin out and flicked a patch of black velvet across his face. He spoke through his teeth:

'What about the Pentagon Building, if you want a souvenir?'

'What would I do with the Pentagon Building?'

Louie turned round. 'Look, Joe, you know how things are. You know the cost of space-freighting. There isn't a quarter-ounce of cargo weight that isn't accounted for. What do you want to fit in, anyway?'

'This is for old Hans. I thought of taking him a Christmas tree.'

Louie didn't say anything for a moment. He had brushed the powder well in, but you could still see the crimson network underneath. At last he said:

'OK. Get it up here the night before we blast. I'll fix it for you.'

'Thanks, Louie. When will that be, by the way? Have they told you?'

'Nineteenth. Now go and raise hell for nine days. But don't forget the Medical tomorrow.'

I looked at him sharply, but he was brushing in another layer of powder. Medical was a routine, always taken between eighteen and twenty-four hours after cushioning. The doctors knew why, or said they did. It wasn't the sort of thing you'd forget. But it wasn't worth taking him up on it.

The *Arkland* touched at Washington every fifth trip. I knew quite a few numbers and had my usual haunts. There was a sombre moment once when one of the girls relaxed and the wrinkles stood out, but it passed. There's always the younger generation. I let it get round to the day before blasting before I dropped in on the company's office. They've got a block of masonry on Roosevelt Boulevard that's bigger than Luna City. Welfare is on Floor 32. It makes me airsick to look out of their windows.

There was a cute little blonde at the desk and it occurred to me that next time I might contact Welfare at the beginning of a furlough. She looked as though she could get through my back-pay as well as any.

I said: 'You can help me out. I want to buy a Christmas tree.'

She looked surprised and rather disappointed, but she was business-like. She waded through a pile of directories like a terrier after rats.

'Christmas trees,' she said. 'Your best bet is the Leecliff Nurseries. Mr Cliff. About fifteen miles out. You can pick up a gyro on the roof.'

'Don't tell me there's a roof on this thing,' I said.

She just smiled very nicely.

'Keep a week free next November,' I told her as I turned to leave. 'I'll be back.'

★   ★   ★   ★

The gyro did the trip in just over ten minutes. Where it put me down you wouldn't guess such a place as Washington existed. One way there were a lot of low sheds and a few glasshouses. The other way there were just fields and fields of plants growing. I realized that it was more than ten years since I'd been outside a city on an Earth furlough. You get into habits. For the first time it occurred to me that I might have been missing something.

They had phoned Mr Cliff I was coming; 'Good Service' is the Company's motto. He was waiting when the gyro touched. A little round fellow, with a look as though something had surprised him. He said:

'Major Davies, I'm delighted to see you. We don't see many spacemen. Come and see my roses.'

He seemed eager and I let him take me. I wasn't breaking my neck to get back into town.

He had a glasshouse full of roses. I hesitated in the doorway. Mr Cliff said: 'Well?'

'I'd forgotten they smelled like that,' I told him.

He said proudly, 'It's quite a showing. A week before Christmas and a showing like that. Look at this Frau Karl Druschki.'

It was a white rose, very nicely shaped and scented like spring. The roses had me. I crawled round after Mr Cliff, seeing roses, feeling roses, breathing roses. I looked at my watch when it began to get dark.

'I came to buy a Christmas tree, Mr Cliff.'

We left the rose house reluctantly.

'Christmas on Earth for a change, Major Davies?'

'No – Luna City. It's for someone there.'

He waited for me to go on.

'A guy called Hans,' I said. 'He's been nearly forty years in Luna City. He was born in a little village in Austria. Halfway up a mountain, with pines all round and snow on them in winter. You know. He gets homesick.'

'Why doesn't he come back, Major Davies?'

It's always a shock when people show how little they know about the life you lead, though I suppose you can't blame them. The exciting parts are news – spacewrecks and crashes and mad orbits – but the routine's dull. I suppose there are some things the company doesn't pass on to Publicity. Not that there's anything they're ashamed of – they just don't talk about such things.

'Mr Cliff,' I said, 'the doctors have it all tabbed. It's what they call cumulative stress. You can't bring a boat in or push her off without an initial strain. It varies with the planets, of course. For Earth, with an average sized vessel, the peak's about five or six gravities.'

I flexed my shoulders back, breathing this different air.

'You've got to be tough physically,' I went on, 'but even so it tells. It's the heart chiefly. They give you a warning when it begins to flicker; you can drop out then with a pension. Of course there are some who can carry on. They're used to the life, and—'

'And—?' promoted Mr Cliff.

'There's a final warning as well. They check up on you after each trip; vet you for the next. Then one time it's just plain No. You can argue, but the answer's No. Another take-off would finish you. So they say. There's no way of testing it; they just don't let you on a boat after that.'

'They're very considerate, Major Davies.'

I laughed. 'Oh, very. The only thing is – they check you each landfall. Hans got his final warning at Luna City.'

'Oh.' Mr Cliff bent his head to smell the red rose in his coat. 'How long ago did you say?'

'Hans is an old man. Over seventy. Generally you get your first warning when you are about thirty.'

'And how big is this Luna City?'

'That's easy,' I said. 'It's in the guide books. A couple of blocks long by a block wide. It goes underground a bit as well.'

'That's terrible, Major Davies. Forty years like that. No trees, no birds – and young men know that and still take the risk? I can't believe it.'

It was an old story but I'd never felt myself getting so mad about it before. I reined myself in. He was a nice old guy.

'You don't understand, Mr Cliff. There's something in the life. And sometimes there's more than five years between first and final warnings. One guy went ten. There's always one more trip that's worth making before you settle down for good. They don't recruit spacemen who give up easily. And you may always strike lucky and get your ticket at this end.'

'When did you get your first warning, Major Davies?'

I flushed. 'Three years ago. So what? Now this matter of the Christmas tree, Mr Cliff—'

'I'll show you. The Christmas tree is on me. Please.'

He led me away to show me the fir trees, and the scent of roses gave way to a rich piney smell that made me remember being a kid, and holidays up in the lakes. Mr Cliff finally broke the silence:

'I've been thinking, Major Davies. I've got a proposition that may interest you—'

★　　　★　　　★　　　★

I didn't see Louie when the tree went on board; one of his boys handled it. There wasn't a sign of any of the company police around, and I guessed Louie was distracting them with a friendly game of poker. Skinning 'em too, if I knew Louie. I didn't see him until the end of my second shift on the trip. The radar screen was a beautiful blank; it was a clear season for meteors. Louie was lolling in front of it reading a book.

'Louie, I always knew I slipped up when I majored in Nav. Do they pay you for this?'

Sometimes there's ill feeling about the large stretches of easy time radar-ops manage to corner, but Louie knew I'd been in space too long for that. Until the automatic relays smarten up a lot there's got to be a man on the screen. And the company doesn't give time away; the radar section handle the quarter-mastering, too. Every third furlough they lose two days.

Louie grinned. 'I've got a weak heart. Didn't you know?'

I tossed him a cigarette. 'Thanks for getting baby on board. What did you throw out – gold bars?'

He shook his head. 'Just my own brand of math. If that orbit you've laid us turns out bad enough, we'll hit the sun approximately ten minutes sooner than we would otherwise. And I've got to pep my meteor deflection up by three thousandths of a second. It's a big risk.'

'My orbit's good,' I said. 'I'll never lay one better. Next trip I'm going to lay the tightest Moon-Earth orbit since Christiansen came in on the Leonids. After that you needn't worry about my failing eyes, Louie.'

'I'm glad, Joe. I always knew you had sense. I'm dropping out the moment they give me a hint. It's not worth it.'

'Yes, Louie, I'm really going.'

'You'll miss it, Joe, but you'll get over that. You'd have to anyway before long.'

'It's out in the country, Louie. A nursery. Growing plants, all kinds of plants. Fir trees and chrysanthemums and daffodils – and roses at Christmas. And the moon's no more than something you plant by. I shan't miss anything.'

'You're lucky, Joe. That's what it is – you're lucky.'

★   ★   ★   ★

We cushioned at three G's and I felt it again; a long ache inside my chest as though my heart and lungs were tied up with strings and someone was twisting them nice and slowly. It was all right after a few minutes and I got up, light and active under Moon gravity. I wasted no time getting through the main lock. I looked for old Hans amongst those who stood by, but there was no sign of him. I called Portugese, who runs the grog shop.

'Portugese! Where's Hans? I've got something for him.'

He came waddling over. With a bulk like his I could almost understand why he had chosen Luna City. He shrugged, lifting everything – hands, shoulders and eyebrows.

'Too late now,' he said. 'He died just after nightfall. We're taking him out in a few hours.'

★   ★   ★   ★

In Luna City there are no extras. You don't waste anything that has to be freighted a quarter of a million miles; and that includes oxygen. When men die there, their bodies are kept until nightfall when, for three hundred and thirty-six hours, darkness freezes into rime the last traces of the Moon's atmosphere. Some time during the night the body is taken out in a caterpillar and committed, with duly economical rites, to some cleft in the antique rocks. With the sunrise the thin air melts, the grey lichen runs like a sickness along the crater bottoms, and in that microscopic jungle the minute lunar insects awaken to fight battles as real as Tyrannosaurus ever knew. Long before the crater shadows lengthen towards sunset the cleft is empty again. No flesh, no hair, no scrap of bone escapes them.

307

Right overhead was the Earth, glowing with daylight.

Portugese drove the caterpillar out through the air lock. Louie and I sat behind him with old Hans' body, covered by a sheet, on the floor between us. We were silent while the little truck jolted on its metal tracks across granite and pumice and frozen lava. And I don't think it was the death inside that silenced us; we had liked old Hans but he had had his time, and was released now to infinity from the narrow confines of Luna City. It was the death outside that quietened us, as it quietens any man who goes out among those age-old crests and pinnacles, under those glaring stars.

Portugese halted the caterpillar on the crest of a rise about midway between Luna City and Kelly's Crater. It was the usual burial ground; the planet's surface here was crosshatched in deep grooves by some age-old catastrophe. We clamped down the visors on our suits and got out. Portugese and I carried old Hans easily between us, his frail body fantastically light against lunar gravity. We put him down carefully in a wide, deep cleft, and I turned round towards the truck. Louie walked towards us, carrying the Christmas tree. There had been moisture on it which had frozen instantly into sparkling frost. It looked like a centre-piece out of a store window. It had seemed a good idea back in Luna City, but now it didn't seem appropriate.

We wedged it in with rocks, Portugese read a prayer, and we walked back to the caterpillar, glad to be able to let our visors down again and light up cigarettes. We stayed there while we smoked, looking through the front screen. The tree stood up green and white against the sullen, hunching blackness of Kelly's Crater. Right overhead was the Earth, glowing with daylight. I could make out Italy, clear and unsmudged, but farther north Hans's beloved Austria was hidden under blotching December cloud.

We didn't say anything. Portugese squeezed out his cigarette and started the caterpillar up, turning her round again towards Luna City. We ran into B lock, and Portugese stabled the truck and came out again to join us. He put his fat arms around our shoulders.

'Come on, boys. Always a drink on the house after a burying party.'

'Medical first, Portugese,' Louie said. 'We'll look in afterwards. Keep the rum hot for us.'

We saw him glide away, and turned back ourselves towards the Administration Building. The others had been through the Medical while we were out, and we had a doctor each without any waiting. We sat in the anteroom afterwards, waiting for them to write our cards up before we could collect them. At last the call came through on the speaker:

'Major Davies. Lieutenant Enderby. Cards ready now.'

Louie got his first. He looked at the big blue stamp on the front – FIRST WARNING. He grinned.

'We'll go out in harness, Joe. Any chance of a third partnership in that flower business?'

I didn't say anything. I could see my card before the doctor gave it to me. I saw the red star splashed on it, and I'd seen too many of them not to know what it meant. It was the mark of the exile, the outlaw who had waited too long to get out. It was the beginning of such a story as the one whose end, forty years later, I had witnessed in the lee of Kelly's Crater under the mocking globe of Earth.

'This is my last trip,' I told the doctor. 'When we hit Antwerp I'm retiring.'

He shook his head. 'I'm sorry.'

'I don't care if it's a million-to-one chance, Doc. I'll take it; and no hard feelings if it doesn't come off. I'll sign any disclaimer the company wants.'

'It's no good, major. You know the regulations. These things are too foolproof now. We're not allowed to let you commit suicide.'

I knew it was no good, too. Louie had gone. We all knew better than to stick around when someone got the red star. I had time to look at the doctor. He was very young and didn't look very happy. I guessed he hadn't handed out a star before.

'It could be worse, major. It could have been Phobos.'

★   ★   ★   ★

From the top level in Luna City you can see the sky; at night the stars and the softly glowing Earth. Down to the west Sirius blazes over Kelly's Crater. I've been up here for hours watching them.

I keep thinking I can smell roses.

The Stainless Steel Rat

Harry Harrison

When the office door opened suddenly I knew the game was up. It had been a money-maker – but it was all over. As the cop walked in I sat back in the chair and put on a happy grin. He had the same sombre expression and heavy foot that they all have – and the same lack of humour. I almost knew to the word what he was going to say before he uttered a syllable.

'James Bolivar diGriz I arrest you on the charge—'

I was waiting for the word *charge*, I thought it made a nice touch that way. As he said it I pressed the button that set off the charge of black powder in the ceiling, the crossbeam buckled and the three-ton safe dropped through right on the top of the cop's head. He squashed very nicely, thank you. The cloud of plaster dust settled and all I could see of him was one hand, slightly crumpled. It twitched a bit and the index finger pointed at me accusingly. His voice was a little muffled by the safe and sounded a bit annoyed. In fact he repeated himself a bit:

'. . . On the charge of illegal entry, theft, forgery—'

He ran on like that for quite a while, it was an impressive list but I had heard it all before. I didn't let it interfere with my stuffing all the money from the desk drawers into my suitcase. The list ended with a new charge and I would swear on a stack of thousand credit notes *that* high that there was a hurt tone in his voice.

'In addition the charge of assaulting a police robot will be added to your record. This was foolish since my brain and larynx are armoured and in my midsection—'

'That I know well, George, but your little two-way radio is in the top of your pointed head and I don't want you reporting to your friends just yet.'

One good kick knocked the escape panel out of the wall and gave access to the steps to the basement. As I skirted the rubble on the floor the robot's fingers snapped out at my leg, but I had been waiting for that and they closed about two inches short. I have been followed by enough police robots to know by now how indestructible they are. You can blow them up or knock them down and they keep coming after you; dragging themselves by one good finger and spouting saccharine morality all the while. That's what this one was doing. Give up my life of crime and pay my debt to society and such. I could still hear his voice echoing down the stair-well as I reached the basement.

Every second was timed now. I had about three minutes before they would be on my tail, and it would take me exactly one minute and eight seconds to get clear of the building. That wasn't much of a lead and I would need all of it. Another kick panel opened out into the label-removing room. None of the robots looked up as I moved down the aisle – I would have been surprised if they had. They were all low-grade M types, short on brains and good only for simple, repetitive work. That was why I hired them. They had no curiosity as to why they were taking the labels off the filled cans of azote fruits, or what was at the other end of the moving belt that brought the cans through the wall. They didn't even look up when I unlocked the Door That Was Never Unlocked that led through the wall. I left it open behind me as I had no more secrets now.

$$\star \qquad \star \qquad \star \qquad \star$$

Keeping next to the rumbling belt, I stepped through the jagged hole I had chopped in the wall of the government warehouse. I had installed the belt too, this and the hole were the illegal acts that I had to do myself. Another locked door opened into the warehouse itself. The automatic fork-lift truck was busily piling cans onto the belt and digging fresh ones out of the ceiling-high piles. This fork-lift had hardly enough brains to be called a robot it just followed taped directions to load the cans. I stepped around it and dog-trotted down the aisle. Behind me the sounds of my illegal activity died away. It gave me a warm feeling to still hear it going full blast like that.

It *had* been one of the nicest little rackets I had ever managed. For a small capital outlay I had rented the warehouse that backed on the government warehouse. A simple hole in the wall and I had access to the entire stock of stored goods, long-term supplies that I knew would be untouched for months or years in a warehouse this size. Untouched, that is, until I came along.

After the hole had been made and the belt installed it was just a matter of business. I hired the robots to remove the old labels and substitute the colourful ones I had printed. Then I marketed my goods in a strictly legal fashion. My stock was the best and due to my imaginative operation my costs were very low, I could afford to undersell my competitors and still make a handsome profit. The local wholesalers had been quick to sense a bargain and I had orders for months ahead. It *had* been a good operation – and could have gone on for quite a while.

I stifled that train of thought before it started. One lesson that has to be remembered in my line of business is that when an operation is over it is OVER! The temptation to stay just one more day or to cash just one more cheque can be almost overwhelming, ah, how well I know. I also know that it is also the best way to get better acquainted with the police.

Turn your back and walk away – And live to graft another day.
That's my motto and it's a good one. I got where I am because I stuck to it.

And daydreams aren't part of getting away from the police.

★   ★   ★   ★

I pushed all thoughts from my mind as I reached the end of the aisle. The entire area outside must have been swarming with cops by this time and I had to move fast and make no mistakes. A fast look right and left. Nobody in sight. Two steps ahead and press the elevator button. I had put a meter on this back elevator and it showed that the thing was used once a month on the average.

It arrived in about three seconds, empty, and I jumped in, thumbing the roof button at the same time. The ride seemed to go on forever, but that was just subjective. By the record it was exactly fourteen seconds. This was the most dangerous part of the trip. I tightened up as the elevator slowed. My ·75 calibre recoilless was in my hand, that would take care of one cop, but no more.

The door shuffled open and I relaxed. Nothing. They must have the entire area covered on the ground so they hadn't bothered to put cops on the roof.

In the open air now I could hear the sirens for the first time – a wonderful sound. They must have had half of the entire police force out from the amount of noise they were making. I accepted it as any artist accepts tribute.

The board was behind the elevator shaft where I had left it. A little weather-stained but still strong. A few seconds to carry it to the edge of the parapet and reach it across to the next building.

Gently, this was the one dangerous spot where speed didn't count. Carefully onto the end of the board, the suitcase held against my chest to keep my centre of gravity over the board. One step at a time. A thousand-foot drop to the ground. If you don't look down you can't fall . . .

Over. Time for speed. The board behind the parapet, if they didn't see it at first my trail would be covered for a while at least. Ten fast steps and there was the door to the stairwell. It opened easily – and it better have – I had put enough oil on the hinges. Once inside I threw the bolt and took a long, deep breath. I wasn't out of it yet, but the worst part where I ran the most risk, was past. Two uninterrupted minutes here and they would never find James Bolivar, alias 'Slippery Jim' diGriz.

*　　*　　*　　*

The stairwell at the roof was a musty, badly lit cubicle that was never visited. I had checked it carefully a week before for phono and optic bugs and it had been clear. The dust looked undisturbed, except for my own footprints. I had to take a chance that it hadn't been bugged since then. The calculated risk must be accepted in this business.

Goodbye James diGriz, weight ninety-eight kilos, age about forty-five, thick in the middle and heavy in the jowls, a typical business man whose picture graces the police files of a thousand planets – also his fingerprints. They went first. When you wear them they feel like a second skin, a touch of solvent though and they peel off like a pair of transparent gloves.

All my clothes next – and then the girdle in reverse – that lovely paunch that straps around my belly and holds twenty kilos of lead mixed with thermite. A quick wipe from the bottle of bleach and my hair was its natural shade of brown, the eyebrows, too. The nose plugs and cheek pads hurt coming out, but that only lasts a second. Then the blue-eyed contact lenses. This process leaves me mother-naked and I always feel as if I have been born again. In a sense it is true, I had become a new man, twenty kilos lighter, ten years younger and with a completely different description. The large suitcase held a complete change of clothes and a pair of dark-rimmed glasses that replaced the contact lenses. All the loose money fitted neatly into a brief case.

When I straightened up I really felt as if ten years had been stripped from me. I was so used to wearing that weight that I never noticed it – until it was gone. Put a real spring in my step.

The thermite would take care of all the evidence, I kicked it all into a heap and triggered the fuse. It caught with a roar and bottles, clothes, bag, shoes, weights, et al, burned with a cheerful glare. The police would find a charred spot on the cement and micro-analysis might get them a few molecules off the walls, but that was all they would get. The glare of the burning thermite threw jumping shadows around me as I walked down three flights to the one hundred twelfth floor.

Luck was still with me, there was no one on the floor when I opened the door. One minute later the express elevator let me and a handful of other business types out into the lobby.

Only one door was open to the street and a portable TV camera was trained on it. No attempt was being made to stop people from going in and out of the building, most of them didn't even notice the camera and the little group of cops around it. I walked towards it at an even pace. Strong nerves count for a lot in this business.

For one instant I was square in the field of that cold, glass eye, then I was past. Nothing happened so I knew I was clear. That camera must have fed direct to the main computer at police headquarters, if my description had been close enough to the one they had on file those robots would have been notified and I would have been pinned before I had taken a step. You can't outmove a computer-robot combination, not when they move and think in microseconds – but you can out-think them. I had done it again.

A cab took me about ten blocks away. I waited until it was out of sight then took another one. It wasn't until I was in the third cab that I felt safe enough to go to the space terminal. The sounds of sirens were growing fainter and fainter behind me and only an occasional police car tore by in the opposite direction.

They were sure making a big fuss over a little larceny, but that's the way it goes on these overcivilized worlds. Crime is such a rarity now that the police really get carried away when they run across some. In a way I can't blame them, giving out traffic tickets must be an awful dull job. I really believe they ought to thank me for putting a little excitement in their otherwise dull lives.

★   ★   ★   ★

It was a nice ride to the spaceport being located, of course, far out of town. I had time to lean back and watch the scenery and gather my thoughts. Even time to be a little philosophical. For one thing I could enjoy a good cigar again, I smoked only cigarettes in my other personality and never violated that personality, even in strictest privacy. The cigars were still fresh in the pocket humidor where I had put them six months ago. I sucked a long mouthful and blew the smoke out at the flashing scenery. It was good to be off the job, just about as good as being on it. I could never make my mind up which period I enjoyed more – I guess they are both right at the time.

My life is so different from that of the overwhelming majority of people in our society that I doubt if I could even explain it to them. They exist in a fat, rich union of worlds that have almost forgotten the meaning of the word crime. There are few malcontents and even fewer that are socially maladjusted. The few that are still born in spite of centuries of genetic control are caught early and the aberration quickly adjusted. Some don't show their weakness until they are adults, they are the ones who try their hand at petty crime – burglary, shop-lifting or such.

They get away with it for a week or two or a month or two, depending on the degree of their native intelligence. But sure as atomic decay – and just as predestined – the police reach out and pull them in.

That is almost the full extent of crime in our organized, dandified society. Ninety-nine per cent of it, let's say. It is that last and vital one per cent that keeps the police departments in business. That one per cent is me, and a few others like me, a handful of men scattered around the galaxy. Theoretically we can't exist, and if we do exist we can't operate – but we do. We are the rats in the wainscoting of society – we operate outside of their barriers and outside of their rules. Society had more rats when the rules were looser, just as the old wooden buildings had more rats than the concrete buildings that came later. But they still had rats. Now that society is all ferroconcrete and stainless steel there are fewer gaps between the joints, and it takes a smart rat to find them. A stainless steel rat is right at home in this environment.

It is a proud and lonely thing to be a stainless steel rat – and it is the greatest experience in the galaxy if you can get away with it. The sociological experts can't seem to agree why we exist, some even doubt that we do. The most widely accepted theory says that we are victims of delayed psychological disturbance that shows no evidence in childhood when it can be detected and corrected and only appears later in life. I have naturally given a lot of thought to the topic and I don't hold with that idea at all.

A few years back I wrote a small book on the subject – under a nom de plume of course – that was rather well received. My theory is that the aberration is a philosophical one, not a psychological one. At a certain stage the realization striked through that one must either live outside of society's bonds or die of absolute boredom. There is no future or freedom in the circumscribed life and the only other life is complete rejection of the rules. There is no longer room for the soldier of fortune or the gentleman adventurer who can live both within and outside of society. Today it is all or nothing. To save my own sanity I chose the nothing.

*   *   *   *

The cab just reached the spaceport as I hit on this negative line of thought and I was glad to abandon it. Loneliness is the thing to fear in this business, that and self-pity can destroy you if they get the upper hand. Action has always helped me, the elation of danger and escape always clears my mind. When I paid the cab I shortchanged the driver right under his nose, palming one of the credit notes in the act of handing it to him. He was blind as a riveted bulkhead, his gullibility had me humming with delight. The tip I gave him more than made up the loss since I only do this sort of petty business to break the monotony.

There was a robot clerk behind the ticket window, he had that extra third eye in the centre of this forehead that meant a camera. It clicked slightly as I purchased a ticket recording my face and destination. A normal precaution on the part of the police, I would have been surprised if it hadn't happened. My destination was intersystem so I doubted if the picture would appear any place except in the files. I wasn't making an interstellar hop this time, as I usually did after a big job, it wasn't necessary. After a job a single world or a small system is too small for more work, but Beta Cygnus has a system of almost twenty planets all with terrafied weather. This planet, III, was too hot now, but the rest of the system was wide open. There was a lot of commercial rivalry within the system and I knew their police departments didn't co-operate too well. They would pay the price for that. My ticket was for Moriy, number XVIII, a large and mostly agricultural planet.

There were a number of little stores at the spaceport, I shopped them carefully and outfitted a new suitcase with a complete wardrobe and travelling essentials. The tailor was saved for last. He ran up a couple of travelling suits and a formal kilt for me and I took them into the fitting booth. Strictly by accident I managed to hang one of the suits over the optic bug in the wall and made undressing sounds with my feet while I doctored the ticket I had just bought. The other end of my cigar cutter was a punch, with it I altered the keyed holes that indicated my destination. I was now going to planet X, not XVIII, and I had lost almost two hundred credits with the alteration. That's the secret of ticket and order changing, don't raise the face value – there is too good a chance that this will be noticed. If you lower the value and lose money on the deal, even if it is caught, people will be sure it is a mistake on the machine's part. There is never the shadow of a doubt, since why should anyone change a ticket to lose money?

Before the police could be suspicious I had the suit off the bug and tried it on, taking my time. Almost everything was ready now, I had about an hour to kill before the ship left. I spent the time wisely by going to an automatic cleaner and having all my new clothes cleaned and pressed. Nothing interests a customs man more than a suitcase full of unworn clothes.

Customs was a snap and when the ship was about half full I boarded her and took a seat near the hostess. I flirted with her until she walked away, having classified me in the category of MALE, BRASH, ANNOYING. An old girl who had the seat next to mine also had me filed in the same drawer and was looking out of the window with obvious ice on her shoulder. I dozed off happily since there is one thing better than not being noticed and that is being noticed and filed into a category. Your description gets mixed up with every other guy in the file and that is the end of it.

★   ★   ★   ★

When I woke up we were almost to planet X, I half dozed in the chair until we touched down, then smoked a cigar while my bag cleared customs. My locked brief case of money raised no suspicions since I had foresightedly forged papers six months ago with my occupation listed as *bank messenger*. Interplanet credit was almost nonexistent in this system, so the customs men were used to seeing a lot of cash go back and forth.

Almost by habit I confused the trail a little more and ended up in the large manufacturing city of Brouggh over one thousand kilometres from the point where I had landed. Using an entirely new set of identification papers I registered at a quiet hotel in the suburbs.

Usually after a big job like this I rest up for a month or two; this was one time though I didn't feel like a rest. While I was making small purchases around town to rebuild the personality of James diGriz, I was also keeping my eyes open for new business opportunities. The very first day I was out I saw what looked like a natural – and each day it looked better and better.

One of the main reasons I have stayed out of the arms of the law for as long as I have, is that I have never repeated myself. I have dreamed up some of the sweetest little rackets, run them off once, then stayed away from them forever after. About the only thing they had in common was the fact that they all made money. About the only thing I hadn't hit to date was out and out armed robbery. It was time for a change and it looked like that was it.

While I was rebuilding the paunchy personality of Slippery Jim I was making plans for the operation. Just about the time the finger-print gloves were ready the entire business was planned. It was simple like all good operations should be, the less details there are, the less things there are that can go wrong.

I was going to hold up Moraio's, the largest retail store in the city. Every evening, at exactly the same time, an armoured car took the day's receipts to the bank. It was a tempting prize – a gigantic sum in untraceable small bills. The only real problem as far as I was concerned was how one man could handle the sheer bulk and weight of all that money. When I had an answer to that the entire operation was ready.

All the preparations were of course, made only in my mind until the personality of James diGriz was again ready. The day I slipped that weighted belly back on, I felt I was back in uniform. I lit my first cigarette almost with satisfaction, then went to work. A day or two for some purchases and a few simple thefts and I was ready. I scheduled the following afternoon for the job.

A large tractor-truck that I had bought was the key to the operation – along with some necessary alterations I had made to the interior. I parked the truck in an 'L' shaped alley about a half mile from Moraio's. The truck almost completely blocked the alley but that wasn't impor-tant since it was used only in the early morning. It was a leisurely stroll back to the department store, I reached it at almost the same moment that the armoured truck pulled up. I leaned against the wall of the gigantic building while the guards carried out the money. My money.

To someone of little imagination I suppose it would have been an awe-inspiring sight. At least five armed guards standing around the entrance, two more inside the truck as well as the driver and his assistant. As an added precaution there were three monocycles purring next to the curb, they would go with the truck as protection on the road. Oh, very impressive. I had to stifle a grin behind my cigarette when I thought about what was going to happen to those elaborate precautions.

I had been counting the hand-trucks of money as they rolled out of

My ears were numb from the roar of the exploding slugs and I could just make out the thud of running footsteps.

the door. There were always fifteen, no more, no less; this practice made it easy for me to know the exact time to begin. Just as fourteen was being loaded into the armoured truck, load number fifteen appeared in the store entrance. The truck driver had been counting the way I had, he stopped down from the cab and moved to the door in the rear in order to lock it when loading was finished.

★   ★   ★   ★

We synchronized perfectly as we strolled by each other. At the moment he reached the rear door I reached the cab, quietly and smoothly I climbed up into it and slammed the door behind me. The assistant had just enough time to open his mouth and pop his eyes when I placed an anaesthetic bomb on his lap; he slumped in an instant. I was, of course, wearing the correct filter plugs in my nostrils. As I started the motor with my left hand I threw a larger bomb through the connecting window to the rear with my right. There were some reassuring thumps as the guards there dropped over the bags of change.

This entire process hadn't taken six seconds. The guards on the steps were just waking up to the fact that something was wrong. I gave them a cheerful wave through the window and gunned the armoured truck away from the curb. One of them tried to run and throw himself through the open rear door but he was a little too late. It all had happened so fast that not one of them had thought to shoot, I had been sure there would be a *few* bullets. The sedentary life on these planets does slow the reflexes.

The monocycle drivers caught on a lot faster, they were after me before the truck had gone a hundred feet. I slowed down until they had caught up, then stamped on the accelerator, keeping just enough speed so they couldn't pass me.

Their sirens were screaming of course and they had their guns working; it was just as I had planned. We tore down the street like jet racers and the traffic melted away before us. They didn't have time to think and realize that *they* were making sure the road was clear for my escape. The situation was very humorous and I'm afraid I chuckled out loud as I tooled the truck around the tight corners.

Of course the alarm had been turned in and the road blocks must have been forming up ahead – but that half mile went by fast at the speed we were doing. It was a matter of seconds before I saw the alley mouth ahead. I turned the truck into it, at the same time pressing the button on my pocket short wave.

Along the entire length of the alley my smoke bombs ignited. They were, of course, home made, as was all my equipment, nevertheless they produced an adequately dense cloud in that narrow alley. I pulled the truck a bit to the right until the fenders scraped the wall and only slightly reduced my speed, this way I could steer by touch. The monocycle drivers of course couldn't do this and had the choice of stopping or rushing headlong into the darkness. I hope they made the right decision and none of them were hurt.

The same radio impulse that triggered the bombs was supposed to have opened the rear door of the trailer truck up ahead and dropped the ramp. It had worked fine when I had tested it, I could only hope now that it did the same in practice. I tried to estimate the distance I had gone in the alley by timing my speed, but I was a little off. The front wheels of the truck hit the ramp with a destructive crash and the armoured truck bounced rather than rolled into the interior of the larger van. I was jarred around a bit and had just enough sense left to jam on the brakes before I ploughed right through into the cab.

Smoke from the bombs made a black midnight of everything, that and my shaken-up brains almost ruined the entire operation. Valuable seconds went by while I leaned against the truck wall trying to get oriented. I don't know how long it took, when I finally did stumble back to the rear door I could hear the guards' voices calling back and forth through the smoke. They heard the bent ramp creak as I lifted it so I threw two gas bombs out to quiet them down.

The smoke was starting to thin as I climbed up to the cab of the tractor and gunned it into life. A few feet down the alley and I broke through into sunlight. The alley mouth opened out into a main street a few feet ahead and I saw two police cars tear by. When the truck reached the street I stopped and took careful note of all witnesses. None of them showed any interest in the truck or the alley. Apparently all the commotion was still at the other end of the alley. I poured power into the engine and rolled out into the street, away from the store I had just robbed.

Of course I only went a few blocks in that direction then turned down a side street. At the next corner I turned again and headed back towards Moraio's, the scene of my recent crime. The cool air coming in the window soon had me feeling better, I actually whistled a bit as I threaded the big truck through the service roads.

It would have been fine to go up the highway in front of Moraio's and see all the excitement, but that would have been only asking for trouble. Time was still important. I had carefully laid out a route that avoided all congested traffic and this was what I followed. It was only a matter of minutes before I was pulling into the loading area in the back of the big store. There was a certain amount of excitement here but it was lost in the normal bustle of commerce. Here and there a knot of truck drivers or shipping foremen were exchanging views on the robbery, since robots don't gossip the normal work was going on. The men were, of course, so excited that no attention was paid to my truck when I pulled into the parking line next to the other vans. I killed the engine and settled back with a satisfied sigh.

The first part was complete. The second part of the operation was just as important though. I dug into my paunch for the kit that I always take on the job – for just such an emergency as this. Normally, I don't believe in stimulants, but I was still groggy from the banging around. Two cc's of Linoten in my ante cubital cleared that up quickly enough. The spring was back in my step when I went into the back of the van.

The driver's assistant and the guards were still out and would stay that way for at least ten hours. I arranged them in a neat row in the front of the truck where they wouldn't be in my way and went to work.

The armoured car almost filled the body of the trailer as I knew it would; therefore I had fastened the boxes to the walls. They were fine, strong shipping boxes with Moraio's printed all over them. It was a minor theft from their warehouse that should go unnoticed. I pulled the boxes down and folded them for packing, I was soon sweating and had to take my shirt off as I packed the money bundles into the boxes.

It took almost two hours to stuff and seal the boxes with tape. Every ten minutes or so I would check through the peephole in the door; only the normal activities were going on. The police undoubtedly had the entire town sealed and were tearing it apart building by building looking for the truck. I was fairly sure that the last place they would think of looking was the rear of the robbed store.

The warehouse that had provided the boxes had also provided a supply of shipping forms. I fixed one of these on each box, addressed to different pick-up addresses and marked paid of course, and was ready to finish the operation.

It was almost dark by this time, however I knew that the shipping department would be busy most of the night. The engine caught on the first revolution and I pulled out of the parking rank and backed slowly up to the platform. There was a relatively quiet area where the shipping dock met the receiving dock, I stopped the trailer as close to the dividing line as I could. I didn't open the rear door until all the workmen were faced in a different direction. Even the stupidest of them would have been interested in why a truck was unloading the firm's own boxes. As I piled them up on the platform I threw a tarp over them, it only took a few minutes. Only when the truck gates were closed and locked did I pull off the tarp and sit down on the boxes for a smoke.

It wasn't a long wait. Before the cigarette was finished a robot from the shipping department passed close enough for me to call him.

'Over there. The M-19 that was loading these burned out a brake-band, you better see that they're taken care of.'

His eyes glowed with the light of duty. Some of these higher M types take their job very seriously. I had to step back quickly as the fork lifts and M-trucks appeared out of the doors behind me. There was a scurry of loading and sorting and my haul vanished down the platform. I lighted another cigarette and watched for a while as the boxes were coded and stamped and loaded on the outgoing trucks and local belts.

All that was left for me now was the disposing of the truck on some side street and changing personalities.

*　　*　　*　　*

As I was getting into the truck I realized for the first time that something was wrong. I, of course, had been keeping an eye on the gate – but not watching it closely enough. Trucks had been going in and out. Now the realization hit me like a hammer blow over the solar plexus. They were the same trucks going both ways. A large, red cross-country job was just pulling out. I heard the echo of its exhaust roar down the street – then die away to an idling grumble. When it roared up again it didn't go away, instead the truck came in through the second gate. There were police cars waiting outside that wall. Waiting for me.

For the first time in my career I felt sharp fear of the hunted man. This was the first time I had ever had the police on my tail when I wasn't expecting them. The money was lost, that much was certain, but I was no longer concerned with that. It was me they were after now.

Think first, then act. I was safe enough for the moment. They were, of course, moving in on me, going slowly as they had no idea of where I was in the giant loading yard. How had they found me? *That* was the important point. The local police were used to an almost crimeless world, they couldn't have found my trail this quick. In fact, I hadn't left a trail, whoever had set the trap here had done it with logic and reason.

Unbidden the words jumped into my mind.

The Special Corps.

Nothing was ever printed about it, only a thousand whispered words heard on a thousand worlds around the galaxy. The Special Corps, the branch of the League that took care of the troubles that individual planets couldn't solve. The Corps was supposed to have finished off the remnants of Haskell's Raiders after the peace, of putting the illegal T & Z Traders out of business, of finally catching Inskipp. And now they were after me.

They were out there waiting for me to make a break. They were thinking of all the ways out just as I was – and they were blocking them. I had to think fast and I had to think right.

Only two ways out. Through the gates or through the store. The gates were too well covered to make a break, in the store there would be other ways out. It had to be that way. Even as I made the conclusion I knew that other minds had made it too, that men were moving in to cover those exits. That thought brought fear – and made me angry as well. The very idea that someone could out-think me was odious. They could try all right – but I would give them a run for their money. I still had a few tricks left.

First, a little misdirection. I started the truck, left it in low gear and aimed it at the gate. When it was going straight I locked the steering wheel with the fraction clamp and dropped out the far side of the cab and strolled back to the warehouse. Once inside I moved faster. Behind me I heard some shots, a heavy crump, and a lot of shouting. That was more like it.

The night locks were connected on the doors that led to the store proper. An old-fashioned alarm that I could disconnect in a few moments. My pick-locks opened the door and I gave it a quick kick with my foot and turned away. There were no alarm bells, but I knew that somewhere in the building an indicator showed that the door was opened. As fast as I could run I went to the last door on the opposite side of the building. This time I made sure the alarm was disconnected before I went through the door. I locked it behind me.

It is the hardest job in the world to run and be quiet at the same time. My lungs were burning before I reached the employees' entrance. A few times I saw flashlights ahead and had to double down different aisles, it was mostly luck that I made it without being spotted. There were two men in uniform standing in front of the door I wanted to go out. Keeping as close to the wall as I could I made it to within twenty feet of them before I threw the gas grenade. For one second I was sure that they had gas masks on and I had reached the end of the road – then they slumped down. One of them was blocking the door, I rolled him aside and slid it open a few inches.

The searchlight couldn't have been more than thirty feet from the door; when it flashed on the light was more pain than glare. I dropped the instant it came on and the slugs from the machine pistol ate a line of glaring holes across the door. My ears were numb from the roar of the exploding slugs and I could just make out the thud of running footsteps. My own ·75 was in my hand and I put an entire clip of slugs through the door, aiming high so I wouldn't hurt anyone. It would not stop them, but it should slow them down.

★　　★　　★　　★

They returned the fire, must have been a whole squad out there. Pieces of plastic flew out of the back wall and slugs screamed down the corridor. It was good cover, I knew there was nobody coming up behind me. Keeping as flat as I could I crawled in the opposite direction, out of the line of fire. I turned two corners before I was far enough from the guns to risk standing up. My knees were shaky and great blobs of colour kept fogging my vision. The searchlight had done a good job, I could barely see at all in the dim light.

I kept moving slowly, trying to get as far away from the gunfire as possible. The squad outside had fired as soon as I had opened the door, that meant standing orders to shoot at anyone who tried to leave the building. A nice trap. The cops inside would keep looking until they found me. If I tried to leave I would be blasted. I was beginning to feel very much like a trapped rat.

Every light in the store came on and I stopped, frozen. I was near the wall of a large farm-goods showroom. Across the room from me were three soldiers. We spotted each other at the same time, I dived for the door with bullets slapping all around me. The military was in it too, they sure must have wanted me bad. A bank of elevators was on the other side of the door – and stairs leading up. I hit the elevator in one bounce and punched the sub-basement button, and just got out ahead of the closing doors. The stairs were back towards the approaching soldiers, I felt like I was running right into their guns. I must have made the turn into the stairs a split second ahead of their arrival. Up the stairs and around the first landing before they were even with the bottom. Luck was still on my side. They hadn't seen me and were sure I had gone down. I sagged against the wall, listening to the shouts and whistle blowing as they turned the hunt towards the basement.

There was one smart one in the bunch. While the others were all following the phony trail I heard him start slowly up the stairs. I didn't have any gas grenades left, all I could do was climb up ahead of him, trying to do it without making a sound.

He came on slowly and steadily and I stayed ahead of him. We went up four flights that way, me in my stockinged feet with my shoes around my neck, his heavy boots behind me making a dull rasping on the metal stairs.

As I started up the fifth flight I stopped, my foot halfway up a step.

Someone else was coming down, someone wearing the same kind of military boots. I found the door to the hall, opened it behind me and slipped through. There was a long hall in front of me lined with offices of some kind. I began to run the length of it, trying to reach a turning before the door behind me could open and those exploding slugs tear me in half. The hall seemed endless and I suddenly realized I would never make it to the end in time.

I was a rat looking for a hole – and there was none. The doors were locked, all of them, I tried each as I came to it, knowing I would never make it. That stairwell door was opening behind me and the gun was coming up, I didn't dare turn and look but I could feel it. When the door opened under my hand I fell through before I realized what had happened. I locked it behind me and leaned against it in the darkness, panting like a spent animal.

Then the light came on and I saw the man sitting behind the desk, smiling at me.

★   ★   ★   ★

There is a limit to the amount of shock the human body can absorb. I'd had mine. I didn't care if he shot me or offered a cigarette – I had reached the end of my line. He did neither. He offered me a cigar instead.

'Have one of these, diGriz, I believe they're your brand.'

The body is a slave of habit, even with death a few inches away it will respond to established custom. My fingers moved of their own volition and took the cigar, my lips clenched it and my lungs sucked it into life. And all the time my eyes watched the man behind the desk waiting for death to reach out.

It must have shown. He waved towards a chair and carefully kept both hands in sight on top of the desk. I still had my gun, it was trained on him.

'Sit down diGriz and put that cannon away. If I wanted to kill you, I could have done it a lot easier than herding you into this room.' His eyebrows moved up in surprise when he saw the expression on my face. 'Don't tell me you thought it was an accident that you ended up here?'

I had, up until that moment, and the lack of intelligent reasoning on my part brought on a wave of shame that snapped me back to reality. I had been outwitted and outfought, the least I could do was surrender graciously. I threw the gun on the desk and dropped into the offered chair. He swept the pistol neatly into a drawer and relaxed a bit himself.

'Had me worried there for a minute, the way you stood there rolling your eyes and waving this piece of field artillery around.'

'Who are you?'

He smiled at the abruptness of my tone. 'Well, it doesn't matter who I am. What does matter is the organization that I represent.'

'The Corps?'

'Exactly. The Special Corps. You didn't think I was the local police, did you? They have orders to shoot you on sight. It was only after I told them how to find you that they let the Corps come along on the job. I have some of my men in the building, they're the ones who herded you up here. The rest are all locals with itchy trigger fingers.'

It wasn't very flattering but it was true. I had been pushed around like a class M robot, with every move charted in advance. The old boy behind the desk – for the first time I realized he was about sixty-five – really had my number. The game was over.

'All right Mr Detective, you have me so there is no sense in gloating. What's next on the programme? Psychological reorientation, lobotomy – or just plain firing squad?'

'None of those I'm afraid. I am here to offer you a job on the Corps.'

The whole thing was so ludicrous that I almost fell out of the chair laughing. Me. James diGriz, the interplanet thief working as a policeman. It was just too funny. The other one sat patiently, waiting until I was through.

★   ★   ★   ★

'I will admit it has its ludicrous side – but only at first glance. If you stop to think, you will have to admit that who is better qualified to catch a thief then another thief?'

There was more than a little truth in that, but I wasn't buying my freedom by turning stool pigeon.

'An interesting offer, but I'm not getting out of this by playing the rat. There is even a code among thieves, you know.'

That made him angry. He was bigger than he looked sitting down and the fist he shook in my face was as large as a shoe.

'What kind of stupidity do you call that? It sounds like a line out of a TV thriller. You've never met another crook in your whole life and you know it! And if you did you would cheerfully turn him in if you could make a profit on the deal. The entire essence of your life is individualism – that and the excitement of doing what others can't do.

Well that's over now, and you better start admitting it to yourself. You can no longer be the interplanet playboy you used to be – but you *can* do a job that will require every bit of your special talents and abilities. Have you ever killed a man?'

His change of pace caught me off guard, I stumbled out an answer.

'No . . . not that I know of.'

'Well you haven't, if that will make you sleep any better at night. You're not a homicidal, I checked that on your record before I came out after you. That is why I know you will join the Corps and get a great deal of pleasure out of going after the *other* kind of criminal who is sick, not just socially protesting. The man who can kill and enjoy it.'

He was too convincing, he had all the answers. I had only one more argument and I threw it in with the air of a last ditch defence.

'What about the Corps, if they ever find out you are hiring half-reformed criminals to do your dirty work we will both be shot at dawn.'

This time it was his turn to laugh. I could see nothing funny so I ignored him until he was finished.

'In the first place my boy, *I* am the Corps – at least the man at the top – and what do you think *my* name is? Harold Peters Inskipp, that's what it is!'

'Not the Inskipp that –'

'The same. Inskipp the Uncatchable. The man who looted the Pharsydion II in mid-flight and pulled all those others deals I'm sure you read about in your misspent youth. I was recruited just the way you were.'

He had me on the ropes. He must have seen my rolling eyes, so he moved in for the kill.

'And who do you think the rest of our agents are? I don't mean the bright-eyed grads of our technical schools, like the ones on my squad downstairs, I mean the full agents. The men who plan the operations, do the preliminary fieldwork and see that everything comes off smoothly. They're crooks. All crooks. The better they were on their own, the better a job they do for the Corps. It's a great, big, brawling universe and you would be surprised at some of the problems that come up. The only men we can recruit to do the job are the ones who have already succeeded at it.

'Are you on?'

It had happened too fast and I hadn't had time to think, I would probably go on arguing for an hour. But way down in the back of my mind the decision had been made. I was going to do it, I couldn't say no.

There was the beginning of a warm glow, too. The human race is gregarious, I knew that even though I had been denying it for years.

I was going to keep on doing the loneliest job in the universe – only I wasn't going to be doing it alone.

Spectator Sport

John D. MacDonald

Dr Rufus Maddon was not generally considered to be an impatient man – or addicted to physical violence.

But when the tenth man he tried to stop on the street brushed by him with a mutter of annoyance Rufus Maddon grabbed the eleventh man, swung him around and held him with his shoulders against a crumbling wall.

He said, 'You will listen to me, sir! I am the first man to travel into the future and I will not stand—'

The man pushed him away, turned around and said, 'You got this dust on my suit. Now brush it off.'

Rufus Maddon brushed mechanically. He said, with a faint uncontrollable tremble in his voice, 'But nobody seems to care.'

The man peered back over his shoulder. 'Good enough, chum. Better go get yourself lobed. The first time I saw the one on time travel it didn't get to me at all. Too hammy for me. Give me those murder jobs. Every time I have one of those I twitch for twenty hours.'

Rufus made another try. 'Sir, I am physical living proof that the future is predetermined. I can explain the energy equations, redesign the warp projector, send myself from your day further into the future—'

The man walked away. 'Go get a lobe job,' he said.

'But don't I look different to you?' Rufus called after him, a plaintive note in his voice.

The man, twenty feet away, turned and grinned at him. 'How?'

When the man had gone Rufus Maddon looked down at his neat grey suit, stared at the men and women in the street. It was not fair of the future to be so – so dismally normal.

Four hundred years of progress? The others had resented the experience that was to be his. In those last few weeks there had been many discussions of how the people four hundred years in the future would look on Rufus Maddon as a barbarian.

Once again he continued his aimless walk down the streets of the familiar city. There was a general air of disrepair. Shops were boarded up. The pavement was broken and potholed. A few automobiles travelled on the broken streets. They, at least, appeared to be of a slightly advanced design but they were dented, dirty and noisy.

The man who had spoken to him had made no sense. 'Lobe job?' And what was 'the one on time travel?'

He stopped in consternation as he reached the familiar park. His consternation arose from the fact that the park was all too familiar. Though it was a tangle of weeds the equestrian statue of General Murdy was still there in deathless bronze, liberally decorated by pigeons.

Clothes had not changed nor had common speech. He wondered if the transfer had gone awry, if this world were something he was dreaming.

He pushed through the knee-high tangle of grass to a wrought-iron bench. Four hundred years before he had sat on that same bench. He sat down again. The metal powdered and collapsed under his weight, one end of the bench dropping with a painful thump.

Dr Rufus Maddon was not generally considered to be a man subject to fits of rage. He stood up rubbing his bruised elbow, and heartily kicked the offending bench. The part he kicked was all too solid.

He limped out of the park, muttering, wondering why the park wasn't used, why everyone seemed to be in a hurry.

It appeared that in four hundred years nothing at all had been accomplished. Many familiar buildings had collapsed. Others still stood. He looked in vain for a newspaper or a magazine.

One new element of this world of the future bothered him considerably. That was the number of low-slung white-panel delivery trucks. They seemed to be in better condition than the other vehicles. Each bore in fairly large gilt letters the legend WORLD SENSEWAYS. But he noticed that the smaller print underneath the large inscription varied. Some read, *Feeder Division* – others, *Hookup Division*.

The one that stopped at the curb beside him read, *Lobotomy Division*. Two husky men got out and smiled at him and one said, 'You've been taking too much of that stuff, Doc.'

'How did you know my title?' Rufus asked, thoroughly puzzled.

The other man smiled wolfishly, patted the side of the truck. 'Nice truck, pretty truck. Climb in, bud. We'll take you down and make you feel wonderful, hey?'

Dr Rufus Maddon suddenly had a horrid suspicion that he knew what a lobe job might be. He started to back away. They grabbed him quickly and expertly and dumped him into the truck.

The sign on the front of the building said WORLD SENSEWAYS. The most luxurious office inside was lettered, *Regional Director – Roger K. Handriss*.

Roger K. Handriss sat behind his handsome desk. He was a florid grey-haired man with keen grey eyes. He was examining his bank book thinking that in another year he'd have enough money with which to retire and buy a permanent hookup. Permanent was so much better than the Temp stuff you could get on the home sets. The nerve ends was what did it, of course.

The girl came in and placed several objects on the desk in front of him. She said, 'Mr Handriss, these just came up from LD. They took them out of the pockets of a man reported as wandering in the street in need of a lobe job.'

She had left the office door open. Cramer, deputy chief of LD, sauntered in and said, 'The guy was really off. He was yammering about being from the past and not to destroy his mind.'

Roger Handriss poked the objects with a manicured finger. He said, 'Small pocket change from the twentieth century, Cramer. Membership cards in professional organizations of that era. Ah, here's a letter.'

As Cramer and the girl waited, Roger Handriss read the letter through twice. He gave Cramer an uncomfortable smile and said,

335

Back in the cubicle the technicians were making the final adjustments.

'This appears to be a letter from a technical publishing house telling Mr – ah – Maddon that they intend to reprint his book. Suggestions on the phone and see if you can raise anyone at the library who can look this up for us. I want to know if such a book was published.'

Miss Hart hastened out of the office.

As they waited, Handriss motioned to a chair. Cramer sat down. Handriss said, 'Imagine what it must have been like in those days, Al. They had the secrets but they didn't begin to use them until – let me see – four years later. Aldous Huxley had already given them their clue with his literary invention of the Feelies. But they ignored them.

'All their energies went into wars and rumours of wars and random scientific advancement and sociological disruptions. Of course, with Video on the march at that time, they were beginning to get a little preview. Millions of people were beginning to sit in front of the Video screens, content even with that crude excuse for entertainment.'

Cramer suppressed a yawn. Handriss was known to go on like that for hours.

'Now,' Handriss continued, 'all the efforts of a world society are channelled into World Senseways. There is no waste of effort changing a perfectly acceptable status quo. Every man can have Temp and if you save your money you can have Permanent, which they say, is as close to heaven as man can get. Uh – what was that, Miss Hart?'

'There is such a book, Mr Handriss, and it was published at that time. A Dr Rufus Maddon wrote it.'

Handriss sighed and clucked. 'Well,' he said, 'have Maddon brought up here.'

Maddon was brought into the office by an attendant. He wore a wide foolish smile and a tiny bandage on his temple. He walked with the clumsiness of an overgrown child.

'Blast it. Al.' Handriss said, 'why couldn't your people have been more careful! He looks as if he might have been intelligent.'

Al shrugged. 'Do they come here from the past every couple of minutes? He didn't look any different than any other lobey to me.'

'I suppose it couldn't be helped,' Handriss said. 'We've done this man a great wrong. We can wait and reeducate, I suppose. But that seems to be treating him rather shabbily.'

'We can't send him back,' Al Cramer said.

Handriss stood up, his eyes glowing. 'But it is within my authority to grant him one of the Perm setups given me. World Senseways knows that Regional Directors make mistakes. This will rectify any mistake to an individual.'

'Is it fair he should get it for free?' Cramer asked. 'And besides, maybe the people who helped send him up here into the future would like to know what goes on.'

Handriss smiled shrewdly. 'And if they knew, what would stop them from flooding in on us? Have Hookup install him immediately.'

The subterranean corridor had once been used for underground trains. But with the reduction in population it had ceased to pay its way and had been taken over by World Senseways to house the sixty-five thousand Perms.

Dr Rufus Maddon was taken, in his new shambling walk to the shining cubicle. His name and the date of installation were written on a card and inserted in the door slot. Handriss stood enviously aside and watched the process.

The bored technicians worked rapidly. They stripped the unprotesting Rufus Maddon, took him inside his cubicle, forced him down onto the foam couch. They rolled him over onto his side, made the usual incision at the back of his neck, carefully slit the main motor nerves, leaving the senses, the heart and lungs intact. They checked the air conditioning and plugged him into the feeding schedule for that bank of Perms.

Next they swung the handrods and the footplates into position, gave him injections of local anaesthetic, expertly flayed the palms of his hands and the soles of his feet, painted the raw flesh with the sticky nerve graft and held his hands closed around the rods, his feet against the plates until they adhered in the proper position.

Handriss glanced at his watch.

'Guess that's all we can watch, Al. Come along.'

The two men walked back down the long corridor. Handriss said, 'The lucky so and so. We have to work for it. I get my Perm in another year – right down here beside him. In the meantime we'll have to content ourselves with the hand sets, holding onto those blasted knobs that don't let enough through to hardly raise the hair on the back of your neck.'

Al sighed enviously. 'Nothing to do for as long as he lives except twenty-four hours a day of being the hero of the most adventurous and glamorous and exciting stories that the race has been able to devise. No memories. I told them to dial him in on the Cowboy series. There's seven years of that now. It'll be more familiar to him. I'm electing Crime and Detection. Eleven years of that now, you know.'

Roger Handriss chuckled and jabbed Al with his elbow. 'Be smart, Al. Pick the Harem series.'

Back in the cubicle the technicians were making the final adjustments. They inserted the sound buttons in Rufus Maddon's ears, deftly removed his eyelids, moved his head into just the right position and then pulled down the deeply concave shining screen so that Rufus Maddon's staring eyes looked directly into it.

The elder technician pulled the wall switch. He bent and peered into the screen. 'Colour okay, three dimensions okay. Come on, Joe, we got another to do before quitting.'

They left, closed the metal door, locked it.

Inside the cubicle, Dr Rufus Maddon was riding slowly down the steep trail from the mesa to the cattle town on the plains. He was trail-weary and sun-blackened. There was an old score to settle. Feeney was about to foreclose on Mary Ann's spread and Buck Hoskie, Mary Ann's crooked foreman, had threatened to shoot on sight.

Rufus Maddon wiped the sweat from his forehead on the back of a lean hard brown hero's hand.

The Hypnoglyph

John Anthony

Jaris held the object cupped in his hand while his thumb stroked the small hollow in its polished side. 'It's really the prize of my collection,' he said, 'but there isn't any real name for it. I call it the hypnoglyph.'

'Hypnoglyph?' Maddick said, putting down a superbly rick-racked Venusian opal the size of a goose egg.

Jaris smiled at the younger man. 'Hypnoglyph,' he said. 'Here, take a look at it.'

Maddick held it in his palm stroking it softly, letting his thumb run gently over the little hollow. 'This, the prize of your collection?' he said. 'Why, it's nothing but a chunk of wood.'

'A man,' Jaris said, 'may be described as not much more than a chunk of meat, but he has some unusual properties.'

Maddick, his thumb still stroking the little hollow, swept his eye over the treasure room. 'I'll say he has. I've never in my life seen more property in one room.'

Jaris' voice gently brushed aside the edge of greed in the younger man's voice. 'It has not been the longest life to date. Perhaps it even has something left to learn.'

Maddick flushed a moment, then pursed his lips almost imperceptibly and shrugged. 'Well, what's it for?' he said. He held the thing in front of him and watched his fingers stroke it.

340

Jaris chuckled again. 'It's for exactly what you're doing. The thing is irresistible. Once you've picked it up, your thumb just automatically strokes that little hollow, and it just automatically hates to stop stroking.'

Maddick's voice took on the tone that the very young reserve for humouring the very old. 'It's a pleasant gadget,' he said. 'But why the rather pretentious name?'

'Pretentious?' Jaris said. 'I had simply thought of it as descriptive. The thing actually is hypnotic.' He smiled watching Maddick's fingers still playing with the thing. 'You may recall a sculptor named Gainsdale who fooled with such things towards the end of the Twentieth Century. He founded a school of sculpture called Tropism.'

Maddick shrugged, still absorbed in the object. 'Everyone and his brother started a school of something back there; I guess I missed that one.'

'It was an interesting theory,' Jaris said, picking up an Arcturian space-crystal and watching the play of light rays from it. 'He argued – soundly enough as I see it – that the surface of every organism has certain innate tactile responses. A cat innately likes to be stroked in certain ways. A heliotrope innately moves to face the light.'

'And the leg,' Maddick quipped, 'innately likes to be pulled. So far we've covered some basic facts about tropism with a small *t*. What of it?'

'It isn't the facts so much as the application that's interesting,' Jaris said, ignoring the younger man's rudeness. 'Gainsdale simply carried his awareness of tropism farther than anyone had before. Anyone on earth at least. He argued that every surface of the body innately responds to certain shapes and textures and he set out to carve objects that – as he put it – made the bodily surfaces innately happy. He made objects for rubbing up and down the neck, objects for rubbing across the forehead. He even claimed he could cure headaches that way.'

'That's nothing but old Chinese medicine,' Maddick said. 'I bought an Eighth Century talisman for rubbing out rheumatism just last week. Curio stuff.'

'Gainsdale must certainly have known the Oriental glyptics,' Jaris agreed, 'but he was trying to systematize the idea behind them into a series of principles. He took a fling at reviving the Japanese netsuke, those polished hand-pieces the old Samurais dangled from their belts. But Gainsdale wanted to carve for the whole body. He tried psychic jewelry at one point and designed bracelets that innately pleased the arm. For a while he got to designing chairs that were irresistible to the buttocks.'

'Quite an art,' Maddick said, turning the object in his hand, working the little hollow around and around in his fist and then bringing it back to where his thumb could stroke along the tiny hollow. 'You might say he got right down to fundaments.' He smiled at Jaris as if looking for acknowledgment of his wit, but found no response there.

'He was, in fact, quite a man,' Jaris said seriously. 'Maybe the chairs and buttocks gave him the idea but after that he got to experimenting with gimmicks that would preserve sexual potency. The League of Something or Other made him stop that, but it is worth noting that his last child was born when he was eighty-four.'

Maddick leered. 'At last – a practical application!'

Jaris looked down at Maddick's hand still stroking the hypnoglyph, the fingers moving as if they had entered a life of their own. 'After that,' he said, ignoring Maddick's still lingering leer, 'he got to designing sleeping blocks – wooden pillows something like the Japanese porcelain block, but moulded to give the head pleasure. He claimed it produced good dreams. But most of all he sculptured for the hand, just as the Japanese carvers of talismans finally settled on the netsuke for their definitive work. After all, the hand is not only the natural tactile organ in one sense; it also has the kind of mobility that can respond to texture and mass most pleasurably.'

Jaris put down the space-crystal and stood watching Maddick's hand. 'Just as you're doing,' he said. 'Gainsdale was after the object the human hand could not resist.'

Maddick looked down at the thing in his hand, the fingers working over it as if they were alone with it somewhere apart from the arm and mind they grew from. 'I must say it is pleasant,' he said. 'But isn't all this just a bit far-fetched? You'd hardly argue that pleasure is absolutely irresistible. If we have no control over our lust for pleasure why aren't we strangling one another for the pleasure of stroking this thing?'

'Maybe,' Jaris said gently, 'because I want less than you do.'

Maddick let his eyes sweep the treasure room. 'Maybe you can damn well afford to,' he said, and for a moment there was no suavity in his voice. He seemed to be aware of the gaff himself, for he changed the subject immediately. 'But I thought you collected nothing but extra-terrestrial stuff. How come this?'

'That,' said Jaris, 'is the curious coincidence. Or one of the curious coincidences. The one you're holding *is* extraterrestrial.'

'And the other curious coincidences?' Maddick said.

Jaris lit one of his poisonous cheroots. 'I might as well begin at the beginning,' he said through the smoke.

'Something told me there was a story coming,' Maddick said. 'You collectors are all alike. I've never known one that wasn't a yarn spinner. I think it's the real reason for the collection.'

Jaris smiled. 'A professional disease. Do we collect so we can tell yarns, or tell yarns so we can collect? Maybe if I tell the yarn well enough I'll collect you. Well, sit down and I'll do my best: a new audience, a new opportunity.'

He waved Maddick into an elaborately carved bone chair, placed the humidor, the drug sachets, and a decanter of Danubian brandy within easy reach of him, and sat down behind the desk with a wave of the hand that told Maddick to help himself.

'I suppose,' he said after that pause-before-the-yarn that no story teller can omit, 'I suppose one of the reasons I prize the thing is because I got it on my last blast into deep space. As you see,' he added, waving his hand about him lightly, 'I made the mistake of coming back rich, and it killed the wanderlust. Now I'm earthbound by my own avidity.'

Maddick sat stroking the smooth little hollow with his thumb. 'Being filthy rich is hardly the worst fate imaginable, I should think.'

But Jaris's mind was on his story. 'I'd been prospecting for space-crystals out towards Deneb Kaitos,' he continued, 'and I'd really struck bonanza, an asteroid belt just popping with the luscious things. We had the ship bulging with enough of them to buy Terra twice over, and we were starting back when we found that Deneb Kaitos had a planetary system. There had been several expeditions out that way before with no mention of the system and we had been so busy hauling in space-crystals that we hadn't been doing much looking. But I realized then that what I had thought was just an asteroid belt was really a broken-up planet orbiting around its sun. With the fragments running about eight per cent pure diamond, it was no wonder we'd hit the mother lode of them all.

'We ran a quick survey on the system and decided to put into DK-8 for the specimen run-over and life-forms data. DK-6 gave some indications of life-forms but hardly enough to be worth the extra stop. DK-8, on the other hand, ran high. So high it looked like a good chance for Federation Prize Money. With a ship load of space-crystals, even a million Units seemed small change, but it would be a kick to turn up a new Intelligence Group. The Columbus complex, you know.

'At any rate we put into DK-8, and that's where I got that thing you're holding. On DK-8 it's a hunting implement.'

Maddick looked puzzled. 'Hunting,' he said. 'You mean the way David got Goliath? Zingo?'

'No,' Jaris said. 'It's not a missile. It's a snare. The natives set them out and trap animals with them.'

Still stroking it, Maddick looked at the gadget. 'Oh come now,' he said. 'You mean they just set them out, wait for termites to invade, and then eat the termites? That kind of snare?'

Jaris's voice stiffened for an instant. 'There are queerer things than that in space.' Then his voice softened. 'You're young yet,' he said. 'You have time enough. That gadget, for instance: you wouldn't believe a culture was founded on it. You're not ready to believe.'

Maddick's smile said: 'Well, after all you can't expect me to swallow this stuff, can you?' Aloud he said, 'A yarn's a yarn. Let's have it.'

'Yes,' Jaris said, 'I suppose it is incredible. In a way, that's what space is: the constant recurrence of the incredible. After a while you forget what a norm is. Then you're a space hand.' He looked off a moment across the shining collection around him. 'DK-8, for example. Once the indicator told us to expect intelligence, it was no surprise to come on side-humans. By that time it had been universally established that you can expect intelligence only in primate and quasi-primate forms. Unless you've got the prehensile hand and the supraorbital arch there's just no way for intelligence to get started. A monkey develops a hook for swinging through the trees and an eye for measuring distances between leaps and he's fitted for his environment. But it just happens that the hand is good for picking things up and the eye is good for looking at them closely, and pretty soon the monkey is picking things up and examining them and beginning to get ideas. And pretty soon he's beginning to use tools. An ungulate couldn't use a tool in a billion years; he has nothing to hold it with. There's no reason why there mightn't be some sort of lizard intelligence I suppose, except that it just doesn't seem to happen. Probably too low-grade a nervous system.'

Jaris suddenly caught himself, realizing that his voice had been running away with the enthusiasm of his argument. 'I really haven't been back very long,' he said with a smile. 'That's the sort of argument that gets hot in space.' His voice softened again. 'I was saying we weren't much surprised to come on side-humans once we'd got an intelligence indication . . .'

'Odd that I've never heard of it,' Maddick said. 'I keep pretty well posted on that sort of thing. And surely a really close siding—'

'The fact is,' Jaris said, interrupting in his turn, 'we didn't make a report.'

Maddick's voice sharpened with surprise. 'Good heavens, man, and you're telling me? What on earth's to keep me from turning you over to Federation Space Base and getting your mind picked for it?' Once again his eyes swept the treasure room as if running an inventory and his lips pursed shrewdly for an instant. Then his voice loosened. 'If I believed you, that is.'

Jaris leaned back in his chair as if buried in thought and for a moment his voice seemed to be coming up from a cave shaft. 'It doesn't really matter,' he said. 'And besides,' he added with a smile, his voice growing near again, 'you don't, as you say, believe me.'

Maddick looked down at his hand still stroking the polished sides of the gadget. The thumb snaked out over the little polished dimple. In, up and back, in, up and back. Without raising his head, he raised his eyes to meet Jaris's. 'Should I?' he said. Once more his eyes flicked over the treasure room, resting longest on the cabinet of space-crystals.

Jaris noted his look and smiled. 'I've often thought myself what a lovely target I'd make for a blackmailer.'

Maddick looked away quickly. 'If the blackmailer could believe you.'

Jaris smiled. 'Always that doubt,' he said. 'What would you say if I told you the siding was so close that Terrans can mate with DKs?'

Maddick paused a long minute before answering, his eyes fixed on

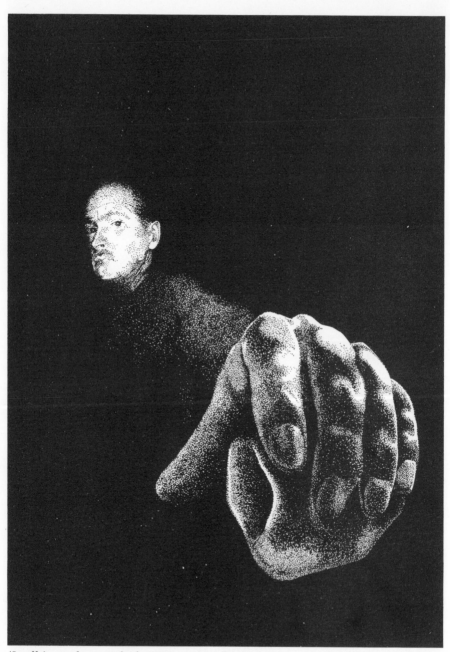

'I call it my hypnoglyth. Here, take a look at it.'

the thing in his hand, watching his fingers curl about and stroke it. He shook his head as if putting something out of his mind. 'I seem to be beyond surprise at this point. Strangely, I believe you. And strangely, I know I should be arguing that it's impossible.'

Suddenly his voice flared up. 'Look here,' he said, 'what is all this rigmarole?' Again his voice calmed abruptly. 'All right. Yes, sure. I believe you. I'm crazy, God knows, but I believe you.'

'Enough to turn me in?'

Maddick flushed without answering.

'I'm afraid they'd only tell you it's impossible,' Jaris said. 'Pity too,' he added wearily. 'As I was saying I'd be such lush pickings for a black-mailer.' He paused a moment, then added gently, 'Don't worry about it, son.'

Maddick's voice did not rise to anger. He looked down at his hand still stroking the thing. 'Is that a threat?' he said indifferently.

Jaris shook his head. 'A regret,' he said. He blew out a cloud of smoke and spoke again more brightly. 'Besides, all the arguments against its being possible are too sound. Life-forms can mate across some of the branches of divergent evolution if the species are related by some reasonably proximate common ancestor. The lion and the tiger, for instance, or the horse and the jackass. But it doesn't work for convergent evolution. You can evolve a species somewhere in space that resembles man, and with space enough and time enough you can evolve a lot of them, but the chemistry and physiology of egg and sperm are too tricky to come close enough without a common ancestor. Nevertheless, Terrans can mate with DK women, and have mated with them. That may sound incredible, said in this room, but after a while you find nothing is incredible in deep space.'

'Deep space,' Maddick said softly. His voice sounded as if it were stroking the words with the same sensuous pleasure his fingers found in stroking the polished thing in his hand.

Jaris caught the movement of his voice and nodded. 'You've time yet. You'll get there. But to get back to DK-8. The only real difference between DKs and humans is the hair and the skin structure. DK-8 has a dense and tropical atmosphere. It's rather high in CO_2 and perpetually misty. The sun's rays have a hard time getting through the atmosphere. Also, the planet is all-tropical. Consequently, the animal life from which the DKs evolved never had to develop a fur covering. Hair is unknown on the planet. Instead, the DK life-forms developed a skin structure extremely sensitive to whatever diffused sun rays they can get. The skin is soft and pallid as a slug's. If a DK were exposed to the direct rays of Sol for a few minutes, he'd die of sunburn.'

Jaris held up the cheroot before him and blew a puff of smoke over its lit end. 'Nature,' he said, 'always has a trick of trying to deal two cards at once. The prehensile hand developed for one reason and became useful for something else. Just so, the DK's tremendously sensitive skin developed originally to absorb the most possible sun, but became in time the basis for a tremendously developed tactile sense.'

'That goes for the lower animals too. Their tropisms are fantastically dominant over their other responses. Once an animal starts stroking one of those gadgets as you're doing, it simply cannot stop.'

Maddick smiled and looked dully, and his thumb ran down into and over the little hollow. Down into and over. Down into and over.

'You might almost say,' Jaris continued, 'that the DKs have developed a tactile science to a degree unknown to us. The energy we have put into a tool culture, they have put into a tactile culture. It isn't a highly developed society in our terms: a rigid tribal matriarchy with a few basic tools that only the women are permitted to operate, and at that only a special clan of the women. The other women lounge about on delicately arranged hill terraces and just lie motionless soaking up sun energy or working up a little voodoo mostly based on hypnotism and tactile gratification.'

His voice grew softer and slightly distant. 'As you might expect, they grow incredibly obese. At first it seemed repulsive to see them lying so. But on DK-8, obesity is really a survival characteristic. It makes for more surface to absorb sun energy. And the women have such perfect control of their skin surfaces that their bodies remain strangely well-proportioned.'

He leaned back and almost closed his eyes. 'Amazing control,' he half whispered. Then suddenly he chuckled. 'But you're probably wondering how they work such hard wood so perfectly with practically no tools. If you look closely you'll find that what you're holding is really grainless. Actually it isn't wood at all, but a kind of huge seed, something like an avocado nut. As you know, you can carve a fresh avocado nut almost as easily as you mould clay, but when you let it dry, it becomes extremely hard. Extremely hard.'

'Extremely hard,' Maddick agreed distantly.

'The women of the proper clan work these things, and the men set them out in the forests. As you might suppose, the men are a rather scrawny lot, and would starve soon enough if they had to depend on their own muscular prowess as hunters. These gadgets take care of all that, however. The animals, with their extremely high tactile suggestibility, come through the forest and find one of these things in their way. They begin to stroke it and feel it, and they just can't stop. The men don't even kill them; all slaughtering is handled by the ruling clan of women. The men simply wait till the animal has worked itself into the right state, and then lead it back to the slaughtering compound – still under hypnosis of course.'

'Of course,' Maddick agreed, his fingers working softly and rhythmically.

Jaris leaned back. His politeness was unfaltering, but now there was a touch of triumph in his voice. 'There's really only one other thing you need to know. The men used to have unmanageable spells. As a result, it has become traditional to hypnotize them practically at birth. The practice is untold centuries old.

'Unfortunately, however, nature still deals a tricky hand. Keep the species in abeyance long enough and it stops thrusting towards its own development. The generations of hypnosis have had the effect of breeding the life-wish out of the males. It's as if the genes and the sperm were just slowly quitting. When we landed on DK-8 there were hardly enough men left to work the traps.'

He leaned forward, smiling. 'You can imagine what a treasure our crew must have seemed to the tribal leaders, once it was discovered that we could interbreed: new vigorous males, a new start, fresh blood for the life stream.'

He paused and his tone became steady and dry. 'I think perhaps you will understand now why I came back alone. The only male ever to leave DK-8. Although,' he added, 'in one sense I've never really left it.'

'. . . never . . . really . . . left . . . it . . .' Maddick said.

Jaris nodded and came around the desk. Leaning over Maddick, he blew a puff of smoke directly into his open eyes. Maddick did not stir. His eyes remained fixed straight ahead and he remained fixed motionless in the chair. Only the fingers of his right hand continued to move, curling about the polished thing, while his thumb flicked out and over the little hollow.

Jaris straightened, still smiling sadly, picked up a curiously wrought little bell from the desk and tinkled it once.

Across the room, a door swung open on a darkened alcove in which something huge and pale showed dimly.

'He is ready, darling,' Jaris said.

Acknowledgements

Grateful acknowledgement is made to authors, publishers and proprietors for permission to include the works listed below:

First Contact by Murray Leinster, reprinted by kind permission of Street & Smith Publications.
Pictures Don't Lie by Katherine Maclean, by kind permission of World Editions Inc.
Knock by Frederic Brown, by kind permission of Elizabeth C. Brown.
Romp by Mack Reynolds, by kind permission of Conde Nast Publications Inc.
Flying Dutchman by Ward Moore. Copyright Wart Moore 1951.
Who Can Replace a Man? by Brian W. Aldiss. Copyright Brian W. Aldiss 1959.
What Thin Partitions by Mark Clifton and Alex Apostolides, by kind permission of Street & Smith Publications.
The Fun They Had, from *Earth is Room Enough* by Isaac Asimov, by kind permission of the author and Doubleday & Co. Inc.
Crossfire by James White, by kind permission of New Worlds SF.
Allamagoosa by Eric Frank Russell, by kind permission of Street & Smith Publications Inc.
The Drop by John Christopher, by kind permission of Galaxy Publishing Corporation.
I'm a Stranger Here Myself by Mack Reynolds, by kind permission of Ziff Davis Publishing Company.
The Luckiest Man in Denv, from *The Marching Morons* by Cyril Kornbluth, by kind permission of Ballantine Books.
Obedience by Frederic Brown, by kind permission of Elizabeth C. Brown.
Not For an Age by Brian W. Aldiss. Copyright Brian W. Aldiss 1959.
Manners of the Age by H. B. Fyfe, by kind permission of Galaxy Publishing Corporation.
Christmas Tree by Christopher Yond, by kind permission of Street & Smith Publications.
The Stainless Steel Rat by Harry Harrison, by kind permission of Conde Nast Publications Inc.
Spectator Sport by John D. MacDonald, by kind permission of Standard Magazines.
The Hypnoglyph by John Anthony, by kind permission of Fantasy House Inc.

Every effort has been made to clear all copyrights and the publishers trust that their apologies will be accepted for any errors or omissions.

The editors acknowledge the contributions of the following artists:

Paul Desmond: 144, 221, 226, 343
David Mitchell: 24, 45, 63, 86, 93, 100, 158, 164, 209, 253, 264, 270, 290, 307, 321
Graham Townsend: 117, 185, 237, 333